SACRED
SEED · OF · THE

Sisters

JOCELYN · OADES

"Self-Published" Jocelyn Oades
Auckland New Zealand

ISBN: 978-0-473-73302-5
Printed in New Zealand

I honour

With immeasurable love for my family, where timelessness echoes unlimited faith and reassurance that we are all seeds continuing to re-unite in the infinite flower of life.

The universal connection to my Goddesses, Priestesses, and Pharaohs, anointed by Elestial Crystal Star 2.11, within the Temples of Saqqara Mystery School.

I N T R O D U C T I O N · T O

Sacred Seed of the Sisters

Akila is a young High Priestess initiate from a revered bloodline known for their extraordinary gift of time travel. Born into a dynasty that has long protected the secrets of the universe, she possesses the unique responsibility of preserving her lineage. Her journey spans vast geographical and time distances, connecting ancient Egypt with the lush landscapes of New Zealand, thousands of years apart.

As she navigates these worlds, Akila is driven by a profound purpose; to assist women in their rising up for the Great Awakening in the future

With each leap through time, she uncovers hidden truths and faces challenges that test her abilities and resolve whilst striving to keep her dynasty's legacy alive.

In the vast realm of historical fiction, a unique space emerges where imagination intertwines with the essence of the past. This captivating novel introduces Akila, her sisters Safiya and Tanith, and her cousin Kalina. They invite you on an extraordinary adventure, weaving events, characters, and emotions that resonate deeply with human experience. You will embark on a journey through a world crafted from imagination, woven with threads of creativity and fantasy.

Set in a world that echoes our history yet unfolds in an alternate reality, this portrayal of time travel breathes life into lost civilisations, forgotten challenges, and uncharted territories. You are drawn into a compelling story that fascinates the mind and stirs the soul, reminding us that the lessons it imparts are not bound by time. They are timeless, resonating with us in the past, present, and future.

The characters and events you will encounter outside the scope of historical records in these chapters are entirely fictional, born from the author's imagination and not based on real individuals or events. Any similarities to persons, living or dead, are purely coincidental. As you navigate this tale, take a moment to reflect on your own journey, contemplating the fine line between history and mythology and the boundaries of truth and imagination. This narrative invites you to explore new realms and perspectives, urging you to suspend disbelief and embrace the wonders of the unexpected.

The writing is rich and evocative, painting a vibrant ability to travel between timelines that feel as real as our own experiences. This novel allows us to be more than mere spectators but to engage as participants in a vivid world, sharing its triumphs and tribulations.

Beyond exploring unfamiliar historical times, this book delves into themes that resonate through the ages. Loyalty, betrayal, love and sacrifice intertwine, challenging us to reflect on our choices and paths. As readers, you are encouraged to ponder the blurred lines between history and myth, truth and fiction, liberating your imaginations to explore the realms of possibilities.

As you delve into this story of Akila, her lovers and her family, may you find joy in the unfolding drama and connection in the shared human experience and recognise the freedom of fiction to roam unbound by reality. As you embark on this adventure, may you discover intrigue in the journey, inspiration in the stories, and perhaps a deeper understanding of our quantum world - viewed through the lens of an ancient historical time of fascination.

THE · DEEP · DIVE

The dive into the cool blue ocean was deep and purposeful. I could feel thousands of tiny bubbles caressing my naked skin. After observing the sun shimmering its dancing rays on the surface of the sea, I succumbed to the depth. My aura cleanse was a way to release the stresses of life as it gathered its pressure around my soul, aching for freedom. A deep dive was all I needed to re-engage my desire to keep motivated. The water seemed to swirl endlessly around me, pure and soothing, like a spiral of bubbles within a whirlpool. The peace and sanctuary of the depth was timeless and captivating. Rising now to the brink of reality, I could see the sunlight lighting up the water and feel the heat of her rays penetrating the surface to warm and envelope my body. I gasped in the air as though the breath of life had been squeezed from me. It was hot and dry, and I sucked in the last remaining breath to fill my aching lungs.

Intense splashing and noise assaulted my ears after the peaceful dive only a few moments before. They were calling my name with urgency and crying on the riverbank. Two tall Nubian warriors were thrashing the water with the ends of their spears as I rose to the surface between them. I was mesmerised by the happenings as memories flooded my mind and blurred my reality. My sisters were huddled together, screaming my name as they suddenly exploded with joy and disbelief that it was me. Where did they think I had gone?

I remembered that I had been paddling by the edge of the Nile, relaxing in the mist-filled presence of the morning, listening to the stunning turquoise kingfishers as they hovered above the water, fluttering from the papyrus stalks and then diving to collect small fish. The call of the ducks in the rushes by the riverbank had been soothing and mesmerising. Feeling anxious after hearing the news from Mother this morning, I had briefly swum out a little further to be free of the eyes of our guards and had dived beneath the surface to watch the tiny turtles flurry around on the river's sandy bottom.

I waved my arms to my sisters, calling out their names as they rushed into the water to greet me, crying, thinking that I had been taken by a crocodile, which had rolled and submerged me. I laughed. "Sisters, I only went for a dive to watch the turtles fossick in the sand. What is wrong?"

"You were down there for so long. No one could hold their breath for that length of time!" Safiya cried. "We were sure that the crocodile had taken you," she stammered, her eyes swollen and red.

I gracefully emerged from the water feeling refreshed and energised, my light-tanned skin drying rapidly in the blazing heat. Our guards rushed to me, babbling in their native tongue. They were scared as if an apparition had risen, and they quickly ushered me ashore to the scolding words of our nanny, Keket, who was waiting for me.

"Do not fuss, Keket," I said as I slapped her hands. She was prodding me to see if I was alive and immediately wrapped me in a fine-textured, soft woven linen cloth, raising her fingers to show me the amount of time that I was submerged. "It is impossible that you are here. You have been given the gills of a tigerfish!" she exploded.

Tanith, my youngest sister, was sobbing uncontrollably. As I soothed her with a song that she loved, I told her, "I would never leave you Tani," as we sisters affectionately called her. She calmed down but was still shaken. We hugged each other tightly, and each sang notes we had practiced, joining in unison in a cascade of melodic sound. Only us sisters knew the meaning and words I had taught them from my other world. We were bound together by the sacred unity of the asp and the circles of the seed of life. We drew pictures in the sand of the seed with six circles, each overlapping. We had two circles each, our full lunar circle, and our new moon circle. If we drew two, we were safe, but if we drew only one, we needed help. We were living to the code of our destiny, our secret of the mysteries of life.

I shuddered momentarily in the hot sun as though a chill had washed over me. I knew I had travelled through a vortex of time, from my dive into the Pacific Ocean to emerging in the Nile. I had often travelled the pathway of the stars, never knowing where I would end up, as the time wall rushed to gather me into the silence, or The Hush, as I referred to these wanderings through the vortex.

The annual flooding of the Nile was complete, and all life was bustling with new growth. We three sisters jumped on our carrier and lying down, snuggled up to each other as we had done our whole lives, with Tani in the middle. Our four guards picked us up as though we were feathers. Keket strolled beside us, muttering about the episode and how she would refer this to Mother. I closed my eyes to return, in my mind, to the rushing of the waves of the beautiful ocean and my other life. I felt annoyed and cloistered with the feeling of being controlled.

I had stripped all my clothes off in abandonment of my other life, just to feel the air brushing against my skin in preparation for my colour cleanse in the cool, refreshing water; when fifteen minutes later, I found myself travelling back three thousand years to my Egyptian homeland. It was a smooth transition as the flowing memory of this fluctuation of life seemed to slip into the present moment. There was always a time-lapse of only ten to fifteen minutes, but anything could happen in that short time. I could not protect my sisters if I were swept back at any time. This caused me to notice the fine hairs on my arms standing poised and my body trembling with trepidation. I would have to define when this time travel would occur and what triggered it. We were so close as sisters. We were inseparable, and I could feel the trickle of tears silently running down my cheeks in gratitude that I was here with them now. I reached out to Safiya, and we wrapped our arms around each other and squeezed Tanith's warm body between us.

I was sixteen years old, with the alluring soft looks of feminine power. Safiya was a year younger than I, and Tanith was thirteen. We were all slim but tall, strong, and wiry. I was initiated into the realm of a High Priestess and took my role seriously.

Communing with the goddesses was my constant joy to feel the presence of such ancient power and wisdom which fortified me in times of renewal and changes in our household. I heard the whispers of the voices in the temples, and their words gave me direction for the growth of our spiritual practices. I was working in the mysterious schools of thought and linking our intuition to connect through our mind's eye. I must draw the women and children into their purpose, collecting those ready to transcend to the higher realm.

Father insisted that we learn the bow and arrow and all the activities boys were conditioned for in defence and combat. We were direct in our aim with the bow. Slick and fast with the loading of the arrow, and we let fly with rapid precision, competing daily between ourselves and our tutors.

Safiya and I were well past the age of marriage, as most of our friends were joined at the age of thirteen. We were insistent that we would choose our own partners, but no one seemed to be the right one, and stretching the timeline to be together as long as possible was causing anxiety for our mother. Keket kept telling our mother that we would need to be married soon to have babies so our lineage could continue. She had been with us for as long as we could remember. Every day, with the help of the other carers, we were pampered and looked after, as daughters of the royal family should be.

I glanced up at my favourite guard, Nef. His eyes were like deep pools of knowing. He was strong and patient and the first to grab me, ushering me out of the water. I had glimpsed the look of desperation on his face. He seemed transfixed as I rose from the waters of the Nile, not believing I was alive. Now, I smiled at him and gave him a slight nod in gratitude for his constant care. I knew it was the type of love and care he would show as a father to the daughter he may never have. His strong arms rippled with tension as he and his three companions carried us effortlessly through the rushes onto the sweltering sand toward our palace.

My desire for freedom is to feel the energy flow uncharted.

*To allow the ocean's water to anoint my body, to gift myself
the weightlessness of the waters washing over me.*

Oh, how I release the fragmentation of the physical life.

*I draw into my soul the wonder, the purity of the mighty
surging of the waves to bring the salty taste to my lips.*

*My other world calls me, echoing the hidden wonder of life
through The Hush, a serene and tranquil state of being.*

*Move me through the veil of forgotten worlds. Let me
encapsulate my soul and free myself from the tension
and bewilderment that arises in the human form.*

*I will be in the guise of the mermaid who dives
deep to discover coral on the ocean floor.*

*Let me embody the grace of the whales, moving their majestic
form to the surface to breathe. They symbolise enduring
strength and beauty in the face of continuous shift and flow.*

*I am life, I am alive, and I feel the rush of life embodying
every cell of my being. My soul light is rejuvenated
as I discover in my freedom the fullness of my gifts,
in perfect harmony with the natural world.*

THE·HAPPENING

Mother was the regal wife, and even though there were a few lesser wives, our father could not stay away from her. She spent her days in the apothecary creating healing salves and balms to counteract venomous snake bites. She was the most wondrous healer and taught us the combinations of the ointments and how to harvest the small herbs and water flowers for their healing properties. She took her time with her craft, to perfect her skills, exploring her knowledge and inspiration for her tinctures and oils, and then distributed them to all the households in our kingdom. In addition, the salve that she made for the wounded soldiers and children inhibited infection, and consequently their healing was rapid. Her expertise and knowledge were well sought after, as her healing powers resonated with people throughout the land.

Her fame followed the capability of her mother-in-law Nefertari, who had left for her afterlife, and whose magnificence was written in her temple. The complete twin temples are carved into the sandstone cliffs along the Nile in Abu Simbel; the large one dedicated to the gods Amun-Ra, Ra-Horakhty and Ptah, and Grandfather himself. The solar star's revitalising energy enhanced Grandfather's image at sacred times during the year, so that he could take his place next to Amun-Ra and Ra-Horakhty.

Our beloved Nefertari's smaller temple was also magnificent, alluring and captivating, and the splendour of the powers assigned to her temple was breathtaking. The land of the goddess Hathor blessed Grandmother's memory each year on the annual autumn equinox, when the sun's rays penetrated the sanctuary and illuminated the sculptures on the back wall.

Mother spent time with the women and children, helping in all areas of personal care. The children of the concubine women were our siblings. We were linked through blood ties and would play together sharing games and laughter, yet we were aware that the royal bloodlines of our mother and father were to uphold the principles of Egypt's protection.

She was beautiful and dreamy; her deep blue-black eyes were pools of knowing. She understood my moments of passing through The Void, and I knew hers as she had that distant faraway look when she returned to us, yet she never uttered a word about her first-hand experiences. Once, I tried to connect with her about this when I was younger, but she hushed me and said, "Akila, use your gift wisely and always be prepared." After this happened, I asked her what had triggered it, but she never replied.

Before our morning swim, we were told that we were to relocate to another area of the palace. Father's brother was now residing with us. Back from his wanderings throughout the Mediterranean, he was in training to become the ruler. Uncle had never settled in one place for long, but now he had been requested to appoint himself a royal bride.

"Mother! Mother!" I yelled, as we raced into our household and down through the maze of rooms leading to the apothecary, "I need to talk to you about my travels and the other world. It is a totally different way of life, and I want to share it with my sisters," I exclaimed.

Her hands were shaking, and the faience bottle she was holding smashed onto the stone floor. Her lip was quivering now, and she said, with such a stern countenance, "You must not take your sisters there. They could be lost in The Void." "But why Mother?" I insisted.

"Life is easier there," she said, low so that no one could hear. "Akila, it is a constant battle to stay focused on the different unusual time frequencies on the body and then to come back here to this old way of living. Sometimes it is heartbreaking, leaving the other world."

I wondered what she meant by that remark. I knew it was difficult, and the other life seemed less complex, with more freedoms than one could ever experience here. As I went over to the other world, my life became dull in my memories, and I was fully immersed in the one I was in. The only feeling I had was the pull of my sisters, bringing me back.

"It is all so difficult to explain Akila, but you must harness your gift as you have two lives. Use your gift to learn from the timeline and recall the wisdom," she said quietly, as she led me away from the other women, and we sat together. "Bring back useful knowledge and continue to gather it to help your family here, as I have, with healing, growing, and harvesting certain plants in our gardens and making the tinctures with oils. There is much to do. The Ancient Priestesses have chosen you to harness this power."

"Do you know when the transition is coming?" I asked, becoming bolder and more inquisitive in my approach.

"For me, it is when something traumatic happens. You may feel a vibrating sensation over your body a few minutes before you go," she said. "Now that is all, Akila, you must be strong and fearless. You are protected by the goddesses, but it is difficult for others to understand this, and you must be careful of the High Priests in Thebes. They are not ready for female power. Never show your gifts to others." She held my hands and kissed my fingers.

"You would leave as a baby," she cried, "And I never knew whose arms were holding you. You have the gift, but it worries me that you are crossing The Void. You need to find someone you can trust to tell, so that they may help you by calling your name if you become trapped. For me, it is Keket. I trust her with my life. However, even though she knows you have the gift, she always gets upset when we are travelling."

"Akila, I had a child, a boy who I lost in The Void. Your father was devastated. There is a time in The Void when all life stands still. It would help if you never travelled when you were carrying a child. You must also pass 'The Gift' on to your child, Akila. You must marry soon to have an heir to our family line. Father is also pressing for this to happen. He is looking for a suitable husband for you now, and all the deities are requesting that you make a union," she whispered.

"No, Mother," I cried. "I will make my own choice! You can tell him, but I assure you, I am not afraid of my father."

Mother rose and said calmly, "Think of what we have spoken about. You must be a royal bride in your own right, in your own household, before Akhet, the upcoming flooding of the Nile."

I sat in silence, my mind racing through all the levels of what this meant. It was severe, and it was time for me to relinquish my childhood ways and rise to the challenge. I was so elated that Mother had opened up to me with her story.

I had glimpsed a moment of her life and why her knowledge was so vast. I wondered if Father knew of her journeys. I pondered, but she said only to trust one person and tell no one else. I shivered with the anticipation of what was to come.

Who do I trust? I trust my sisters, but they would request I take them with me. My precious soul sister and cousin Kalina? I would talk with her. We held secrets together about the way we wanted our future to be. We shared intimate thoughts about the boys in the kingdom. Kalina was in love with the magician's tall handsome son, who was kind and reassuring. In the evening, Kalina, Safiya and I would dress as boys and slip out in disguise into the streets of the bustling marketplace where we observed life as if through the eyes of the villagers. We tasted food from the stalls and smiled at strangers, even giggling about how we were treated as waifs or troublemakers. We explored the city's dark secrets, learning and seeing the underworld of the ways of men. I always glimpsed the great towering shadow of Nef following us from a distance and felt safe.

The whispers of a million voices were in my head. Hearing those thoughts of others, I concentrated on the skills I was developing. I could feel the concepts as if they were alive in my own mind, see colours dancing around people, or visualise pictures of their actions if I closed my eyes, and it was enthralling.

I gathered up my garments from around my ankles and ran to Kalina. Her name was very unusual and beautiful, though not Egyptian by origin. Mother had named her sister's daughter and said she was honoured to choose it. She told me that it meant a bright flame, a flower on a faraway tropical island, Kalina was undoubtedly stunning. Her dark hair cascading down around her shoulders was thick and lustrous. She held the gaze of many suitors, and I knew she would choose one of them before the striking star over Egypt entered the night sky.

"Kalina, I need to sit with you. There is much I have to talk with you about." I held her hands in a gesture of connection. "I can trust you, my dear sister. We are bound by the blood of our mothers and are inseparable. Can you hold everything I say to you sacred without telling anyone?" I stammered.

"Yes, my dearest," she answered carefully. Then I started slowly explaining my journey to her whilst hiding my emotions and preventing them from bursting out.

"I live two lives at once in two different places and timelines and I am fearful for my sisters here and unsure what will happen if I get lost in the void, the time-space between my lives," I explained.

Kalina moved closer and wrapped her arms around me. "I can see that you are distraught and at a loss with your words. I find it hard to understand you," she said lovingly. "What do you mean?"

"I need you to trust me and hear my story. I am alone with my inner turmoil, and I have no one to turn to," I said.

I did not leave anything out as I explained my understanding of The Hush, my description of when all life stood still while I travelled between the two worlds.

"I don't know what will happen or what the future holds for me, and I need you to call me to verbalise my name with intent, so that I may re-appear if I get lost in The Void." With this, I let out sobs of pent-up emotions.

Kalina was stunned. We had heard of the time travellers in the voice of Mother's stories. Mother recited her own father's journeys into the unknown.

"I had no idea you held this gift too! Be assured, my beloved sister," as we called each other. "Your secret is safe in my heart."

I felt lighter for the first time in years, as though I did not have to carry this alone. I was free to be me and celebrate this freedom before the next rising of the Nile. We hugged each other tighter, renewing our love and support for one another and delighted in feeling the beating of our hearts in synchronicity with one another.

DREAM · TO · DANCE

The crystal beads that adorned Tani's neck collar and headdress were her favourite colours, turquoise, gold, and green. They sparkled brightly, sending out light shimmers from the reflections of the torches.

"I am so excited and nervous," exclaimed Tani. "I have been practicing since my first flower, and now I can finally show my dance," she said, clapping her hands.

Both Safiya and I had been watching her as she practised her routine to give her encouragement. She danced with slow, steady movements to the whimsical sound of the harp, and as the tempo increased, Tani allowed herself to become lost and free flowing with the music, celebrating in her light. For the first time tonight, Tani (whose formal name is 'Tanith', but we sisters call her by her nickname, 'Tani'), would lead us in the dance. The palace was waiting for this moment, and then we would follow her performance, three sisters dancing together.

We would honour our Uncle's homecoming tonight with a ritual for his return and a grand celebration. The boats had arrived at sunrise yesterday, and the delta was congested with their presence. The Palace housed our guests in the homes surrounding the main roads. With the best linen and finest pottery laid out for them; priests, priestesses and nobles, female and male scientists, physicians and dignitaries were present. They came from as far away as Philae and Abu Simbel, honouring the temple of our Grandfather and Grandmother, which was majestically carved into the bluff. From the Mediterranean Sea they came, in their golden embellished ships. They were joining us for the banquet and the celebration. The smell of the freshly prepared feast and fine incense wafting through the temple into the main hall, was intoxicating.

Kalina and I were excited too, as we knew her boy Dakarai and his father, the Magus, would be present. With help, I squeezed into my fine costume with its beaded neck adornment and headdress, and I was ready to dance. Kalina and I ran to Tani and Safiya, holding hands in a circle and closing our eyes. We were performing a sacred dance together. I called in the goddesses to bring joy, clarity and love, and we sang together harmoniously and raised our arms in celebration, feeling the magic encapsulating and mesmerising us. I hugged Kalina before she darted away to prepare her wooden harp.

Her fingers flicked lightly on the strings of the instrument, and we could hear the melodic sound of the tambourines and flutes as the musicians played. The music swam before us as the troupe reached their crescendo. Then, it dropped low into a softer tone, and Tanith took to the floor. Her beautiful, lithe, animated energy was captivating. Mother looked on in complete admiration as we shed tears of joy for our darling younger sister, displaying the enchantment of her dance. Tani's soft, delicate linen gown enhanced the swaying of her body as she moved with power and grace. Safiya and I looked at each other, and then we joined her, our bare feet adorned with beads, lightly moving across the cold stone floor, dancing in time to the rhythm of the musicians. Our hands created the story of the harvest and the richness of the fertile land.

We danced, depicting the ducks as they elevated themselves from the marshes and the papyrus waving in the gentle breeze. We represented the ritual of Goddess Nut as she adorned the night sky and lit up the stars in the cosmos.

I was so caught up in my movements that at first, I did not see the young man standing to honour us so vigorously as we finished the ritual dance. Then, as his enthusiastic clapping continued, I noticed how handsome he was, wearing a full headdress, and his High Priest, who had the most unusual light green eyes. They were both standing, and he was observing me, his eyes locked on mine as if in recognition. My eyes, heavy with black kohl makeup were riveted on him also, and Safiya grabbed my hand to draw me away from the applause. Safiya spluttered, catching her breath, "The young man had eyes for you Sister," she mocked. "He was absolutely mesmerised by you."

He was like a rare jewel of a man, such as I had never been attracted to before, yet it was just a moment, a mere glimpse of his beauty.

"You must not say that too loudly," I laughed, "or Father and Mother will be arranging the union in no time."

We quickly caught up with Tani, who was being assisted in getting changed into more formal attire. We too, were being helped to undress and re-adorn when Keket came marching up to us.

"Tanith, you were delightful with such a creative, flowing dance," she purred as she warmly hugged Tani's slim form. "Your parents were so proud, as was your grandfather, and the guests were in raptures with your performance."

Keket quickly drew me aside and whispered, "Asim has noticed you. It would be a good time to mingle while the other performers prepare."

"Please do not push me, Keket; there is plenty of time. I do not want to rush out to meet him."

Although I was highly intrigued, my stubborn streak showed, and I did not conform easily to being told what to do. My other world had diminished in my memory, but I already knew I had strong feelings for my love there. Was it possible to be attracted to two men in different worlds? And what was it about the green-eyed High Priest that was so soulful? I shook my head. It was all too much trying to figure it out. Right now, I was here, my heart pounding and excitement filling my every breath.

The little people had begun their lively entertainment while we encircled the tables waiting to be seated near our guests. My eyes darted to Asim, who was focused on our entry. We held each other's gaze for longer than usual, and then I lowered mine timidly.

The beautiful palace maids served a feast of the most refined foods, roasted succulent meats, pastries, and scented spiced delicacies with abundant wine. Asim shared his increasing delight by staring at me and giving me his fantastic smile.

It was infectious, and I could not help but reciprocate. Safiya, noticing this, kept nudging me under the table, and we both giggled.

My heart pounded as I sipped the sweet, delicate wine, which tasted divine, like honeysuckle. My head was light and ecstatic, my mind filled with alluring thoughts of the future when I was jolted back to reality with the gentle whispering of Asim's voice close to me.

"Would you delight me with your presence by walking with me?" he murmured, his voice deep and melodic.

"Of course, Prince Asim," I replied, fumbling with my gown upon rising. Safiya tugged at my garments with a glint in her eyes and a nod of approval as if saying, 'If you do not go, I will.'

As we walked, we spoke of the recent alignment with the Nubian forces to the southern borders of Abu Simbel and the richness of trading the prized Nubian gold, the finest pottery, copper, ivory and ebony. The ability to have the highly skilled Nubian archers as part of the Egyptian forces was favourably regarded, and Prince Asim spoke highly of them. Safiya would have found this conversation invaluable as her love for the military forces of Egypt was her passion. She would spend hours with Father, planning and strategising all aspects of protecting Pi Ramesses, our beautiful city. I brought myself back to the moment and was enraptured by Asim's passion for life, which was evident from his words.

Suddenly my hands were being held together in earnest as Prince Asim suggested I call him by his name without using his title. I smiled and gazed into his intense brown eyes and very quickly, we became close and deeply connected.

"Akila," he murmured, his voice deep and husky. "You are the most beautiful woman. Why are you not married?"

I shuddered, thinking of my other life with a yearning.

"I have not yet been attracted to a man who can express his desire for me. I know that my father and mother would have chosen for me if they knew the right person, but they, too, have not found him," I said.

"I hope that I may be the right one for you," he whispered. "You know our families would be in good alignment."

"I know. They would be perfect," I blushed. My face felt so hot in the moonlight and I was sure that Asim could feel it.

Nef suddenly moved forward one step to show his presence, but I was already basking in the tingle of Asim's kiss on my lips.

Afterwards, we held each other close for a long time, which I knew was against a young woman's etiquette, but I was physically enamoured with this young man holding me as though there was a fire in his being. His breath was warm and sensual, and his voice deepened as he whispered, "I would love to see you tomorrow. We can go sailing on my father's felucca."

We pulled ourselves apart, still holding hands, gazing into each other's eyes. We could see the promise of what the future may hold for us, to celebrate a union such as ours.

Tomorrow felt like a long time away. How long would it be until I would see him again, after he returned to Thebes? I stood on my tiptoes to kiss him lightly on his warm lips and say goodnight, and he drew me towards him again, kissing me passionately. That spellbinding kiss lasted so long that I heard Nef clearing his throat in the distance to signal that we were becoming too entangled.

As we strolled back to the celebration, I felt alive in every cell of my body. The rest of the evening was filled with wine, dancing, and entertainment, and as I glimpsed Kalina in conversation with her man, I smiled to myself, as now I could tell her of the exciting moments that I had spent with my new love.

Safiya and Tanith were seated next to Mother, talking and gesturing like archers on a battlefield. Finally, I succumbed to the fragrant smell of incense and let my eyes wander once more to the man who now held my attention.

Asim's High Priest was also observing me with those piercing green eyes. His energy was solid and unwavering. I was perplexed by my feelings for the High Priest and the connection between prince and priest. However, I excused myself effortlessly for the rest of the evening as I had the promise of seeing my prince in the morning.

Keket was fussing over me, undressing me, and bathing my feet in water, scented with the petals and oil of neroli from the wild orange trees in our surrounding gardens. I was waiting for her explosion of words to admire or admonish the prince's presence. Instead, to my delight, Keket's soothing voice was as soft as I remembered it when I was a baby. She was full of praise for the conquests of Asim, and she spoke in admiration.

"Prince Asim has already shown his skills recently in battle, protecting our upper borders against the Cush tribes. Also, his father is aligned with your grandfather, and only the High Priest's underhand control from inside the palace threatens the peace in Thebes. If something went wrong, we would not easily be able to come to you because it is such a long distance from here," Keket murmured.

"What are you leading up to Keket? Asim and I have only just met, and Father would have to be in agreement with our union," I faltered.

I realised that I had mentioned his name without a title. Keket spun her head to look me directly in the eyes.

"You have talked?" she asked intently. "Why do I have no knowledge of this? I know everything about you sisters," she said.

"Keket, there are many things that you are not aware of. Of course, we have secrets in the royal household, but this is not one of them. Asim and I are sailing on the Nile in the morning at first light. Would you care to join us?"

"Nef and one of the handmaidens will have to go with you," Keket stammered. "I have been assigned to your mother to start moving the household immediately when all of the guests have gone after the next sundown."

My feet felt fresh and pampered, and my heart was light and warm. The gentle aroma of the soothing oils made me feel loved and secure. I tucked myself into my freshly laundered soft linen bedding, closed my eyes, and the next sound I heard was the gentle tapping on the door.

The music notes floated, creating a profound
transformation, offering hope and healing to the soul.

All noise faded as the power of the therapeutic caress
of music influenced my body. Oh, to feel the subtle
flow of energy moving around like filtered sunlight,
wrapping my essence in a nurturing frequency.

I feel a harmonious balance, a sense of tranquility
and rejuvenation. Movement, like a symphony, heals
my body by allowing the electrical impulses within
the human form to express these melodic tones.

I detect delicate moments of silence between the structure
of the harps and flutes. Feel the dips and highs as the music
plays lightly over the skin's surface. The body's creation and
natural ability to respond to the delicate rhythm and sound.

We soared on the waves of emotion, the musical
instruments tuned to bring out our elation.

To dance is more than mere movement; it is to be granted the
liberation of release. Feeling the sensual movement of the physical
form, the graceful sway of the hips, and the elegant extension
of the arms in unison with the sound, is beholding beauty.

The desire to dance, the aesthetic movement, captivates
us. It is a pleasure to observe, inspiring us with its
grace and presence, which allows this wonderous
human experience and the language of the soul.

KEYS·TO·THE·VOID

The taste of the saltwater on my lips suddenly brought me to my senses. Cool and refreshing, the auric cleanse in the sea was exhilarating and I felt stunned by the swift change in atmosphere from my relaxing bedtime ritual, to rising from a deep dive. The sand was firm beneath my feet, and I squelched my toes as if trying to reconnect to the land I was in. The gentle breeze on my naked skin was wrapping me in the sensation that I was alive as I moved out of the water towards the beach.

My vision captured my clothes, lying strewn around the rocks where I had left them. This stunning secluded beach lay desolate and forgotten, like an untouched island. Why had I returned here so soon? I felt a quickening and questioning in my mind as I bent down to write Asim's name in the sand. My heart fluttered with excitement as I recalled his warm sensual kiss, his strong arms holding me close, and his breath on my face. "I do not want this memory to fade," I heard myself say to the breeze. "Please let me keep this intense feeling within me," I whispered into the wind. I plucked a strong shell out of the sand and ran to the rocks to preserve my feelings. I carved 'ASIM' into the stone and called his name out loud and long, "A-S-I-M". I felt the magic of the ancient wisdom and the goddesses surrounding me, and the wind picked up and encircled my body. It was 1978. What would the future in two years, 1980, mean to humanity? Jonas' Jeep came speeding up the track and he powered down the vehicle.

"Hey babe, have you finished your swim and cooled down? Oh wow! Has the goddess risen from the waters?" he yelled.

I laughed as I threw my arms open to show him the entirety of my naked body. He vaulted out of the Jeep and ran towards me, stripping his clothes off as he ran. He grabbed my hand, and we both plunged into the ocean naked and free, frolicking like two dolphins, diving and swimming. The sun was warm on our bodies as we made love in the ebbing tide. He kissed me intensely as we held each other, rolling over and over, laughing and childlike as the sand collected in our hair. We leapt up and immersed ourselves in the sea once more. The memory of my sisters and the strong young prince was fading into the foam on the waves, tossed and torn from one dimension to another.

"Who is Asim?" Jonas asked, as he traced the lettering in the sand.

"I had a dream of a faraway land as I dived under the water," I recalled, hoping my heart would not give me away as I felt that faraway feeling come over me.

"Come on you romantic, and I am sorry about this morning," he murmured, looking longingly at me. "Let's open a good red and celebrate us, as we have to head back to the city in the morning."

Jonas was two years older than me. We were engaged to be married next January; and it was almost March. We both worked long hours to purchase our hideaway within the natural bush in a small private cove in Northland, New Zealand.

We were blessed and in love. Jonas was a great hunter-gatherer and an expert in diving for seafood. As a chef in a restaurant owned by his family, his cooking skills were always in great demand, and our time together was limited, so we valued each moment in our hideaway by the sea.

As a reporter, my role in the media sometimes presented problems as I reported on events that did not always align with my values, and as a result, I often felt voiceless. Reading the autocue with a sense of commitment was challenging for me to convey and look convincing that this was my truth. However, our big, exciting news was that we had established an 'EEZ' (Exclusive Economic Zone) around New Zealand with a two-hundred-nautical mile radius to protect deep-sea fishing. In addition, Jonas and I supported and were involved in the Bastion Point protest for tribal land reclaim. The government was trying to sell ancestral land to build luxury housing. With the Vietnam War ending, the aftermath and difficulties experienced by the soldiers returning to their everyday lives was harrowing. These issues were foremost in my mind as I considered returning to the city.

We locked up the Jeep, closed the door on our hideaway lodge, and drove our Zephyr along the track to the road leading to the highway. We were living the dream. As the sun rose gallantly in the sky on a stunning summer morning, Jonas put his hand on my knee, and we smiled, remembering our love-filled night.

"You took the words right out of my mouth," we sang at the top of our voices, when a truck suddenly appeared which seemed to be on a mission to head straight at us.

"Hang on!" Jonas yelled.

He swerved, and our tyres got caught in the loose metal of the track. Our car spun out of control when the truck violently hit the back of it. We were oblivious to everything as our car was catapulted over the bank and down through the thick undergrowth.

I regained consciousness and was, unbelievably, okay, though I was covered in broken glass as I hauled myself up inside the vehicle.

"Jonas! Jonas!" I cried. "Are you okay? Can you hear me?"

We were lodged in a thicket of trees held fast by the surrounding bush and the strength of the mighty totara trees. People were scrambling down the bank to rescue us, yelling to get our attention and calling to ask if we were okay. I didn't even have the strength to respond.

"Jonas, my love, are you okay?" I asked him again. Blood was evident from an open wound on his head, but he just moaned. "Stay with me, my love; help is nearly here," I cried.

A while later, I could hear a siren screaming in the distance. Soon, there were voices right next to us. The men stabilised the car and tried to get Jonas to respond and pull him free. The truck driver, wearing a short-sleeved jacket, felt familiar as he approached me. I batted his arms away.

"What the hell! Why did you come directly at us? Were you trying to take us out?" I was shaking uncontrollably in shock of it all.

The ambulance crew wrapped a collar brace around Jonas' neck, and others cut branches to free him. Lifting him to the ambulance was treacherous. He was alive but incoherent, just moaning and mumbling. Pain relief and prompt attention was critical.

It made me think; *what if I had been killed in this accident? What would happen to my light body through time and space? Would I continue to exist in my other dimension? Maybe they would find me in eternal sleep in my bed? Or would I wake in another realm?* So many scenarios were racing through my mind that I had to seek answers to.

Jonas remained semi-conscious for two days and then slowly came around. He saw me, and his eyes lit up as he tried to speak my name.

"Akila," he whispered, barely audible, as I leapt close to put my ear to his lips.

"Whose name did you call me, darling?" I whispered.

Had he called me Akila? Had I heard him, right? My name here was Lily. I shuddered. Had he gone through The Void, and was he somehow tangled up with all of this? Could that even happen? I had not left my vigil from his hospital bed, and he had been out for two days. He must have travelled to my other world. But who was he, and did he know who I was? I had so many questions, the answers to which were left unexplained.

I lifted a glass to his lips to give him sips of water, anxious to know more without pushing too much. When he finally was fully awake, he called me Lily.

"Lily darling, are you okay?" He struggled. "I can't move my legs, babe. I can feel them, but I have no control over them."

I questioned him immediately. "What about after the accident? What do you recall, darling?" I said in earnest. "What thoughts did you have? You called me by someone else's name. Do you remember who that was?" I asked with determination that he would give me an answer.

"I can't move my legs," Jonas kept repeating.

"Nurse! Nurse!" I yelled out of the door. Pushing the buzzer, I hurried back to pacify Jonas, who became agitated.

The days were long trying to get a diagnosis as well as a prognosis. Jonas had called me Akila. How did this fit? Could he travel along the timeline like me? I was excited to find someone else like me here, and I was excited by the fact that he was also my lover. However, it seemed that he was oblivious to his ability. Or was he?

My work was on hold. I had taken leave and decided that I may never return to the media, which had never been in alliance with me anyway. I would set up my healing practice for holistic wellness.

We needed hands-on energy work now more than ever, and I felt drawn to activate women and families for the years ahead as we catapulted ourselves towards 'The Awakening'.

It may take twenty or forty years, but we were rushing towards it. That was unimportant at this moment, however. The only thing of any importance was that Jonas would heal and walk.

All the tests had shown that there was nothing physically wrong. His brain was trying to unscramble the messages for what his body was supposed to do; to move his legs. The connections were not linking up correctly. I had been healing him, but there was resistance in his mind.

Laying my head back on the chair beside his hospital bed allowed me some rest and activation in my mind of what I needed to do next, being quiet and still, letting the magnitude of creativity for my emotional brain go to find a solution.

I must get Jonas back through The Void to my other realm. I knew my mother could heal him with her medicines and tinctures, along with my goddesses' gifts and the Magus's ancient healing magic. I could feel the tendrils of the fragmented memory of my other life becoming stronger.

Jonas became increasingly anxious, saying, "The doctor's diagnosis is that this could be permanent. Who is going to look after you, babe? I cannot protect you." He was not even thinking of himself.

I did not need protecting, and from whom? I was strong and athletic and regularly practiced at the rifle range with Jonas to perfect my aim. My tutors had told me I was also a pro at archery, a born natural. They would understand why, if only they knew of the many years of practice I had had with my father's soldiers in my other world, so I knew I was well equipped to protect myself.

"I am okay, my love. You just get better. We will find a solution," I said consciously and with determination.

It was a calm night, with a slight breeze, and the city's lights filled the night sky. I could see from the balcony of our flat that it was soon to be a full moon. I felt alone and bewildered like I had uncovered a dark secret as I went over and over the accident. The truck driver had not seemed concerned when he came down to check on us, as we were in a daze of confusion. He could not wait to get his hands on me. Why did he keep coming at us when we spun out of control? His energy had felt familiar, making me shudder to recall this. Okay, so my brain was becoming overactive. I thought the cloak and dagger stuff was behind us in this day and age. We had been so close to losing our lives, and what would that have meant? I knew my work was not over here, but what was my real purpose?

I knew I was a light-being; and it was time to fully shine and incorporate my goddess guides into my life. My purpose, I felt, was to help amass the women, mothers, and grandmothers who would be potent in 'The Awakening'; allowing them to rise and see their own strengths. To see the power as we united would unleash an irreplaceable force. Since I was a child, I have known about this role, but now I know that I must learn more about time travelling. But why this, and why now?

I would have to go home through The Hush, but how would I program the transition? Could I take Jonas with me? Jonas was blond with bright blue eyes and would have been very distinctive if he had already been in The Realm. So, who was he? I was similarly accepted in both worlds; my eyes were green here, and my hair light brown. My complexion and skin colour in The Realm was darker, with amber cat eyes.

All the sensory information was at my fingertips as I started to remember with more clarity. Concentrating was bringing the memories closer. If I connected more intently, I could feel the nearness of The Realm and almost smell the desert sand. Maybe I could 'will' myself back there.

I needed to find the key to unlock the travel. It seemed to happen at a whim, but perhaps I could define the intention and choose when to switch.

Pulling out my journal, where I had logged all my journeys since childhood, I started combing through the data. I recalled times and moments when the transitions began. Even before my last auric cleanse and deep dive off the rocks, I had been angry with Jonas. He was becoming paranoid about my safety and control, and I had called him negative and overprotective. So, I wrote 'anger' down. Coming back, I was the opposite, content and feeling love. I wrote 'love' down. So those were the triggers. It was the two emotions. Looking back on the journeys, I see it has always been love or anger! Oh my gosh, I was elated. To move away from, or to move to where I needed to be.

If I were to go through The Void consciously, I would have to invoke love, which would be love for Asim. Now the memory of him was strengthening. I would have to feel more love for Asim while being with Jonas. The feeling for Asim though, was distant. My passion for Jonas was right here, right now, and strong. The other feeling was anger. Could I invoke anger? Yes, I could. I was angry about what had happened to Jonas, and I recalled that I had been furious that morning on the Nile when we were told that my sisters and our whole family would have to move from our royal house so my uncle could occupy it. We would be relegated to another place in the royal palace, which made it more difficult for my mother to be close to the apothecary, and I was angry and upset for her. It was all returning now, so I could use my anger as the trigger. The solutions formed, and the positive impact consumed the trepidation of what might happen on the journey, and what it would feel like to have Jonas back to his full strength.

THE · LODGE

Feeling drained and uneasy, the staid hospital building, although relatively new, held a feeling of dread as we pulled up outside the main doors. I continuously felt like I was being watched. Jumping out of the taxi, I felt the hairs on my arms tingle and my hands went hot. Quickly turning around, nothing unusual was visible. Visitors to the hospital were soberly walking through the self-opening doors, like robots on their way to fulfilling their destinies. I was prepared to move swiftly inside the lift to have my back against the stainless-steel wall facing the door, but no one unusual entered the lift.

"Jonas darling," I said as I walked into his room to be by his side. "Are there any changes?"

"No, nothing has changed. The doctors want to move me to a rehabilitation ward." He sounded angry, frustrated and in an argumentative mood.

"I have arranged all the insurance papers; you will just need to sign them. It could be months before we can get another vehicle and I feel that the best way forward is for me to go up to the lodge and bring the Jeep back. Kate will take me up. We'll spend the night, and we can be back the next day," I confirmed softly.

I had not seen Jonas in this light before, but he was adamant that I wasn't to go. I thought it may have been because he could not come up to our hideaway and we would not be able to make love. He was so adventurous and such an ardent lover, so I teased him, saying everything that he loved to hear. He drew me to him, kissing my lips and telling me passionately that he would always be my man in this timeline.

"What did you say?" I jerked away from him. "What other timeline is there?" A nervous twitch was happening in the corner of my mouth.

He chuckled and held my face in his hands. "I love you, Lily. You are the wonder of my life. You keep me on my toes and feeling alive as though I can beat this."

I was lucky to have him, but I wanted him back in his complete agile form, and I had a plan. He wasn't paralysed, although he could not move his lower limbs. His brain just wasn't signalling effectively so he didn't have any movement in his legs. Then, with a determined mindset, I knew that I would take him through The Hush and that he would be healed in the ancient world.

"See you soon my love. Remember what we must finish," I said softly. Kissing with longing, we filled ourselves with the connection that blended our souls together, wrapping ourselves in love and tasting the sensation of our endless desire. Separating from him wasn't easy, leaving him in this vulnerable state, but I assured him I had a plan.

Kate arrived to pick me up. She was packed for the night and was toting a bottle of bubbles, holding it up to show me as she grabbed my bag from me and threw it into the boot. Again, I felt a sense of freedom, as though I was sixteen instead of twenty-two. The morning was fresh as we drove out of the city and across the harbour bridge, paying our toll at the other end. Then we were free.

"Wahoo!" we both yelled at the top of our lungs. "Freedom! Freedom!"

Kate was happy to be out of her mother's house and have some time to herself. It had been ages since she had been up north and I was excited to be able to show her the changes we had made to the old bach. We chatted non-stop about everything, catching up on the accident and our respective work situations. As childhood school friends, our friendship had remained unchanged. No matter how long we were apart, we always picked up where we had left off, as though it was only yesterday.

As we pulled off the main road, there seemed to be that familiar chill in the air that I had felt at the hospital. I rubbed my arms as though to warm up, but it was another brilliant summers day and there was no need for me to feel cold. The lodge looked loved and tranquil, nestled in the native forest. Tui birds were hustling each other, diving, and flitting through the trees in a welcoming song to greet us. I inhaled deeply, smelling the earth and the bush and feeling deeply connected to it.

Opening the windows and doors to air out the lodge, I yelled, "First, a swim. Let's go!"

It was only a few hundred metres to the beach, so we grabbed our towels, kicked off our jandals and launched into a run, feeling the beach emptying her stunning blue ocean at our feet.

We always swam naked, even as children, when no one was around. We didn't have hang-ups, but today I felt vulnerable and had worn my togs under my dress. Kate had too, so we let our bodies meet the water full-on, sucking in our bellies as we plunged into the water and dived together. We laughed as we rose, spitting out the water, brushing our hair back off our faces and then going under again. What a paradise. I had to pinch myself to think we had been so lucky to find and create our little hideaway. Our sanctuary was practically gifted to us by the couple that Jonas knew, who lived in the farmhouse on the hill. I hadn't even seen or met them yet, which was odd.

I happened to gaze back at the shore during our salty sea play, when I saw a burly figure crouched way back, down the track, as if trying not to be noticed. I saw the aura colours first, emanating from him; a display of dark grey and red, like the shadow of the sunglow, which was in stark contrast to the surrounding landscape. I didn't warn Kate. I was trying to act normally, which was the only way this could look legitimate, as Kate would have become nervous or started screaming if she knew anyone was watching us. We finished our swim and, with enthusiasm, we grabbed our towels to briskly dry ourselves and headed back to the lodge. Thoughts were rampaging through my head on what was happening. I had to get next to my bow or knife to feel safe.

"Let's get our things and settle in," I said stiffly.

Kate was laughing as she threw my bag at me and grabbed hers and we headed inside. While we were at the beach the lodge had been left open, so I skirted around inside, checking the rooms, with my long knife tucked up my sleeve. I went through to the adjoining garage to check the Jeep. All seemed good, but then I noticed the flat tyre.

"You okay, Lil?" Kate called out. You're acting freaky."

"Yeah, just checking for critters, but it's all clear. We've got a flatty on the Jeep though, so that's a job for you in the morning," I smirked.

The lodge looked fantastic. It had been completely rebuilt. Jonas had almost built a fortress, I thought to myself. He had just kept the bones of the old bach. Everything could be latched down, even the windows could be covered from the outside, and it had a sliding metal door to completely close us in.

He had made a trap door in the floor to go under the lodge to get out if needed. I loved it and I had used the trap door many times just to try it out. It was still only late afternoon so we didn't want to close the place down for the evening just yet.

Kate put out the nibbles and popped the champagne. "Here's to Jonas getting better and to me leaving home," she said, raising her glass. "C'mon, time to chill."

Sipping my champagne, I remained on high alert. The tyre was flat but it had been slashed, which meant that someone didn't want us to leave.

A person, or maybe two, out there were up to no good, but what did they want? I had that icy feeling again, but I got up and showed Kate her room, which was decorated in natural soft shades of sage. She was ecstatic and, spotting the red wine on the rack, said that she didn't expect to get much sleep.

"Oh, you'll sleep well up here," I replied. "We have windows in the ceilings to see the stars and the night sky." I called the strengthened glass skylights, my 'picture book windows'.

Unlocking the cupboard and pulling my bow from the archery rack that Jonas had made for me, I felt relieved. He had had my bow crafted from the description I had given him, which was highly accurate to the double composite bows we used back home in my other world, in Egypt.

"Gosh, Lil, are we going hunting?" Kate said sarcastically, making me almost jump out of my skin.

"Hmmm, maybe we will. Who knows what the night may hold."

But Kate was already off that conversation, topping her glass up again, relaxing and saying how good it was to get away.

Jonas had a licensed gun to eradicate possums, but the gun was not my natural weapon. It was the bow that made my body come alive. I felt at one with the bow, as if we were masterfully joined. I visualised how, as the bow tensed, I tensed. We were in absolute unison. As the arrow catapulted, my energy would fly with the shaft to its target. Holding the highly polished composite frame now gave me strength, and the instrument would sing to me the sweetest note as it reverberated when the arrow was released.

The evening sunset dimmed quickly like the shades being pulled down. It was only 7.30pm, but I jumped up to secure the lodge.

Kate pulled out more snacks, saying, "We don't need to cook tonight, do we? We can just graze?"

I opened a bottle of Pinot Noir, and we swapped from the empty bottle of bubbles to the red. When I heard the sounds outside, Kate was talking about her mother and how hard it was to leave home. The sounds were delicate and muffled through the wood, but I definitely heard them.

I whispered, placing my finger on my lips, "Hey, keep talking to me."

Kate got the message and talked unfalteringly, her eyes big and her eyebrows raised. My body was alive like a cat, poised, waiting to spring as I slid back the mat, unlatched the trapdoor, and disappeared underneath the lodge.

I saw the shape of his legs easing alongside the wall near the garage, no doubt trying to locate a crack in the windows.

He was alone and cleverly moved as though familiar with the night without the light, just the evening sky to help him to manoeuvre. He was stealthy and purposeful. I came out from under the lodge, and my arrow was nocked, ready for flight. As I moved away from the wall to get a direct hit, he lunged at me, weaving almost sideways. He had a strange gait I thought. I put all of my energy into my limbs and focused on my body, releasing the power into the string and aimed for his upper torso, away from his heart. He ran at me like a madman as I let the arrow fly. I only wanted to scare or maim him if I could get an accurate shot. The arrow flexed. A good shot, but it didn't stop him. He lunged at me with big hands. His eyes were deep black, his face unshaven. His nails scratched down the side of my neck. His breath was dank and foul, and then he dropped like a stone.

I panicked and kicked him briefly. Moving fast, I slid back under the lodge and up through the trap door, bolting it behind me. Kate was jumping around the room. "Oh Lil, what the hell is happening?"

"Oh man, I've killed him, I've killed him!" I shrieked. We had no landline to call anyone for help.

"Kate, we'll have to go outside and see. I might have just wounded him. We'll need to check."

I re-nocked the arrow while Kate unlocked the door. We were poised and ready and shuffled lightly and slowly around the side of the house, Kate holding on to me.

"Oh my gosh!" I exclaimed as I lowered my bow.

There was a massive hairy possum on the roughly trodden earth with an arrow in his upper torso, his beady eyes still open. I started retching.

"What the hell?" Kate was ecstatic. "You got him Lil, you got him! Great shot!" as she slapped me furiously on the back. I was still retching.

I kicked the possum and shuddered. This was a form of magic or shapeshifting, but who had possessed the beast? I wasn't sure how to handle it, but I did know that I wasn't telling Kate about it. She would have freaked out, but of course I wasn't planning to tell anyone until I had figured it out for myself. At least the icy feeling had gone. There were only the welts on my neck left to show for the episode.

I had to retrieve the arrow now, knowing that I couldn't face it later. We would bury the beast in the morning. This was 'the big one' that Jonas had been after. He had said that it was a real persistent pest that kept hanging around, but always at a distance and Jonas hadn't been able to get him in range. I ran and grabbed my gloves and we tried to yank the arrow out. Kate tried, but she couldn't move it and stood back in disgust. I rocked it back and forth as Jonas would have done, and managed to dislodge it and threw the heavy pelt on the ground, trying to escape the creepiness of it all.

"We'll deal with you in the morning," I squirmed.

The evening's horror, followed by relief, was too much and Kate poured me a large glass of pinot.

"Always fun and happenings when you're around Lil. You keep me on my toes and make me feel alive."

"Thank goodness you were here too," I replied and I meant it, as I thoroughly washed and rewashed my hands as if to cleanse myself from experiencing such a foul incident, but unfortunately, I could still taste the smell of the beast's breath.

"So much better to share the excitement," Kate said and seemed animated by the whole event.

I had to shower to wash away the stench and the nauseous feeling which engulfed me, making a note, with the fresh rainwater cascading over my face, that a deep dive and swim in the morning must be a priority. Drying myself briskly again made my skin come alive and I checked the mirror and felt shocked by my reflection. I hardly recognised myself as Lily but looked more like my memory of Akila now, strong and in control. I made a blend of essential oils, patted them onto my welts, and returned to sit with Kate.

Wrapped up in blankets and sipping wine, we talked until late about the future. Since Kate's brother had drowned and her dad was gone, Kate said that she had felt more obligated to look after her mother. I encouraged her to see beyond this. She must prioritise finding a special love as there was also a life to be lived. Each of us has our calling, and we must live this life to the max and live it to our life code, otherwise we are just living someone else's destiny.

"Be strong Kate," I urged. "You deserve the magic of love and the feeling of your man loving you in return and sharing your passion."

Sleep, when it finally came, was disturbed. I was reliving the scene over and over throughout the night and woke up late. I grabbed the shovel and spent twenty minutes digging a deep hole in the bush. Leveraging the shovel under 'the beast' as Jonas called him, I carried him into the bush balancing him precariously on the shovel, my arms straining under the weight. Sliding 'the beast' into the hole and covering him with the damp earth felt like a massive release. I uttered a short blessing over him, sending him back to return to the ground and I asked the shapeshifter to be set free and liberated from his intention. I sprayed and washed the shovel, releasing any energy of him, and washed my hands thoroughly again.

"C'mon, Kate," I said excitedly. "Let's have an aura cleanse before we clean up."

She always laughed at my sayings as she gave a chuckle. The luxury of the pristine cool water to wash away any trace of the encounter was perfect. We leapt in naked and with abandonment this time, feeling that life was for living and releasing.

A warm breeze lifted the atmosphere and, feeling the gentle breath of wind and the sun's heat lightly caressing our skin we felt breathless and, as we rose like goddesses out of the rolling foam, the sea kissed the sand, and our footprints were gently erased with the trace of the tide's energy.

"Who is Asim, Lil?" she asked. "Who is Asim?" She repeated.

Oh, the memory of him flooded every crevice of my being. I recalled the kiss and how he had lifted my hair and held my face in his hands. Bringing that memory into the moment, my heart started pounding. I wanted him. I longed for him, like an echo inside me. 'Asim' ... I loved hearing Kate say his name like a forbidden dialogue.

I admired my youthful strong body as I wrapped the towel tightly around me.

"He's like... a friend of mine," I sighed.

"Like a friend? What type of friendship do you have for you to be carving his name in the rock?" she asked.

I tried to ignore her probing tone whilst also wanting to share my story, but I couldn't even begin to tell her because it sounded, and was, too unreal for anyone to understand my complicated life.

"He is a friend and I have used his name as a highborn prince of The Realm in a historical story I am writing," I expressed exuberantly.

"Ooh, I would love a man to take me away from my boring existence," Kate murmured. "In fact, I'm making it a priority to find my own prince," she said with purpose. "After our talk last night, I WILL make it my priority."

"Okay, let's do this!" I exclaimed. "We will prioritise it when we get back, Kate."

I felt blessed. I had a lover in two different worlds. How privileged was I? Now it was Kate's turn to find romance and I was going to encourage that.

We felt free, refreshed and full of life and all wrapped up, we strolled back along the track to the lodge, preparing ourselves to return to the city.

Kate yelled from the garage, "Hell Lil, this is one slashed tyre, like it happened with a knife."

Or maybe the sharp talons of a possum shapeshifter, I thought to myself as I touched the welts on my neck.

We struggled with changing the tyre and then cleaned up to go.

I wondered how it would happen, getting Jonas through The Hush and having Mother tend to him. She would not like me bringing someone through The Void, and how strange would it be for Jonas? How would I even explain to him what I planned to do? I was determined now to encourage the venture as soon as we returned. We would only be gone for ten to fifteen minutes, so I would have to set up my intention as to how it would happen amidst the staff in the rehabilitation ward.

RETURN

Exhilarated and ready for new beginnings, Kate was determined to tell her mother of her decision to go flatting. Her eyes were alight with emotion and heightened by the thought of free living and finding love. Hugging tightly, our hearts beat in unison, and we separated with a promise to each other that we would catch up soon.

"Make this a new reality, Kate. Don't let anyone coerce you out of your choices. Your life belongs to you, and you deserve it," I said with love, encouraging Kate to believe in herself.

All the recent thoughts of Asim made me miss my Egyptian sisters. They were with me through the dulled veil behind the timeline. I could hear them calling me as if waiting for our journey to continue.

The drive home was quickened as my mind wandered off, trying to unravel the mystery of why I had been targeted and by whom. I was tired of the weight of the two worlds, as though they were crashing around me, entwining two sets of circumstances, heavy and shrouded in caution.

"Jonas, my love," I cried as I ran to him. We reached out and embraced intensely, touching and holding each other.

"The day apart felt like an eternity, my love," Jonas whispered. "Are you okay? Did it go well?"

"I killed the beast," I said in a proud statement. "He was huge and fierce, like a savage. He lunged at me instead of running off. Look at my welts." I pulled back my hair, and Jonas let out an expletive. "I got him with my bow at close range. What a night!"

I shuddered at the thought of the beast as I recalled how he had thrown himself at me with those intense black eyes and a desire to kill me with his bare hands.

I heard myself saying, "If I had not reacted so quickly, those claws would have pierced deep into my carotid arteries, and a huge possum would have been the killer." I thought then no one would have ever known his shape-shifting form.

The rehabilitation ward felt heavy, as though we could feel each person's individual struggle to get well. It permeated the corridors and infiltrated every crevice. The anxiety and earnest desire to heal were enveloping the whole department. I wanted us out of there perfectly healthy and to pursue our lives with our future stretched out before us.

Sitting down and holding Jonas's hands, I whispered, "We are going on a journey together, like into a dream or an escape for a short time. Are you willing? It will be more intense than when I do intuitive healing on you." I stared deep into his eyes. "This may be strange and confronting but trust me," I gently assured him. He seemed okay with it all, even excited that we were about to go on an adventure together.

When the evening came, and before visiting hours ended, I summoned the anger that this had happened. The offence was that someone had tried to kill me. What rights did they have?

I was getting agitated and fragmented, and I sat on the bed next to Jonas and held him close so that we were enmeshed and conjoined in our energy fields. I could feel the intense anger propelling me forward. I had found the key to unlocking The Void. I could feel The Hush as all sound and energy stilled into nothingness. Within the emptiness, we were boosting ourselves forward without movement, and we clung to each other and held our sacred love for each other, which time nor travel could never diminish.

I stared in disbelief, clutching my hand over my mouth for fear of screaming. We were back in Egypt, entwined on the floor by my bed, holding each other tightly. My arms encircled my Jonas, the High Priest and the same High Priest who was standing next to Asim at our celebration, a few hours ago.

We were clinging to every shred of our identity in the familiarity. His eyes, which were like pools of light green, were wide open yet hooded as he gazed at me, his handsome features outlined in the dim light of the evening glow, recalling he had knocked gently to awaken me moments ago, stumbling into my room.

"Akila, forgive me. I have yearned for you in this world, but we are prohibited from being together."

We both gasped, drawing long breaths as we leaned forward and kissed passionately, holding onto the acute awareness of our mutual touch. I wanted Jonas to entice my longing for his body as he touched my face. His kiss burned my lips, bringing blood to the surface. Our eyes held the gaze of deep love as the other world slowly dimmed.

I should not have had these thoughts and desires for a High Priest of Thebes when I was going on an excursion with his Prince in the morning. It was unacceptable, and I would be scorned or even cast out. Immediately, I went into action, remembering why we had crossed The Void.

"Wait, Jonas, I am going to get my mother," I murmured. We desperately need her help. "My name is Herihor," he impressed upon me. "We must remain in our status, in our roles here. I love you in our other world, but we cannot be together here."

"Our love is enchanted and deeper than The Void we cross. Hold on to that," I whispered. "This world will consume us the moment that we are in it, but we must always recall our love. It is forever and timeless."

I fled through the opening, barefoot on the stone floor. I was racing towards my mother's room when suddenly, the booming voice of my uncle echoed around the stone walls.

"Where are you fleeing to Niece?"

My uncle's tone was questioning. He grabbed me by the shoulders and spun me around to look at him.

"You performed well tonight, child. We are proud of you and ready for you to take your rightful place in allegiance with Upper Egypt."

"Thank you, Uncle," I replied, breathless, respectfully lowering my head before him. "We are pleased that you have returned to take guardianship over the palace to support Grandfather as he creates his temple tomb for the afterlife."

"Go now and wish your mother well. I hold the deepest admiration for her. If times were different, she would have been my Queen."

He gave me that all-knowing glance, and then a faraway look came over him as I grabbed my robes and fled into the darkened corridors lit only by the dancing light of the oil torches to show the way.

"Mother, Mother, I need you! Come quickly. Can you summon Nef, please? I have a patient who is suffering."

Nef was already off his couch and present as we rushed back to my space.

"You will be in shock, Mother, but I will explain."

We looked around, hoping that no one would be in the halls. Mother was in total shock that a High Priest was in my room but seemed very in control as she and Herihor (Jonas in my other world), nodded at each other with a knowingness that I did not understand. Nef immediately kneeled, scooped Herihor up, and pushed past us. His long strides led us down the corridors to the clinic and the low couch in the room where he placed Herihor as though he were a child. I knelt to hold his hands, but Mother quickly pulled me away and said with determination in her tone.

"Akila! Go back to your room. You must not be here. It is inappropriate."

I did not have the chance to tell her what had happened. It was as though she already knew what was going on. Only a few hours of sleep were left, and I wondered how Jonas was feeling and if he was comfortable. He did not have any of his medication from our other world, but my mother's antidotes were the best in the land.

The morning light struck the landscape with a burst of heat, accompanying the glow of the beating sun. Keket came quickly into my room, followed by Tani and Saf.

"You are going sailing this morning with Prince Asim. We are all prepared."

She excitedly spoke about the adventure I was to go on. I grabbed my sisters and hugged them as though I had been apart from them for a long time. We drew our six entwining circles on the smooth bedding to connect our devotion.

Finally, Keket hissed, "Enough of that. Those rituals with the circles will not be enough to keep you connected forever."

We looked at each other, held hands, closed our eyes tightly, and squeezed our hands together. Yes, we will always be connected as children and adults. It was our destiny.

Freshly bathed, Keket anointed my skin with neroli and pure blue lotus blossom oils. I smelled divine, but my emotions were awash with unusual scenarios. Everyone was in a festive mood, and I too was drawn into the joy and delight of my impending connection with the Prince. I had not seen Mother this morning, but my sister's chatter told me about the priest in the infirmary, which kept me fully engaged with the news.

Safiya gently plaited my hair, folded it under my headdress, and whispered, "You look like a Goddess already. Let me help with your make-up." The maidens had already started applying it, but Saf took the colour palette and began her mastery.

Tani piped up. "Do you feel good about the Prince? Will you move away and live with him?"

"I want us to stay together, but I feel that we are growing up too fast, Tani," I said with reluctance, which she heard in my voice and came closer to hug me.

"Remember, we have made a pact to always look out for one another. We are connected forever as sisters of the light, and our symbol of circles will guide us."

Her questions made me nervous as our world was changing rapidly. We came together and embraced as Saf held the mirror to show me her art. I looked intently at my reflection in the self-discovery of who I was.

The white robe with the turquoise and gold studded collar hugged my slim hips, accentuating my athletic body with my feminine curves spilling over the bodice. I was excited and naïve, not knowing what was expected of me and how I would perform in front of the keen eyes of the Prince's entourage. If I could maintain my feminine poise, I would feel the balance of beauty and natural synergy within my surroundings and know I would get by. Nef and my guards were ready to escort me on my adventure with Asim, as it was a big occasion for the house of Pi Ramesses. Although dimmed, thoughts of Jonas came to me, as I was highly aware of the purpose for which we were here back in Egypt.

A fluttering of excitement about my rendezvous kept me elevated as I glimpsed Asim in the distance, already on board his father's ship. What transfixed me was the blazing colour of the man next to him, that dark red aura I had seen before, but where exactly was that? It was a blur at the moment, but I was caught up in the wafting aroma of my perfume, and my suitor's dazed eyes.

Nef helped me onto the felucca, and the canopy was in place to deter the blazing sunlight. The day's heat was already bringing droplets of perspiration to my arms and forehead as my maid patted my skin and assisted in manoeuvring my gown so that I could be comfortable. Asim came directly to me, grasped my hands, and held me captive with his warm, gentle eyes.

"It is such a pleasure to have you here with me," he smiled, the creases of his eyes amplifying his genuine care. "Please be seated. My oarsmen are ready to depart."

The craft was magnificent, built with strength and a high prow with a sculptured golden head of an antelope. The large white sail was rolled up and could be opened if needed. The wind was mild, and the glistening waters of the Nile sparkled her magic, dancing around us like angel dust.

I glanced up to see the man before me, wishing to be introduced. His countenance was severe and stern as he eyed me with contempt. Asim introduced him as his father's main guardsman. He told me that his priest, Herihor, had been taken ill and was being cared for in the infirmary.

"Do you remember my priest? He was with me last evening," Asim said. I was hesitant in my response.

"Yes, yes, your priest was very attentive. I hope he will heal rapidly."

My skin crawled, and I was on high alert as the bodyguard held an air of superiority. However, I would not let this ruin mine and Asim's celebrated time together.

"Thank you, Asim," I uttered, bowing my head demurely.

We were mesmerised by our willingness to be ourselves and talk freely out of the earshot of his rowers and Nef. Laughing, we recalled some of our childhood experiences in the royal households. He told me that his priest, Herihor, had told him of my beauty and how he had been in our presence many times growing up.

"Herihor suggested I come to watch you dance, as he knew I would be enthralled," Asim told me.

The sail was billowing in the slight breeze as we sailed smoothly towards Pelusium on the Mediterranean Sea, where the azure, blue ocean was reaching out to draw us into her bountiful beauty. There was much excitement along the riverbank as hordes of farmers and their families skirted the edge of the Nile, throwing petals and flowers into the flowing waters in honour of our visit as we sailed past their villages. I visually captured the acknowledgement of the people waving gently in appreciation. Asim was following my every move. He too, gave a wave here and there, much to the delight of the people shouting well wishes as the children were jumping into the shallow water.

They laid out the cheese and bread with figs, honey, and small dainty delicacies for us as we sipped the sweet honey nectar and celebrated our budding endearment with each other.

Suddenly, Nef lunged towards me, knocking my goblet to the boards of the boat as, in one sharp move, he sliced the head off the horned viper snake as it drew its coils together, ready to spring. The sandy-coloured body kept slithering momentarily, hanging out of the basket, as the dismembered head lay limp on the wooden floor. We were shocked that the snake was there.

"Clear up this mess," Asim ordered his guard. "How did this come to be here?"

Nef eyed me with concern, but he calmed down when he saw that I was not perturbed. One of my goddesses of protection was Wadjet. We were in her territory, so I knew I was protected. Without speaking, I nodded again to honour Nef, noticing that the colours around the guard had deepened in rage as he tried to appear concerned about the attack.

Our eyes met, and those piercing black eyes made me shudder as I recalled where I had last seen them. My skin was prickling as I tried to stop myself from being sick. Swallowing, I managed to keep myself from showing any form of recognition.

We were sailing now, picking up the breeze nearing the mouth of the delta. It had been a long day, and the afternoon heat had kept us under the canopy. We languished on the couch and scanned the water's edge for submerged hippopotamuses. There was danger lurking everywhere in the Nile. Massive rock pythons that could swallow a crocodile were prolific along the riverbanks. Crocodiles were everywhere, slithering silently into the river as we passed by, with only the clustered ripples of the disturbed water showing their presence.

Asim was excited as he talked about Africa's beauty and his kingdom. His tales of hunting the hippopotamus and antelope were full of detail, so much detail that I recoiled from the gruesomeness of the encounters.

"Akila."

Asim suddenly spoke my name and faced me. I shifted my body to accommodate his sudden change of position and brushed away the tendrils of hair from my face to get a better view of him. My skin felt warm, and I could feel the droplets of sweat trickling down my back. The moving current of air from the fan that Nef was gallantly using kept our breathing light as Asim continued.

"You have captured my heart, and it has been beating faster hearing of you and more so since meeting you last evening. The effect you have on me is tantalising and all-consuming. When in your presence, my world is all about you, and here you are, like the divinity of the gods and goddesses in perfect harmony. I would be honoured if you too, shared the happiness that you bring to me and the pleasure that I may offer you. We were born for each other, and our lineages are perfectly aligned for the greater good of our country, mighty Egypt. Will you share your world with me until almighty Ra, creator of all life, leads us into our afterlife?"

I felt these words deeply, and Asim's graceful way of describing our union was divine. My heart was a flutter of possibilities, and my purpose intensified to the point that I blurted out, "Yes!"

I knew that I was meant to be more reticent, yet my body wanted this man to hold me, to entice me, and to make love to me.

"Oh, I am honoured that you have chosen me, and I have chosen you. We are a perfect fit!" Asim's eyebrows raised as he took in my words and looked curiously at me.

"We will make plans on our return to Pi Ramesses, and I will not be returning home until we have planned the day we unite."

We grasped each other's hands, and I held the gaze of the man I was to marry. Love and desire had found me here. Glancing up at Nef, I noticed his unique smile that showed he was happy. I nodded slightly to show him my care and silently hoped he would accompany me to Thebes.

In the background, I felt a rush of chilly air blasting me, emanating from Asim's guard, who did not deserve even a glance from me, as I held the look of love with Asim.

HEALING

The morning was filled with the noise of geese and ducks squawking endlessly as the rich sounds of birds on the Nile came alive. A cascade of amplified calling filled the air, enveloping us in the vibrant sounds of Egypt.

I was immersed in the excitement of my impending coupling with Asim. I had not dreamed I could feel as connected to this land as I felt now. Lying back on my tapestries, the time to ponder life as a lover and wife was an alluring pleasure. My goddesses, who respected and honoured our prayer, stood firmly beside me, and their strength filled me with an intense vibration of crystalline light. I was the physical embodiment and the voice of the goddesses themselves.

My thoughts drew me back to the task at hand. How could I find peace of mind that Jonas was healing when I was excluded from my rightful duties and from knowing all the activities going on in the palace? My sisters seemed more knowledgeable about what was happening, especially Tanith, as she was stealthy and quick and could penetrate any place without being noticed. No one would be any the wiser if Tani was there.

She quietly slipped into my room as if on cue, so I casually asked the question that had been playing on my mind without wanting to sound too keen.

"Tani, can you tell me how the priest is healing?" She excitedly replied that he was recovering well and had sensations back in his legs.

"Oh!" I said in relief, letting out a big sigh of gratitude as Tani continued.

"Mother has been brewing very strong broths every few hours and making the priest laugh, which helps him relax. From being a stern, quiet person to now, there is quite a shift in him. I have been taking notes of the ingredients so that we know the secrets and can copy the potions." She lifted her papyrus scroll to show me that she was serious.

"Most of it is here," she smiled as she tapped her head. Her beautiful skin was glowing, and her face lit up, indicating she knew some of Mother's secrets.

"Tani, you are lovely. Keep it up. You will be just like her one day," I said.

"No, I won't!" she immediately snapped back. "I will be on the battlefield with Father driving a chariot at the head of the army. I will be heralded as a warrior. Safiya and I have been invited by Father to view the new horses, especially for our battle chariots. Do you want to come, Sister?"

A feeling of foreboding came over me as I glimpsed through the veil and saw, at that moment, a vision of a chariot smashing up against another chariot and Tani being thrown into the mass of marauding foot soldiers and disappearing.

I shook my head to make the vision dissipate. "Come on, sweet Tani, be a young, free girl for a little longer. And yes, I would love to attend with you as Father is purchasing a horse and camel for me this season. He may have already chosen them."

Father had invited Asim to view the horses bred primarily for him from the Bedouin tribes. The Arabian horses and chariots would make a great spectacle to show off the finery and power of the regime. Since my grandfather's conquests during his rule, especially at Kadesh, the sea people and the tribes to the west of the delta have been calm and peaceful. This was the perfect time then for my grandfather to show the kingdoms of Upper and Lower Egypt, that his power was not lessening. Moreover, Father's control of the army as 'General' gave him licence to have the best weapons, the best animals, and the fastest chariots.

Safiya strode in, her long-legged stance promoting her boyish attitude as she slapped the flail against her thigh.

"It is so exciting that we will be watching the chariots tomorrow. I will ask Father if I can drive one with a pair of the finest horses."

Tani burst forward. "So will I!" she shrieked loudly to reinforce her determination.

"I will be content to have the fastest horse and the most splendid camel for trekking," I smiled.

I dressed with assistance, and we held hands and strolled into the palace for our morning feast. Our belongings and household had been moved so we were further away from the main hall and closer to the other houses of our family. I was happy that Kalina and I would be more in touch, so I went straight to her house after eating. She was stunningly dressed and with full makeup and was excited as she saw me enter.

"We must talk, Sister," she said, grabbing my hand. "I am going to be the wife of Dakari. He is the most alluring, powerful man and can command wondrous magic. Even though I know his father is the Magus, the seer, who holds the visions of Egypt, Dakari's power has intensified. He has been telling me things of which you have spoken. I did not mention your travelling, but he told me there is danger for you in another world. A shapeshifter is hunting you, and even though you overthrow him in that world, you still have a heavy burden to carry here with the priests in Thebes."

"Phew, I'm glad I told you, Kalina," I said with relief, "but there is more."

I licked my lips and smoothed my hair, wondering how much I should divulge to her. Kal listened intently to the whole story. Then, when I came to the connection between Jonas and Asim's priest, Kalina grabbed my shoulders and her look intensified as she exhaled.

"What are you going to do? If you marry Prince Asim, your other lover will be at your side. That will be so difficult if you cannot reach out to him," she cried.

"But that is just it. I do not have the same burning passion as I do in my other world. It becomes pale or faded; do you understand what I mean?"

"Hmm, I do understand," she stammered. "Dakari is concerned for your emotional well-being and safety here in Pi Ramesses."

"Ha! I am fine. No need to worry," I scoffed. "I am protected by my Goddess Wadjet. "I showed her my beautiful arm amulet of the snake coiled around my arm. "Mother had a golden Wadjet crafted for me to always bring me protection. My physical spirit snake is black, like the evening sky, and rises out of the sand to protect me from all magic unless it's my own," I laughed, throwing my head back. My hair cascaded down my back, and I felt my snake rise around my throat to view Kalina.

"When is your wedding?" I asked. "We have much to get ready."

"You have your own wedding to prepare for, now that Prince Asim has stolen your heart," she replied. "Akila, can I ask you personal questions about when you are with your lover in the other world?"

"What would you like to know?" I tried to appear calm, but my heart had intensified its beat.

"Physical love is not the same for everyone." I could feel my breath quicken as I recaptured the memories of lovemaking with Jonas. "You must guide him to what your desires are. Start from the beginning and show him how to caress you, and where you like to be touched. We were born to pleasure our man, but if you want to be the only one for him, make your body move seductively and enthral him every time. Guide him to touch you, taking his time. You can breathe in his energy and be led to where that energy takes you. Let him kiss you in all places as you gift your bodies to each other. He wants to pleasure you just as much as you are a gift for him."

Kalina looked flustered and hot; as no one had ever spoken to her this way.

"Well, you did ask Kal," I said with a laugh.

We spent the morning talking explicitly about our role as women and how to hold that power.

"There is so much more, but we will continue when you are ready, at another time," I sighed.

Kal's handmaiden had just announced that Dakari was presenting himself outside, waiting to be ushered in. Kal waved her hand to say yes and allowed him to enter.

When he stepped into the room, it was apparent that he was overwhelmed with love for Kalina. His eyes were all over her, and she bowed her head demurely. She was blushing and could not speak after what we had been talking about, so I tried to excuse myself.

Dakari came over immediately, to warn me of the imminent danger to me.

"The guard is extremely dangerous and has the backing of the priests in Thebes. There is much unrest there. He knows that you have power, and they do not want you to breed to increase your lineage. If you do, they will most certainly take the child to have control over him in the priesthood," he spoke softly to me, out of earshot of the handmaiden.

"You will have to be wary, and keep yourself armed," he continued.

"I must go to the Temple of Isis in Thebes and beyond, to align with my goddesses," I insisted.

"It is my role to appease the gods, to hold the balance for Egypt, and that I shall do. But what would happen if I killed a highborn? I too would have to die?"

"You could never do that, just protect yourself from the guards. You may have a fair trial, but the priests are the ones who wield the judgement," Dakari mused. "Thebes is a powerful place, with our Pharaoh Ramesses, mortuary, temple, and the House of Millions of Years."

"I already feel that it is a lost cause, my going there, but I know that my child will be a royal boy, a Prince in his own right, and he must be born in Thebes to be recognised," I replied.

"Oh, sorry, Dakari I almost forgot. Congratulations! We are celebrating Kalina's and your union. You are a powerful Magus too. Thank you for your insight and care."

I left and strode smartly back towards our quarters, but first I was going to see Jonas. Walking along the corridors to the apothecary, I felt ready to consult my goddesses and the papyrus scrolls in the library of the healing temple. Mother was not there, so I continued walking until I was outside the infirmary, then, hearing the hushed voices of Prince Asim and his priest, I listened intently, placing my hands on the cool stone walls in order to hear more clearly.

Jonas's voice was low and guarded, "I will return with you to Thebes after our time here. I am nearly healed and can walk quite steadily now with the aid of sticks. The Nile is slowing; and the parched fields will show through after the harvest. We must gather the ships and sail before the water level falls."

"I am genuinely concerned with the guard Dhoser, your father's minder," Herihor whispered. "He was able to move between worlds but he no longer can, as his form has been extinguished from that world. His anger will increase though, and he will try to destroy your love for Akila. What do you foresee?"

"I will not let anything happen to her. She is my passion, my light. Her connection to the goddesses and how the gods favour her is a gift. She brings the unity of the sceptre of Isis. I have seen her call her in. She will have my full protection, but I need your help," replied Prince Asim angrily.

I shuffled nervously but kept my ears keen on their conversation.

"You will be appointed her High Priest, which alone will keep Dhoser away. He will not cross you for fear of his miserable life."

I could hear footsteps behind me and turned to see Mother coming up to hug me saying, "Child, what are you doing here?"

"I have just arrived to see how Priest Herihor is. How is he, Mother?"

"Well, let us find out, my daughter." She grasped my hand and pulled me into the dimly lit room.

All eyes were on me as I held out my hands to the prince, who at once held my fingers securely in his. His eyes told me I was his love, whilst his hands were getting warmer as he grasped mine.

"Thank you, my Prince," I stammered awkwardly as I lowered my eyes in respect. "Mother says that you are nearly healed, Priest Herihor," I said, using his rightful title.

She glanced disapprovingly, wondering why I had said that when she had not given me any information about his condition, but I pressed on, trying to get more information.

"You look like a new man," I continued.

"Yes, I feel better than I ever have, and I am sure we will be making arrangements to return home soon." He spoke with such eloquence, but I understood the double meaning.

"We will not be rushing anything," Asim said very directly, not knowing what we were referring to. "Surely we have much to discuss in planning our royal wedding, Akila?"

"Yes," Mother agreed. "We have many formalities to address. We must ensure that all dignitaries know the importance of the union between Upper and Lower Egypt."

Mother's regal stature was a breath of fresh air as she came to stand next to me, and she was very emotional.

"My daughter, the first to be married, and to enhance the bond, and solidify and strengthen the borders to the South. After that, Upper Egypt will truly have a strong, forthright High Priestess."

KHONSU

The flirtatious morning breeze teased at my hair as if trying to unpin it. Tied up with coloured glass beads, my tresses were held firmly in place as we made our way out of the gates just before dawn to position ourselves. Orderly and with guards flanked on either side, we waited. Dust and sand were ingrained in our skin and hair and, with every deep breath in, we could taste it. I ran my hand down my neck brushing away any visible signs of dust and pollution, appearing relaxed and calm.

Saf, Tani and I were dressed in the attire which was best suited for our excursion to the soldier's encampment near the livery, where the prized horses were housed. Excitement filled our bodies as we held hands and squeezed each other's fingers in anticipation of learning more about the ways of our armies. The swish of the marching soldiers and the pounding of the feet from the military sent a shot of adrenalin through me as I realised that I too loved the power of our infantry, and how the advancement of our foot soldiers would send shivers down the spine of any enemy. Crowds were gathering to catch a glimpse of their leaders and an army full of vigour. Father led the entourage with a light, brisk step as we moved towards the animals. I could smell the sweet damp scent of the horses, and the yells of the men in preparation for our visit there were intense.

Letting out a deep exhale, I clasped my hand over my mouth as I saw the finest Arabian horses already groomed, with their coats lustrous in the morning sunlight.

"Sisters, look how gallant and intelligent these horses are. We have an array of the finest steeds. I hope father has chosen the best for me."

I could not help but speak rapidly, for I was animated and longed for an elegant ride.

Father yelled out for the men to halt, and the foot soldiers moved away, allowing us full access to the ring of horses as they were paraded in front of us. My eyes flitted from horse to horse, and I gasped aloud as the most beautiful animal snorted and bowed in front of me. I knew he could feel my energy and I willed him towards me as I moved swiftly to return his acknowledgement. He was dappled grey, proud, and strong, with a silver and black mane which shimmered when he moved. His intelligence and connection to the activity surrounding him was in his ability to take it all in. I called him 'Khonsu', after the Moon God, as he held the moon's colour at its zenith.

Saf, Tani, and Kali were enthralled by the display of the horses, bred for royalty in battle. Father turned and summonsed me forward.

"Akila, you are my eldest daughter and I honour you for your devotion to your sisters. You are connected to the wisdom of the goddesses and you have the ability to call in the answers and the protection of our armies. I have seen you in the temples, bowing low, paying homage to our Goddess Isis the protector, and Goddess Sekhmet the destroyer of our enemies and the healer of disease. Your constant calling of the goddesses to safeguard us has made me proud of you as my daughter."

I could feel the tears trickling down my cheeks and I tried not to wipe them away, as it would show that I was emotional.

"I promised you the finest horse to care for. A brave swift horse that will be at your command. I relinquish my choice and allow you to recognise the animal you desire. I must leave it to you to choose my daughter."

A sudden golden flash flickered in the sky, like an electrical storm without the rain. Goddess Isis commanded that her throne be honoured. The horses, who were restless and uneasy, were still being paraded, but the one who had bowed to me was strong and proud and holding his rightful place.

"This magnificent stallion has chosen me, and I lay claim to him, but first Father, I can only accept if my sisters have had their choice of a magnificent beast from this herd."

Father looked flushed and seemed impatient with my request; he could never refuse the heart's desires of his daughters. Saf, Tani and Kali were ushered forward, and they too eyed the selection of thoroughbreds.

I noticed a new commander and having not seen him before, I was intrigued by his graceful movements. He hurriedly stepped forward to assist, then snapping his fingers, he drew a symbol in the air as the men took a step backwards in response to his signal. As the commander spoke firmly, the rising sun made a shimmering pathway in the morning sky as though in obedience to his command.

"Make way for the palace princesses," he said firmly. I noticed that his eyes were trained on Safiya, and as the light touched her smooth features, he took a deep breath as though to take in her beauty. "But first, allow me to introduce myself. I am Yahya, the second commander of the Pharaoh's forces."

Another flash of golden light lit the morning sky, and I knew that Isis had agreed with the transaction, and the recognition of Yahya. The clouds parted and a dazzling display of light danced around us all as we gathered in front of the stables. The girls moved with lithe animation so as not to startle the animals, and each stroked and spoke gently to the horses until they had chosen their prize.

To my joy, Prince Asim had entered the front line of onlookers and caught my eye with a nod of proud recognition that I knew my horses. Thank goodness his father's guard was not in sight as I looked lovingly at Asim. I ran my hand down Khonsu's shoulder, gently touched his muzzle and tousled his forelock. He had been handled well and did not shy away from my touch. I was in complete awe of my very own Arabian stallion.

Glancing at my sisters, our looks to each other immediately conveyed that we had chosen our horses. Then without speaking, we each focused on our father for his approval.

"You have all chosen well, and this will enhance the training of these Arabian horses to our liking by the Bedouin tribesmen."

Father ordered us to venture to the paired horses for the chariots. Although at peace with the Hittites, he was always prepared for battle with his charioteers. His army was still in place as Grandfather had divided it into four separate divisions in order to make it more manageable.

Named after the Gods Ra, Seth, Amun and Ptah, the infantry was well equipped and proudly on display today and the chariots were brought forward to be inspected. The Egyptian army followed the Hittite concept of one charioteer and two marksmen, famous for their precision bowmanship. The horses were led out in pairs, prancing, and pulling in perfect symmetry, and the chariots, polished and gleaming, showed no sign of being battle-worn.

Safiya moved up close to Father to ask his permission to ride in the back, and Tani was right behind her. To my surprise, he nodded, and they brought two chariots forward, one for each of my sisters. This skilled chariot riding was a show for all to see, as Saf and Tani climbed up, one into the back of each chariot.

They were armed with bows and set off at an incredible pace, the dust whirling as the soldiers crammed in along the line that the chariots would follow. Finally, the girls nocked their arrows into their bows whilst flying forwards, expertly balancing their bodies as the chariots raced ahead, and they yelled out for the wooden shields to be held up as targets. The horses' hooves thundered as they galloped around the track, with the wheels of the chariots spinning lightly and quickly.

It was exciting to see the show put on by the two powerful young fighting women, balancing precariously on their chariots, as they drew back their bows to release their arrows into the targets.

Tani's chariot suddenly veered off course and crashed into Safiya's at such a high speed that the wooden and leather frames graunched and Tani was thrown into the throng of soldiers and disappeared. She was athletic though, and rolled on the ground and came up unhurt, and full of adrenalin, determined to regain her ride.

On the beaten hard sand slithering away from the scene was a rock snake, the same type of snake that had been in the basket on the felucca, which was an unusual sight this far away from the river. As though it had never been there, it suddenly disappeared and I noticed Asim's father's guard in the distance, dusting himself off and holding his arm. I immediately thought that the shapeshifter was no match for the goddess's power, but it was apparent that he was still out to destroy.

Tani bounded back onto the chariot as it came around again and slowed to collect her, then sped around the track again for showmanship.

Finally, they came to a halt, the dust whirling and to the full appreciation of the infantry, who were clapping loudly. The arrows had penetrated deep and true into the grain of the wooden shields. The girls were heralded as true warriors, and there was a thick smell in the air of horse sweat and human perspiration as we all baked in the sun's intense heat.

I saw Tani's eyes grow large and full of excitement as she gasped and exhaled through her lips, as though she had narrowly escaped her ordeal to now be standing next to Kal and I. We held each other for longer than usual until I finally relaxed, feeling blessed that she was okay and that my foresight and vision were here and not on the battlefield. She could not understand how that snake was slithering on the track as the guards had checked it thoroughly before the race. The horses had shied precariously away but had managed to hold their gait due to the expertise of the Bedouin trainers.

"Sister," she said wisely, "there will be many snakes as we venture into the desert. However, this experience has helped me to become more cautious. I will need my mother's healing touch on some of my scrapes today and I look forward to a soak in the bath."

"You were magnificent," I said, still shaking a little from the incident. "Tani, you were so quick to get back on your feet. It is such a huge advantage that you are light and agile. Keep it this way as it is your superior edge over others. Father was proud of you both, and so am I my beautiful sister."

I kissed her forehead and sent direct healing energy from Hathor into her heart and body. As Father marched over the parched sand to us, Safiya, covered in dust, was fully engaged in conversation with Yahya.

"Tani, I have not seen such skill in any of my warriors as I saw in you today. I am so proud of you and Safiya, you are all priceless seeds of our royal house and faultless in your aim and precision," Father said.

"What do you say, Prince Asim? Were you proud of your upcoming wife's family?"

Without waiting for a response, he continued with passion.

"My daughters are precious. They are born of the highest realm and carry a sacred bloodline that you must cherish. Do you understand your role in protecting this line, Prince Asim? You hold a great weight upon you, to take my daughter to Thebes. She must be in safe hands, for she will bring significant power if you honour her destiny, or she will destroy Thebes if you forsake her," he said, holding full eye contact with Prince Asim and, not waiting for an affirmative answer to any of his questions, he spun on his heels and headed back to his infantry.

I was spellbound. Father had completely expressed his knowledge of our worth as 'Sisters of the Light'.

"Your recovery was bold and brave as you remounted, Tanith. I too, am proud of you and Saf," Asim said with calm assurance as he smiled at me and grasped my hand.

Prince Asim held me in a long deep gaze as he said something that chilled me to the bone on this steaming muggy day.

"Tanith has excellent qualities as a woman and a warrior. I did notice that two of the guards who rushed forward when she went down were not from here. They were part of the group of prisoners that your grandfather brought back from battle, to work for their freedom. I will have them watched, but I did see a look in their eyes that she is a prized possession."

Breathe into the shallow mist and allow reality to dissipate.
Feel wonder and enchantment of yesterday's world.

May you be the one to see and sense beyond the veil of now.

Only in the essence of being in awe of this life
will we see the space that allows worlds
to collide simultaneously in unison with one another.
May we tread quietly in the space.
May we detect the winds of change.

Knowing this, the gateway to self-discovery
and enlightenment opens and waits for us to discover it.

Only then can the courageous enter through the timeless
vortex of space within time, a realm where the past, present,
and future coexist, the molecules that exist in silence.

Are you the enlightened being to pass through these caverns?
Have you allowed yourself the request to know that the
gateway exists? Or are you waiting to be told through
science that this reality has always existed?

Maybe we have been unable to grasp this in our innate intelligence
while waiting for humanity's knowledge to confirm it.

Seek now; do not wait until your physical form
has been extinguished in this life.
Allow faith and fearlessness to guide you
on your journey of pure enlightenment.

DESIRE

"Mother, please try to be more gentle," Tanith protested in discomfort.

"You deserve a scolding, not being pampered, for even riding the chariots like that. But, of course, your father will always push the limits by allowing you girls such freedom. I would never have agreed to let you ride on the war chariots under any circumstances. The risk you have taken has left you in an extremely precarious position. If anything were to happen, we as women in our family would be left vulnerable."

"That is why we did not want you to come, Mother. You would have forbidden us even to choose our own horses. You are so overprotective."

Mother turned slowly, her eyes bright with anger.

"Horses! Who allowed such foolishness? Next, you will be riding off on a desert safari, oblivious to all the danger," she said with heavy emotion. "You girls are our possibility for future generations to continue our bloodline, to be seeded for thousands of years into the future. We cannot jeopardise this with acts of mortal danger."

"What bloodlines Mother? Thousands of years. What are you saying? Anyway, you want us to be survivors, strong and unafraid. How can we develop these elements of courage if you keep us locked up here in the palace?"

Tani tried to get her questions answered, but she was completely ignored. There was so much tension in the room that it hung like a storm cloud, unable to leash its fury.

While Mother tried calming herself and attending to Tanith, I slipped away to engage with Herihor. As I entered the apothecary, he leapt to his feet, and I noticed that he appeared robust, eager, and ready to return to our other life, which was now far from my intention. I wanted to turn and walk out, back into the arms of Asim, but I was mesmerised while gazing into Herihor's sea-green eyes, and I stammered, "I am not ready to return yet. I see that you are healthy and have gained the connections to your legs that we had hoped for, but Tani has had an accident and I need to ensure that she is going to be alright."

Herihor knew that I was stalling for time, but he was gentle as he acknowledged my feelings that were holding me firmly to stay here. He reached out to me, and we held hands, a strange feeling of desire washing over me as we connected.

"I will return soon, within the coming moon, and we will depart," I murmured as I pulled away and stood to bid him goodbye.

I needed a little more time to fulfil some of my fantasies with Prince Asim before he returned to Thebes. My desire for Asim grew even more potent as I visualised his handsome, sturdy features. It was painful to be apart from him, even for a few hours.

I bathed, dressed and gathered my skirts, and ran lightly in my soft sandals through the palace to his rooms. His guard lifted the thick hessian partition as I bent down to go inside. Asim was bathing in Frankincense and Blue Lotus water, and my nose tingled with the familiar captivating scents of the divine concoction of soothing, healing, and anointing oils.

"Ahh, my sweet goddess, you have come to release me from my yearning for you and to comfort and console my aching heart, but I must leave soon and return to Thebes to prepare for your homecoming," he murmured in a low husky voice.

I moved to kiss him, then pulled away, slowly unpinning my hair and untied my light-tanned linen dress, letting it slip to the floor and stood naked and unashamed before him. The water dripped and splashed into the bath as he stood and grasped his towel to dry himself. His eyes were all over me and a pleasurable surge of energy spilled into my veins. The day's warmth still tingled on our skin as we came together. His body was all I remembered from when I had observed him on the felucca. The taut muscles in his arms and his muscular thighs were captivating. His maleness was solid and proud, and he was a perfect male specimen as I viewed his torso. Oh, my goddess Hathor would approve of our connection. I let my hair caress his chest, still damp from bathing, and scented with the neroli blossoms.

He inhaled my essence as I lightly touched his chest and ran my fingers over his arms. His muscles bulged as he flexed them, then he grabbed my arms to encircle his waist. He drew back my hair, and his lips caressed my neck and shoulders as we stood. He moved gently down to my breasts and kissed and teased me with his tongue. Heaven was colliding with my heart in that moment, and his breath's warmth created circles of delight over my stomach. He moved downward, caressing, and igniting my aching desire for his touch. As he lifted me effortlessly and laid me on his bedding and cushions, our bodies sang the notes and played the melodic tunes of our lovemaking. The longing in my soul to be fulfilled and feel his magnificence inside me made me shudder with desire throughout the evening. I claimed him deep within me, with gratitude for him being my chosen one. The goddesses had favoured us wisely as we felt all the elements of love cascading around us. Lying together, our fingers entwined, squeezing them tightly said all that needed to be heard, as we had offered our sacred ritual of commitment to each other.

Asim's guard announced Herihor's arrival for a discussion. We dressed quickly, and I moved behind a wall into the room's shadows as Herihor entered.

"Prince Asim, we must embark on our journey homeward after the next moon. We should make haste as there has been conflict and hostility since you have been away."

"Your father has left for Thebes already with his guard Dhoser, who is very displeased with the protection of Thebes and your aligned marriage with the Pharaoh's granddaughter."

"Let us not shake the temple walls, Herihor. As soon as you are officially assigned to Akila's protection, she will amass her power to protect us all in Thebes with you as her High Priest. Those who are devious and have tried to take control of the temple will be punished, and we have the right to instil this, with trust from the Pharaoh himself," Asim replied.

"I do not like this latest unrest as soon as the city lacks its leader, when the masterminds of betrayal come forward," Herihor expressed with deep concern.

"You are a loyal friend of the Gods, and I have placed my trust in you," Asim said. "Therefore, we will leave on our flotilla after the next moon, which will guide us."

As soon as Herihor left, I moved cautiously from the shadows and into the arms of my Prince.

"Thank you for your protection, my love. You honour me with your complete care. However, I have one request for you. I do not wish to share you with a concubine of women in Thebes as my father does. I want to be your every dream and our children will bear the bloodline of high nobility from the Goddess Hathor. They will be ordained and will hold the sacred representation for thousands of years into the future," I said, keeping a strong, steady voice as I continued.

"You, my love, will be the direct seed from which I will sow the garden of our lineage."

"Come here, you temptress. You are my one and only, and I pledge that love to you now. Maybe you are already with child," he said gently. "If so, we will have to marry before the subsequent flooding of the Nile."

"It will not be possible yet, my Prince, as I have an unfulfilled journey," I said with sadness. I held my lower belly and instinctively knew that his seed had already connected to mine, but I also knew that I could not save this baby if I crossed through The Void. Fate had already chosen. I must return to the other world for Herihor, but could I defy destiny and hold off the impending journey?

I steadied myself, my hand lingering on the large wooden storage chest elaborately decorated with scenes and inlaid with precious gems. I let my fingers trail over the artistry, pondering our relationship now that we had offered our sacred ritual to each other. Re-pinning my hair rapidly with a quick motion, I was preparing to leave when Asim came close and thrust himself against me, pressing himself into my pounding chest.

Feeling our breath rise together, I could see his gaze on my throat, where my pulse was pounding. The shortness of my breath caught in my throat as we again allowed ourselves to be lost in the passion of our lovemaking. Still, this time, I took the liberty of being in command, showing him all the moves that instinctively came to me from an echo of my other life.

"You are gifted with the body of a goddess and with the enticing art of an enchantress. How could I share my seed with another?"

he sighed, languishing on the mattress, his naked body glistening with sweat and the sweet smell of our union filling the room.

As I locked eyes with him, I felt an unbreakable bond forming between us. It was as if I could see into the depths of his being, and in that profound moment, I knew without a doubt that I was the sole person of his desire. A warm smile spread across my face, and I was filled with a sense of completeness, knowing that I was the only woman who could truly satisfy him. The idea of sharing him with anyone else was inconceivable to me. It was crystal clear that we had discovered our eternal soulmates in each other.

CALL · FROM
THE · DIVINE

Waking early with Prince Asim on my mind, my body recalled our connection. I could feel my temperature rise as my breath caught in my chest, and I flowed with the feeling, allowing it to warm my body as I briefly closed my eyes.

There was an overshadowing premonition within me that everything was about to change. Nervous and trembling, I shook myself and then dressed with help from my maids, but I found their fussing was very frustrating.

Stepping outside, I sucked in a deep breath as I felt the sun casting her warmth over the waking city. The long, warm days gave me a feeling that time would linger on forever, but not today, however. Everything felt different, as though I needed to improve my tempo of accomplishing things.

I began the journey to the massive North Temple set down by the water. Moving quickly with Nef and with two other guards accompanying me, we strode down the long avenue lined with sphinx. The obelisks and immense statues of my goddesses stood tall and indestructible, glistening in the morning light.

Guards lounging by the eight metre thick walls of the North Temple jumped to attention as we entered the court. My strongest and tallest of all the Nubian warriors, Nef, commanded attention as he glared in their direction. We breezed through into the magnificent Hypostyle Hall. The hieroglyphics and pictures of the great warriors were inscribed and painted on all the walls and columns which held their tales in the magnificent colourful depictions of the power of the Pi-Ramesses kingdom.

Raising my hand to infer that I would go into the sanctuary alone did not faze Nef. He went in first to inspect that the Holy Temple was safe, then stepped back as I swept past him.

I fell to the base of the breathtaking image of my beloved Isis. Crying and pleading to my goddesses about what was happening did not seem to affect a release. All my pent-up emotions had surfaced as I was to hear the implication of what was to unfold. Here, in the stillness, the message was clear. It came with a power and the tremble in my body forced me to grip the granite tightly.

"Akila, hold the sceptre of Isis with both hands. The sky will darken, and the clouds will fall, but all is in alignment with the will of the goddesses. You will surrender a chosen one, a sister, who will move between cities. She will be an ally to tie the bloodlines to a blue-eyed race of people across the seas to the far north. She is well equipped for this and has been training in her agile, supple way to elude danger. Prepare yourselves for this event. The Seed of The Sisters must flourish if we are to have many preparing for the events to come."

I fell to the temple floor in terror of what had been ordained. *My sisters, my precious sisters. What was to become of us? I must gather them and talk, and they must know the will of the goddesses.*

We will seal a pact. Thoughts were crashing around in my head as I looked for scenarios to stop this rampage of time moving forward.

I felt the tender hand of Isis caress my forehead, brushing away the tears from my face. Her light surrounded me, bringing warmth and a glow to the coolness of the temple. My body felt deep healing penetrating my being, finding the recesses of my soul. Finally, reaching the depth of my aeons of light-years, I surrendered to her wisdom. I questioned aloud.

"How will this happen?"

I knew it was Tanith, our baby. She was the one who was able to move between walls. Yet, like the silkiness of the mist, she was almost invisible as she had the grace and strength of Grandfather's lion and the softness and resilience of Mother's tenacity and love.

My snake had now appeared, feeling my anguish. Slithering up my neck, my black cobra uncoiled the long, slender form with the hood fully extended and forked tongue flicking as he gazed around the inner sanctuary. The teardrop marking below his eyes made him look almost emotional, but I knew his power and intent were all but that. Then hissing, with his forked tongue flicking and his hood fully flaring, he was prepared to strike. I knew he was Nef in his shape-shifting form, so I calmed his tension, which helped me calm mine.

Goddess Isis collected herself and continued.

"You will not be fully aware of how this will transpire but leave each other with the seal of nobility fully imprinted in your heart, knowing your lineage. You will consistently, throughout time, be able to call on us. We will be here to change the energy and assist you with messages and sacred scrolls as you open portals in other worlds light-years away."

"Goddess Isis, I feel weakened by this information, as I have told Tani that I will always protect her. I have taught her the symbol we share as sisters. You instructed me, Goddess Isis, to revere these markings as circles of life," I stammered through my tears.

"I will not stop trying to help her wherever she may be," Goddess Isis's words reverberated around the temple.

"Thank you for your constant connection and guidance for me. I revere and honour your wisdom," I choked, as I clung to the magnificent statue of Goddess Isis with her headdress of a massive solar disc between two horns. Her form was soft and subtle as a mother to a child embracing me through my tears.

Instantly, my black cobra slid back and disappeared as I collected myself and drew my gowns around me to connect back to my role. Then, wiping my tear-stained cheeks, I rose and took some deep breaths to inhale the energy in the sanctuary. Bowing low and long to Goddess Isis, her stature had returned as a solid representation of her power to heal the sick and bring life and magic to the throne.

I honoured her insight bestowed upon me, and then stepped out into the Hypostyle Hall. The brightness caused me to squint as I realised hours had passed and the sun was at its peak.

Nef had sent a guard to bring our horses, and we waited, sitting on the stone bench surrounding the hall. He came close and stamped his sceptre on the stone paving to recognise what I had just been through. Sparks leapt and then disappeared as the baton hit the stone. There was a long tone of sound that was hardly audible, but which grew intensely as it resonated out and beyond, like a cry of grief, I thought. I glanced at his firm, calm face to see if he gave away any sign of apprehension, or to acknowledge that he knew what Isis had told me. Still, he remained solid and unwavering in his role of protection. Beads of sweat were trickling down the sides of his face and covering his chest. I wanted to jump up and hug him but knew the breach of protocol would be unforgiving.

We rode in silence back through the city, viewing the houses. People were lining up to wave and acknowledge us. Only a few of the nobility would ride through the town unescorted as we did, but I always felt safe with Nef at my side. I prayed here at this moment that nothing would ever happen to him.

I loved our beautiful city surrounded by water from the branches of the Nile Delta. We had a plentiful supply of food; grain was stored in the warehouses, and the wineries on the Westside were always well-stocked. Camel trains were due to arrive at the port in two days from the West Bank of the Nile with rich Frankincense oils, perfumery oils, and fabrics from faraway lands. We were to join Father on an expedition to gather more camels, beautiful rugs, and supplies from the continent. This may take our minds off everything I thought.

Khonsu held his head proudly; his Arabian breeding made people draw in their breath when they saw him. Finally, I trotted up beside Nef.

"Are you assigned to come to the coast with us as Father takes his troops and acquires supplies?" I asked.

Nef nodded. "Yes, princess, I will always be close," he replied, his deep voice hanging on to the words drawing them out to assure me he would be there. I immediately felt better, as though my world was safe. However, my briefing with Goddess Isis had left me shaken.

Our guards took the horses back to the stables at the palace, but first they would bathe in the canal.

"Mother is looking for you," Safiya scowled. "Where have you been? Tanith, is she with you?" Saf was becoming the military wife, organising and commanding with an authoritative tone and demanding to know where everyone was.

"No," I jumped up immediately. "Where is Tani? I must find her."

"She will not be far, but she has been missing all morning," Saf snapped.

"Let us look for her. She must be at the stables. Tani is so invested in the horses," I replied, panicking inside. We grabbed each other's hands and ran down toward the stables. It was a burning, sweltering day, and we were exhausted when we reached the canal where the horses were bathing.

"Tanith!" I yelled, with all the grooms coming out of the stables to see what the commotion was about.

"Princess Tanith is down by the pools bathing with the horses," one guard yelled.

"She is such a boy," I said to Saf, and then, seeing her in the water with Khonsu washing him down, made me scribe a picture of her boyish form in my vision. Then, like a memory, I would hold her beauty in my mind as she was in that moment, excited and animated. Looking after the horses was paradise for her.

"Tani, we all need to talk urgently when you have finished here," I said.

"I am coming, Sisters, just a few more minutes," she promised.

Saf and I waited as we observed the stable hands when I noticed a very attentive groom trying to help Tani.

"Who is that young man Saf?" I queried.

"I do not know, but he is one of the prisoner's our Grandfather captured. He is of the Ocean People, I believe."

"Those two are close. I will have to speak with this young groom," I responded.

We edged our way under the palms to the bathing pools, and I called out to him.

"Hello, groom. Where are you from?"

He was keeping his head down but, when I called him again, he finally lifted his face to look at Tani and then turned to Saf and me.

My heart jolted like I had been punched, and I stumbled backward. This boy had the brightest piercing blue eyes. I had never seen anyone here in this timeline with eyes like his. It took my mind back to Jonas, his beautiful blue green eyes, and how he looked at me.

"Tani, please tell us what you are doing, and who is this young groom?" I questioned her.

"His name is Khan. He does not speak our language but is learning and teaching me his language. "Isn't he beautiful?" She beamed, a broad smile creasing her cheeks.

She spoke a few strange words to him and pointed to us, saying our names. He bowed his head in humbleness. Saf and I smiled back and then looked at each other inquisitively.

"Tani, we must hasten. It is the time of the feast, and we must talk. Mother is looking for us," I said, trying to keep my voice light, to refrain from showing my desperation.

The day's heat made me wish I could jump in the water with her as Khonsu was pulling, trying to get away from her and come to me. Soothingly and calmly, I spoke to Khonsu to put him at ease.

Tani turned to Khan, spoke a few more words, and placed her hand on his arm. Then, she gracefully drew herself out of the water and sauntered over to us.

"Let's go," she said cheekily.

We all held hands and, swinging our arms, we walked off, with Tani turning to have a last look at the boy. Her wet clothes clinging to her body showed clearly that she was a beautiful, budding young woman.

We were heading straight to Kalina's for Tani to change out of her wet, steaming attire and for us to get ready for the afternoon feast. Our maids came running with our clothes, beautiful colours, and striking hues of soft-dyed linen.

"Now that we are together, I must share this message," I whispered. "We must talk as the goddesses have communed with me."

They sank onto the large cushions on the floor as I ushered our maids out.

"What is it that you are so desperate to talk about here?" Kal asked inquisitively.

"We are on the edge of an unusual happening."

I had no idea how to start, so I just blurted it out.

"We must be prepared for changes in our world. Tani, you are young, but you are strong and courageous. We will be separated. Tani will be taken to live in another country," I wailed.

"What?" Everyone cried in unison as we huddled closer.

"I have spoken to the goddesses, and Goddess Isis told me directly of Tani's union with a blue-eyed prince."

We all stared at Tani, who clapped and seemed excited.

"Khan is my prince," she said slowly. "He tells me he is the son of a king in a foreign land and that they are searching for him."

"There is more. I must talk to you all together, as Kal and her man know of my journeys."

I looked at Kal, who was twisting her hands together and moving restlessly.

"I was not going to say anything for fear of unease; however, I must reveal the secrets of us as sisters, as Kal's mother and our mother are sisters who share a common ancestry. We are a unique bloodline that can transcend timelines. This is inherited from our mothers."

I looked at each of them individually, as though I would see a solution, but nothing came.

"We are aligned as 'Sisters of the Light', to travel through and along the timeline. I can travel to another life where I am living another destiny. Our mother can also do this. Your mother Kal was a traveller also. When you were born, you were facing the wrong way. The birthing woman tried to change your position; however, and we are unsure why, but your mother went into The Void and could not fully come back into her body as she was in too much discomfort and pain. There is a space in The Void where all time stands still, and she was caught in that. She persisted and was able to birth you before she passed. I call this time, 'The Hush', and she could not fully come back through. That is the grief our mother holds for her sister as she had tried desperately to call her back through The Void. That is the grief of you not having your mother, Kal. So now you know, and I am sorry to have delivered this knowledge so abruptly; however, we need to be aware of our advantages and tragedies," I said with care. It was as though I had shaken the world of Egypt to its foundations.

We all went silent as we hugged Kal and each of us felt deep sorrow for what could have been.

"Mother could never tell you. She has only just finally explained to me what happened to your mother, Kal, and she feels responsible for this," I continued. "As yet, you girls have not gone through The Void. Although it could happen at any time, your children may also be time travellers. We do not know when it can be activated. Mother asked me never to take you through The Void for fear she may also lose you girls. However, I will if needed and if the time comes," I stumbled with my words.

"This is much to consider, but with Goddess Isis's information in her Holy Temple today, she insisted that we must be prepared. Tani, you must be careful when the time comes and know that this transition to another country will bring many risks.

However, you must not fight so bravely and lose your life when you know this is your pathway. The goddesses will guide you if you open your heart and listen. We will forever be linked, and we will find you and come to you. You will never be forsaken. We hold your life as a sacred part of our lotus. Life-through-life."

Our combined intake of breath of all that had been revealed at this moment had us clutching onto one another in our huddle. When we drew back and felt what was happening between us, we knew that they would never deceive us, and so, in the joy of living, we realised the truth of our birth.

"So, our evening feast will be about our honour to each other and to remain in our purpose, which is more significant than ourselves. We will unite many times, and in the future, we will arrive from many destinations to come together and recognise each other. This is the will of the goddesses."

Where had the time gone? Where had the years gone? We solemnly made our way to the banquet hall in the failing light, and even though the music was thrilling and enticing, there was an air of loneliness hidden in the recesses of the hall.

Tani was exuberant and excited as she hummed a strange melody upon entering the hall, and lightly sashayed forward to place herself next to Mother. I saw her slip her arm around our mother's waist and push herself close while raising her face to deliver a sweet smile to her.

Be with me, Goddess Isis, protector and guardian.

Mother of Horus, I abide by your wisdom and magic.

You grant me an extension of your powers,
by which I am honoured you have faith in me.
I bring commitment to my role.
I am shielded by your divine protection
even when the gathering of danger surrounds me.

Your sheltered love is a potent force,
capable of healing and resurrecting the ailing.
I feel your mighty force and magnificence
as you extend your wings, preserving the magic
and wisdom for eternity throughout our sun-kissed Egypt.

As the daughter of the Earth God Geb and the sky Goddess Nut,
your richness is steeped in the Earth
and connects with the star-studded universe.
Goddess Isis, your power transcends
that of all the other gods and goddesses.
Grant me the anointing of your hands on my head
so I may feel your intense passion for all life.

I see your magical prowess collecting the golden thread
in the thunder of the skies to bring lightning fire
over the oceans and blaze a trail before you.
Your unlimited protection and endearing love fuel
a light that will never diminish in my soul.

T H E · O A S I S

"Come quickly, Kal. Everyone is nearly ready."

Kalina and Safiya were taking their time. We wanted to reach the oasis before the sun was low in the sky for our entourage and guards to set up camp. There was at least a half-day ride and then another half-day to the encampment, where the traders would meet.

Dakari conversed deeply with Asim, who looked regal in his short wrap. I knew I was blushing as Asim turned to look at me and smiled boldly, his smooth-shaven face charmingly boyish.

Tani had already been to the stables to help the groomsmen as they shipped the horses across the delta. She came running up breathlessly and fled past us to get changed, the distinct earthy smell of the horses was all over her.

"I will not be long, Sister," she almost sang in a melodic voice filled with excitement.

I observed her with her strong-willed determination and relaxed a little. I just wanted to enjoy each precious moment with her as a young woman. *Why? She is so young to be away from us. Why did the goddesses choose her?* I cried inwardly.

Suddenly we were swept up in the excitement, as my mother came out to wish us a safe journey. Her face was lined and weary as though she had not slept, and a few tendrils of her hair had slipped out of her headdress. Although her countenance was regal and collected, she seemed very agitated. The five of us held each other tight in a circle, with Kalina tucked between me and Tani.

I noticed the long lingering embrace Tani had with Mother and the tears rolling down Mother's cheeks. Was she aware of something? Of course, she knew everything. Nothing escaped her knowledge. She clasped Tani's hands and whispered a loving endearment to her, kissing her on both cheeks. They moved into each other's arms, holding on tightly for as long as possible. Whatever was to come we were held in the fragile whisper of the sands, moving silently with the intention of change. I wiped my eyes and spun on my heels, my sandals squeaking on the stone floor.

Looking highly tailored in his uniform, Yahya was in the front of the entourage. He nodded to us, particularly Saf, who fluttered her eyes at him. Kalina stood with Dakari, holding his arm to steady her emotions. I smiled and moved to my man's side. With his height towering over me, I looked lovingly up into his eyes. My body shook as I felt a tingle of desire for him. Then a fleeting feeling of sadness about Tani's impending departure overcame me.

Herihor, observing us, moved out of the shadows of the Main Hall, and prepared to join us.

"Herihor, we will embark on this journey without you," Asim explained. "You will fully recuperate and be fit to travel to Thebes on my return."

I felt relieved and I am sure Herihor noticed the sigh of relief that escaped my lips as my shoulders relaxed. We quickly made eye contact and smiled at each other. A fleeting vision of us in the hospital came unannounced into my mind. It reminded me of that far-away lifetime for just a moment.

Our procession was ready, so we walked briskly with urgency, heading for the flotilla to take us to the opposite banks of the Nile.

I took a deep breath, and as royal children, we moved together in silent synchronicity, holding hands as we viewed the magnificent array of palm trees and listened to the squawking of the ducks and geese lifting their laden cumbersome bodies out of the reeds as we floated past.

The punts carried us to the other side to disembark and mount our horses, which were waiting patiently, with lines of guards surrounding our entourage. Significantly, empty wooden cases were being carried on carts pulled by donkeys, to bring our spoils home.

I was looking forward to finding material for my wedding, as Kalina and I had previously been excitedly discussing the colours of our gowns and robes and noticed the young groomsman leading two prized stallions, who were snorting restlessly in anticipation of a fast ride: between the guards, up to our father and uncle.

Where was Tani? I could not see her, and I whirled around, flustered and in a panic. Finally, I saw her with Safiya, her head thrown back in laughter like a joyful child as Saf was teasing her.

The wave patterns on the sand gently moved in the distance as Father and Uncle led the way forward, with a surge of horses ready and willing to race. There was only a slight movement in the air as we moved along the beaten trail. Singers kept pace, and excitement and carefree harmony filled the air.

It may have been minutes or hours before I settled back into my body. I knew I had been travelling, not through The Void, but carried on the gentle movement like a papyrus seed floating on the current. Khonsu was plodding rhythmically onward, shuddering as he felt me re-enter my body.

I had been on a timeless journey of teachings and instructions, all with Goddess Hathor, who was showing me the birthing of many extraordinarily gifted children. One after another; hundreds, millions, who all had telepathic abilities. They connected through sound vibration and were calling to each other, like the whales in the oceans. Human children who were growing into adults, sending their cosmic vibrations to each other to reconnect.

They were sensitive children, energetically enhanced children, but many lacked the communication skills and language. Nevertheless, they were experts in their field, each drawing on a valued viewpoint for themselves. They must not be stemmed or quashed from their unique qualities. Many would be labelled and numbed down but, if given the right path of the wayfarer, some would rise to greatness. I realised how small we were individually, yet collectively we were a mass of human families borne of the same knowledge, to come together at a time in the future. The stars and the planets will align when we are needed most for 'The Great Awakening'.

"Aki, look at how well Khan holds himself," Tani said softly, as she rode beside me. "He holds the bearing of a great prince. Even in his acts of service, he already displays strong character for a young man."

"You are fanciful of him, but Father will never agree to you being associated with a groomsman," I replied. I checked Tani's facial emotions and saw her curl her lips in determination and then change to smile sweetly at me.

"Well, he may not have a choice as Khan is my Hittite prince, and I will not let Father decide for me."

I looked intently at Tani and realised she was telling her truth.

"Well, my darling sister, the goddesses will decide for you, and I believe in whoever you choose. However, it will be unforgivable if Father learns of these thoughts of betrayal. I will talk with him when I have the opportunity, but we must not let on that Khan is a prince as you say he is. If the military considers him a threat, he will undoubtedly be put to death," I said earnestly.

"Please do not say anything to anyone. I trust you and need an ally on my side if the time comes. But, Sister, let us enjoy the journey to the market and choose the fabrics for your wedding robes," Tani whispered as she reached out for my hand.

Every moment was priceless as I squeezed her small strong hand and held the look of sisterly love between us. She drew her two circles in the air precisely and I drew mine back to her as we laughed at life's sheer delight.

Setting up camp was a fast and efficient task. The main tent was erected first with the smell of warming loaves of bread, meats, and spices within to tempt our taste buds.

Asim and I walked away from it and felt the day's heat diminishing as we discussed our future. The horses had already drunk from the pools of water bursting out of the ground forming a shallow lake. They were now tied in pairs and being fed grasses and sweet honey sugars by the stable hands accompanying us. Khonsu neighed as we walked close by him but then, head down, he ate hungrily from the baskets held up to him. Our soldiers thronged to the site and guarded the small oasis, and we felt safe and secure, protected and in safe hands. However, Nef, still holding his bearings standing at the tent's entrance, was unable to let his guard down.

Out of sight a little, I stood up tall to brush my warm lips on Asim's, and he reacted by moving his body next to mine and I felt his manhood pressing and eager to be with me. It was such a wondrous feeling to be so close yet it was so tantalising and seductive that we could not immediately use the sacred energy of our impending union when I could wrap myself around him. Instead, our energy would build, then in time, we would consume it together and breathe our sensual release in the afterglow of our lovemaking. I was breathless again and so was Asim, as we gazed longingly at each other, hoping the time to lay together again would be soon.

The stars beckoned as the night sky fell with a dazzling display of meteorites lasering through the galaxy at speed, a golden tail of light trailed from them, piercing the depth of infinity. My Goddess 'Elestial Star' was prominent in the dark night sky, bold and twinkling in anticipation of all the years in the future that she would continue to exist.

Still in awe of her magnificence, I silently crept into the tent I shared with Kalina and my sisters. Together, we allowed the love generated by our ancestry to flow through us as we whispered stories of joyous childhood adventures while sharing dreams for our futures.

Kalina spoke up, suddenly talking about her mother.

"I wish I had known her. The sadness of her passing has tortured me. Now I know how it happened and how she could not return to me. My father left to go south to the gates of Nubia to be in the army, which left me feeling abandoned.

I would love to know my father and learn why he left me as a baby. Did he not love me? Would he recognise me today? Would he be proud of me? Did my aunt ever say she met my mother in the other timeline? Does she still exist there?"

"I have no idea where or who she is, dear Cousin. Now you are close to marriage, will your father come up to be at the celebrations? We will approach my father and attend to his wishes if he wants him there."

I pulled the covers over Kalina and held her tight as we all snuggled up, each thinking of the unknown aspects of our world.

The morning noises and awareness of the aromas outside returned to me immediately on waking, reminding me of where I was, as I leapt up to wash in the basin of freezing water, with towels placed neatly on the stool ready for us.

Strolling down to the makeshift altar, I could see that Father had already summonsed his gods for the day, as I bowed in reverence to my goddesses. A soldier walked briskly past me, and I felt my snake quivering as he rose around my throat. I reassured him that all was well, although I hesitated in thinking that so quickly. He remained in the defensive position until the soldier was out of sight.

It was the start of an exciting day as we left our encampment, leaving thirty soldiers behind to guard the oasis. Riding gallantly for hours before the sun was too high, we reached the outskirts of the town's Per Amun House, or Temple of the Sun God Amun. The sounds and pungent smells assaulted our bodies in the market, yet we continued with enthusiasm toward the bustling centre.

Many foreign strangers from unusual origins and with different languages milled around the main stands. Nef constantly remained on alert, and as I observed his stern features, I felt more love and compassion for his presence. Camels were herded into areas corralled by a ring of herdsmen, and I remembered how father would acquire more of these beasts to use for necessary travel across the desert.

"We will choose mothers with a calf to breed from," Father told Uncle. "These beasts are such a commodity here. We can use them on strategic missions across the desert. They can go without water for two weeks or more, and because of their double layer of eyelashes and because they can close off their noses and breathe through a slit in their upper lip, they can survive the sandstorms."

Fascinated, I wanted one more than ever now, I thought, as I eyed the almost fully grown calves milling around their mothers.

Leaving the men to check the animals, we set out for the merchant's stalls. There were numerous oil merchants, and our purchasers were selecting jars of the liquids for use with the priests and embalmers.

"Saf, are you coming with us?" I asked, as I saw her moving away with Yahya and his guards.

"I will be okay with Yahya. You go on with Nef." Saf replied, trying to shake me off.

"Tani, come look at these and feel the softness of the fabrics. What do you think? Would you like robes of these colours for our weddings?"

Tani shrugged with disinterest. I knew she was not interested in clothing; just the basics were all she ever wanted.

We admired the thick rugs, their colours like the softness of the marshes, and the magical sunsets of reds and oranges.

"Mother would love one of these," Tani beamed as she smoothed the fabric. "I have chosen this for her," she said, turning to our guards to collect the goods.

Kalina and I were engrossed in fabrics and textures and did not see Tani move away from the stand. It was Nef who drew her back to our group.

"Come along, Tani, do not look so severe. We are here to have fun while away from Pi Ramesses. We will soon be home, so let us just enjoy ourselves." I was getting frustrated with watching Tani and trying to keep her amused.

Late in the afternoon, we began the journey back to the oasis and I noticed that the clouds were thickening, which was usual here on the coast, where we had the most rainfall.

Father was organising to have the supplies loaded and our herdsmen to bring the camels, while the donkeys were moving ahead, pulling their cases loaded with cargo.

The oasis was a welcoming sight as we came in exhausted from our day of haggling to get the best deals. My sisters, quiet and ready to dismount, were hungry and tired. With the groomsmen tending to the horses, we moved into the main tent, where tasty dishes had been prepared. We were ravenous and sat down to feast. Tani was the only one who still needed to enter.

Leaping to my feet, I moved swiftly outside to find her and walked over to the horses, where I knew she would be.

"Come now, Tani, our father and uncle are waiting for us all."

She rested her hand on Khan's, intimately just for a moment as a gesture of care. He swallowed when I looked at him, observing the starkness of his blue eyes in the fading light as though they were pools of the sea that spanned the oceans. He bowed slightly, and a flash of lightning lit up the sky at that exact moment. The horses reared and moved against each other, some kicking out in frightened backlash from the noise. It was odd. There was no rain. Only the skies darkening and the blackened rolling clouds which covered the last remnants of light. Still, the lightning persisted far away in the night sky, lighting up the darkened clouds.

I could hear the voice of Goddess Aset, or Isis. "Akila, hold the sceptre of Isis with both hands. The sky will darken, and the clouds will fall, but all are aligned with the will of the goddesses."

Grabbing Tani's hand, we returned to the tent, the swirling sand picking up the energy surrounding our feet. Immediately, Nef was at our side, and he picked Tani up as we ran for shelter in the tent, which was being laced up.

The night felt mysterious, seducing our world. Magus held his sceptre, raising it to the sky and muttering his spells. I knew the Storm God Sutekh was here, creating the battering of the desert. I called on Goddess Aset as she held us, her faith strengthening us.

We lay quietly together, hearing the whirling and cries of the wind picking away at the tent's base. The trees around the oasis sheltered us, but I felt far from restful.

The girls had drifted off to sleep lulled by nature, giving us her bountiful breath, so I waited while the storm quietened, then drew myself stealthily out under the bottom lace, moving silently like the wind herself, whipping the hair out of my tied headband, I crept to Asim's tent.

"Asim, my love," I whispered above the restless animals and wind noise. "Can you unlace and let me in?"

Momentarily there was shuffling then a slight opening allowed me to slip through.

"I could not sleep," I murmured, my voice husky with desire. "The goddesses are stirring the land and my passion for you is electrifying."

"My heart and body are always awake and ready for you, Child of the Light. I am entrusted into your care," he said, stroking my face.

Tonight, I wanted Asim to be the strong one, enriched in his lovemaking and taking me to the heights of my Goddess Star.

"Lead me, my love, and take me to the world of pure pleasure and soul discovery," Asim teased and taunted me, lightly playing his fingers down my arms and thighs. Finally, he drew my thin gown aside, revealing my slim naked belly. He kissed me on my navel and kissed me everywhere until I was lost in the moment, moving beyond the stars to feel the breath of the gods, breathing their whisper-light touch on my soul. Then Asim moved to be inside me, collected by the goddesses he was taken and drawn into my hidden sacredness where he was urged to release his power, which sent shivers of timelessness for me to draw on, as we clung to the others' release and fullness of surrender.

Quivering in the afterglow, we had abandoned all thoughts, when suddenly we heard shouts and someone yelling for guards. The horses were loose! I listened to them jostling and squealing with the fierceness of their panic. Khonsu, I must get to him! What was happening? Slipping out under the laces, I ran instinctively to the horses.

"Khonsu!," I called. It was dark, and the torches only partially lit the area around them. I noted that the winds had subsided, but the thick dark clouds hung heavy in the night sky, suppressing the moon's light.

Nef was immediately there, his large form commanding and forceful as he moved me aside. Armed with his knife, he was moving in the darkness toward the sound of the horses as they were bolting off into the distance. I glimpsed a lithe figure, which I knew was Tani, dressed as a boy, with her bow slung low off her shoulder, running with her horse as she flung herself onto its back. Then, they disappeared into the night, being swallowed in the darkness. Nef was already mounted as he too galloped off, with soldiers in quick pursuit.

"Wait! Stop!" I yelled to Nef, but the surging wind swallowed my voice up.

Father, Uncle, and Asim quickly mounted their horses as they realised Tani was missing. All the women were in the large tent crying and wailing.

My sisters and Kal were crying, too, as they reached out to me. We huddled and sobbed as we knew the prophecy of the goddesses had been delivered. Goddess Aset had come on the wind.

"Please Goddesses, protect Tani and Khan, for they are destined to be together. Ride like the wind Tani. Be where you are born to be," I stuttered through my tears.

I knew however, that Nef would not give up. He would ride to the end of the earth to protect our sister. At that moment, I wished I had confided in him and told him what the goddesses had ordained, but instead, my black snake was struggling to raise his head. His hood was down, and he was suffering.

We waited for hours, and I felt the energy of my snake wilting, until we heard yelling for us to bring the priest and physician. Someone had been hurt and I prayed it was not Asim, then corrected myself, as all our strong men were there. We prepared liniment salves and a place to bring the wounded. When they came through the tent, two men supported Nef, covered in blood, but he was still trying to shrug them off. An arrow with the quill broken off was embedded in his right upper chest. I checked the head and knew it was Tani who had fired it. She could have killed him easily, but no one was able to shake her desire to be free with her young man.

"Nef, thank you! I am so sorry this has happened to you. It is my fault. I should have confided in you," I whispered.

He recognised what I was saying and was ready for the Magus to perform his rituals. The physician was preparing to pull the barb out of his chest but decided not to hold him down, as it would be worse if he fought. I sent the breath of life to my snake, as I could feel his weakness. 'Goddesses, I pray that this will be easy for Nef, for he does not deserve the pain.' A lone lightning bolt let loose from the heavens and its light lit up the tent.

"Thank you for hearing my plea," I whispered to my goddesses.

The graunching of flesh and sinew made a squishing sound as the barb was manoeuvred to the surface. It was not as deep as it could have been. She would have had to hold back for it to lodge just in the surface layers.

Father was tired and angrier than I had ever seen him, furious that Tani was taken and the horses! How many horses were missing? Had they seized them, or were they wandering the desert?

He sent soldiers to follow them and bring them back, or return with news of the abduction, so we were to camp here for a few days more to see what the outcome would be.

"Akila," my father boomed. "Commune with your goddesses and Goddess Hathor to see where Tanith is. She has been captured and taken against her will. Will they use her as extortion tactics?" Father moaned.

"Your guard has been injured, and you are responsible. You should have been more in service with your goddesses as they have not stood by you."

I cringed at the harshness in his voice but stood my ground, knowing that the goddesses had already spoken, but I could not pass this information to Father, so without explanation, I walked out and strode to the altar. The intention of my prayer was for Nef not to get an infection, but Mother would be able to sort that out. I took a deep breath as the light in the morning sky struggled to push her way through the clouds as they hung oppressively overhead. What could I say to everyone? The truths that I did know must remain concealed.

I called in the winds of the desert to create a storm between Tani and the soldiers. I felt the power of the wind's breath curling her mighty source, to shift the sands and make a cover for Tani to escape. I could see the stinging sands whirling through the veil, turning the soldiers, halting them in their pursuit. Two other riders with her and Khan were skirting on both sides to protect her. Tani could sense me there through the sand and she turned to gaze directly at me, drawing me into her, as we reached through the distance to each other in an earnest, emotionally charged farewell gaze.

Goddess Isis immediately entered the vision and touched my aching heart for Tani, letting me know the words I must use to placate the Kingdom. I bowed in honour and prayed for a decisive resolution for our sister's safe return.

"Aki, come and see Nef. He asked you to attend him," Saf called, ushering me into the healing tent.

"Nef, I know you are suffering." His skin was hot and damp, a sign of the beginning of an infection. As I touched him, he flinched and raised his arm to stop me.

"You must listen, Akila. Tani has killed two soldiers. She executed them with fine precision, firing her arrows one after the other. I pulled the arrows out and buried them deep in the sand even though I was wounded. I snapped the quill off my arrow so as not to arouse suspicion. Hopefully, the ravens will have feasted on their souls by now, so the gods will be favourable, and the ravens will have guided their souls into battles for our Pharoah in their afterlife. They represent luck, and this must be our soldier's sacrifice. You must express this to your father and uncle when they do not return."

Taking a deep breath, I gently placed my hands under Nef's ribs to reassure him and help him rest. My dear Nef. Once their souls are reclaimed, the sands will cover the men. It is imperative that Tani remains free from any entanglement in controversy with my father.

The healers came in unannounced and opened the bandages on his wound, which looked ugly and swollen.

"Please bring the Frankincense, Lavender and Myrrh oils we have just purchased for the embalmers immediately," I said with authority. The heavy flasks were placed beside the bed, and I waved for everyone to leave. Then, dipping a corner of linen in the oil, I dripped a little of each oil into the gaping hole as I had seen Mother do. Then, re-covering the wound, I kissed Nef and urged him to rest.

In the distance, I heard a loud neighing as the dust stirred on the horizon. *Oh, please be Khonsu,* I thought. I knew that Tani would never take him. Suddenly his proud form came galloping towards the oasis. As I called out, he changed direction and headed directly towards me; his coat was wet with sweat and covered in a fine layer of desert sand, which showed he had travelled some distance and behind him trailed the mares and the other missing horses. Father came out and slapped Khonsu on the rump, happy to see him.

"What is this, Akila?" Father looked bewildered and then angry. "Your childhood circles are written with blood on his coat. What do you make of it?"

Khonsu was snorting and trembling, stomping his hooves. Father immediately wiped them off and stared at me. He knew that drawing two circles meant that we were content and safe and that we used only a single circle if there was danger or fear. The frown covered his face as his inquisitive eyes drilled into me, and it dawned on him in that moment that Tani had not been taken against her will.

HOMEWARD JOURNEY

The sombre movement of our return trip seemed to drag on. Safiya, Kalina, and I stayed close as though trying to insulate ourselves against the wave of sadness blanketing our entourage. The soldiers too, were affected. My father and uncle, who were riding in front of the soldiers, were not speaking. My father had not expressed his feelings to me since the event when he understood Tani had chosen her destiny.

During our journey, we faced a three-day delay due to a surrounding storm, making it challenging to care for Nef. Nef's delirious state led to moments of urgency, with him even yelling at times and urging Tanith to turn back. His delirium resulted in him providing an undue recollection of information, suggesting Tanith resisted her rescue. If this account of the details were to fall into the wrong hands, it would threaten our family.

We had not anticipated the depth of sorrow we would feel without the radiance of our little sister by our sides. Our hearts ached in her absence, and we worried about the challenges she might be facing. Although her departure was difficult, I chose to have faith that all was well, knowing that higher powers had sanctioned it. I felt nauseous the whole time on the homeward trek. I had been conscious I wanted to be sick but kept swallowing the bile that rose in my throat.

I continued to pray to Goddess Hathor to guide Tani wherever she was heading. Although she was the strongest of the four of us, she was still our baby sister. I could feel the almighty Goddess Hathor wrapping herself around Tani, breathing her strength upon her. Tani was headstrong in the face of adversity, and I prayed she would not upset her comrades by overusing her combat skills. Tani loved to show her talent with her ability to use various tactics, especially two-weapon fighting skills and sneak attacks.

I recalled how she could throw the knife so swiftly that any creature she threw her blade at died instantly without even knowing that they had been struck, but, on the other hand, she never killed without purpose, always taking her trophies back to be skinned and prepared for feasting. Tani could slit and pull the pelt from a rabbit effortlessly, her little wrists and fingers working meticulously to skin her prey. Tani would strip the sinew from the pelt, flicking it away as she cleaned the hide. Her life seemed designed to use every skill her body possessed, always appearing fearless. She had trained on her own terms, often disappearing to be with those who could teach her something. Of course, some men and women felt threatened by such a small yet powerful force of a girl.

I found myself overwhelmed with emotions as I recalled memories of her as a young child. My veil hid the tears, but like the other girls, my shoulders gave away our feelings as we were caught up in our moments of sorrow. It was unimaginable to think what my mother would do, which would be in our father's thoughts as he rode silently with his head bowed.

I blinked and wiped my eyes as I recalled the lovely memories of my sister. Then, nudging Khonsu forward to walk beside Asim's mighty steed, I felt connected and supported. Even though Asim was silent, lost in his thoughts about letting Tanith slip into the night unaccompanied, he smiled briefly as we viewed each other. Asim was putting his faith and trust in Khan, hoping he would be her protector as she ventured into unfamiliar territory. We were very aware that this was what Tani had chosen - to be with her Prince; as she would never have been able to share her life with him here.

As I rode steadily beside Asim, the picture of him lavishing his attention on me, blessing me with his love, and holding me in the evening, flickered into my mind. How blessed was I to have a man of courage and diplomacy be aligned with me. I held one hand on my stomach as we rode, trying to calm the rushing wave of sickness. This journey was taking its toll on me as well.

Nef's makeshift cradle jolted periodically, and he moaned softly, pained by the motion. However, now that we had stopped again to rest, he was forcing himself to get up, knowing he was becoming more conscious as the infection had subsided. I leapt from Khonsu to give water to Nef, and even though his minders were attentive to his every wish; I wanted to bathe his head to cool and wash him.

"I am here for you, Nef," as I placed my hands on his chest, sending the circling golden energy of light into his body. Lifting his Ba, lifting his spirit, I called his guides and my goddesses to surround him and nurture him, healing his body.

We all dreaded arriving home. Tani's disappearance would forever change our family's life. Our mother had always been extremely vigilant about her daughters' safety, ensuring no harm would ever befall them. She was the warrior woman. If I considered my other life, she would be the Amazonian woman protecting her tribe.

Mother's screams echoed around the walls as she ran from us to go inside, calling Tanith's name. Grandfather tried in vain to comfort her and commanded us to send an army to bring her home. Father was trying to speak, to tell them that she had gone of her own free will but, unfortunately, there was nothing we could do. Two of our father's soldiers were lost without a trace, and Tani's tracks also had been erased in the desert storm. I hung my head, knowing I had been heavily involved in Tani's escape. Even though I had not been present in the planning, I owned my guilt in supporting her vanishing into the desert storm.

Herihor's appearance as he walked quickly into the palace entrance gave me a twinge of uncertainty about returning to the other world. How could I abandon all that was happening here? I could come back at any time, but there was a realisation within my soul, a knowing that this was not the time to return to my other world. I spoke quietly to Herihor as he tried to console and protect me against the tide of emotion washing over us all.

"Put all thoughts of returning to the other time out of your mind. Be safe, knowing there will be a right time in the future, but it is not now. I am here for you as your priest to be at your will and command and to forever protect and care for your wellbeing and that of your goddesses," Herihor opened up to me with support.

"I feel fragile and ill. This event has upset my stability, and I feel faint and unable to eat," I spoke with a releasing sigh.

Herihor's voice purred as though he were emotional as well. Even though he understood the determination of the Goddess Isis, he was aware of the toll it had taken on our family. Our eyes met briefly, and then he turned and looked away. Herihor pressed my hand, bowed, and moved toward Asim.

On our return, Nef was taken to the infirmary, where Keket supervised his care and looked after his wound. As she took over, she released our mother from the intense state of monitoring his healing. Mother had been crying and muttering about her baby, causing us all concern that she was losing her mind. We were unsure about giving her the gift from Tani, but she accepted it as if it were the most precious carpet she had ever seen, unravelling and stroking the fibres as she lay it beside her bed.

During this time of great uncertainty, Saf, Kal, and I lounged in the bathing pools and bundled up, drawing closer together as we shared countless stories of Tani. Despite the nauseating waves of emotion, sipping on peppermint and fennel-infused tea brought us a sense of calm to recollect our thoughts. I seemed continuously nauseous, as though the blame was resting on my shoulders.

Father chose to find solace and happiness with his extended family, creating joy and anticipation of more visits with his other wives' children. Despite the different nature of their bond, he held a special place in their hearts. At times, I felt a lack of warmth from Mother, and our family seemed restrained in expressing emotions. As Father formed stronger connections with his other children, especially his sons, I also longed for a deeper bond with him. He ignored my presence, denying that I existed as he brushed past me numerous times. He was dealing with his grief internally. Tani was his favourite child, as she had spent much time with him growing up, executing her battle skills. I think he created the sons in her and Safiya that he had lost with our mother.

I felt sad for my grieving mother, but I was also relieved to see my uncle being so attentive to her feelings. Their close friendship comforted her; he was always there when she needed someone to talk to. Seeing him as such a supportive friend helped ease her pain. They must have had something special together when they were younger.

The weeks went by in a holding pattern, as no one had heard any news about Tani's whereabouts until finally, one day, the massive doors of the main hall were pushed aside, and a scout was ushered in. Father was summonsed, and he and our uncle pressed the scout for information. Saf, Kal, and I were standing in the background, intent on listening to hear about our sister's fate.

"What news do you bring?" Father urged the scout. "Is she alive? Is she still in Egypt? Who has seen her?"

We waited for the barrage of questions to cease before the scout could answer. He could not interrupt and remained silent until Father had finished speaking. Mother came quickly into the main hall, appearing fragile, but she propped herself up straight, looking as though she had been dealt a death sentence. There was silence in the entrance to the hall, and the scout felt compelled to speak.

"Princess Tanith has crossed the Great Sea. She is in the Hittite stronghold, probably on her way to the Upper City of Hattusa. She is safe and escorted by the young Prince, who had been previously captured and put to work here as a stable hand."

The scout regained his composure and continued.

"Her mare, which it has been said she was reluctant to leave, has been re-purchased, so we know that she was not bound or held as a hostage but was free to travel without bondage. She was flanked by two of our soldiers who had abandoned their military posts and returned to Hittite."

Now that we knew that Tani was safe and protected, we felt life flooding back into our bodies like we had been holding our breath for the past few weeks.

That night, I silently waited until everyone was sleeping. Dressed as a traveller, I left the fortress to be alone under the sunset tree to focus my thoughts on Tani. She was easy to connect to, as though her line of communication was finally open and waiting for me to come to her. I went deep into a meditative state and called her name, honouring my goddesses and favouring Goddess Hathor to assist with the connection.

Tani, I called her in my thoughts, *I can see and feel you close. Are you safe and secure?*

As she came through the mist, there was a nod of agreement, and I saw her bowed head move. Her concern was for the lost souls she had taken out, and her guilt for wounding Nef was immense. She had been carrying an enormous weight in her regret of unleashing her arrows to kill. I assured her Nef was safe and that he had set the souls of the soldiers free with the call to the ravens.

You must relinquish your feelings of guilt as you know you will attract situations that will keep you feeling that way. Tani, I set you free! As your older sister and High Priestess, I urge you to release these emotions, which keep you bound to the code that is not serving you. It is your sadness that keeps you accountable for adverse situations. Let the strength of your insight and training with our soldiers be your sturdiness.

I held my stomach for a moment in nauseous response.

Are you under stress, Sister? I notice you are not well. Tani's soft voice responded in a soothing and calm tone.

Yes, I am fine now that I have connected with you. My sister, your surroundings are mountainous regions and rivers. I can see by the valleys and ravines that this is rugged terrain. I have never seen such a country. It is breathtakingly magnificent. You must love it.

My thoughts and words were transmitted to Tani, who received my clear communication. However, I felt resistance when I probed about Khan, as though she was protecting him, so I relinquished my questioning and turned my contact back to her.

It seems like you are carrying a more mature and subdued manner, Tani. I pray that you never lose your childlike passion for life, I sent my thoughts to her.

I found comfort in sending a stream of radiant, golden energy, infused with love towards her. We both held onto the understanding that everything was unfolding as it should, and we would have the opportunity to reunite as time and the open vortex permitted. As we closed our personal interaction, I emphasised that my Elestial Star would always be a guiding presence for her. I assured her that whenever she focused on it, she could count on feeling my presence, drawn to her like an emblazoned light of moonbeam.

Transmitting a message across
immeasurable space is a motion of harmony.
The sender and the recipient perfectly sync with
each other's essence, creating a profound connection.

Projecting our frequency and receiving it
as audible communication is a powerful act
that requires a clear intention,
empowering us to choose what we wish to convey.

As all senses focus on the message,
they must grasp the emotional vibration
from which it is channeled.
This emotional depth amplifies
the information and directive.

Children of the light,
you are born to channel your message
imprinted in vast memory chambers.
Each has access to the global significance of your role
in conveying the revelation that lies behind the purpose.

He who chooses to be the envoy
must use all reasonable measures to complete their task.
It is of you, and for you, we exist in this time and space to reveal
this intelligence of truth and light, bringing the world back to love.

A · U N I T E D · F R O N T

Fine dust particles were dancing, illuminated by the sunlight streaming into the courtyard, where a throng of villagers gathered waiting for any news about Tanith. Everyone was stunned that a royal daughter of the palace had disappeared so suddenly and dramatically. Finally, the whispers fell silent as Grandfather addressed the people. Turning directly to his household, he honoured us for being strong and holding space for Tanith's return. Then, in a sombre voice that boomed around the palace walls, he expressed what his military forces were doing to find her. She had disappeared completely, but it was believed that she and her captors had crossed the Great Sea. My father and grandfather would have been notified if there was more information.

I felt ashamed knowing I was holding secrets, but the goddesses knew the meaning of the extraordinary developments. They incited and allowed me to activate the storm, so I trusted implicitly that it was all for Tani's highest good.

Mother had not been seen since the scout informed us of what had happened, and she was unwilling to see her daughters or Kalina. I knew she would have returned to her other world to feel safe, as I would have. However, she did understand Tani had been meant to travel to sow the seed of our family lineage into new continents. Even though Mother knew what was happening and was aware of the situation, it did nothing to ease her heartbreak.

After Grandfather's address was given to the people, I quickly left to find my mother. She was alone in her room and had not allowed her handmaidens to serve her. Her hair had not been washed or wrapped, and her face was tired and crumpled with grief.

"Mother, you will need to lift yourself. The goddesses pre-arranged this journey for Tani. I am sorry I never told you, but I saw you saying goodbye, and your colours said you knew."

"Yes, I knew. I was hoping for more time with her so she could be a child a little longer," she said, sobbing.

"Let us try to gather ourselves Mother, and even though we are sorrowful, we must provide a united front so that all is well in the palace. It has been several weeks now, and we do not want to show a family weakness to the lines of the military. It makes us vulnerable and puts our beloved Egypt at risk. I am so sorry about Nef, but he is healing well. Our girl is a perfect archer and did not want the wound to be fatal."

"I cannot believe she would purposely aim at Nef," Mother replied, lifting her eyes to look directly at me and then narrowing them in disgust.

"She had to slow him down and stop him. I should have expressed to him what the goddesses had pre-ordained. Her intentions were already solidified, and there was no return to the past, so we must deal with what we have right here and now," I replied.

I felt more vital than ever. I knew we were unstoppable in the past, present, and future. It was all entwined.

Kneeling next to my mother, I asked for the goddesses blessings. I asked for protection for Tani, and I asked that Mother would see her again before this life extinguished her breath and led her to her afterlife.

"I have pushed Keket away," Mother sobbed, then whispered, "Would you find her and bring solace to her aching heart? It is not necessary to reveal the goddesses wisdom. Please, just tell her I hold remorse for not confiding in her and comforting her in her loss of Tanith. She is like a second mother to the four of you girls. Your father has not entered my chambers since the event. I have also pushed him away, and his concubine is easing his hurt. I will have to recollect myself or lose him forever," she said sadly.

"Mother, how can you be happy with him being with other women and the children he has? It is rather strange for me. I want to have my man to myself," I said intensely.

She sighed and looked into the distance, viewing another life she could have had here.

"You may have to learn to share, if Asim disagrees with you, my daughter. Men have an appetite; just look at your grandfather. He has a hundred or more children."

Feeling unsettled by my mother's explanation of Father's behaviour, I switched focus, calling out loudly to her handmaidens, who immediately responded. They came rushing in with bowls and preparations to tend to her needs and return her to her beauty. It was as if they were waiting to be summonsed to re-establish her care; for this is a duty they were expected to perform.

We smiled at each other, and as she turned away, ready to be adorned, I understood why her delicate features of extreme beauty were still the talk of the city.

"Your beauty is captivating, and you hold such regal power in your personal presence. Dress in stunning robes of rich blue and gold tones which suit you. All the people of the palace will see your strength and will follow you. We await your guidance Mother, to hold strength for all parents feeling your loss," I spoke from my heart.

Leaving Mother's quarters, I met my uncle in the hall as if he was waiting to hear news of her well-being. As he drew me aside, I tried to move away from him as though he would reveal secrets he had been holding, which I was not ready to hear. He looked so handsome, and I admired the detail of the finery he was wearing. A long natural robe that hung loosely over his tunic looked striking. A solid golden ribbed collar connected to the scarab was adorned at his throat with vibrant green and blue eagle wings.

"Thank you for instilling faith into your mother. I have not seen her for days and have been concerned. Is she favourable, Niece? Is her mind still strong after her loss? You have always been a treasure to me, and I admire you like your mother; strong and determined."

"Yes, Uncle. She dresses now and is ready to face the people and be the strength they all need now."

He seemed genuinely delighted, and his face held a deep, open smile. I knew that he loved my mother and that they had a unique bond... but why? It always left me curious, and I knew my curiosity was showing on my face as he addressed me.

Clasping my hands, he looked at me directly and strangely. "You would be the daughter I aspire to have. You have shown bravery and tenacity when situations have not gone your way. Your implicit trust in your goddesses, that they will deliver harmony and justice strikes genuinely within my heart.

Thank you for enlightening me on cultivating harmony and peace within our royal palace. I have been observing you, and it would honour me, as you being a High Priestess, if you were my advisor. This time could come later, as you are young and have many life goals you are still discovering," he said genuinely.

I watched his eyes as they lit up and crinkled at the corners, just like mine did. I then observed his facial expressions and noted they were similar to mine. His smile when he had suggested I be his High Priestess was soft and caring. I stood back and observed him. His mannerisms were like mine.

Uncle lowered his eyes, his long lashes sweeping down his high cheekbones. A warm countenance enveloped him, unlike Father's natural, unemotional stance. I was intrigued. He held discernment, a deeper knowing inside, and was sincerely spiritual. I took a breath in, and many scenarios flashed through my mind. *I will hold all this information for another time.*

"I will ponder on your request, Uncle. However, I see my role from quite a different perspective. I wish to engage with women and families to illuminate the spirit and assist them in stepping into their divine and activating their intentions."

He pulled back, nodding. He paused and thanked me again several times before leaving the hall with a noticeable lightness in his step.

I went in search of Keket and found her in the apothecary. She was very irritated and cranky. Maybe her joints were hurting her again, I wondered. She was snapping at the maiden helpers my mother was training, and they were visibly upset with her scolding words.

"Keket, can we talk? Mother wants to apologise and tell you she is sorry for abandoning you," I asked quietly.

"It is not for her to be sorry. I am just upset with myself for allowing this to happen. Why did I not go with you on the journey?" she asked herself in frustration.

"Please, Keket, sit down and hear me. Tani will be safe. I would feel it if she were not. I feel she has been crying and carries a sharp pain down the side of her face when I call her. I have pulled aside the veil and seen her on a journey of great danger that lurks all around her. However, I feel that her prince and many others protect her, and I just know that all is well."

Keket eyed me with a shrewd look. "This is the first time I have felt more peace. Thank you for coming to me. I will now attend to your mother and take my rightful place beside her." She dabbed her face, chose a liniment, and rubbed it frantically on her knees.

"When are you planning to marry and take a husband, little one?" she asked quietly, eyeing me steadily. "I can see you are with child. Your hair is luscious and thickening, and your cheeks are full and flushed."

"Keket, you must be silent about this, but yes, I feel the mothering in me is growing more powerful. I know you are my mother's confidant, and you call her to return from her journey if she gets waylaid. Well, I too, travel through The Void." I stopped and waited, deadly quiet, to hear what Keket had to say.

She sighed deeply and acknowledged what I had said, looking at me intently as she replied from her heart.

"If you go through The Void in your condition, you will lose this regal child. Look at the grief it has caused the women of your lineage. You cannot undo it, and you may never give birth again if there are complications. I never wanted to acknowledge your travelling in the hope that it would diminish, but I see you will not stop as it is in your destiny."

She expelled her breath loudly and then continued, "Do you know what triggers the travel? If you do, keep away from those moments."

She hesitated for a moment before asking, "What is the connection between you and the priest, Herihor? I have seen you together. Besides being a nephew of your mother, he can also travel; I have seen the signs."

"I cannot consider such musings of importance, Keket, but I am happy that he will be assigned to me as my High Priest. I have not decided what to do about my child yet," I pondered slowly, gently rubbing my stomach.

"Think with wisdom, Akila. Destiny is constantly weaving her magic. Also, when your decision is made and if you decide, will you allow me to be your carer and your guardian for you and our little one? If you do, your mother will assign me to go to Thebes with you."

Keket seemed very intent on escorting me to Thebes, so much so that she grabbed my arms with both hands, looking straight at me, almost willing her decision with urgency upon me. My snake stirred, rose, hissed and stared straight back at her. Though she could not see him, I am sure he would have struck out at that moment if I had not pulled my bodice together.

I deliberately walked out to the palace gardens and found myself breathing in the silken air as though I was in perfect harmonious alignment with the flowers, the bees, the butterflies. I was blending into the garden. I could see the radius of symmetrical patterns of circles spanning outward throughout the perfectly laid foliage. This garden was created using the geometrical spheres of our entwining circles pattern. Even though it was not apparent initially, I now see it so cleverly laid out in sequence. I could see the circles within the circles, the seed of life within the flowers of life, continuous circles of the seven connecting. I could see the star within the star. In this perfectly aligned garden, I could hear the music floating from the flowers, the trees, the wavelengths and harmonies of the music, and the dimensional levels were all interrelated. The beautiful tones of the music drew me to sit on the grass and extend more than my ears, but to feel the vibration in my third eye deep within my brain, within my soul. I could feel the oscillation and frequency of the music played with perfect precision. My heart connected to my mind, and my mind signalled to every cell in my body, calling in the instrumental orchestra of the sweet-toned melodies of nature.

I knew what the circles on the ceilings in the temples meant. I could see the power of the magnificence of Egyptian wisdom and the connection to the light beings. I could see my Elestial Crystal Star in the heavens guarded by our red star Sirius and the direct connection to the eyes of The Great Sphinx, showing the pathway to home. I knew of the great cities under Egypt and the temples in alignment holding the space of all creation. Lying down on the softness of the grass, I could hear the language of the moss and toadstools. I could feel the pulse of the Earth connecting to my physical being and sending shivers of waves down my spine. I elevated my lightbody to view the garden from above, and the music grew louder and floated through the foliage. The perfection of the symmetry of the circles was crystal clear. The sound waves of the mystical garden lifted the opening to a pure portal of time travel healing.

This was the garden of the Pharaoh, designed for his longevity. Instantly, I knew what I must do. I will bring Mother to the garden to heal, lie or sit among the vibration of the creation of all life, and listen to the sound healing of the Earth to renew her Mer-Ka-Ba.

THE
MOON'S·SLIVER

I shivered involuntarily as I called Goddess Nut to shelter us from the night's reflection. The evening felt eerie, perhaps a premonition, as I shook myself to cast aside any doubt of going out and getting swallowed up in the secrets of the night.

To blanket our bodies, we wrapped our breasts tightly to conceal our womanhood. It was painful for me as my breasts felt the tender fullness of the beginnings of mothering. Safiya and I had chosen this night to explore the city's darkness and find information from the back-end world of those who may have information about Tani. I was usually fearless as I had been trained in the temples for initiates, and we had spent our childhood learning the military ways with our father.

We had heard in the camps that some knew where Tani and her prince were heading, and we needed more relevant information about our sister before the trail was cold and covered by the endless waves of the ocean.

I felt resistance and fear for the first time, leaving the sanctuary of the palace grounds now that I had a life inside me to protect and nurture. However, brushing those thin whispers of thoughts aside, I concentrated on checking that my hair was tied and tucked away and my old and tattered breeches were covering my lower legs. Saf was the same. We worked in unison to perfect our old, ragged look while covering our faces with grime and foul-smelling fat from the cooking fires stolen from the kitchen. Finally, I could feel the cold steel of my knife as I tucked it close to my thigh, and we were ready.

We planned to skirt the city and end at the wharf area, where the punts moved across The Delta to bring wares to the town. It was here that we would listen to the stories and keep open to the opportunities of learning more about the young prince's rescue, but unfortunately, we would have to wait until the drunken men filled themselves with the honey-sweet beer to loosen up their tongues. They were a foul group of unruly men on the harbour where the boats anchored. We knew of their drunken behaviour from the servants in the hall.

Looking directly at each other, we drew our circles in the air and stealthily slipped into the shadows of the blackened night. It did not take long to become accustomed to the dark coolness of the late evening. We had rubbed roots on our teeth to stain them, and it looked like we were weather-beaten as part of the city's darker side.

Soldiers were everywhere around the palace, but we were well-versed in our ability to scuttle past and around them without being detected. However, Nef was not following us or in the background this time, so we were utterly alone.

It took us nearly three hands of the sliver of the moon's movement to skirt the city. After that, there was just enough light to keep our steps quick and light, taking care of whether we encountered Apophis, the snake trying to take out Ra, the Sun God, as he travelled through the underworld. Then the snake, Mehen, would coil around the Sun God Ra to ensure Khepri would roll the sun across the sky to bless the coming morning.

Our thoughts were on the mission we had carefully planned, when we were suddenly amongst the rabble and the raucous laughter of the seediness of the city's nightlife. The putrid stench filled the night air from the dockyards, and it was hard not to hold our noses in disgust. Saf and I stayed close, grunting if we were pushed or elbowed. We listened, filtering all the information. Finally, with the pretense of being slightly drunk and driven by the desire between fear and curiosity, we managed to saunter our way to the back of the group of casual, rowdy drinkers.

Hearing of a flotilla anchored west of Pelusium with an escort of twenty men, it was said that the rescuers men took the King's youngest son across the Great Sea to Tarsus. They were making their way through to the stronghold in the Tarsus mountains.

"She's a feisty one, that young maiden. I heard she took the breath of a seaman who tried to touch her. We would hold her down and show her what it would be like to be with real men," one of the drunken men spat.

There were lewd remarks about what would happen to the princess, which made us squeeze our hands together, but we kept our heads down. The drunken men became fouler in describing what they would do to the young beauty if the men got their hands on her. Laughing loudly as they theatrically portrayed how they would abuse her while becoming more graphic with their words, almost spitting out their vile language, causing the eruption of laughter of the other onlookers.

No more information was forthcoming, just more laughter and drinking, but at least we knew their direction of travel, which may be of help to us when we start our voyage to find her.

The anger inside me felt dark and enraged, like an Apis bull with a courageous heart fighting for supremacy. The men's foul words and descriptions had heated my blood to boiling point. Now, the thickness of the night hung like the stench coming from the stale beer and the smell of the men.

An argument was brewing, with raised voices of anger and frustration. There was an imposing group of three men right next to us, when suddenly one turned directly to Saf, taunting and spitting, saying there was a rotten smell in the area where she was slumped. She kept her head down, but he was intent on harassing her. We rose and moved stealthily away from the group when he started yelling, bringing attention to us.

"Hey, where are you going? Come here, you little vagabonds. Your kind is not fit to drink with us," he slurred.

My snake was up and flaring his hood. I pushed him down, took a deep breath, and hurried away from the men gathering to create a bigger audience. Saf was animated and lightning-fast, providing a stance of protection against attack. However, there were now six strong men with bellies full of wheat beer and heads full of brazen anger, launching an attack.

They tried to circle us, but we kept moving to keep a clear way out. The bloodlust looks in their eyes had turned into a pack mentality, but they were slow and lumbering.

Saf flicked out her knife, and I also had my hand on the hilt of mine when the first one lunged.

I aimed for the soft space to the side of his jaw and sliced his throat in one clean backhand movement. His death froze the look in his eyes of a savage killer while his blood gushed forth with a bubbling sound.

It was all on then for Saf and I, fighting for our lives, with the advantage of being quick and supple. We fought hard, with two more casualties injured and moaning, before we backed up and disappeared into the night. Heading back the way we had come, we were sure they were following us, but as the night wrapped her blanket around us, we realised we were on our own and free from pursuit. Praising each other for keeping calm, we made our way back as Khepri struggled to light up the morning sky.

Covered in blood, we washed away some of the vile stench in the cold waterways and slipped back into the palace and entered Saf's room. Without time for fully washing away the night's horror, we stripped and bundled our clothes together, pulled on our night attire over our weary bodies, and cradled each other. Shaking from the experience, we curled up and slept until the handmaidens came in to rouse us, talking about the smell in the room.

We washed and freshened ourselves, stripping away all signs of the previous night, from our skin. I was bruised, and my arms ached from the severity of the attack. We were both covered in tell-tale signs of a struggle. Saf and I did not speak of the incident that morning. We had wrapped it up and sent the energy back to the goddesses to manage.

By noon, we felt more positive, like we had escaped an horrific outcome. Feeling lucky, Saf and I wandered down to the palm trees and sank down with our backs against the trunk of one of them.

"How did that go so wrong?" Saf started. "We were minding our own business."

"Yes, but maybe we were too quiet not chiding in with the banter," I recalled. "Father will not discover it was us. Who would think that we could do anything like what happened? There were three men down, at least one dead. It will be spoken of, but we will see how it unfolds with the soldier's inquiry when you talk with Yahya."

We held hands, our fingers entwined, gripping our hands tightly as I placed my other hand over my belly.

"Saf," I said quietly. "I have a mothering inside me, and I feared for my baby's life last night."

"Oh, Sister," Saf exclaimed. "I did not know. We should have just run, but we did not have time. It happened so fast. Are you okay?"

"I am good, but it has made me realise I cannot go through The Void until my baby is born. I have too much to live for now, and you will be an aunty, Saf. I need to tell Asim and Mother as soon as possible."

We sat in the sun's warmth, feeling the wonder of being alive, lost in thoughts of our future and that we still had one another. How different we felt now, like our childhood had dissipated, all in one evening of horror.

"At least we know where Tani is headed. We must keep that in mind for the future when we search for her," I said seriously.

Saf turned to catch my look. "Yes Sister, we will."

Spoken or unspoken, we knew the time would come when we would embark on the journey across the Great Sea to find her and bring her home.

PENANCE

Waiting patiently for Saf to return with news of the last evening, kept me on edge. I was hesitant to come out to see the family as I was sure there was guilt written all over my face. Nausea had built up in me, with visualising the menacing face of the man staring at me, blood gushing from his wound. I could not get the smell out of my nostrils, so I covered my face with my linen hand towel doused with blue lotus oil.

Kal had come looking for me, and we curled up together. She reiterated how pale and forlorn I looked.

"Aki!" she exclaimed. "You are with child. I can tell. You look pale and are retching at seeing the food the maidens have brought for you. Mother said you were poorly. Now I know why. Your union should be brought closer so we can celebrate you and your baby. Oh, there is so much to do." She clapped her hands with glee.

"There has been a rough night at the docklands," she suddenly announced. "Two men have caused mayhem. There has been a death, and others with injuries caused by sharp blades, who may not survive. The victims have been terrorising the docklands, and many bodies have been discovered, partially devoured by crocodiles. The soldiers believe these men are responsible for the previous deaths but are baffled as no one knows where the two brave men who inflicted these recent injuries came from, as they have not been seen on the docks before. One death was clean and precise, execution style," she said rapidly to get it all out in one breath.

"They were described as well versed in combat, maybe even trained by the military. A full inquiry is being held. The wound on the deceased was not deep but had been clean and purposeful," Kal continued, filling me in on every detail and then again, I felt nauseous and was retching as she recollected what she had heard.

I had not considered myself or Saf as executioners; it had been self-defence. We would have to be redeemed by our goddesses and go to the North Temple for forgiveness. I did not want to carry that energy into my unborn child. Saf and I would go alone. We could not take Kal as she would be horrified. She gave me that all-knowing look, and I wondered what Saf was doing. *Why was she taking so long?*

She arrived at sundown, and Kal was ready to reiterate the news. Saf looked calm and self-assured, so I relaxed, knowing no one suspected us. However, they had traced movement towards the outer city limits, heading in this direction before losing the trail. The soldiers were keen to find the perpetrators, but Saf said Yahya was convinced that the victims were known troublemakers, and this may be the blessing they needed to stop the ongoing trouble in the docks.

"Saf, we must go to the North Temple right now," I insisted. We waited until Kal had to return to her duties with the Magus to perform the daily rituals of blessings for this day of abundance for Egypt before we could leave.

"Really, Sister? It is so late," Saf started to protest, but I insisted we could not leave this as it was. This soul whose life I had taken would be causing chaos in the afterlife on his way to The Hall of Two Truths. Osiris would judge him, and his heart would be weighed against the feather of Ma'at. Then, if his sins outnumbered his honourable deeds, he would be devoured by Goddess Amit, devourer of the dead who held the head of the crocodile, the front legs and body of the lion and the back end of a hippopotamus.

"We must immediately atone for our part in these actions and ask the goddesses for forgiveness," I insisted, the emotions caught in my throat. "Let us pay homage to the goddesses, Saf."

I called the guards to request Nef to guide us to the temple. "We will answer to the will of the goddesses, and they will hear our case."

I could feel the goddesses gathering in the evening sun's glow as burnt orange and gold colours covered the landscape. They were gathering on the breath of the wind. The rays of intense light lit up the sky, beaming on us through the lines of palm trees, holding firm in the gentle sway of the breeze.

I was ready for our atonement. Nef led the way, and two soldiers flanked us as we moved down the Avenue of the Sphinx.

Oil lamps illuminated the Hypostyle Hall, where more guards were stationed, adding an eerie glow to the carvings on the walls as though they had come to life. They must have thought this was an unusual entourage gathering here this evening. These thoughts ran through my mind as Saf and I moved closer, holding each other tightly and clutching one another's arms to steady ourselves.

"Saf, hold no fear," I said quietly. "We were protecting ourselves from the enemy. We will answer the call of the goddesses, and they will hear us."

Nef entered the sanctuary, checking the space to see if no one else was present. For a large man, he swept gracefully past us, leaving us to await the goddesses' retribution.

I pulled Saf down to lay prostrate on the ground in front of the glorious statue of Isis. She must know that we are repentant of any mortal sin we have created in our Ka, our life force, and we will want to be free of any sins we have collected. As the forty-two gods and goddesses preside over our judgement, we must be forgiven before we die for the sin of taking a life.

I was trying to hold back the nausea, banishing the act of purposeful execution from my mind. Saf was already crying and shaking, not knowing what was expected from our goddesses.

Suddenly, a hush fell over the temple, and we bowed before Goddess Isis. I felt her warm hands extend to envelop Saf and I. Saf shuddered with the connection as a beam, a pillar of light, emanated from each of our crown chakras, and we rose and lifted our heads, to sit on our haunches. The soul of Isis, her pure white light, was pouring from our soul star chakra above us through our Ba, the physical manifestation of our soul bodies, which then beamed into the Earth. Healing grace and power were pouring into us, blessing our lives and the land through our bodies.

Our penance was clear. We were to develop great strength and presence through this stunning pillar of light. We were to manifest our deeds of service by visualising this light penetration into our bodies. The light hovered over our heads and descended into the Earth, drawing energy from the heavens and my Elestial Star planet, embedding itself within us. This flow of light then connected with the ground like a river of light flowing into the earth. We were to perform this ritual at least once daily for as long as this physical life held its divinity through us, in this life or the many other lives to follow. We will never forget this day.

There was no need to state our case as all was known through Goddess Isis. Her warm hands of envelopment surrounded us as the light played and lit up the temple, so we sat with the communication of spiritual connection pouring through us. At this time, my womb was celebrating the life force held inside my sacred space.

Our legs felt numb as we crouched. Slowly, the light reduced its luminosity, and we heard the voice of the goddesses hail our names as they withdrew the power of their presence. We both cried with the joy of being redeemed, and our souls' light was strengthening, climbing the ladder toward the heavens to retain our immortality.

The goddesses' grace held us in their favour as we left the temple, the sanctuary of light. Once again, our guards surrounded us, staring at us as though we were an apparition descended from the heavens.

We could not speak as we ambled back through the Avenue of the Sphinx, tightly holding hands as though the eyes of each statue held us in their gaze of knowing of our atonement. Guards had assembled at the entrance to the palace to usher us in, nodding with recognition as we passed.

Finally, Saf broke the silence. "Sister, I feel so pure and cleansed as though I must never waiver but hold myself as a Priestess of the Temple. We have both been given this day to honour our life as a commitment."

Turning to Saf, I held her shoulders and gazed responsively at her.

"Sister, there is so much more we need to do, which may require the battle skills for which we have trained ardently, and we will do it all in allegiance with the knowledge of the goddesses. Remember, we have been ordained to serve with our mind, body, and soul as the ever-enlightened wisdom of the ancient ones. Now, we register our penance as a gift to the Earth, to draw in from the heavens and my soul star, the pillar of eternal light, and beam it in through our bodies to connect to our planet. We will hold this commitment for all the passing days of eternity as we live life-through-life."

The strength Goddess Isis had given us this day captivated and reinforced our spirits as we entered our quarters.

"We must be prepared to present a united front that all is well. How are your commitment plans with Yahya? I will talk with Mother about us uniting with our men as a communal occasion for the three of us," I said with conviction. "We all need a divine distraction."

L O T U S · P E T A L

I let the curve of my body match Asim's. Just touching the heat of each other's skin felt like flames from the firelight dancing in front of us. Asim hugged me from behind. As I drew his hands in front of me, I held them over my slightly protruding belly as we allowed the moment to be present for us. I was deep breathing and taking Asim to that quiet place of surrender. Asim quickly regained his emotions and turned me around to look at him.

Our lips still tingled with the kisses lingering on them. The scent of sandalwood was strong in the air as my long, thick hair, free and untied, caressed Asim's skin as I turned over. He looked at me in awe at what his heart had just discovered. He wasted no time questioning me, his voice quivering, and then let his eyes use their intuition. Moving down and kissing my bare skin, he knew the truth of what he felt. His son, his child, had been given his form and was growing steadily in my womb. Safe and nurtured, our child was now letting himself be announced.

Our lovemaking intensified at this moment as Asim pinned me to the soft mattress of rush fibres. He wanted to consume me with his love. He wanted to connect deeply within me to feel himself as close to me as physically and emotionally possible. Then I drew him in to inhale his breath to absorb his glow and show him the gift of our joining, which was blessed with his seed growing inside me.

He whispered endearments as he came closer and called me his little Lotus Petal. I laughed at the name, but secretly, I loved how it rolled off his tongue as he pulled back my hair to place the name delicately in my ear.

It had been a cold night, so we kept warm, tightly cloaked together. Asim looked tired when I moved to dress and ready myself to return to my room.

He gestured for me to come close and whispered, "I am excited about where this will lead us, Lotus Petal. Make the arrangements, for we will live under one roof before the next moon."

I was humming, but then I took a deep breath and stopped to return quietly to my quarters. I was dreaming of the time we could wake up and lie together, waiting to feast for breakfast.

As I turned the corner of the hallway, Herihor gave me such a fright. His grave face expressed his feelings. He looked stressed and rather haggard, and his handsome features looked weary.

"Akila, we should address our situation," he said with compassion.

For a moment, I was caught up in his deep green eyes and the memory of our other life. Then, when he moved towards me, his presence was surprisingly companionable, and I felt my heart flutter with excitement.

"Herihor, I cannot return to our future at this time. You will have to trust me. It will be some months before we can. Can you be honest and unguarded for a moment? Can we talk openly?

I am honoured you are my priest, but it is at this time that I am in love with Asim. You are related to my mother. How is that?"

"Your mother is my aunt. My father, her youngest brother, was killed in the fighting, and I was sent to Thebes to become a priest. However, my mother was one of the concubine women. Then, when it was discovered that she loved my father, she was sent away. I have no word of where she is, but she is looked after, that I know. I will find her one day and revere her for giving me life," Herihor spoke openly and was mindful of how I was taking this all in.

We moved inside my room to talk in a more private place. Still whispering, Herihor continued, "I have always loved you from a distance, but I know my place in Egypt, and it is not as your lover but your priest, your protector, and your ally in Thebes."

"Everything is being revealed so quickly, Herihor," I stammered. "But I have found a true deep friend in you, and I am pleased that when we travel to Saqqara and Thebes, I will have you by my side as our protector." I pulled back my gowns to reveal the light linen wrap covering my belly and let my hands rest lightly.

He drew a breath and lifted his head to show a genuine smile. "Know this, your child will have my devotion and protection; it is my sworn oath to pledge myself to you both," Herihor responded as he bowed slowly and held aside his robe.

"All these years, I have studied history, the arts, the languages, and spiritual knowledge with my heart and dedication. I have assisted in the sacred arts, working with the artisans and decorating and embellishing the tombs in The Valley of the Kings. However, it is here at this moment that I have found my calling; to serve Egypt through the lineage of future generations. To your children, I pledge my life. I know my destiny is here with you, supporting, admiring, and protecting you when needed. I have found my place," he spoke with reverence.

My eyes welled up with tears, tears of joy. My children would have their faith and education through Herihor's undaunting devotion. His authenticity was his strength, whilst his regal commitment to the families in the palaces was inspiring. I reached out to him to clasp his hands with mine in a gesture of reverence for his words.

Suddenly, the electrical current of connection catapulted through my veins as the veil of time faded to reveal my feelings for Jonas. He felt it too and acknowledged its magnetism. We held for a moment longer, then let our hands fall away, knowing there was nothing we could do about this association.

"Thank you, my priest," I stammered. We are honoured to trust you with our lives and our children's lives. You are my confidant, my faithful friend and family. We will know when it is time to return to the other world.

Herihor retracted from the doorway into the passage and disappeared into the early morning awakening.

My desire to remain in Egypt dissipated for a moment, and I felt like chasing after Herihor and returning to Jonas's strong arms. I knew now that I could no longer travel through the time warp.

My womb supported the growth of my treasured child, an embryo of divinity. I could feel the impact the prospect of becoming a mother was having on me. Instead, snuggling back into my bed, I drew my legs up, curling like a foetus I was hugging myself, and fell directly to sleep, with the warmth of my complicated emotions filling me up.

Mother was ecstatic and utterly energised as she listened in such patient silence. Her face was animated, and all the pain of Tanith's disappearance was erased as the lines on her face creased with joy.

"We want to hold a binding relationship for all three of us Sisters of the Light - Kalina, Safiya, and myself; an event to bring festivities and celebration to Pi Ramesses and joy to the nation. Then, Asim and I will need to return to Saqqara and Thebes before the lessening of the Nile," I said excitedly.

"I promise my daughter that you will have a feast for your joining like no other, but also, this will be a good time to celebrate. We will have a council meeting and see how we can bring this together in such a short time."

Mother had gone into organisational mode. The occasion was undoubtedly giving her a distraction, helping her to relinquish her pain. Her colours lit up intensely around her body. If only she could set herself free. Sometimes, her rigidity was to her detriment. At this moment, though, Mother was excited and had regained her passion.

With the fullness of her heart, she set about making plans in favour of her girls. Kalina had always held a special place of recognition in Mother's life. As Kalina was a year younger than me, it meant our mother loved us both equally and dearly. When her sister died, she cherished Kalina because of the loss they had both felt as they clung together in grief. Mother had never changed our names, and even though she was excited, she did not use our shortened names.

It was her turn to shine now; it was my mother's time to put all her love and endearment into us girls for our pending relationships. We did not need a celebration for our connections, as our sacred rites to commit to each other meant we would just stay the night together. It was simple. We just had to move in with each other and tell our parents of our commitment. As young women, we had waited for the right partnership, and now fate had drawn to us good men of standing and perfect alignment to capture the strength of our families.

Seek ye the relationship that is worthy of your favour.

As we entwine our energies,
we must be in constant flow and balance
to bring out each other's most honoured characteristics.

When we experience the closeness of our relationship,
we will discover the keys that unlock the other's potential.
The language of two souls requires coherence
in conveying the same desires and ambitions,
bringing the power of another frequency
to strengthen the union.

We then generate and amplify our intensity to amass
projections and abundance of all we can co-create together.

Be abundant in our thinking,
knowing there is enough for all to share.
Essentially, we will create an immeasurable
wealth source of good things to celebrate.

May we stay within the golden light,
placing precious blessings into our union daily.
Lovers, friends, and family: let us say to ourselves,
"Through my free will, I join you as a being of light."

S T A R G A T E

A distinct scent of sandalwood permeated the room, with the heavy smell of potent wine, which was especially fermented for royalty. Beautifully crafted faience glass goblets filled with wine were held high, some of the red nectar spilling over the edges to fall unceremoniously on the banquet tables. We were honoured with dancing and acrobats during the ceremony, which was highly entertaining. Now, ready to display our dancing skills for our men, we led the movement of expression and covered the floor gracefully with maidens flanked on both sides. The music and beat were woven into our bodies and brought a vibrational sense of freedom to express our dance of love, fertility, and praise of the goddesses for their protection and sacred honouring of our world. The energy was electric, pulsing and alluring, with the rhythm beating out the passion on the drums and tambourines.

As we caught a glimpse of each other, Asim held his open hand to me as a proud gesture. My body tingled as though the starlight had touched my soul. The music quietly slowed in time to the sway of our bodies, and we sisters bowed our heads slightly as the raucous clapping filled the feasting hall, and we spontaneously embraced, squeezing each other joyfully, smiling at the thought of our futures. Our men seated at the feasting tables replicated the delight on our faces. We celebrated with the goblets offered to us by entwining our arms, taking a sip, and raising our goblets to the heavens.

For the past few days, we had prepared our bodies to energise the surrounding field of light as the blessings vibrated in our physical and light bodies. Governed by our thoughts and feelings about ourselves, we uplifted each other with expressions of sisterly love, practicing this energy flow so that we could couple with our men and bring the seed of immortality into our womb space. A child and nurturing our own child within is the greatest gift we could offer to our men and to the world to continue our positive imprint on humanity into the future.

Therefore, allowing the seed of life to be planted and nurtured in us is where our power grows, preparing our bodies and female sacred space. I showed my sisters how to activate their lotus flower to open the womb of life. This physical, spiritual nourishment for our intimate lotus was to be replenished regularly with the glow from the man. I was using this precise emergence before coupling with Asim.

Saf, Kal, and I had practised holding our thoughts high and breathing the energy in. For hours, we went over the process and heard the joy of each other's laughter mingling with our voices, raising the levels of energy needed to enter our Mer-ka-ba and beyond. Women's magic was strong enough to bring the emotional power to life and to live within stargate patterns with our lovers.

"Tomorrow, we will be following our star pathways, wherever that may lead," I said with a softness tinged with sadness. "And the inevitable time of letting go of our childish ways. I will be the wife of Asim, Saf of a military soldier, and you Kal, the wife of the son of a most powerful magician. We have big roles to fulfil. How will we be with all this change and uncertainty entering our lives?"

"Thebes is a profound change. How will you manage it?" Kal enquired with concern.

"There is much unrest, Sister. We will pray to the gods and goddesses for your favour," Saf said with unwavering determination.

We embraced one another lovingly, with tears of the moment washing away our childhood, like the great Nile obliterating the debris in her path.

"A new beginning!" I exclaimed, swallowing the words as they tried to forcibly spring from my lips. I was holding back, not wanting this inevitable shift in our lives, the moment etched in my heart, knowing that things would never be the same again. We were entering our combined energy field with our partners toward our journey for ascension.

I was returning to the celebration and feeling the trickling of sweat cooling my warm skin. I turned to the embrace of my man, who was now seated at the table.

"Asim, I feel rather dishevelled after our dance, but I love how my body responds to music as though it has its own life that I do not control." Laughing, I gazed seductively into his eyes. "You tantalise me with your good looks and piercing eyes," I teased him as I gently leaned over to place my hand on his.

"And you, my love, bless me with your beauty and ways that enrapture my heart. You will be more dishevelled before sunrise," Asim smiled.

We left the feast to fill the night with the ways of our souls entwining, lifting each other to reach the heavens and the stars. That night, I felt the glory and pathway of the stars leading me, calling me, pulling me in the direction of the future. With Asim's strength and protection anchoring us to Earth, I ventured on my golden thread out into the solar system to see the stars of my future children, grandchildren, and great-grandchildren; all travelling in unison, reproducing the sacred seed of the sisters into the open stargate.

As preparations began for our southern journey, I noticed Nef was pulling away and becoming slightly distant, so I seized the moment when he was alone to ask him his reason.

He quickly bowed his head and muttered, "I am unable to embark on this distant journey with you. My orders from your father are to allow your priest and husband's family to escort and care for you. I am beside myself, unable to protect you in our dangerous southern lands, close to my homeland on the Nubian border."

I was frozen, his words vibrating in my ears as I repeated them silently.

"Nef, you are my rock, my strength, and you are always with me as my spirit snake, but you are also needed here with my sisters," I replied. "Maybe you will have a message from Tani and be sent to rescue her. The goddesses will bring us together again, Nef," I said, shaking and holding back my emotions as I resigned myself to his staying back. I asked him, "May we take one last stroll to the Temple of Isis together?"

We left immediately walking past the Avenue of the Sphinx. I had had a lifetime of protection from my dearest companion and guard, and I could see his heart beating out of his ebony chest, with the arrow's scar standing proudly on his skin. The beat was replicated in my snake as it slithered toward my neck and wrapped around my throat.

"I am here with you forever, my little Akila."

Nef had broken his silence and spoke of his respect for my role.

"I will travel through the stargate with you as a representation of protection through this life and the many others in which you will dwell. My role as caretaker and bodyguard will abide within the asp around your neck. My spirit soul, the snake, will guide you to Thebes and beyond. I will know when I am needed as I will feel the beating of your heart, hear your call, read your thoughts, and feel your breath on my skin."

Unbridled tears were released from my eyes as I shuddered momentarily from the fear of him not being by my side. Together, we strolled through the Great Temple Hall, holding our heads high as we passed the guards at the entrance. Nef checked the sanctuary and returned, bowing low, indicating that all was well. I looked at him, taking his hand, pulling it toward me, and gesturing for him to enter the sanctuary with me. He stared at me wide-eyed.

"Nef, you are my closest strength and have always been like a protective father. Please enter here with me in front of my goddesses. We are called here for a blessing."

Kneeling in front of the iconic stature of my Goddess Isis, Nef looked uncomfortable, as his size and presence dominated the space. He had no idea what to expect.

"Goddess Isis, we are here to pledge our lives to the realm," I said with clarity and power, as I could feel the sanctuary filling with other goddesses, who gathered in reverence of Nef and myself. "We are here to honour the travel I am to embark on with the protection of Nef's spirit animal as comfort and protection for me."

At that moment, my snake raised his energised hooded face and slithered down my body to wrap himself around the statue's base. All was quiet for a moment, and then Goddess Isis' melodic, hypnotic voice sent shivers up my spine as she voiced words from an ancient language which then turned into the tongue we understood. Nef was immediately subdued beside me.

"The waters will fall and rise," Goddess Isis continued. "There is danger in the hidden rituals ascending our temples in middle Egypt. Beware of the disguise of the nurturer, for they are preparing to undermine their loyalties and betrayal is like a mist creeping slowly and surrounding their existence. The unforeseen magic must be dampened before your Prince of Thebes is born. His birth will be in Waset, where his soul duality and placenta must be buried in the land to anchor in the new light."

At that moment, I felt my baby flutter in my belly like a little bubble, a blip of acknowledgement stating, 'I am here.' My snake suddenly uncoiled from the statue, slithered up around my legs and belly, and settled back around my chest.

I reached out for Nef's hand and clasped it in thankfulness that he was here. We could feel the warmth of Goddess Isis wrap around our hearts as her blessing was showered upon us.

"Your journey will lead you back here," Goddess Isis's voice reverberated around the walls.

"Travel up the river towards where the flow source pours from the mountains, where the great lake and the hills carry their silt to enrich the waters of Upper and Lower Egypt. You will soar on the extended wings of Goddess Nekhbet, the eagle representing Upper Egypt. She will guide you to protect the Pharaoh, honour the land of past ancestors, and ensure that we continue the inundation of our beloved Nile..." Her voice trailed off, then suddenly boomed out. "The gods and goddesses have requested this of you and your unborn child. You must not fail."

"To our gallant protector of the light", Goddess Isis's voice continued, now in a soft yet powerful tone, and I knew her reference was to Nef. "We honour your wisdom and courage to adhere to your position even though you could have broken free from the bonds of service. You have given us the ability to trust again. Like you, your totem viper is strong and will survive many lifetimes. You will always be placed where you are needed the most. Because of our gratitude for your protection of the royal sisters, we will bestow upon you the gift of your own wife and child in the future with our blessing."

We had tears of gratitude welling in our eyes as Nef and I held the enormity of our duty and blessings for the future. The whispering in the sanctuary diminished as the voice of Goddess Isis was hushed. We felt the surge of power filter through our bodies, warming our blood and connecting us back to our senses and our place here in the temple. I stood with my head lowered in honour, and Nef followed as we moved out through the great courtyard into the warm sun.

"What an experience," Nef muttered. "The energy has shaken me, but I am now more confident of my new role here in Pi Ramesses. I will miss you, Akila. I will miss being your protector and knowing you are safe under my care. My observation of you growing in your role has given me purpose throughout the years."

He pulled out a cord from his robe and tied to it was a highly polished black tourmaline coiled asp with a bright green peridot third eye, such a precious stone in Egypt.

"This is your protection amulet, renowned for being a stabilising shield against negative, destructive forces. It holds safety within its space as a forcefield around the keeper, the one it was made for," he said warmly, in his deep quivering voice as I choked back tears of love and thankfulness.

"I must travel and give birth to my son on the land of the great Pharaohs. Grandfather's Temple of a Million Years, with forty-eight towering columns in the Great Hall, has been completed for all eternity. You will not physically be with me Nef, but your soul spirit is always here."

My emotions heightened as I abandoned all protocol and tiptoed, embracing Nef as my warrior and my friend. His return hold was full of inner turmoil as he cradled me like a child.

The guards never lifted their eyes from the stone floor, each feeling the honour of this compelling moment. The winds whipped up a force of sand, spinning in circles and stinging our faces as we covered them with our hands. Instantly, all fell silent and still.

As the scarab beetle follows the sun,
so too are we ready to follow our visions and pathways
into the illumination of our new life.

We go with courage, for surrendering any fears
liberates our ability to experience new pathways.

Each river carries out a new course over time,
so we will also pattern ourselves to a different horizon.
These perspectives give us an alternative range of encounters.

We intend to trust more in the process,
understanding that our intuitive growth is not a destination,
but a continuous journey that depends
on valued experiences and alliances.

We will view the sun's rising over another mountain
from a different perspective,
reassured by our visual magnificence.

As we return to the Stargate of our existence,
travelling through the portals of space,
we are inspired by the value of our innate power.
Experiencing new optimistic outlooks
allows us to grow in our ascendance.
We place intimate appreciation of our
spiritual growth life through life and are humbled
by our role in the resurrection of our new earth.

DAUGHTER · OF
THE · NILE

Khonsu was proud and prancing on our ride this morning as we left the confinement of the stables. His smooth coat and highly brushed silver mane danced hypnotically as we ambled. I spoke lovingly to him, whispering gently as we walked, and then I lay across his neck, hugging him. My emotions were difficult to hide, and I knew he could feel them as he continuously quivered. Thoughts of leaving him here while I travelled south touched my heart, and I feared he would feel abandoned as we were used to spending all our free time together. Father had chosen a prized young camel for me, and no one but myself and the trainers had ridden her. She loved our excursions as she plodded behind, her reins held by Nef. As we proceeded on our daily outings, we appeared to be a strange procession. I called my camel Akhet after the morning light, as her coat was the colour of the sunlit sand. Her bridle was adorned with precious glass beads, and her saddle, crafted by the Bedouin people, was beautifully embellished with threads of coloured cotton.

Today felt like a funerary march, grief-filled and sombre. Even the kingfishers fluttered and dived as though trying to strengthen my heart to bring me joy. However, I was lost in the knowledge that today was the last time we would spend together until they were brought to me after the inundation of the Nile. The only hint of what lay beyond the slight breeze of this morning was that I would be with the man I adored. As I cradled my belly, I felt the miracle of our child's life blossoming within me. Becoming a mother reminded me how precious life was and filled my heart with a profound joy that now overshadowed everything else. At that moment, nothing else seemed to matter.

"Promise you will care for them Nef," I urged in a grief-filled voice. "They are a part of my soul path. They feel my heartbeat and are matched with my emotions. I will feel if they suffer Nef. You know I will."

Nef wore a billowing tunic covering his broad shoulders. His eyes pierced mine as he connected and gave me his full attention.

"Your journey is mine," he said in a commanding voice. "I will be here as your eyes and ears, so we will still be banded together whilst we will have the full and mighty force of the goddesses igniting our purpose. Bring back our little prince, born of Thebes, a place of majestic power, as he has an influential role to fulfil."

Nef wiped the sweat from his brow, urging us to return to the palace for my departure to the south.

"Kal, can you call Mother through The Void if she needs you?" I implored. "You will be here in the city; she will need you to be close. You will feel her urgency, and you must call her by her full name to pull her back if she needs you. Keket is coming to help me as my confidant and nanny for our baby; however, rest assured that I will not travel through The Void with my baby in my womb."

Kal looked nervous but stretched herself tall, her clenched hands holding desperately onto her robes. There were so many things to say to each other, yet few words were passing our lips as we would be out of contact from here. I laid my hands on her shaking shoulders.

"I will come to you, my sisters, in a dream state, or when you see the aqua turquoise kingfisher, the white-collared sacred bird of the canal, you will receive the message of the goddesses," I stuttered emotionally.

"Kal, I will miss you dearly. We are forever connected, and I feel my loss already. Saf, I know you will help strategise to make Egypt the most vital force in all the lands, though your husband will have to take the credit," I laughed. "Think of yourself and rest, as many pampering maidens will be at your beck and call. Too much worry and stress can stop you from having a child, dampen your soul light, and rob you of your beauty."

Saf worried and took it upon herself to fix everything, which is why she was such a clever strategist.

"Next time we meet, we may each have babies," I said lightly.

Saf's face was darkened with emotion, and she gave a lopsided smile of resolve that said this was truly happening. Two of her sisters were now gone. I felt deeply for Tani out there somewhere, forging her path, but I was trying to stay uplifted.

"You and Kal still have the gift of one another," I attempted to sound cheerful while the sour taste of regret lingered in my mouth.

There was a broken sound in her voice as Saf spoke quietly.

"I knew when you travelled, Sister, that I would wait for your return like the time on the riverbank, but the fear was overwhelming that you may not return. Those minutes were the hardest," she whispered, her brow furrowed in worry.

So, this is where it has stemmed from. I reached for Saf's warm hands and squeezed them so hard that she trembled.

"I will always return," I replied assuredly, even though my heart leapt out of my chest at the thought of making such a rash promise, not knowing if I could keep it.

Dropping my hands, I smoothed my delicate linen gown, letting my fingers linger on the ripples in the fabric. Then, I pulled my sisters together and held their hands over my slightly protruding belly.

"His aunties need to be strong and self-willed to support the new life that we are creating. May the gods and goddesses preserve and protect us," I prayed out loud.

My snake shifted, tossing and moving his head, as I placed my hand on my chest. "My star will guide us through the eternal night and day, and when we view it together before sleep, we will transmit the golden threads of light between us."

I murmured farewell behind my tears as we held onto the flicker of energy that matched our breathing.

The flotilla of six ships signalled they were ready to leave. As I was ushered onboard, I was distracted, I noticed Hori, who was emotionally distraught, waving frantically to those left on the shore.

We caught each other's eye, and I saw his dewy tears glisten like the morning dampness on the papyrus. Hori was travelling with us as far as Saqqara. He was stationed in Memphis and training to become The High Priest of Ptah.

I was excited to travel to Saqqara again. It was the sacred place where I felt the most incredible connection to life-through-life, as there was a doorway to all the secrets and the world of my other star warriors. I called Saqqara my place of worship, the oldest pyramid, home of my Mystery School training.

As a child, I had been to this wondrous site many times, with the majestic walls around the courtyard where the uraeus heads signalled protection and power. It was here I was immersed in my

Priestess training. I would sit on the ledge of the blue lotus pool, mesmerised by the magnificence of this place, whilst dipping my fingers in the water and washing my forehead. The subtle scent of the flowers released upon her unfolding petals stimulates the brain in a euphoric, hypnotic sense. I felt hypnotised. The opening of the blue lotus was magical, as the intense gold from the centre against the vivid blue petals was like the sun rising in the indigo-blue sky. I would ensure that I was there by the pool at first light to see the wondrous glory of her daily ritual.

I honour Nefertem, the God of the Blue Water Lily, for the healing, beautification and euphoric effect they released, and for bringing out of the well of darkness the most precious flower in all of Egypt. I envisioned this as the place where Nef got his name at the sacred pool in Saqqara, where I called him in as a child and felt my snake wrap around my chest as protection.

Bringing myself back to the moment, all hands hoisted the sails, and with the winds behind us, we sailed south to Memphis City.

"Akila my love, the winds are blowing us rapidly towards my home. Are you feeling any apprehension?" Asim whispered. "Everything will be prepared as messengers have gone before us."

"I am so invested in you, my sweet lover. Nothing could dampen my heart, for we are united and hold our child's blood and soul light. Together, we will do great things for our Pharaoh and our country," I replied.

I could see Keket sit up, trying to listen to our conversation against the slapping wind on the tightened sail. This was the first time Keket and I would be constantly in each other's company, so I did not want her overbearing approach, as I was married now and would make my way with my husband. Yet, I felt secure with her presence, even though she could sometimes aggravate me. I would have to compromise and be thankful.

The long voyage was rhythmic and lulling, and finally, Memphis and Saqqara loomed in the distance on the Nile's West Bank. We were all sweltering in the heat, so it was a welcome time to arrive at the edge of the Nile delta in Memphis to restore our energy and bathe in the palace's luxurious pools.

The land awoke after a night of starlight from Goddess Nut. The frogs' chorus of unending calling had helped me to sleep as I connected with and belonged to the Nile.

The daylight called the great Ibis birds to launch out of the papyrus reeds, and the ducks scattered as we walked hand in hand and entered the waterhole down by the river. Children were already laughing and bathing in the silted water, unaware of the lurking danger to which the birds had alerted us. Too many birds had scattered, aroused by our presence, and Asim's hand was on my arm, poised in trepidation that something was amiss.

We had heard the morning roars of the hippopotamus as they greeted the sunrise. Although we feared them as they could outrun us or tip our boats over in the river, they also represented the regeneration of the life cycle and protection, just like the Goddess Taweret in the form of a hippopotamus. I recollected how the most feared and dangerous creatures become more protective in the breeding season, as they have just one calf every two seasons of the fall of the Nile.

We tried calling the children to be aware that something was among the rushes, and then suddenly, with immense speed and aggressive pounding, a female hippopotamus launched herself into the group of children, savaging one of them. Her baby rambled beside her as she used force to protect her offspring.

Roaring loudly with her mouth wide open, she was a fearsome creature. She lunged back at the moaning child, grabbing his arm again. The sound of splintering bone sent him into a blood-curdling scream, and Asim moved deftly, leaping the distance, all sense of self-protection gone as he flung himself at the mother, his knife slashing into her flank. Her baby too, was roaring, and for a split second, she released the child and turned to her calf. The full weight of her body lumbered towards Asim, his lungs straining for breath as he viewed the hippopotamus's mouth wide open in the attack.

I was terrified and at a loss as to what I could do without a weapon. Our guards threw their spears at her, blindly trying to reach their target. Lurching sideways, she spun towards them, their arrows bouncing off her thick hide as they were too close to have full force behind them. Her calf bellowed again, and miraculously, she recoiled, abandoning the charge to guide her calf into the river, and they rapidly submerged. Swimming along the river bottom, they were well out of range as the next spears hit the water.

The children were in a state of panic as I leapt into action, pulling the rope from my dress and using it as a tourniquet around the child's damaged arm, stemming the flow of blood. The blood, squirting soundlessly, slowed to a stop as I tightened the rope. I retched violently as the sight of it emptied my already queasy stomach into the blood-stained rushes. Pulling myself together, I lifted my overskirt off and wrapped it around the dismembered arm, tying it as a sling around his other shoulder to secure it tightly.

The little boy was whimpering and moaning, looking disoriented and shaking violently as his body went into shock, causing the other children to clamber around in support. Our guards hoisted the boy out of the river and quickly left for the Memphis House of Life, 'Per Ank'. The children, shocked and crying, scattered, and Asim and I clutched at each other in disbelief at what had just transpired. Even the morning sun made me shiver on our return walk.

"My love, you were so moved to action and knew exactly what to do," Asim said with emotion as he wiped his forehead with his arm. "I admire your strength and see you as more capable each day than other women who spend hours with their maidens being pampered."

"Would you prefer me as a spoiled woman?" I teased, poking him in the stomach. "Or are you content with me being the strength beside you to support you as you lead, to protect Thebes as a place of power?"

"I could not stop you if I tried, as I find these traits so admirable, and know that with you by my side, we will survive our harsh life," Asim grinned. His broad, handsome smile made me feel weak at the knees, and I could sense my immediate desire for him growing.

Leaving the shore of the Nile and the plantings of rushes behind us, we walked briskly back to the palace in the city. Two guards hurried toward us to escort us and took their places at our side.

They said that the hippopotamuses were being pushed further south up the river, but the crops in the fields around the city were drawing them back. We knew we could never feel safe around the marshes as they could swim underwater at such an incredible pace.

Quickening our stride, we went directly to the House of Life to see how the child was. The surgeons could not save his lower arm and were taking it off below the elbow. The physicians Asim talked with were highly skilled and held high positions of honour. They gave the boy concoctions to make him sleep, containing as much pain relief as necessary, and with the prayers of our High Priest, were such a blessing.

I rubbed my thumb over the green peridot eye of the black tourmaline amulet Nef had made for me. Given my intention for the child to heal, it felt suitable to leave it in the boy's care until his operation and recovery was complete or until he was out of danger from infection.

Coming out of the hall, I heard the boy's mother, Anippe, wailing and pleading with the surgeons to preserve his life. I went to her and held her as she cried, passing my black tourmaline snake amulet to her for protection until she could return it. I prayed to the goddesses to care for her heartache and mend her little boy so that he would grow into a strong young man. She told me that he was her only child, just six years old and that her husband was killed in battle as a soldier when he was just a baby. This tragedy had left her clinging onto the only love she had, her son. I understood the feeling now that I was having a child. It made me realise even more what a precious gift our children were, and I held my stomach as I felt the tiny flicker of life within me, but nausea still gripped my belly.

Asim was attentive and ensured the boy was to be tended to with the utmost care. He spoke compassionately, saying he would provide the boy and his family with financial support. Anippe bent and kissed Asim's hand, clutching at him with gratitude. I noticed her beautiful, young face, tear-stained, and eyes filled with pain, fear, and uncertainty. Anippe, meaning daughter of the Nile, spoke with power as she stood to thank Asim.

"You are a true honourable saviour going in with just a knife to save my boy. Your child, also a son, will have the courage of his father." She blessed Asim as she faced me, nodded, and placed her hands on my stomach. My undergarments were stained with her son's blood, and she looked directly at me as she wiped her hand over the blood.

"My son and yours are already connected like blood brothers. My son's name is Amon. Please hold him in your prayers, for I wish to see him become a man, and if the gods take him, I know we will have done everything. His heart is so pure like his father's, it will weigh as light as a feather when he meets Anubis."

I knew exactly what must be done.

I asked his mother, "I would like to take him to Saqqara with me in the next few days for a blessing by the blue lotus pools where my goddesses will gather for his healing."

She was beaming, her beautiful brown eyes glistening as she knew of the magic of the sacred pools. We hugged and surrendered his fate to whatever the gods may have in store for him.

Priests and priestesses had gathered graciously on our arrival at Saqqara as they invited us to join them in rituals for the prosperity of Egypt and the preservation of the afterlife of those buried in the tombs for their eternal journeys. Leaving Amon and his mother to rest in the sanctuary, Hori vocalised his blessing on Saqqara's healing temples and tombs to uphold the energy for the future Pharaohs and our grandfather to prosper and have strength for his life path to continue.

"Please bring Amon to the sacred blue lotus pool," I invited Anippe.

Our guard lifted him, and he seemed comfortable with the medication and oils, so we moved into the courtyard as the day's heat brought beads of perspiration to our faces. The scent was encompassing, and the fullness of the open petals with the golden glowing centres made the blue lotus shimmer in the sunlight.

As always, I kneeled to dip my fingers in the pool, when suddenly an electric energy current rippled from my fingertips and up my arm. I shivered but continued and rubbed my fingers on Amon's forehead, reciting an incantation the goddesses were saying to me in their ancient tongues.

I lifted the covers from his arm and dipped my fingers in the water again, feeling the electrical charge each time, and washed it around his swollen flesh. The end of his arm immediately seemed to calm, and the angry red blotches around the stitching quelled. After bathing for several minutes, the heat and swelling were diminishing, and I could see a distinct difference from only a few minutes earlier. The wound smelled clean, there was no rotting flesh, and the healing salve of the blue lotus water was energising the boy. I plucked the lotus petals, counting six, one for each of my sacred circles, and lay them gently on his flesh, and then I bathed his forehead, intending to wash away the hurt and trauma of the incident.

He strengthened and started murmuring and talking for the first time since his attack, and his words were prophetic.

"I will be a great swordsman and protector of my brother," he said, gesturing at my belly with his left hand as he spoke. "We will walk together among men and bring light to the darkest places. The hidden valley in the mountains will shield us from those who hunt the lion, but when our backs are against the wall, the mountain will open, and the star will guide us out of the lands to prosperity."

We sat back and tried to take this in, and I had to try to recall each word as it tumbled out in the voice of a young man - a powerful, self-assured young man, not the voice of a timid six-year-old boy.

Standing next to me, cousin Hori said quietly, "How profound. Is he hallucinating, although his fever seems to have diminished?"

The magic of the sacred blue lotus had given her powers of sight to the boy in his healing moment. He saw himself as the man that he was to become in the future. Was my child his brother?

Amon and Anippe left Saqqara, and I stayed with Hori for a day. The next morning, we rose to observe the blue lotus, which was open again to bless the sunrise. Hori and I were close, as first cousins, and we had a bond that connected us spiritually.

We sat now by the pool talking about our future. We bathed each other's foreheads in a gesture of care. At the same time, the electric energy still tingled from the touch of the water to the centre of Hori's third eye. I bathed the blue lotus water around my navel and rubbed my hand over my stomach, my short top exposing my solar plexus. It was a tonic for my baby as I felt him drawing upon the energy. I thought I must always have our sacred blue lotus essence around, realising that my nausea had subsided entirely.

"My time here is important," Hori said. "I work under my uncle so he can hold the position in Memphis as High Priest of Ptah. There is unrest in Thebes, Akila. Please be aware of the safety of your baby. A child of his bloodline would wield power for the priests, especially if something happened to you, sweet cousin."

I shivered with dread, thinking that my baby would not have his mother. I would certainly be on the lookout for any untoward situations brewing.

"Would you have any insight, or if you hear whispers, could you pass this on to Herihor? He is my Priest to support the Temple of Isis and my grandfather's Temple of Amun," I implored.

"You trust Herihor implicitly, cousin?" Hori questioned, lifting his eyebrows and looking at me directly. "We must be cautious about who we are in alliance with. There is betrayal everywhere."

"Yes, I do trust him. He is the priest of Asim. I have perfect faith in Herihor and his sense of dedication," I continued. "Goddess Isis stated that our baby must be born in Thebes near the Valley of the Kings and closer to the southern borders to form a greater alliance with Nubia. How is Grandfather's Temple of a Million Years? I also hear great unrest within the temple walls, like spiders preparing to ensnare their prey. I will cast my eyes over the running of this magnificent fortress. I have heard so much about it since its completion."

"Go well," Hori said discreetly. "You are my closest ally; I am your eyes and ears. We must do anything necessary to appease the gods and goddesses to hold Egypt in her rightful power."

Speak to me of the prophecy of new lands.

Tell me from where the Nile originates.
My journeys are pathways to the stars,
as in my meditations,
I become more sustained to higher vibrations.
I trust with love that all is perfect
in the divine possibilities of life,
bringing reassurance and hope.

In the world of death, there is life.
There is nothing to fear.
I have walked this path before and will walk it again,
all in alliance with the fullness as an initiate.

There is no need to hold onto the past.
I have been released and hold onto
the healing power of shift and change.

I walk with strength and courage,
allowing the divine plan to serve me.

Lead me so that I may be free from all encumbrances.
Letting go, I feel the flow of life, sensing the signs
of choice so I may respond to birth and live again.
I feel a sense of liberation in the freedom I choose for myself.
My eyes are open with a deep sense of gratitude.

THEBES

The tedious journey to Thebes, set by the Valley of the Kings, which usually took four to six weeks, was taking its toll on me. We were nearly sixteen days into our sailing, and each period of twenty-four hours was ten hours of sunlight. Ra, the god of the sun, with the falcon's head, carried the solar disk on his head as he travelled. One hour on each side is either dawn, dusk, or twilight, and then twelve hours of darkness. It was relentless. I used lotus oil to soothe my unborn baby, chewed on peppermint leaves, and drank tea made from peppermint leaves to relieve my nausea.

I kept my vow of daily penance, directing the divine light of the heavens through my body into the ground and felt more robust and connected to my body by performing this ritual. Manifesting a stronger relationship with the universe and Earth made the days feel more valuable. I felt more appreciative of my life and repentant for the life I had taken. I was haunted as I kept seeing that filthy man lunge towards me, and most of all for the ease and force without emotion, by which I had placed the blade on his throat and keenly sliced him.

I wanted to be happy, knowing my baby was feeling every emotion that I was, however, with these images constantly distracting me, I was continuously feeling nauseous and had hoped that the winds would pick up as the length of the journey depended on the swiftness of the southern breeze.

The water lapping against the craft made me feel queasy as I had not eaten much in the past few days and my strength was diminished. Keket was constantly putting food close to me in an effort to tempt me to eat, which only made me feel worse. She seemed to have changed somehow, appearing less caring now that my mother was not around. I detected it when I needed her most, calling out as I vomited over the side of the felucca, but she just squinted at me with disdain and moved away. Hardly having the will to call out to her again I felt detached, as though I had outgrown her like a well-worn pair of sandals when it is hard to give them up, but you know they will not do the job they were designed for anymore.

Asim was always attentive and brought damp towels to cool me down. We had soft linen nets at night to keep the mosquitoes from biting us, but it was a difficult time with cool nights and sweltering days.

I dreamed of the rains in Alexandria in winter and wished we could have a lashing from a wild storm like those on the Mediterranean coastline to cool the days. I could almost imagine the rain on my face as it was when I had felt it for the first time as a child, exhilarating, like we were being bathed from the heavens. It hardly ever rained in Egypt so I was living in my memories, feeling the water droplets cascading down my face as I closed my eyes to the sky. I quickly moved back under the canopy as the vision faded.

Our stops along the river brought relief, but I must admit I was becoming thin and pale. My belly was swelling slightly, and it was only my love for my baby and Asim that kept me from wanting to cross The Void. The world had dimmed slightly for me, whilst the sight of the children and families lining the riverbank were failing to make me joyous like they used to.

The evenings were cooling now as the temperature dropped, and I watched the fires flickering on the shoreline and felt homesick and alone, wondering about my mother, my sisters and Nef.

I recall feeling like this when I was in my other world. Did this feeling of homesickness never cease? It seemed as though it was etched into my body, like stretch marks on the skin after giving birth to a child.

Herihor was always there at every stop, encouraging and blessing me with his incantations, as though I was possessed and needed cleansing. When we were on our own, and he was praising the gods for their deliverance, I yelled at him in frustration.

"We will be leaving this forsaken place as soon as possible! I want to return to a civilisation where it is not so difficult."

Herihor gawked at me as though I were crazy.

"What civilisation?" He sounded annoyed at me. "Where is it you want to go?"

I realised then that I had broken through the timeline on a thread of remembrance and that he was oblivious to our other life. Just like Jonus, Herihor had obliterated his other life almost entirely, yet only a few weeks ago, he had said that we needed to return. Now, he was fully immersed in his life as a priest, as though he had just flicked a switch, a figure of speech from my other life as well.

The realisation made me think of my parallel world and I looked at Herihor, gazing up and down at him, covering him with my eyes, thinking how I would react to being intimate with him, to making love with him, and I could not imagine it at all. He looked so different and seemed so weak here in Egypt, not the strong, sexy, courageous Jonas that I recalled. I knew, too, that I must forget that time and concentrate on what was right here, right now. All that mattered was my baby and my husband Asim, who had been rejected by me recently. If I were to stop the hierarchy from resorting to a concubine, I needed to be more aware of his needs, and what we had as a couple. My hot tears and dry throat reminded me of the intensity of our life, tearing at the pain and ache inside my chest.

That night, the magnetic full moon was glowing with moonlight, trembling on the water's surface, her essence spilling across the river, lighting up her pathway and the shapes of the flotilla as we docked for the night.

Comfortable in our small but private cabin, we let ourselves explore the beauty of our bodies. Asim was amorous, but any slight movement meant the ripples from the craft sent all the other boats into a rocking motion. I had felt it before when the men relieved themselves over the side of the boats. Quietly and gently, I filled Asim's mind with thoughts of what I could do to him, teasing and taunting him until he could not take it anymore; feeling the blessings of life and the power of a man and a woman and what they could create together if they let go of restraints and restrictions. How unshackling it was, feeling the depth of the water beneath us, and the warmth of love within to fuel us. Asim locked his arms around me as I snuggled into his shoulder.

To feel protected and loved, like they are the only one, is every woman's dream, so why is it then that men and women constantly compare themselves to others and search for the elusive dream that there is always someone better? Why is it we cannot improve ourselves so we can be the only ones? I allowed these thoughts to linger, falling asleep while Goddess Nut took us on the long journey into the night sky.

There were essential ports along the way. It was time to pause, fill the temples with blessings, and meet many hierarchies, dignitaries, and spies who needed confirmation of what was happening in Pi Ramesses and Memphis. Hearing the news from Asim, who had been briefed by the Pharaoh, made the information believable, and all were fascinated by me, his bride and daughter of the chief commander.

Spies and messengers, as my father called them, had already laid the foundation for what to expect from us. There was the deciphering of the codes sent by secret agents to have clandestine meetings regarding the running of the temples and the security of Egypt's borders. I was not interested in the hushed whispers of secrets like Safiya would be, but I was fascinated with the inner sanctuaries of the temples.

I moved in and out of the holiest places as though floating through the mist, hidden yet exposed at the same time. I could not hide from the goddesses but remained as an observer of the life patterns of power, ego and control. I moved stealthily away from the hustle of the marketplaces to experience the vibrancy of the women, connecting to their world of children, food and the support of one another. How simple and free life could be if you were focused solely on your family. Children were the assets of all parents, from inside the great walls of Memphis to the small villages along the Nile. My commitment was to my unborn child's health, so I created times of stillness in the temples to go inward to commune with my son. We passed miles of lush green pastures, growing grain for bread and barley to make beer. Such a narrow belt of farmland and villages between the Nile and the searing desert.

As we sailed closer to Asim's home, I could see his body tensing, his jaw clenched as he remained aloof and seemingly deep in thought. We discussed the preparation of meeting with his father and introducing us to his family. I was apprehensive. I had been drawn to the middle of Egypt to embark on learning, finding it all a new experience, but I was a willing pupil. My hunger to learn the way of the people here, the life of the priests and priestesses and how they honoured the gods and goddesses would be how I would spend my time, learning to absorb and communicate with my mystical guardians.

The port in the distance, the entrance to Thebes, emerged on the skyline. Rotting food and fish stench filled the air as we drew closer. With such high temperatures, food spoils quickly if left for too long and it would be discarded and washed into the Nile for the crocodiles to feast on the offal. The difference in the traders here was rather astonishing, with many nationalities, skin colours and languages, and I felt like a stranger here amongst them all.

Preparations had been made from when we docked to when we were escorted off the ships to reach our final destination and we were well attended to, with strong guards gently waving large fans to circulate the heat.

Asim's father was waiting to greet us, and there beside him was his main guard Dhoser, standing tall and erect, though looking passive, he seemed unresponsive to all the noise and chaos of the unloading of wares.

I had tried to arrange my hair and clothing as much as possible, however after weeks of travel, I felt somewhat dishevelled, though it seemed to go unnoticed, so I continued as though we were well-groomed for the official meeting.

Keket was considerate, kind and caring, helping with our personal belongings, and I thought she must be happier now that we were on shore, and soon we would be able to bathe properly and feel clean again. She seemed to only have eyes for Asim's father, or was it his guard? She appeared to be caught up in her thoughts as Dhoser immediately came forward to assist us and, as they locked eyes I could see the physical response between them, and my snake reared his head in that moment. I quickly turned away and arranged the luggage for the servants to carry inside as the handmaidens came forward and curtsied, assisting us along the walkway to our rooms then, once we were settled, they left in a flurry of giggles and chatter.

"Keket," I called directly. "We must prepare for the celebrations tonight, where I will formally meet Asim's mother, Amunet."

She clicked her tongue as she always did when annoyed and continued to arrange my bath, becoming the loving adviser that she had always been to my mother, eyeing my naked body as I stepped into the tub.

"You have curves now and the body of a woman. You cannot hide your maturing and your gift of a new life," she said softly.

"I want the whole of Egypt to know that I have the gift of a little lion within me," I giggled. "I love him so much already that my heart bursts with pride."

Keket patted me dry, but I noticed she would not go near my belly, instead offering the towel for me to finish drying myself.

Pinning my hair up and laying out a fitting gown of pure white silk with a thick golden neckband, Keket stood back and admired her choice.

"You could wear this wide beaded waistband which would make you look demure and feminine," she said softly, holding it out to me.

"Yes, you are right. That matches the golden amulets perfectly," I replied exuberantly, clapping my hands. "I never want to get old and dreary. I want to live like the young forever."

For a moment, I wished I had not spoken those words as I realised that Keket had become all of those things. Bearing no children of her own must have hardened her heart, I thought to myself .

My sickness had subsided and I felt refreshed, rejuvenated, and ready to strengthen my connection to this beautiful city and to my new family.

Stepping out into the courtyard, the view overlooking the Nile was magnificent.

The evening was calm, subdued almost, and we followed the maidens into the dining hall where I noticed only a small gathering for the celebration, which seemed very different to our banquets at home. There were not even any musicians. Everyone was seated, and Asim rose to offer me his hand and escort me to his mother. I curtsied, which was entirely unfamiliar to me, but respectful, and she promptly held out both hands in a warm gesture of affection.

Relaxing immediately, I felt the tension in my shoulders lessen and realised that I had indeed been nervous about this meeting, as if my happiness here depended on her liking me.

She spoke with a smile that made her face light up.

"Asim has been telling me of your beauty and charm, and although we have known of you, to meet you is such a pleasure."

Her genuine care put everyone at ease as they glanced at each other and relaxed, while my racing heart skipped joyfully. I felt relieved. She liked me. It was as if I had another mother who had welcomed me, putting my soul at peace. *Thank you, goddesses,* I smiled to myself. I am in the right place, right here and now with my husband's family, and I am safe. I returned the warm smile, bowed and moved toward my seat.

Jovial banter resumed around the table as though time had been forgotten, and all had returned to the usual pattern of the family discussing their time apart. The voices mingled until they became a solid mass of dull sound which overwhelmed me and, as Asim's family members spoke to me, they did not give me a chance to respond before continuing with their own stories. Being one of the privileged now, to be a member of a large, opinionated family was quite a step for me to deal with.

"Hello Akila, I am Heqet, Asim's youngest sister," a girl said softly into my ear as the dull monotone seemed to die down, and I could hear only her soft, melodic voice. She appeared quietly like the smooth desert sand which would sweep unannounced into the temples.

I nodded a greeting in acknowledgement of her presence.

"Hello, Heqet," I managed to respond. "It is refreshing to hear your voice. I am feeling rather fragile," I said with a sigh. "It has been a long, arduous journey in my condition, and I do feel very tired."

"I pledge to be your new sister as I know you have left your blood sisters in Pi Ramesses. We will make a pact on the rose thorn to be true and honourable to each other. If you need me, I will come to you, and I can be your guide here in Thebes," she said gently, showing concern.

I had not expected someone to be so forthright and helpful, and I knew instantly we would be as close as sisters. My heart leapt with excitement as I had previously felt alone, as though the walls were closing in on me.

"You must tell me all about your family, the dignitaries and what I could learn about their roles," I said inquisitively. "Then I will feel more connected to you."

"Asim should have been more discerning and given you some insight into our family dynamic. I am sure that now he is home he will be consumed with father's business and the engaging tasks here in Thebes," Heqet continued. "I hope he does not forsake you for his work here, as he is a highly revered architect."

All colour drained from my face as I realised that I knew nothing about my love. *Had I been so self-indulgent that I had not asked him about his duties or position? What else would be revealed to me?*

I urged Heqet to continue. She gave me insight into Asim's moods and how he liked to wander through the magnificent Hypostyle Hall, spending hours viewing the scenes of the great Pharaoh's triumph over the Hittite forces in the victorious battle of Kadesh.

"Many of the young ladies here will be heartbroken that Asim has claimed you, as I am sure each had hoped they would be the one," Heqet sighed.

I flushed, my cheeks burning hot as I glanced around the hall to see where Asim was. *Was I jealous?*

"Are you feeling jealous, Akila?" Heqet squirmed in her seat. "Your face looks quite flushed," she said, as though sensing my feelings.

"It is time for me to retire for the evening," I stammered, trying desperately to hide these emotions that were new to me. "I would love to see you again soon, Heqet. Will you excuse me if I say goodnight?" I asked graciously, quietly leaving the dining hall.

Heqet withdrew to leave me to return to my room to rest, but how could I? My whole world had been challenging from the moment I left my mother, and I could feel the nausea rushing up inside me and rising into my throat.

My snake slithered unceremoniously to hiss at Keket as she entered the room to help me prepare for my bedtime routine.

"Thank you, Keket, for your timely care. I am most grateful," I said, as I held my hand to my chest. At least I have someone familiar here to soothe me, I realised with gratitude.

SACRED
WOMEN'S·SECRETS

I was coping well with my pregnancy, and although Keket was living close, she had now chosen to spend her days elsewhere. I was blessed with two highly trained handmaids whom I adored. They were more my age, so sharing my child's progress with them was exciting. I had a specialist physician attend to me, and he was sure I was further along than the timeline suggested. I must be carrying a big baby.

I was travelling with an entourage of Asim's family to visit the magnificent temples of Hut Ramesses Meryamun and the Temple of Ramesses, Beloved of Amun, way down at the Second Cataract. There, the temples of Ramses II and his beautiful wife Nefertari were constructed as a dedication to her and to put fear into attackers if they came from Nubia.

They were arranging passage as I had withdrawn from the room.

The night's sleep eluded me; until the lull of my body and with the sway of the felucca, I eventually dropped deep into a visionary state.

The thin, silken sunlight streams sent a shaft of golden light to emblazon the great eagle. She stooped with poise to collect me. Without disturbing her feathers, I gently lifted my form onto her warm back and buried my knees into the folds of her feathers. Her deadly dark hooked beak with a yellow blaze over her nostrils could tear a carcass apart. At the same time, her beady eyes bore directly into me and made me tremble with apprehension. I could feel my child moving within, fluttering like one of the feathers flicking on my skin.

We lifted off from the courtyard in massive flapping motions to gain altitude. I was pressed between the vast uplift and then the outspread of the wings and felt the air currents flow over the top of us.

We rose unseen, unheard, as though only the oscillating energy of the mist surrounding us was keeping us shrouded in secrecy. I could feel the goddesses push us on as we soared over the city of Thebes and followed the great river. I viewed the expanse of the overland trade route, the trail winding to the Red Sea.

The mountains to the west and the cobra-shaped highest mountain rising from the Theban Hills struck me with wonder as they towered in the distance. Renowned for the mountain's connection to Hathor, the sky deity and Meretseger, the cobra goddess, whose name means 'she who loves silence' and who guards over the Theban empire and the Valley of the Kings, allowed me to feel the silence encompassing us.

The feathers ruffled with a gust of a warm breeze that penetrated our journey. Moments of deep knowing came to me as this would be the rightful birthplace of my child, with the cobra goddess to guard his placenta.

The majestic eagle sliced through the wind with the front edges of her wings flat into the currents. She carried us onward, using the energy of the bubbles of rising hot air to gain altitude. We glided south to the connection of the great rivers, where the waters gathered at the coming together of the massive tributaries and spewed forth into the Nile River. The run-off was dwindling as the torrents beat against the rock face. These distant mountains and lakes carried the nutrient-rich waters to our towns and cities.

Time was irrelevant in this travel. The light of the day and majestic views showed where the Nile waters originated. This was lower harvest time in the valley and in the delta, so the rivers weren't raging. However, they indicated their path with the massive walls where the waters would traverse.

The energy subsided, signalling our return as my eagle spread her wings, turned, and lowered her flight path. We were heading back when we rapidly descended to dive and soar over a well-travelled trade route where three merchants made their way on the road heading north. We then dropped so low I could view the faces of the staggering merchants as they felt threatened. My gigantic bird swooped so close to them that her extended talons looked menacing. One of the men drew his hood back to expose his face and gazed intently at me with his hand now covering his eyes for a better view. I did not think I was visible, just a thought or expression in my vision.

We pulled up again suddenly in the thermal updraft and lifted skyward. Far below, I could view the three travellers who had all come to a standstill watching our departure.

I never knew why we had swooped so low to threaten the travellers. However, the whisper of all thoughts was blown from my mind as we flew with grace and power, and I dug my knees into the warmth of her feathers.

Upon landing silently on the edge of the courtyard's low wall, I manoeuvred myself down from the back of the great bird, placing my hands on her neck in gratitude for the experience. The subdued skies opened as nightfall revealed a mysterious summer midnight glow. A crack of lightning lit up the great eagle as she stood gallantly on the wall, waiting with patience and dignity until I summoned her release to fly. With a shrill scream, she ascended, her talons spread like razor-sharp hooks; she launched into the air, turned, and made her way toward the coast.

Seeing the merging of the rivers and feeling the pulse of the land of thousands of years of history and thousands more into the future was inspiring and magnificent. Only a few were aware of where the inundation of the Nile flowed from. All the incantations from the priests to bring the flow of the waters worked miraculously each year as the star arrived in the sky and the monsoon waters flowed from the highlands. It was such an honour to have been given the journey of this flight of visual magnificence.

I was tossing in my covers, being roused gently, when Asim entered. It was a darkened night sky now, so different from the moments before in my vision.

Asim undressed quickly as he slipped under the covers. He reached for my warm, soft body, I was yearning for his touch, and we joined in unison, giving each other the caress of sacred energy, holding on to the flow of life. I was soaring on the eagle's wings, lifting into the cosmic bliss as we blessed each other with the divine touch.

The sensation was soft and ticklish; however, it kept returning even though I brushed it away. Finally, I awoke with a start, imagining a scarab crawling over my lips.

"Oh, Heqet, it's you!" I exclaimed with relief as I saw the pure white Ibis feather she held in her hand. She was grinning and excited.

"Quick rise, Sister," she said excitedly. "You have been intoxicated with sleep and languishing while the sun has risen high in the morning sky. Come on, let me show you everything about our magnificent Thebes. Asim is already on his way to a meeting with the council, and you, sweet sister, are lounging here like we have all day." She laughed and threw back my covers so I would get up. Again, I felt blessed with her infectious, charming personality.

Such a stunning girl, a little older than me, I presumed. Her round face and smooth skin showed she was a beauty of bearing. Her ebony eyes were touched with genuine warmth, and her lashes were long and thick. Her hair, silken and loose, covered her face as she leaned over me. A waft of the rich scent of sandalwood hung in the morning air. A plain tunic did nothing to hide her sensual body as her breasts pushed against the fabric to reveal her natural feminine beauty.

"I am excited," she said, as she touched my warm, rounded belly.

"A fire is growing in there, and we will want to ensure his flame will always burn brightly. Asim is enriching you with his glow," she said, eyeing the ruffled sheets. "This will be a well-nourished child," she smiled warmly and pulled my hand to help me get up.

I could feel the sway of the voyage was still affecting my balance with the undulation of the Nile journey.

As Keket was nowhere to be seen, I hastily dressed and omitted my beauty preparation.

Then, moving secretly past the kitchen and out into the morning sunshine, we held hands and laughed.

A layer of sand covered everything, so there must have been a wind whipping up at night, but it had since subsided.

Heqet grasped her scarf and wrapped it effortlessly around her hair and face, and I did the same as we skipped out into the square toward the main centre.

It was a bustling day in the market with so much colour and a hustling vibe that I quickly fell into the anonymous role of being here unnoticed.

The stalls and stone floor were sand-free as the stall holders had cleaned and set up after dawn. The rich scent of stewed meats and hot bread wafting around made my stomach tingle with hunger. The vibrant Theban culture transfixed me.

We moved toward the alleyway to the priests' chambers, but Heqet pulled me away.

"Let us leave that stuffy energy to the men and go where all the women reside. They are waiting to hear more about you," she exclaimed. "It is my favourite place as we are all closely connected and are like family."

I felt excited about meeting more women who were on the same wavelength. Would I meet the girls who loved my Asim?

Heqet called out and was answered favourably by several women's excited voices eagerly welcoming us.

As we entered, time slowed, and a stillness came over me. I recognised the energies of all the women in the room. They had been gathering. It was a flash forward into the future as our smiles and union of love were infectious. We embraced individually and then collectively while the children played, some hiding behind their mothers in curious anticipation of excitement and celebration.

Women who looked stunning, more beautiful than I could have believed, were all in one place. They moved forward, surrounded Heqet and me, and started loud rhythmic clapping to begin the connection. They were moving outward and then toward us as if the tides were effortlessly moving grains of sand on the beach.

Each gave my belly a baby blessing, and they spent time laughing and teasing me about Asim. Finally, we all felt comfortable together in our energy field, and I let go of caution of anyone who would wish me harm.

Suddenly, I was transfixed, unable to move, and I began speaking.

"You will be called in the future to reincarnate at a time when we will gather." The words were flowing from my lips. I didn't sound like myself; however, I couldn't stop my words.

"I will reach out to you. Do not hesitate to come forward even if you feel unprepared," I continued breathlessly.

"Each will be in unique situations, learning from your life experience. Release any fear during this unsettling time. Your role is essential, and you must develop even more rapidly during this era. Hold fast to your belief. You will be tested, as dark forces will threaten us. How you handle your truth will be of utmost importance. You will hold this memory of what I utter, but you may need to discover where this calling comes from consciously. It will return to you when you are ready, so be prepared, thousands of years into the future."

I continued without thought.

"There will be a moment when you will be asked by me subconsciously if you are a 'Yes' to hold firm with the vow you make today. You will choose lives that may draw you to other lands, even another gender for your soul to have all experiences. However, you will know when we will connect again before your birthing time. When the calling draws near, you must choose a female reincarnation. I am gathering the women who will be ready for the future. There will be such turmoil for women throughout time, and many will be unjustly forced to their knees, even death, but keep the intention strong, life-through-life. You are here right now, so are you ready to commit to this? Do you understand?"

Once the question was out, the words stopped tumbling from my lips, and I waited and listened. I could still hear the magnanimity of that which I was asking. I had opened myself to my purpose. I felt my ancient goddesses around me supporting this moment. I remembered my sacred words embedded in the walls of the Great Pyramid to be imprinted into the future.

There was silence. Every woman was in shock. Even the children were hushed and had stopped playing to be still.

Then, the moment of decision burst forth, and the comprehension of what was requested here rang true as to why they had gathered. The women thrust themselves at me, nodding and raising their hands in a fist to confirm their intention.

I viewed their beautiful faces and the colours surrounding them and tried to imprint them in my mind, hoping to recall them in the lifetimes to come.

An alarm rang in my thoughts as two women were holding back. I memorised their faces and colours and thought, *I must know them better and see if they had other motives.*

My goddesses' energies evaporated into a mist of babble and hugging.

We were a unification of trust and happiness. So, I knew my sisterhood was growing and gathering. Like in Pi Ramesses, women already held the torch of light for the future.

Food and nourishment were arranged for our lunch, and then we all moved to the pools for a luxurious bathing afternoon.

I met the wise birthing women who were available, and they showed me how to prepare my body to grow a healthy baby and to practice frankincense steaming.

Brimming with happiness and good soul love, Heqet and I closed the gates of the sanctuary of the house of women.

Back past the alleyways where the market thronged this morning, we meandered, the gardens lush and tendered. I pulled up suddenly and held Heqet back. I touched the scarf around my head to reassure myself I was not recognised and looked again. There against the garden wall was Keket in deep conversation with the guard, Dhoser. My snake recoiled as I held my hand over my chest to support and quell his movements.

We waited and watched from a distance. Crowds were moving along the alleyways as if nothing significant was amiss. It was out of context as Keket reached up, and they embraced with care for one another.

My mind was a whirl of what-ifs.

"Heqet, what do you know of your father's guard, Dhoser?" I questioned with suspicion laced in my words.

"He is a favoured guard of my father. He has been loyal and faithful for as long as I have known," she murmured, looking at me with surprise. "Why do you ask?"

She continued without waiting for an answer. "I was told, as a child, he was brought into the priesthood from a woman in one of the villages who said he was born of high ranking. Because of his size, he was suited to the protection of Thebes and worked his way up to be father's main guard."

"I must say," Heqet continued, "He has always given me the chills, and I have avoided his gaze."

"Let us go and make our way back quickly," I said with a slight edge.

The day had climaxed with our bathing in the pools but had then sent me into a spin, witnessing the embrace between Keket and Dhoser.

How are they connected? I asked myself in the quietness of our evening sanctuary.

My mind was elsewhere throughout our evening meal; even Asim was eyeing me quizzically, without words about what had happened. Then, as the evening shadows finally left me, I abandoned the day in my preparations for sleep.

Keket came and bathed me while I tried to get something out of her, but nothing was forthcoming.

Sleep never came quickly, even though the warmth of Asim's body was comforting. When I closed my eyes, I was haunted by a large hairy animal with red eyes piercing my mind, rushing at me, his massive body rocking with an eerie gait. It was an otherworldly creature, in another time, but it chilled me, so I nestled even tighter into the fold of Asim's chest.

I sense the stillness of my body and the colours surrounding me,
embellishing me in the beauty of the prism of light.

As I lay here resting quietly,
I open myself to the whispers of my innermost dreams.
I hear the answers to my desired choice for my future.
I am at one with the miracles of all existence
and draw the proof of my visions to me.

I come from a place of empowerment as I resolve any
outstanding situations that may have been called into being.

My sacred secrets, the intimate truths and revelations
that guide my journey, are observed.
They clearly show me how all my relationships
are based on the truth revealed to me.

I am here in reverence of
the divine journeys of my ancestors.
I honour and place unconditional love
with them for bringing me to who I am.

SACRED
WOMEN'S·WOMB

The massive temples celebrated the power of our Pharaoh, Ramses II. While the vast city of Waset covered both sides of the Nile, the magnificence of the West Nile with the royal tombs in construction was always a bustling enterprise. The houses of the craftsmen, artists, labourers, and priests were on the West Bank. The mortuary temple of my grandfather took twenty years to build, and the majesty of this temple for all to honour was the beautifully constructed Ramesseum.

We went to the northernmost Temple of Millions of Years on the West Bank at Thebes, where Seti I began creating his dream of dedicating the temple to his father and the god Amum-Re. It faces east and was designed to pay tribute to the Hypostyle Hall that resides within the Karnak Temple across the river. Seti I never completed his temple here, but my grandfather had finished the temple and constructed a great wall and massive pylons to commemorate the power of his reign.

In front of this glorious temple was the administrative centre of Thebes, where all the officials ran the city. There was a hub of power where Asim spent many hours in his love of architecture and supporting his father in keeping the town running with its strategic positioning down the river from Edfu and Elephantine.

I was uninterested in all the planning and avoided hearing of the military decisions that would be important to my father. They received daily instructions for the protection master plans from Pi-Ramesses regarding our borders, and I wondered if Safiya was assisting in any strategic groundwork.

Heqet and I stood in the power centre with two colossal stone gateways leading through two courtyards into the Hypostyle Hall with those forty-eight columns within the inner sanctuary. The stunning blue ceilings studded with astral stars were breathtaking. Four great standing statues of Osiris, arms crossed, holding the crook and flail, stood guard against the columns. I noted how the flail, used for threshing (which was separating the grains from the husks), was depicted as the fertility of the land. Osiris held the crook used by the shepherd in honour of kingship and the pharaonic authority.

The massive statue of Ramses II seated on his throne was nineteen metres high and stood at the back with the royal palace to the left. Two statues of the seated pharaoh flanked the entrance to the temple, one in pink granite and the other in black granite. My favourite of all was the pink granite statue with flecks of black. Like all granite, it held the most unique energy; the earth's power was always present. I rubbed my hands over the magnificent marble whilst paying tribute to my grandfather for his exceedingly visionary concept of spectacular mastery.

Heqet and I held our breath in awe as we wandered through the vast magnificence, a testimony to the mighty power of our pharaoh.

Then, we were silent, absorbing the glory of the military victories and the depictions of my grandfather's dedication to the gods.

"Heqet, you can feel the power of the gods and goddesses within these walls. You can feel the insignificance of all the small things when you stand in the glory of this monument. To have the opportunity to have prayer in the sanctuary is such an honour." I spoke with reverence.

"Come, let us go to the smaller temple of my great-grandmothers; Tuya and Nefertari," I spoke with admirable esteem of these two respected and loved women. We entered the temple, our approach unnoticed, we presumed.

"Akila," Heqet said to me as she looped her arm through mine, "this is a true goddess temple where you can feel the love and guardianship of the female role. You can feel the womb of the earth embedded within these walls," she said almost in a whisper, so as not to disturb a breath of air. We knelt to pray in the sanctuary. I felt the red mist enveloping us like the strength of red granite. It held a force to its gentle wafting form. My snake was quivering, and I placed my hand over my chest.

The mist encircled us; it had an unusual pungent smell, almost like cinnamon. We both remained still awaiting what this ritual had in store for us. Heqet moved to place her arm around my waist, and my unborn child pressed his body against her arm, reaching for her comfort.

We had become so close over the past few months. We were inseparable, and I knew Asim and his parents were happy with our deep friendship.

My goddesses came forward, and Hathor held out her arms, welcoming us into the portal she was beckoning us to go through. The mist became thick and protective as we floated like the mist itself down a long, narrow passageway. Heqet was now behind me, freely moving as I was. Finally, we opened up into the shrine of the female womb, the lining thick and full. We could see the glowing eggs like the opal moon, which had just been released from the tubes leading from the almond-shaped ovaries, the nest where the eggs were held in preparation to be released.

We had been ushered into a sacred, timeless space of being present at the beginning of human conception. The two eggs had been fertilised and were beginning the journey to the embryonic stage. We felt privileged to feel the mist of the portal as we were shown two rapidly forming foetuses, now two months in utero. We knew we were in the same space as the two foetuses, floating in their embryonic sacs, knowing each other was close.

We had glimpsed into the past or the future of our souls being together in harmony. The mist gently tugged at our presence as the foetuses kept growing. We were then drawn back down the passageway to deliver us back into the sanctuary, like a birth. Finally, the red mist evaporated as we gasped, looked at each other and hugged fiercely, pressing into our sister souls. What a feeling of belongingness. We were already connected through a kindred spirit, but now we knew why.

The gift of Hathor's vision and the goddesses' protection in the temple during the portal passage made us wonder what had just transpired. Our sacred mother's womb had left us both in no doubt we were soul twin sisters, each living our separate lives.

We thanked our brave women whose temple we had been led through to the portal. I knew we would return as my child grew within me, to come through to his birth.

It was hot in the afternoon glare, and the noises of the community were pressing against our brains; almost too loud. We both clasped our hands over our ears to drown out the voices. Slowly, the voices softened enough so we could speak.

"Wow, that was such an unexpected experience that we were invited into," I said in an excited rush.

"I have never experienced commune with the goddesses like this! We are true soul sisters. Though non-identical, we both have the same purpose," Heqet exclaimed.

"Will you stand by me and be my birthing woman and guide? I need you, Sister, whom I can trust," I spluttered, almost bursting into tears at the immense impact the sanctuary journey had on me. My vessel was going through all these changes to bring our prince into the world, and it was all happening by the innate gift of my body.

"The fascination of childbearing," I said in awe. It is no wonder women here in Egypt are cherished for having children, and mothers are respected and admired. Both men and women here acknowledge a revered status for mothers, the givers of life.

We stopped walking, took a deep breath through our noses, and then exhaled.

"Yes, I am here for you as your baby is born, as his birth is sacred for me also," Heqet said eloquently and with deep feeling.

I showed her the sacred circles and how to draw them, knowing two were for comfort and only one was significant for danger.

We were oblivious to the menacing shadow following us. Only as my snake wriggled to be seen did I turn around quickly to notice movement behind one of the granaries.

"Let us go, Sister," I expressed, to Heqet's surprise. But there was a cloud formation, and suddenly the sky let go of her ultimate deliverance of rain quite heavily, like the gushing waters of birth.

It was such a surprise and without warning, and because of the noise, everyone was drawn out of their homes and workplaces, and the streets were a throng of muddied children soaking up the rain from the skies. This had never happened here before. We hurried back to the guest wing of Heqet's family residence. Our heads were covered with our scarves, and the water was streaming down our faces. The rain subsided almost as soon as it had started.

Laughter and joy tumbled out of our mouths as we each went to change for dinner.

Keket still needed to be found. I enjoyed not being around her as she seemed judgemental of everyone and everything we did.

Asim and two handmaidens entered our room and the handmaidens filled the bath with delicious scents and jugs of warm water.

Asim cleared the room with a brush of his hand and came to undress me. My belly, tight and growing, was such a delight for Asim as he massaged me with neroli oil while talking cutely to our baby.

"And what have you been doing today?" he spoke directly to my belly as though it would give him answers.

I dared not tell him about the sacred woman's womb, because he may not have believed me. But really, he would, as he knew of my commune with our ancient goddesses.

So, I started embellishing my story of the tour through the temples. When he put his finger to his lips to quieten me, I did not need to continue.

Gently bathing me in the scented water was such a loving gesture; as women, we were versed in the art. He then let me wash him, and as he allowed the water to trickle over his body, he became alive. We held on to one another while moving naked toward our bedding.

Our lips tasted our fervour as the fire ignited the tingling in our bodies. I closed my eyes to feel the sensation ripple through every part of me, washing over my being in an energy of desire. I was determined to keep my eyes open to revel in the feast of my husband's body. He was strong, and his stomach taut with nipples erect and tantalising as I viewed our bodies together. We were perfectly entwined in the warmth and soul food of our amorous, tender, yet powerful loving. He always held my hair back briefly to see my face, as though to recall every detail. I was now on top, leaning over him, my full breasts hanging seductively to be teased and tasted. We joined in a coming together of our hearts, each beating with a frenzy as I rolled over and held him with my legs wrapped around his body. He gave me his glow with urgency, and I received it like an azure blue faience chalice waiting to be filled. We both shuddered with release and fell into the afterglow of love, matching our bodies as he wrapped his arms around me from behind, placing his flat hands over our baby in a protective manner.

Then Asim started talking quietly but with a stern, concerned voice.

"My love, Herihor has warned me to be careful. There is powerful magic here, and it is known that a child is descending during Akhet and the star's rising to grace Egypt." Asim spoke gently with long pauses to let it sink in.

"Our son is also due at this time," he continued. "Hundreds of other children are due at this time, but the priests will watch us so that they may monitor our child. Do not place your trust in anyone or give secrets away about your time travelling."

He urged me to face him, moving back slightly to accommodate our baby between us.

"We have so many gifts here right now, and we must protect them," he said, brushing my hair back off my shoulders. "We are creating our masterpiece within our little family; this is the beginning. So make sure your goddesses protect both you and our child. I trust you will know what you need to do. Herihor is here as your priest, so let the people see him with you so they know you are honoured and protected."

I saw the concern on his face, and it stole his handsome features. I embraced him fully and pressed myself against him, complying with his wishes.

We will walk, and I will teach you about sacred women's wisdom.
I thought I heard her say.

The vision of the Egyptian Goddess Taweret
with the breasts and belly of a pregnant woman,
the limbs and paws of a lion
and the back and tail of a crocodile.
She embodies fertility, motherhood,
new life and the nurturing of babies.

Her vision floated before me, a powerful reminder
of the extreme importance of my child.

I called in her magical protection.
"Oh great one, the lady of the heavens, the mistress of the
horizon and pure water, bring your gifts of benevolent love
to my birth house and anoint me with your blessings.

I worship Goddess Meskhenet, who will be present
at my child's birth and breathe his Ka his soul into being.

I am here to hear your prophesies,
envisioning my child as strong as the King of Egypt."

AMULET

Finally, the extensive monumental journey with an entourage of Asim's family was preparing to go to the magnificent temples of Hut Ramesses Meryamun, The Temple of Ramesses Beloved of Amun, down at the Second Cataract. The temples of our pharaoh's power standing proudly were a reminder of his mightiness as a ruling king.

Finally, we prepared for the extensive and monumental journey with an entourage of Asim's family to go to the magnificent temples of Hut Ramesses Meryamun, The Temple of Ramesses Beloved of Amun, down at the Second Cataract. The temples of our pharaoh's power standing proudly were a reminder of his mightiness as a ruling king.

The flotilla was ready, magnificent in all their splendour. The golden and rich brown flags depicting the Pharaoh's Sceptre fluttered gently in the quiet breeze. Dhoser's figure gripped my heart with a sudden bolt of fear as he stood motionless to guard the entourage onto the vessels.

He held a quirky look of satisfaction etched on his face, and it perturbed me in a way that I had felt the night I experienced meeting the beast back in my other world.

Smelling death again alerted me and I knew I could not go on this journey. It was a warning of something about to happen. I shook my head to brush it off, but the smell and feeling gripped even tighter around my chest. I trusted my intuition, knowing my baby's need to be protected. After what Asim had told me, I felt myself recounting all the situations where I may have been at risk. I thought I would be safe here amongst my family; but I could see a significant problem with Dhoser's presence.

I moved, pushing Asim's mother to the side to vomit unceremoniously close to her.

"My dear, what ails you this day? Our voyage has been planned with you in mind for the festivities," she spoke kindly as she rubbed my back gently. "The goddesses are awaiting your arrival, I am sure."

"Mother, I feel unwell and unable to attend. It is such a long journey, and I am apprehensive as I have such a short time before our child is born. I will stay with my handmaidens; it is only fourteen cycles of the night before you will return. I must see the physicians to check on our baby." I spoke with urgency.

"Yes, you have my understanding, child," she spoke with reassurance. "I too, would be concerned as we will be sailing on the water much of the time, which can make one ill."

Immediately, Heqet stepped forward. "I will also stay Mother and assist my beloved sister in her ailing. I have loved these temples and the blessings they give since I was a child. The huge monuments with our pharaoh's image towering above the Nile and the deep-seated knowledge that they pose a threat if you enter our world with negative intent. But I am needed here with my sister."

Built to face eastward to capture the sun rising, the temple lit up the images of twenty-two baboons, who are the greeters of the sun. My intent to go there before our baby is born fuelled my preparation. Relief washed over me when the trip was announced. However, now I knew it was not possible to go.

Uncanny clouds floated aimlessly where there were usually clear, bright blue skies. I noticed a massive eagle with a vast wingspan burst from the clouds above us, circling the flotilla and descending rapidly downward, aiming at Dhoser. The boat was rocking as though there was a great tide of waves, similar to what I have witnessed on the ocean's shores by the great seas in Lower Egypt.

The energy was alarming as everyone grappled with boarding the vessels, and the flotilla rocked dramatically. The River Nile offered her displeasure, with my goddesses guiding the rippling effect. I could feel their dynamic power.

Dhoser boarded one of the vessels in front of the family and turned to stare directly at me, his eyes turning blood red instantly. The magnificent eagle tipped her wings before colliding with the boat Dhoser was on, pulled away, and soared upward, her great expansive wings casting a temporary shadow over the ships.

A lone feather floated gently, softly, enticingly, to land at my feet. Picking it up brought a surge of protection and dignity, filling me with gratitude as I placed it in my hair.

What was meant to unnerve me made me stronger. The vision of knowing I had taken Dhoser's life in my other world gave me a sense of satisfaction that he could no longer travel between worlds. Visualising the picture of a hunched man with glowing eyes covered my thoughts. I had finished his time-travelling using my bow and had taken him out with precision. Here he was, still making motions that would drive fear into my heart. Now, with the entrance of the eagle, the messenger of the highest gods, who depicted loyalty, truth, freedom, and honour, I knew it was time to take action.

Asim and I connected more personally as we viewed the undulated rise and fall of the boats with the rugged landscape looming from behind.

The time before parenthood; the feelings for each other whilst clasping these family moments, surrounding us with an aura of warm anticipation. I viewed these times with appreciation for my husband's family, which made me miss mine even more. Mother would miss Tani and me; I wondered how she was coping.

"My love, we have the world before us, yet I feel nervous as the time creeps closer to welcome our child. This journey would have been refreshing and given us some time together," Asim spoke, trying to understand why I would not be attending the voyage.

Frowning with concern, Asim leapt at the chance to place a protective arm around me. "We are nearly there; our baby will be the highlight of my life and a treasure for my parents."

A chill washed over me as I could not visualise his mother holding our child. *What did this mean? Will he be alright?* "Oh, Asim, I do hope everything will be okay." I felt tormented by not being able to see something so natural as his grandmother holding him. *Were my visions failing me?*

The voyage was to begin for the family, with now cloudless skies and family united for the journey. We seemed to have everything, yet I trembled with a foreboding.

"You go, Asim. It is only for a brief time and I will have plenty to do. Heqet and Herihor will be with me," I said, confidently placing my hand on his arm. "Go, my love. The nights will pass rapidly, and we will be reunited." The air was soft and warm, like a gentle caress on my bare arms as Asim leaned in to kiss me. Then, once again, time ceased to matter, and the spinning of my world showed me how deep my affections were for my husband.

We waved as the boats gently manoeuvred their way out into the waters of the Nile. The slapping sound of the boats on the water drifted off into the distance.

My specialist physician was concerned about the birth. His suggestion of me relaxing with no more water journeys relieved me, as I anxiously awaited the news of Anippe. What caused me anxiety was that I was unsure of who would care for me now that Keket was removed from our palace. It was as though Anippe would be my saviour.

The long-awaited arrival of the feluccas from home and through Memphis caused joyous shouts of excitement. Everyone anticipated good news from both the capital and our families as the flotilla approached. We could smell the pungent goose fat plastered on their bodies to ward off mosquitos wafting to meet us and it brought back memories of our voyage. I had been conscious of my anticipation of news from my family and Anippe as the boats were coming from Saqqara. Also, there may be news from Hori.

Gifts of beautiful handmade linen wraps from my mother and trinkets from Safiya and Kal made my stomach churn as I instantly felt homesick, whilst fighting the tense emotion of being away from my family. I desperately wanted to go home.

Heqet and Herihor stood by my side. We have been constant companions during these times. They both endearingly supported me through all my pregnancy challenges, which seem to be growing just as I was.

I noticed a budding relationship between them as they exchanged loving glances. Heqet dropped her eyelids demurely, which stimulated even more affection from Herihor. I felt a brief rush of jealousy rise within me until I pushed the emotional impulse aside. What was I thinking? *This was a crazy love triangle entanglement I was living in?* Herihor had forgotten our past world entirely and was fully enveloped in this one, yet here I was, still being pulled between returning to my other life and being fully present here.

My knees were weakened, as standing firm in the heat was brutal. I had been advised to wait inside, but my overwhelming curiosity about being right here waiting for news was all-consuming.

Heqet and Herihor gripped my elbows to steady me as I was handed my black obsidian snake amulet wrapped in a linen sash from Anippe. As I unwrapped it, its stunning green peridot eye captured my position from every angle, and I felt immediate protection as I tied it to my dress.

That was much better. I could now feel relaxed and released from distracting thoughts and desires as I was spending much time with Herihor while Asim was on the journey and living his work with passion.

Holding my peridot amulet, I blinked thoughtfully, trying to understand what was happening. A man's voice came with force into my hearing, and then the vision of two young men, one noticeably with an arm missing, holding a warrior's spear as he rubbed his finger along the dart's sharp point. The other young man, strong and supple, brandished a bow, his arms tense and ready. Both were bronzed by the sun with their muscles tight and oiled for protection.

It was Amon who spoke ardently and tenderly to his companion. He leaned sideways and whispered with a clarity I could hear.

"We will practice the stealth of the crocodile."

The other young man turned; his gaze flicked over me. He couldn't see me, but he could feel my presence. His eyes glistened light green like my crystal peridot gem, and his hair was relatively fair.

Instantly, I recalled Jonas's distinct look with a solid square jawline. His pleasing, boyish face was pressing on fifteen summers, and I shivered, a prickling running down my spine, knowing he was my son, and I listened intently as his name sprung from the lips of his friend, Amon.

"Herihor, drop to the ground and crawl as we have practiced," Amon whispered, moving his spear downward.

They both melted into the mist as they bent low to the forest floor.

I sucked in a shallow breath, feeling the air forced through my teeth. *How could that boy be my son?* He looked unlike his father;

my eyes struggled to focus on something my mind could not comprehend.

"Herihor," I whispered. *What an elegant name*, I thought, as I heard it from my lips. To be named after my priest. That is an honour. My eyes darted to the man standing beside me. He smiled as he bent to listen to why I had whispered his name. Those handsome features gave me a moment of far-away recollection, followed by a rush of emotion. Although they did not look alike, there was the essence of Jonas in Herihor. I am sure I saw the exchange of that fleeting glimpse of recognition with Herihor just now, which I would have to get him to recall before we travelled on the timeline.

"Oh, nothing; I was reminiscing about a far-away time," I said whimsically. Herihor wiped his forehead and eyed me intently. The vision had faded, but it already had given me a heightened sense of intrigue. *Will my son here look like the young man whom Amon was talking to? How has that happened?* I grappled with the enormity of what that might mean.

Heqet buried her face in my arm, showing her strong affection for me as a transcript written in her body language. We loved one another dearly; we were all entangled in this divine power of connection.

"Anippe has given favourable news of Amon. He is healing and does not let his small arm affect anything he is doing," I spoke rapidly and excitedly. "She says through her messenger that he is effectively becoming a warrior and practicing tossing a spear and using a knife. He is fighting with his left arm, and the metal workers have made him a smaller spear with a slight tip of bronze."

Ooh! I clapped my hands with pure relief and naturally rubbed my belly to commune with my son, as though the life of Amon was entwined with our baby.

"Anippe wishes to come to Waset and assist me as my guardian to worship Taweret, our goddess of protection. What do you think?" I asked Heqet. I knew because Taweret is known as a pregnant hippopotamus with breasts like ours and a crocodile tail with the mane and paws of a lion. This goddess was fierce to ward off any evil spirits.

"Anippe has given me this protective silver neckband and a carved jewellery box filled with spells and incantations from cousin Hori," I told Heqet. "I feel it is a blessing to have Anippe here as I see very little of Keket nowadays."

I felt someone was observing me; my jaw tightened as I turned slowly to see if the character stood out. No one was obvious, but many people were on the dock, and because my snake did not seem annoyed, we continued.

Heqet agreed, and it was news that needed to be sent urgently to bring her to Thebes. I was overjoyed with her future arrival to help, knowing I could trust her like my sister, Heqet.

The night fell breathless but alive with the voices of insects, crickets and frogs and the occasional roar of the hippopotamus cooling further up the river. I planned to leave the house silently to go to the women's gathering, where Heqet was waiting. We anticipated connecting to practice toning, which is used in the temples for religious ceremonies. It was calming, soothing and healing, and I was keen to not miss out. Excitedly, we would all lie down and feel the deep sounds washing over us to balance and harmonise our bodies' frequencies.

With anticipation, I pulled the wrap around my shoulders, covered my head and face from the cool night air, and said a brief incantation to my goddesses as I stepped out. My hand immediately went to my protective amulet of Goddess Tawaret, which I was wearing, and my wadjet eye of Horus, which I had adorned myself with for extra protection. As I walked, the blade of my knife strapped to my thigh gave me reassuring pressure.

I was praying and calling my goddesses, my lips moving without a sound. I soon got lost in the crowd, looking like anyone on the street. Walking as quickly as possible, I told myself I should have a guard with me; however, I did not want to arouse suspicion that I was stepping out. With Asim away, I wanted to spend as much time as possible rousing the women for our healing and women's mysteries for thousands of years into the future.

I gripped the lower palm fronds to pass through the gardens, and as they sprung back to their original position, I looked up and stood motionless. The figure before me appeared without warning; the moonlight dancing on this stranger's dark face, haloing his features. He was armed with a spear aimed at my stomach. I forced a shallow breath into my lungs to utter a few words, questioning his position. My snake, who had become fully alert and with hood flaring, was emitting a fierce energy that the man was picking up on. He was backing up, trying to figure out how to proceed. I slowly eased my knife to hold it before me, my scarf falling away to reveal my long black hair framing my face.

He twisted to the side to look for a means of escape in the garden and could not move anywhere. My snake's impact and confrontation with him had made him panic. His breath rose from his nostrils in fear, when from behind him, he was struck with such force that his brain matter immediately spurted and seeped from the wound as he toppled forward, his feet flying from under him as he hit the ground. The axe was still embedded in his skull as his body shuddered and made wheezing sounds. The foliage danced in the moonlight, the shadows looking sinister against the backdrop of the palms.

"Who are you?" I demanded of the man in front of me who had killed this villain. My voice cracked with distress; it was my child I feared for. With a blood rush to my head, my vision became blurry, and I swayed. I was sinking and trying to reach out to the tangle of fronds to hold me, my knife spinning from my hand. The tomb bat's wings flashed in the moonlight as they darted through the palms.

The force of his grip to catch me was overpowering, and tremors of effort accompanied his ability to stop me from falling. The wingbeats of spirit were gathering, and as I came around, blinking my eyes, I saw his concerned look as he uttered incoherent chants. The mosquitos buzzed as darkness crept into the crevices of the trees and plants, enveloping us in secrecy.

"I am Badru, father of Kalina," he spoke rapidly, reassuring me I was safe, as I was sure he was on the verge of tears.

"I have been trailing you to have words. It was providence I was here for this man had sinister motives, but your courage held him off. I could not let him leave alive little one, as he would have tried again to take your life," he murmured matter-of-factly.

My snake, who was too precious to name, was my guardian and had held the villain back with force. My snake representing Ra, the Sun God, was now hushed. I knew this man here, saying he was Kalina's father, could be trusted.

We stayed down behind the foliage until I could become more centred. I could smell the sweat of Kalina's father; his closeness was solid and comforting as he supported my head. Looking like a Nubian warrior, although not ebony, his face was oh-so-familiar as I strained to catch another glimpse of him in the soft moon glow.

We were both aware of the possibility of snakes. Still, in the carefully manicured gardens, the mist now encircling the glistening leaves and crickets calling, it was unlikely the earth was being disturbed.

"It is you," I breathed as I struggled to rise, the weight of my baby belly making it challenging to get up gracefully.

"I saw you on the road with two other men making your way along the route from Nubia. I was in a vision to source the waters of the Nile, but now, possibly, it was to look for you, to see if you were coming. The massive wingspan of the eagle's flight had tipped toward you, and you pulled your hood back to reveal your face."

My legs were shaking uncontrollably now, and I clutched my belly. Badru held me up as I adjusted my sandals with my other foot, steadying myself with his gentle embrace like a father.

"You are my uncle, and there is so much to know," I stuttered.

"We must leave here now to not bring attention to ourselves," he said softly.

Wrenching his axe from his victim, he wiped it unceremoniously on the grass and put it back under his cloak.

"My knife!" I uttered as he searched and found the blade glinting in the undergrowth.

We walked silently through the gardens to the house. But before leaving me at the entrance, Badru promised to meet up again and squeezed my shoulders. I was still unstable and held myself against the wall.

"Be wary of Keket," he voiced in a chilled tone. "She is capable of immense destruction. I will reveal all to you soon. How is my beautiful daughter? Because of Keket, I have missed Kalina's whole life. There are secrets you will have to know." Then he was gone, and a shadow wavered against the mudbrick wall.

The rich smells of roasting rabbit and geese restored my energy as Heqet and my friends gathered to change my clothes and anoint me.

"Burn them," I stated as I sat rigidly on the cushions, unable to relax fully.

"What happened, Sister?" Heqet urged me to talk.

"I tripped and tore my clothes. With the bedazzling moon Khonsu, he cast strange and silver contours which made me unsteady." I looked at Heqet as she gazed under hooded eyes, not believing my story.

Our feast was delicious, with bread, fruit, and wine. I raised my goblet high toward the heavens in honour of my goddesses, and all the women followed the gesture, stretching our arms upward as if determined to reach the stars.

Snuggling down to listen to the beautiful cascading melodic toning and the warm envelopment of the women surrounding me, I fought off the descending energy. It was so relaxing to drift off in surrender to sleep.

Heqet must have sent a messenger to Asim's household as I awoke the following day, the golden sunlight sending her filtered shaft of light into the sleeping quarters. I was somewhat disoriented as my eyes adjusted to the comfortable surroundings of the slumbering women. The thick mattresses held the women and children in unison like puppies gathered around the mother to suckle. Getting up to the latrine was difficult as I stretched like a cobra unravelling from a coil. The cold limestone on my buttocks helped sit me up and remind me of the events of last evening.

Safe... I hardly felt safe here; it was like a conspiracy of finely twisted silver filigree thread that you could not untangle. Beyond the walls of the royal household, there was a whisper of knowledge of a language I could not decipher. There seemed to be spies lurking on every corner to tell secrets that did not exist and then pass on messages to degrade and challenge someone.

I kept myself scrupulously open so I would not be the creator of gossip, and Asim's family was a constant protector. It was like being under the wings of that great falcon.

I could hear the goddesses playing the ancient harps as I re-entered our rooms, and a sonnet washed over me while I felt my closeness to Asim's family grow. They kept me focused on my well-being and my baby's health as time moved toward birthing.

Now home, the day crept up on me as I relaxed, pondering the latest events. Keket must be avoiding me; she knows her role in coming here was to look after me during my sacred womb time. How can she be so cold?

She did come in very late to prepare me for my sleeping time. She had sent my maidens away, so I knew she was here to undress me, and I was waiting. My snake was aroused and ready, and the force to hold him down made me shake as my mouth tightened.

"I am unhappy, Keket. You are not fulfilling your duties to me," I said, waving my hands around uncontrollably. "What is your excuse? My mother trusted you; you betrayed her. What are we to do with your role here?" I spoke angrily, trying to keep my voice low. I could feel the blood-hot anger rising like a fire under my nails.

Keket kept her head down, unwilling to look at me. When she finally lifted her face, I saw the courage of triumph burning in her eyes instead of remorse. Immediately, I dropped my deep emotions, recalling one of the most potent triggers that would send me hurtling through The Void. The instant recognition of her manipulating power chilled me. She knew my triggers, and she was trying to use them on me, coercing me into a state of frustrated anger without uttering a word.

I will not be the victim of her fanciful evil destruction. I am keeping my baby, was my burning intention. Slowly, I sank onto the mattress, holding my stomach and ordered her out to never serve me or my family again. I wept a thousand tears of loss as she was our nanny since we were babies. *What dark forces had established themselves inside her?*

When Heqet came in, she was distraught to find me in this state and holding on to me; she unleashed her words.

"She will be removed from Thebes," she threatened; her body was tense and contorted with anger. "I will have her deported for her behaviour. I will have the guards escort her out of our city."

Heqet had no idea what Keket had done; but she saw that my face was swollen from the tears and reacted instinctively. No one would ever need to know of her evil intentions. How she must have manipulated my mother all these years. My mind flashed back to the dealings and power she had with control over my mother's and her family's happiness for my whole life.

Oh, protective amulet, shelter me from
the focused elements that may be against me.
I surrender myself to your healing protection.

I can feel the outstretched wings of Goddess Isis
glowing with light and magnificent power.
I sense the waves of protection
washing over me from Goddess Taweret.

I am held in my beloved's sacred care
and am grateful for your spiritual representation.
I am conscious beyond the physical world
and reassured by your guidance in this lifetime.

I release all that no longer serves me,
and I become more passionate, loving, and caring
to receive ancient knowledge from the highest source of light.

I am your child, unwavering in my thoughts and deeds.
I share my gifts of activation, creativity, healing,
and anointing others in the physical world.

Nothing can distract me
from the divine love I feel within me.
I am always guided and wear this amulet
as a token of your endearing love.

THE · TRUTH
PREVAILS

Nearly ten cycles of starlit nights had passed while I waited, anticipating a meeting with Badru. My mind was burning with questions to clarify why he had given me such a warning about Keket. So it was unexpected for him to have an audience with me here. Requesting a meeting in the house gardens was considered forthright but also open and trustworthy. The maidens were clucking to themselves, and Asim's mother was concerned that I should meet this man without a guard.

The family was home from their journey, and the many festivities they had engaged in within the temples along the banks of the Nile, kept their emotions buoyant and engaging. The celebrations spilled into the days ahead, and the festivities continued as everyone joined in to celebrate.

As the High Priestess for my family and in governance with my goddesses, I should have attended. I furrowed my brow, still feeling the flickers of frustration unnerving me that someone like Dhoser could keep me from my duties; however, I lifted my head, held my bearing, and abruptly brought myself back to the moment.

"Mother, I assure you he is family. He is my uncle. I know you will not request to meet him yet, but I am sure the time will come," I reassured her.

In the creamy light of the morning sun, I stepped out and sucked in a deep breath taking in the most handsome features of the clean-shaven man standing erect and calm before me. Badru looked polished in his smart army uniform, which surprised me. I had not taken it in that he would be in the military and a leader too, by his attire. I could tell by his clean execution of the man the other evening that he was well-trained. No doubt he had been in the Royal Guards.

"I have waited for our connection. I wish to introduce you to my husband Asim, when he is available," I suggested proudly.

He squinted against the stream of sunlight and turned slightly to avoid its intense rays.

"Asim knows me both personally and professionally. When I was banished from Pi Ramesses, I was sent here to the military. I trained Asim in the art of combat from when he was a young man," he spoke officially. "I am one of the deadliest assassins trained by the Pharaoh's military to protect Thebes and its royalty. I have learned the tactics of the Nubian executioners, and it will be an honour to protect you too."

Wow! I was shocked. I pulled my body upright and now had even more surprises to unravel. Sadness burned in my breast for his loss, of him not knowing our beautiful Kalina.

"Let us sit here in the garden, as I have so many questions," I purred excitedly, finally meeting Kal's father and spending time together. We sat on the bench, and I leaned toward Badru.

"Why did you leave? Kalina has grown up heartbroken not to have known you or her mother." It sat uneasily with me that he had never even made an effort to contact us until now.

"It was because of her birth," his face flushed with emotion before he continued. He tried to get his words out without elaborating but was tripping over them.

"Kalina's mother and I were so in love. We were in the happiest times of our lives. I had attained a high ranking in the military, but I was hot-headed and full of aggression as my role demanded it. My impending child was my highlight," he attempted a smile as his eyes glazed, recollecting his joy. "I knew my child would help me be a better man."

"Nashwa, your mother, and my beautiful Sanura were inseparable as sisters are and close in age," he continued. "Keket had massive control over the sisters as she knew the secret of their travelling. I could see her manipulation, but both your mother and Sanura thought Keket protected them as she held the sacred mystery. Keket was in love with their brother, your uncle, for many years, but he was later killed in battle. Her jealousy was worn like a scar on her face and heart. They were lovers, but as he became committed to loving another more regal woman, Keket's jealousy intensified. That beautiful young girl was found killed by a poisonous snake, bitten on the neck. It was unknown how it got into her bedding," he continued.

I gasped at the intensity of the information unravelling. Mother had never spoken of this, so the secrets inside the walls were intended to stay hidden there. My hands reached out to clasp my uncle's. They were battle-scarred and rough as he drew my hands together and placed his big, calloused hands over mine. He then looked directly at me and spoke lovingly.

"It was after the young woman passed that your uncle requested to go to battle, and he never returned. Only his physical body was recovered when his spirit fled, and he was subsequently wrapped in burial cloth to go into the underworld. The sisters never got over the loss of him. Knowing the young girl committed to him was carrying his child, turned Keket's mind into a dangerous mood. His death broke the sisters' hearts as his essence with the young girl was lost forever. He already had another child, a son to a peasant woman, and this boy had been sent into the priesthood in Thebes. Then our baby came early with all the stress. She was not deep in the birth canal with her head down; she was facing the wrong way. We had the birthing women trying to turn her."

His voice was quivering with emotion as if it was yesterday. "I was with her throughout her struggle, stroking her head while she screamed in agony. I was pouring my energy into her to help her relax. They nearly managed to turn the baby, and my love was helped into the squatting position with the birthing women holding her," he said painfully.

I could feel Badru's pain as he recounted his story. "Keket came in and ushered me aside while she whispered to Sanura. The last look was painful as we held on to the link of love. From then, I knew she had slipped into The Void but was fighting to stay present, her body racked in pain. I tried my best to calm her. She could have made it if she had not taken the passage."

His big chest heaved with emotion; this was the only time he had spoken of this in nearly seventeen years.

"I forcibly moved Keket out of the way. I knew she was responsible for Sanura's transition. My love gave an almighty push to deliver our daughter, but it was too late; she could not return. I lost all sense of sanity as I was screaming, calling her. Your mother and I and Keket were calling her, but she had spent too much time in The Void and could never come back to us," he spluttered, his body heaving with grief.

I was crying too, sobbing while holding on to my uncle, rubbing his back, trying to take his loss away, my loss away, all our loss away. I felt the knife twisting in my heart for our family. My baby was squirming and kicking under my ribs as if feeling the tragedy. It was hard to breathe. I was shallow breathing, sucking in as much air as possible before I exhaled loudly.

My uncle continued, "We gently placed her down, and I lay with her, my heart against hers. Mine was shattered into a thousand fragments of faience glass. Her first milk was staining the linen of her tunic. I could not look at my baby. I was so full of uncharted emotion. I leapt up and laced my fingers around Keket's throat, squeezing tightly; and I would have broken her neck if your mother had not stopped me. I hissed at Keket that her time would come as she fled from the room.

Your mother wrapped and passed me our baby, and through her tears, she said quietly, "I call her Kalina after a beautiful flower in a faraway land." My uncle kept on telling his story, "I only held her for a few minutes. She was the most beautiful flower I had ever seen. My tears covered her with my love. She was nestled next to her mother to let her suckle her first milk in honour of the work my love's body had gone through to produce that elixir just for her. We stayed together until Sanura's body was cooling, her life force fading, and I saw her spirit lifting out of her physical home. Kalina was hungry again and cried mournful cries of loss for us both. She was taken to suckle on a nanny, separated from her mother. That was the last time I saw them both.

Because of my hot-headed behaviour, I was sent away to protect the southern borders, and I left immediately, as I would have been a danger to Keket. I heard that Keket too, went away for many months.

I have been tortured by thoughts of, *What if? What if Keket had not spoken to Sanura?* She has dark spirits; that woman is cunning and dangerous. So when I heard you were journeying to Waset and Keket was on the flotilla, I had to come back to protect you.

You are a threat to her, with your child nearly ready to be born. I do not know why, but she is trying to take out the time travellers. I am determined she will not be near you during the birthing, but there are other risks and dangers for you as well," he spoke with apprehension.

My eyes were like saucers. I could feel the pressure behind them and rubbed them furiously. I had my weapons, my snake, my goddesses and Heqet, and soon Anippe would be at my side. My body trembled as I shook myself to shake off this troubling story. The river of treachery flowed all around us while we were trying to manoeuvre our way emotionally through the uprush of water. I tried to untangle all of the words to simplify them in my mind. Many more questions became apparent, such as; *why Mother trusted her? Why did Keket look after us so well, like a nanny, even Kalina? Maybe because she thought we were not travellers.*

We sat for a while, gaining our composure.

"Word must be sent to my Mother about this turnaround of events," I stated. "However, we must not alarm her as I will be birthing here in Thebes so I can bury my son's placenta in this land.

My uncle jerked my shoulders to face him, and I winced and cried out softly. "I have removed Keket from my service," I said purposefully. "I do not know where she has been spending all her time or with whom. Maybe we will track her to see who she is involved with. I saw her embracing Dhoser, Asim's father's guard. What do you know of him?" I questioned, expecting Badru to know.

"You may have to leave here before then; this is my warning," he wet his lips and spoke abruptly. "There is much unrest in the administration here. I have expressed my truth to show you how deep this infiltration is. Dhoser is well-trusted and has never stepped out of line; however, he has never looked me in the eye, so I have been unable to hold assurance about him, especially since he has avoided my gaze. I have traced his lineage, and it is very hidden. He was brought into the priesthood at an early age," he grunted with dissatisfaction.

I swallowed hard to keep the bile from rising in my throat and rubbed my shoulders. "That hurt, Uncle. I am not a child but a High Priestess and a wife and will do my own bidding. You can not tell me what to do." I pushed myself up from the bench and faced Badru, now standing.

"Remember, I am here exclusively for you, like my own daughter," he assured in a soothing voice.

"Well, you will want to remember to tread gently with us; we are not your military troops. We have survived this long without you!" As soon as the words slipped out, I knew I had gone too far at this delicate stage, for he was still feeling the emotions of speaking about my aunt.

I whispered to my uncle, more relaxed, as I released the frustration of being commanded what to do, "Very well then. Sorry, I am listening to you. Maybe you can be my bodyguard and ally. No one needs to know of our blood ties. I will speak with Asim."

"I have already spoken with him, and he agreed after the garden event that I should be your bodyguard. We have hushed the event, and nothing more needs to be said about it. I trust you have not told anyone," he said gently.

I had not even told Asim, and now my face felt flushed and somewhat guilty. I could tell Badru was not used to communicating with women, and I purposefully mentioned this so he could modify his mannerisms and words before he met Kalina.

"My gratitude is much more profound than my words," I spoke with reverence. "My goddesses had shown me your arrival as you trekked through the perilous trails from Nubia. They took me low to see your face, so I have the most heartfelt trust in you because of this vision. I believe in the family, but we must set no foot wrong if you say there is danger; however, I do not wish my child to have this energy of mistrust within my womb space. So, instead of worrying or being concerned about these security matters, I will hand them to you entirely. I will go to the temple tomorrow to converse with my goddesses. Please be with me if you can."

His constant shadow reminded Heqet and Herihor that I needed protection. They felt uneasy about the hidden attention but were reassured we were safe from whatever evil lurked around us. The energy of dark forces hung like heavily laden date palms. It was never knowing when the corrupt force would lash its fury on us.

Anippe's arrival many weeks later brought much more festivity and joy, as there were always celebrations in Egypt. I was so large

I could not believe my body could expand and stretch that much. Fortunately, my sister and friend Heqet constantly reminded me how deeply we loved each other as sisters. We invested much time together daily, meeting with the other women. I was training them in the art of feminine power and how to hold sensual energy in our sacred space. Our women's group multiplied, and genuine connections constantly expanded to deliver total soul food. We could send a nod of reverence across the room, but the hugs we shared filled one's heart.

A couple of women were not displaying colours of truth and when I approached them, they both were hesitant to open up. I said pretty clearly, "I can see you. You are not hidden in the veil you cloak around you. As a High Priestess, I can see your shadow souls accompanied by corruption." From that approach, they never returned to our circles.

Dark clouds gathered on the landscape, and I could feel the constraint around me as though someone had their hands on my shoulders, pushing me down. To stay connected to spirit, I spent many hours visiting the temples in deep commune with my goddesses. I was linked to the vortex of sacred knowledge hidden in the temples and the walls of the spiritual chambers.

I was an advocate and a Priestess of the Rulers of the Light. I embodied the fifth and sixth dimensions as a shadow priestess, invigorating the craft and the knowledge therein.

I was bringing in the galactic force of ancient hidden rituals of the light beings. Millions of years of cosmic sacred geometry were being beamed and aligned into our Earth's grid system. The energy patterns would remain hidden, held in suspended time, until humankind understood the fullness of the codes of nature and all life. My goddesses were evoking their powers so I could be a fearless participant in all physical existence and the deep, hidden knowledge of energy fields. My child was also initiated into The Realm. His stirring in my womb awoke my protective female force, his soul light wrapping around my heart, filling me with exuberant happiness.

Faith and trust in Anippe gave me strength, as we followed the old ways of preparing for my birth. We continued with frankincense rituals, crouching over the warm embers while the warmth caressed and purified my sacred feminine space. These thoughts of birthing preparation were chasing through the fringes of my mind as Heqet and I strolled back from a visit to the temple.

We ambled, basking in the light play. The light danced softly over my body. With Heqet by my side, we started methodically planning my birthing technique, as discussed in our weekly sessions with the wise women. Our physician was still voicing how big my baby was, that maybe I was further along than I thought. That was not possible, but he was reminding me it could soon be time and to be prepared, so we were going over how it would all play out. I chose to deliver at home amongst those close to me. Asim would be there with his soothing voice and calming influence, but through my façade I was unsure. Knowing I could do this, I tried to breathe deeply to calm and soothe myself.

The mingling of people in the square was not strange. However, there were groups whose presence disturbed me and their gathering seemed out of place. Keeping my head down and avoiding people's stares, I grabbed Heqet's hand and hurriedly kept moving. My snake rose in defence of something I could not physically see.

I could smell the tension with a cold chill tracing down my spine. My feet hardly touched the ground in urgency to make it home. A woman came close, and under a hooded scarf, her eyes met mine. She had a terrible smell of rotting flesh about her. I had smelled this often after the battles had raged and when the wounded returned home. The whites of her eyes were bloodshot and creased with pain. My snake rose in pure defiance whilst a mist of anger engulfed me, which I managed to waft away as I kept repeating my love for my child. Fearing I may slip into The Void, I clutched my stomach and turned to face Keket. I hardly recognised her with her dishevelled, slovenly appearance.

"What do you want?" I spat out, determined to make my point relevant.

"Meet me tonight outside your room when the moon time is close. I will be waiting and need to talk. Move hastily now, as you are in danger here," Keket whispered through her teeth.

A dull ache filled my presence and my skin prickled with sudden fear. "Heqet, let us go please," I pleaded as we picked up our pace. My body was heavy, lumbering disjointedly with apprehension, and haste was nipping at my heels.

The gathering of blackness filled the air as we left the square to move as briskly as possible towards home. Heqet too, was trembling as she firmly gripped my hand. My goddesses were whipping up a sandstorm, flicking needle-like flecks to those behind us.

Suddenly, my uncle appeared. His scathing look showed he was upset we had chosen to go to the temple so late in the day without him. Scouting around us, standing tall and threatening, he observed the situation, his footwork spinning his power to push the apparent threat away. Using the sorcery of the goddess power, he blinded the followers with sand as a whirlwind traced our footsteps.

Safely inside the compound, he faced us, making eye contact. He boomed out his displeasure, then lowered his voice, remembering what I had said about him commanding us.

"You have put yourselves in danger, which will never happen again. The vultures circle when the prey is vulnerable," my uncle said sharply.

Heqet and I stood hugging, listening intently. I struggled to sit in the courtyard while we took our verbal punishment.

"You are right Uncle, we will never be that forthright again to believe we are safe freely walking when there is sinister activity amongst us." Heqet then burst into tears, which streamed down her cheeks in a release of pent-up emotions. I had never before had to be so wary of people, but then again at home, we had guards stationed at most points around the royal compound.

Anippe came racing from the household with Amon trailing behind and I stood up, nodding and smiling demurely in gratitude at my uncle for rescuing us. Amon was getting anxious, trying to position himself before me to connect with my baby. I hugged him and drew him close, the recent vision of him clear in my mind. He put his head on my protruding belly as though to listen to the heartbeat. After stroking my snake amulet, he started whispering words I was not familiar with. Anippe gently tried to pull him away as I looked at her with large eyes and raised questioning eyebrows.

"Sorry, Akila, I do not understand his language. It seems like another tongue, a tribal or spiritual language. He uses it when he is alone and thinks he is out of earshot."

"I am fine with him coming and connecting with me, Anippe. There seems to be a bond here I would like to foster," I said tenderly. "Maybe my baby understands his whisperings." We all laughed to lighten the atmosphere.

"Heqet, thank you, my sister. You have protected me once again," I said with encouragement and gratitude as I turned to embrace her. It felt like home with her, such a warm, loving hold.

"Heqet, I urgently need to talk personally with you about Keket's desire to meet. Can you stay awhile with me, Sister?"

Anippe and Amon left hand in hand, Anippe clucking about how I will need to be in soon for my bathing.

"There are unusual happenings here, and I am feeling quite distressed for my child," I said softly, reaching for her arm to wrap around my back and comfort me. "Asim too, is concerned. I have brushed this off, but now I see more to it. Keket wishes to talk with me, and seeing her face today has shaken me, as no doubt this is urgent."

"Yes, that was frightening today as the sun was sinking with twilight upon us. An evil presence lurked in the square as though all those people would have rushed us if your goddesses had not pelted them and your uncle had not made his presence known," Heqet confirmed my unpleasant thoughts.

I hardly noticed the dark shadow of her form slouched against the bench; her body slumped on the ground in total defeat. I knew she was no threat, but what was her intention? Shame was etched in her soul as I stared at her demise as though she was shrinking before me. I held my hand to my chest to quell the energy of my guardian snake as the premonition of death was upon us.

"What evil has become of you, Keket? How has the crocodile devoured your soul?" I sounded possessed but recoiled as I felt the anger welling inside me. I glanced over to where Heqet was standing, huddled and wrapped up warm. Now, this night, I was cold and heartless.

"You have betrayed us all, and now you come crawling like the flies on the carcass," I spat. There was a stench all over Keket, like the decomposing carcass itself.

"I know what you have done. Kalina's father explained it. We have all missed out on family because of you. We loved you and trusted you as our nanny. My mother will be devastated. You were the chosen one to call her through The Void." I sniffed uncontrollably but knew I must stop, as my feelings were getting out of control. I could feel the buzzing and tingling like I was going to travel.

Snapping myself back and repeating, "I love you, my baby," instantly calmed me.

She spoke slowly but still with a fire in her as she turned and looked at me, pain obliterating her ability to relax. "You are in great danger Akila. When your child is born, your use is over and you will be given the potion, which will take you quickly, making the bleeding unstoppable.

There is no escape if you do not listen to me. My time here is almost through, and I feel the long night is coming for me." She sounded cold and lifeless already.

"Dhoser is my son, fathered by the man I loved, your mother's brother, your uncle who died in battle. Dhoser is a traveller and shapeshifter; however he has the darkness in him and does well to hide it. I had to leave to have him and then to keep my position, I had to give him up. I have loved him and protected him as a mother would, but I feel he is going too far to obliterate all travellers he knows, and you are on his radar. I hid it from him that you travelled, as my love for you girls was true like daughters. However, he had been observing you in the other realm," she coughed and held her stomach, her face contorted in pain.

"He wants your child, and your son will be chosen for the priesthood as Asim will want that too if you are not here. From there, he will have control over him and use him to travel, creating havoc in the other realm. Asim would be oblivious to the dark magic.

Go now! Go child, as fast and far as you can or know the loss your child will face with his mother dying in childbirth."

My head was spinning. I knew she was telling the truth; the righteousness of her efforts to speak made me crumble with respect and love for her.

"I have two granddaughters born of Dhoser and I will not be here for them. They are beautiful girls, a blessing and a gift to me for all the wrongs I have done through my jealousy. They are my saviours. They are your blood, too. Please look out for them. They may need your favour if they are travellers. Please give me your blessing, Akila. I know as High Priestess, you convene with the goddesses."

Slowly, her voice trailed off while she steadied her breathing. "I never tried to harm your aunt in her birthing. I thought we could call her back if she went into The Void for a little time, for she was exhausted, and to ease her pain while she delivered. Tragically, her delivery took too long, and it was the pain that was stopping her from returning. What a courageous woman to pull herself through enough to give her daughter a chance. She may never have known she had a daughter. A daughter is a most powerful gift for Egypt. It has haunted me and turned my head," she stammered.

Through my emotions, I could hear my voice affirming, "Yes, Keket, I will meet with my goddesses in the temple. I forgive you, but your heart will be weighed against the feather, and Duamutef will lead you as the son of Horus to your trial. It is out of my hands, Keket."

I knew she was dying, but how? "What is happening to you?" I questioned, the tears welling in my eyes.

She took her hand away from her stomach. The stench was putrid; it looked like she had a knife wound. Not deep enough to kill her, but the lack of medicine had led to an infection, and the foul stench of death was calling for her soul to be released from her body slowly.

"Why did you not seek help? I have my mother's knowledge of medicine. Who has done this to you? Was it Dhoser?" I kept the questions going for fear I was running out of time.

"It was not Dhoser. It was one of the women in your circles. I was trying to stop her from giving information about you to the men who are against your presence here. You have female power, and they are threatened by it and are determined to stop you. Go now, Akila. Leave here and be safe for your son and all the women who need your message in the future." She kept going but was losing her strength.

"I ask for forgiveness from your mother, the one I have hurt the most," she said, looking back and forth as though we were at risk. Her nervous tension was more apparent the longer we were together. "I leave that with you to deliver Akila, for I am being called away."

"Can I get you some plant medicine to help ease the pain? It is the least I can do," I stammered. "Please come with me Keket; all is not lost."

She struggled to her feet, and Heqet, seeking to give help, came forward. We held a long look, knowing this moment was necessary for us. Heqet had witnessed everything with concern etched into her beautiful face.

"I have completed my role. How you take this, is up to you. Please tell me you will leave here and return to Pi Ramesses," Keket pleaded.

I felt sick, my heart pounding with the knowledge that my life and my baby's life were in danger. Heqet and I could only tell the heavens. I closed my eyes and lifted them to a soulful call to Hathor and Goddess Isis for help to take Keket's life force from her body quickly.

DESERT · STORM

"Come here Priestess, the beautiful goddess of light. You have gathered all the women you can bring together here in Thebes, and I hear you are anointing them?" he questioned with a raised eyebrow. "All the men are anticipating their women to be open to the new sensual ways you teach them. We honour more rituals during childbirth, and the children have a morning ceremony to greet the rising of the first light as Goddess Nut arches over the morning sky. You are showing them how to bring back their maiden power," he laughed and buried his head in my hair. "And now you can show me how you manage those teachings."

"My love," I murmured, "I will take your glow to nourish our baby, and I will leave you wanting me with a desire that will always haunt you. You will never experience anything else like that which my energy can give you." I pinched his stomach as he moved to cradle me underneath him. "Our god Min would be proud of your physical body; you are passionate and full of life. Come to me my love, let me take you home to the stars," I whispered huskily.

Our interlocking energy was tender, slow, then fierce in wanting our bodies to connect. I would hold Asim without letting him seek solitude in pulling free, then take him to the heights of eternity and only release him when I was soothing his raw, animated energy. I touched and massaged him in places that sent his body into a wild, intense passion and took him deep inside me. Home to my inner world, to the womb of my baby's sanctuary. I pulled his exclusive colour into my body as his glow cascaded. I felt his energy pouring into me in his delicate way of nourishing my body. My Elestial Crystal Star spun in the solar system and basked in the midnight sky while lighting the flickering comets.

The pain came in waves, gripping and releasing. My baby was on his barque, his vessel into this world. The time was right now, the moment we had eagerly waited for. I was early, for my due time was nearly another moon away.

I breathed out a muffled cry of exasperation as I gripped Asim's hand. "Please go for Anippe and Heqet, and do not alert the birthing women. We can do this. Anippe and Heqet are practised in the art. I will go to the Temple of Isis to birth our son, for he will be protected there. I will listen to the words of Keket as she spilled out her message before her spirit was taken to the afterlife."

I recalled when Keket died; I had cried and forgiven her for all her misgivings. However, I knew she would be devoured when Anubis weighed her heart. Our goddess Ma'at was always truthful, just, and dependable with law and morality, so Keket was in her hands in the underworld. Maybe she will return in the future to right all her wrongdoings and release herself from the harsh lessons she has learned in this lifetime. It was a desolate time for me when they found her body curled up under the bushes in the garden; frozen and stiff, clasped in her hand was the amulet my mother had given her when she left with me to travel south.

I dressed warmly and gathered my robes. The evening sky had a soft pink glow, with only a little light left. Sipping on water, I prepared for the subsequent pain. I was still perplexed by how long the birth could take or what my plan was after my baby's arrival. As long as he was born in the temple, he would be safe, and so would I. Sweat was gathering on my forehead.

"We must look like we are taking an innocent stroll to the temple, my love. Please call Heqet now, as I need her hand."

I stopped abruptly as the next surge of a contraction overtook my senses. I took my time going inward, my innate sense of survival. In my trance, I felt Asim beside me, supporting and rubbing my back. We would have to look relaxed as we moved to the temple, as the gathering dusk dimmed the light.

The palm trees laden with heavy fronds gently whispered to me to hurry. They looked cumbersome and reminded me of how I felt. Briefly turning to check on Badru, I squinted; he looked oblivious to my situation. However, he was scanning the buildings and gardens to see anyone lurking in the shadows. I felt comforted that all was perfect and that the goddesses had me in their care.

Herihor had been urged to go to the temple and would meet us there. I wanted to alert Asim's mother to the birth, but more people might find out. My trusted allies surrounded me. That is all I needed. I focused on breathing, taking awareness into my heart, and shuffling forward with my feet to keep moving.

Strange, raised eyes from onlookers were obvious while we remained solemn, they were almost too intent on our passage. I had to rest again; leaning on Asim and seeing the dazzling golden light behind my closed eyes, I steadied myself and fought off nausea. Anippe, Heqet, and Amon, who were trailing behind, now moved more rapidly towards us. I could hear their breathing as they hovered around and positioned behind me to shield and cover me. I was fearful my waters would break right here on the pathway.

"Whatever are you thinking of?" Anippe asked, concerned. "We should be in the birthing chamber, where you will get all the support and attention you need."

"Just help me to the temple. Isis is calling me not to dally here," I justified myself.

Heqet was carrying blankets, making me wonder where I would give birth to my son. I am sure Herihor, with assistance, will have it sorted as he was always patient, present and organised.

At last, I could smell the familiar surroundings; the mighty walls of safety were musty, yet the distinct scent of frankincense and neroli permeated the exterior of the sacred temple. A gasp and a sigh of relief burst forth; we had made it.

The moment I did that, I felt the gushing flow from my body, wetting my legs, and the floor of the entrance covered in my baby's protective waters. How apt that my waters wash and anoint the temple entrance.

Everyone hastened to help, and as the great doors were pushed open to the temple, we saw that Herihor had prepared the mattress and cushions. Brightly woven fabrics were laced with ornamental braiding, making the scene calm and peaceful. The fire wands burned in their holders to softly adorn and light up the paintings etched into the walls. Frankincense was smouldering in the bowls placed around the sanctuary.

Asim, tentative yet nervous beside me, urged me forward to relax on the mattress. Anippe felt my stomach pushing at the top of my belly to see how far down he was, and then she smiled at us, signalling all was well. My shoulders relaxed as I closed my eyes to bring the energy down through my crown chakra into my baby, connecting to his pineal gland, his third eye. Strengthening our energies together, I communicated to my child, giving him the signal it was time for his grand entrance into the physical manifestation of our world. It was time for his soul light to commit to his earthly home, in his new body here with us.

The intense pains came as Anippe helped me up to lean against Asim. The men moved out of the doors to give us privacy. Asim pushed back my glossy blue-black hair and asked Heqet to pin it up. Hardly speaking, he looked pale and in shock, but his strength and guidance were reassuring.

Hequet gently held me as I now crouched low over a soft cushion. I had prepared my womb space each day with the rich frankincense steaming, and I felt ready and strengthened with my goddesses holding the space.

"Imagine you are in deep connection with the Mother of All Life," I heard my goddesses speak gently, then in soft, lulling mantra sounds.

"You are in a sacred relationship with the Goddesses Isis and Hathor, and our presence here fills the room to welcome your child. The path is enlightened before you, and the wisdom of the solar barque moves your child down the canal.

All energy in the room ceased as I went inward for the deepest contraction. Every element of my being was alive with sacred spiritual healing. Concentrating on delivering gently, I held my lotus while I breathed and waited till the subsequent searing pain gripped me. I opened my lotus fully, and the pushing and bearing down became intense while guiding my child on his solar barque, his boat of deliverance.

I was hot and sweating, with each contraction getting more potent and longer. Heqet handed me a chalice of cool water. My thirst was ripping at my dry throat. As I lifted it to my lips and took a sip, my snake suddenly rose, his energy flinging the chalice from my hand.

The commotion began as soon as the chalice shattered on the stone floor. Anippe quickly snapped, demanding where the water came from. Heqet was beside herself, saying it was already here. She thought Herihor had brought it in.

I coughed harshly as the liquid burned my throat instead of cooling it. I opened my eyes wide in fear, recalling the words of Keket. I started spitting it out, but I had already swallowed a little of the liquid.

The birthing pains were upon me, and my goddesses wrapped their arms around me, whispering, "It will be alright; you must concentrate on this moment. Make it a memory of love here for your baby."

Asim's concern was etched in his worried features. Looking at him gave me a strange peace as though he could look after the worry for both of us. Then, closing my eyes, I drew on my personal energy and focused on going inward again, knowing this was the moment of surrender. I moaned quietly, succumbing to the waves of burning sensation as I gently pushed and guided my child to the crowning of his birthplace.

Nausea and intense pain in my abdomen were washing over me as I took the special moment to observe my beautiful boy. His cries of new life rebounded around the walls, filling the crevices with sound and penetrating through the thick wooden doors. He was rather pale but had light, dazzling eyes and stunning features. The shape of his head was delicate, yet his distinguishing chin and nose held me in shock as the recognition fully hit me. He looked just like Jonas, linking to my other world.

Everyone looking at him gasped, and then silenced as though a prophet had been born. The absence of sound in the chamber was deafening as the baby was quietened, and then the nervousness as the placenta was birthed, as Anippe pressed and rolled her hands down my abdomen to fully release it. I started bleeding after. Exhausted, my thighs still quivering from the intense bearing down made me feel faint.

Anippe had taken our baby to be wrapped and passed him back to me. Heqet had brought a large water vessel and urged me to drink from it. She gave me sweetened goat's milk with a potion she said would counteract the poison and stop the bleeding.

Asim laid me down gently to cradle our son; our eyes met with deep love that we had created a miracle. I felt the rush of delight and protection giving him his first suckle. I was afraid the poison would taint my milk but was assured we would express milk later. I was unwilling to take my eyes off him for fear of slipping away without taking him into my soul. The immediate bonding moments were intense in me, yet I knew I might not make it.

"Asim, Heqet, come closer. Promise me you will bury our baby's placenta here in Thebes," I cried earnestly.

Amon came up, and I gestured to him to come forward. Then he hugged me and then hugged the baby and kissed his head. A blessing of momentous proportions had been witnessed as he wiped the blood from his crown.

The outside sounds were immediately drawn inside as the great doors opened, bringing in a whirling, high-pitched sound of the wind.

Herihor urgently commanded attention to speak with Asim, who leapt to his feet to attend to the happenings outside.

Anippe and Heqet helped me to the chamber to expel the poisoned liquid. Heqet then gave me more soothing goat's milk with the antidote to sip. Slipping in and out of awareness, I felt myself swaddled and blanketed. I was strapped and then lifted by Badru.

A powerful sandstorm whipped up her fury around us as the stinging sand billowed into the chamber now that the doors were fully open.

I closed my eyes and felt my snake wrapping around my baby and me to hold us together as Badru and Herihor struggled against the desert storm to carry me outside. I could not comprehend where I was going, but weakness overtook me. I could hear and smell my camel, Akhet. Was I to ride my barque into the afterlife, where all my loved ones would be?

"Asim," I whispered thickly, "Am I going to the afterlife so soon? I will miss you."

The sand stuck to his wet tears as his hood was dishevelled in the wind.

"We will call him Herihor after your priest. He will be protected with that strong name," he said through tears and the stinging storm. "You must go now my love, Heqet and I will come to you, for there is dark magic here, and your goddesses will surround you and serve you well. For tonight, a prince is born."

I heard a magical voice, like the spirits of the wind, calling my name. A soft hand touched the wrappings around my face, which would protect me, my sister's beautiful voice was calling my name; that voice seemed to echo from a time so long ago.

"Safiya... Saf, are you here? You have come for me," I choked. "Am I going to the afterlife without fully suckling my son for his first milk?"

"We must hasten; no foolish talk now - he is strapped to you to give you strength. We must leave here now; our mother is waiting," she muffled as I could hear the tears in her voice.

"Thank you, thank you, Sister, you are my saviour," I managed to squeeze out before her hands left my face.

Badru lifted me onto Akhet, his arms straining with our weight. He gave me water from his leather gourd, then leapt up behind, holding the reins. Then we were up and we lurched and swayed forward.

We kept a steady gait through the murky depth of the storm, each camel tied together. The sand noise was deafening and obliterated our path as we left Thebes. Holding on tightly to my baby, I could feel his little body warm and safe beside me.

"Isis! Hathor! Hear my prayer," I began as the rhythm of the camels urged us forward. I could feel the life force gently pulling at the edges of my world.

"My goddesses save us to be together again; Asim, baby and me," I cried into the drowning noise of the desert storm.

The storm raged; dark and mind-splitting, while I clutched desperately onto my baby and blankets. Badru's frame was like a solid rock of strength behind me. It felt like hours of slow plodding; the camels would spread their hooves to keep from sinking too deep. The wind howled for hours with sand spinning, biting and tearing at our clothing.

Suddenly, the storm surrendered her force, and we were on the other side. Like the whirling desert was locked in a rolling pattern, we had witnessed a miracle to obliterate all traces of the hoofprints behind us. The whistles of the trail leaders kept us connected. I was feeling more relaxed and soothed, knowing we were safe.

The first light pulling through from the darkness showed the campsite ahead. The lights flickered like beacons, with tents billowing in the gentle pre-dawn aftermath of the storm. Badru leaned forward and pointed in front of me while he passed his water gourd, which I guzzled, licking my lips with the crunch of the sand in my mouth.

The last distance felt like forever till I could see the cluster of people waiting for us to get closer. I was burning inside and must have drifted off again, in and out of exhaustion.

My mother's quivering voice called my name repeatedly while my father's arms lifted me after Akhet lowered her body. I fell into his protection as my baby was unstrapped and passed to my mother. Saf was instantly beside me, brushing the sand from my face, which seemed embedded in every pore. A persistent worry in her voice was evident as she kept repeating my name.

Father carried me through the camp to a tent while my mother, running alongside us, urged me to drink her elixir, trying desperately to pour it into my mouth, though challenged by her awkward gait while trying to keep up.

Herihor signaled he wanted to do a blessing, so as soon as I was washed and settled, he was sent for.

Kneeling beside me, he started his blessing. I immediately felt the buzzing and trembling as he came closer. We locked eyes, gazing deeply into our souls as the timeline suddenly blended. Then, as we reached for each other, we were hurled into The Void, all quiet and soundless, as The Hush transported us through time and space.

Clutching onto one another in momentary bewilderment, we could hear the exaggerated voices of the nursing staff trying to wake us.

Slightly disoriented with the bright lights blinding our vision, I shuffled into a sitting position.

"Are you okay, Mr Blake? The young nurse asked anxiously, reaching to check Jonas's pulse. She fumbled, looking to get a steady reading; however, it was as if it hardly registered he was alive. She looked perplexed and kept trying and in a panicked voice she cried, "I cannot get a pulse!"

"We are fine," I stuttered, looking straight at Jonas. Our extraordinary bond strengthened us as we silently read each other's thoughts.

"Yes, we were tired and needed to rest, but now we are ready to leave," Jonas stated, looking around as though to escape while willing anyone to challenge him.

The three staff in the room looked with open mouths as Jonas swung his legs off the bed and struggled to stand.

"Hang on, please. You cannot move, Mr Blake," the nurse reiterated. "I can't get a pulse," she said, still latched on to his arm, trying to figure out the oddness of the situation. They then all leapt at Jonas to restrain and calm him.

"Thank you, please excuse me, but I feel healed already," he replied, slightly annoyed, as he lifted his arms to bat them away.

"We have discovered the cure for Jonas," I smiled as Jonas stood up and started to walk toward the nurses, who were, by this time, moving backward. One of them fled out the door to get the charge nurse.

His going into the bathroom to change gave me time to thank the nurses who were still riveted on the spot, wondering what had happened.

I felt a little weak with cramping pains and reached out to sit down. I then felt my moon cycle, which had started very late. Oh my gosh, my eyes widened with shock as I realised the impossible had happened. I had travelled through The Void with Jonas's spirit baby.

Searching in my bag for protection, I knocked on the door to the bathroom and swapped places with Jonas, who looked nervously at me. "Are you alright, Lily?"

What had I done? I thought my baby was Asim's. I missed my little boy tremendously, my heart aching with the separation as he was strapped to me a few minutes ago. I will explain my observations to Jonas, and I wondered how he will take all this before he forgets his other life. Thoughts cascaded through my mind.

The staff commotion about Jonas's miraculous walking was far-reaching, as doctors came from all directions to corner us.

"Can we do some blood tests, Mr Blake? What sensation are you feeling in your legs? Would you be willing to have a scan and x-rays?" The questions were endless, but it was time to leave. With gratitude and thanks, we left the ward, walking awkwardly toward the main entrance. Jonas was still unsteady, just leaning slightly on me for balance.

I grappled with the gears and weaved the Jeep out of the car park towards home.

We looked at one another constantly to believe we were here together. Jonas reached out and placed his hand on my knee, and the familiar longing for him returned instantaneously.

We had experienced a profound connection in another land. I had no idea Jonas was a traveller. He, who must forget his other life so rapidly, was now trying to relive the past time together.

"You will want to record or journal your thoughts," I gestured to the back where my work gear was. "You will not have this keen memory for long. We both may not, so we must record as much as possible, especially about our travels, and I want to journal about our baby," I said without thinking.

"What did you say? Lily, what did you just say? Please pull over. We need to talk." He spoke with a surprised, fascinated look as I glanced at his boyish face.

Yes, I observed intently; baby Herihor looked like Jonas, and he deserved to know. How we both handled this was going to be emotional either way.

I pulled the Jeep to a stop in our parking bay, and we clambered out. I ran around the car to hold onto Jonas, knowing we needed to talk. I wasn't sure how long he would keep his memories, but I still felt strong with mine and deeply connected to my baby.

Once inside, I opened the refrigerator and leaned in to feel the cool, refreshing air, vastly different from the hot desert. I flicked the caps off two beers and passed one to Jonas. We drank in silence, tasting the delicious flavour, cold with a burst of fizz.

Looking around, it felt like our apartment had not been lived in for years. After setting the tape recorder to capture our words and memories, I sunk into the chair, tucking my legs under me.

"Jonas, I have a revelation to tell you, which is astonishing," I blurted out. "You know I have just given birth to Asim's child in that horrific situation. Well, I believe the child is ours; yours and mine. He looks just like you. I know you didn't get a clear look at him, but I can assure you he does." I wet my lips with another suck on the beer bottle and continued. "When I took you through The Void, I had no idea you were in our other life. I didn't even realise you could travel. I thought I was taking you for your healing, remember? I believe I had just conceived our baby as I was late with my cycle. How the egg was protected in my womb is a miracle," I whispered. "It is a miracle." I vividly recalled my sacred womb journey with Heqet in the temple. I thought my womb was a powerhouse, and I could feel the excitement of my goddesses gathering around to support us.

Jonas turned the beer bottle, fumbling with the label. His eyes glistened with emotion as he too realised the enormity of this situation.

"We will return immediately." He paused to look at me to see my response.

"Yes, we must, I agree. I wish to see our baby and to assist with my recovery," I said dramatically without thinking.

"First, we must go up to our cabin. There is someone I want you to meet," Jonas exclaimed abruptly.

Jonas looked more alive than I had seen him look for some time. He murmured something I couldn't hear but refused to talk more. A lock of his disheveled hair dropped over his forehead as he ran his fingers through it.

"I suggest we document all our activities to know more about what we are trying to achieve. Then, at least, we can understand it all better," I pressed on, watching Jonas's face as I assuredly spoke. "We have chosen to be together here. What I question is, why?"

"Do you know why Jonas... apart from being attracted to each other?" I said, looking at him quizzically. He lowered his hands, then rubbing them together, he responded.

"Mmmm, there is much corruption here at this time, those exploiting others; with a global takeover of assets and manipulation of countries and leaders, which is happening right here in our home country as well. There will come a time when we will be called to participate. I hope I am here to help," he squinted curiously at me.

"Yes, I feel this too; it is like activating others to all rise together. I know our guides have brought us to this timeline for a great purpose as we navigate this star gateway instead of reincarnating like others."

I yawned, got up and held out my hand. "Let us sleep on it, and in the morning, we will go up north." This act of hand-holding sprung into my conscious thought and reminded me how vital hand expression, hand-holding, and touch were relevant in a sensory aspect in Egypt.

Both tired, we snuggled into the familiar pattern of our bodies. My yearning for my baby kept me awake as I rubbed my hands over my flat stomach, searching for signs of having carried a child, but there was nothing. I stifled the cry coming from my soul, chanting the cry of the loss of our baby, for Jonas and me. My baby hormones were still coming to terms with the fact that I wasn't pregnant.

In the morning, the warmth of our bodies brought us closer together, and skin-to-skin contact sent a river of tingling up my spine. Just having left Asim, our lingering touch felt strange in some ways. The silence continued as if we uttered a word; the spell would be broken. My eyelids fluttered as he gently stroked my arms, and I felt a throbbing in my heart. *Was this loss or betrayal?* I couldn't bear the thought of not being with Asim. Oh, it was all so fresh!

In a constricted voice, I told Jonas I wasn't ready, and I climbed out of the sheets and locked the bathroom door as though a stranger was on the other side - something I would never normally do.

His big hands gripped the wheel. Jonas drove without words, and I stretched out, pushing the seat back. My thoughts were lost with Tanith. How could I find her and bring her home? I could go to the library and find historical records of the lands across the Mediterranean Sea. I can use this time wisely or squander the days until we return, or I can return alone.

The silence screamed at us when we started talking together at once.

"You speak," I encouraged.

"No, you go love, you go first," Jonas replied softly.

"We could celebrate our baby when we return to Egypt, each in different roles. As far as everyone is concerned, he will always be a prince of Thebes. You will probably forget all this soon, or when it gets too hard, perhaps you will just block it out. What do you think?"

"I will try to be more present with the switchover and retain my memories as they are not as crucifying as I always thought. I now realise there are rich messages to bring back to capture a culture with a powerful dynasty." He spoke with a sentimental tone.

"We don't even know if our son is a traveller. I presume he is, as we both are. What if he chose us to come here too?" he spoke longingly.

"What if he didn't?" I said, voicing my thoughts out loud. "Perhaps we would spend our time searching for him. Love cannot separate as it will always lead back to those who hold the flame. I knew he would come to be close to us," I continued with my thoughts.

"I think we need not harness all the scenarios as everything's meant to be as it is," I said frankly. "We must also carry on with our purpose here."

Jonas flicked me a glance of satisfaction. "We have had a major shock which has come out of us travelling for my healing, and I feel responsible for our loss. But you know he is not lost; he was born in another country thousands of years ago, and we will check to see if he is a traveller. However, we don't know yet his entire purpose in Thebes."

We drove quietly, both lost in our thoughts, arriving at the accident scene to face our crash experience. While getting out of the Jeep, I heard a branch creaking and felt flustered as it brought back such vivid memories of the treacherous shapeshifter.

Jonas needed to face his peril; that he could have been paralysed if we had not travelled. Had I known there was a possibility I was pregnant, maybe I would not have gone, so all was what it was meant to be.

"Come on, my love," I urged. "Let's make this a great trip to our unique hideaway."

We were tape recording as much information as possible about our travelling through The Void to play back if our memories dimmed, even laughing at some of our situations.

Instead of taking the turnoff to our cabin, Jonas kept driving until we reached another fork in the road. He held a look of concentration as though he was trying to figure something out.

"What is happening?" I was perplexed. "Where are we going?" I felt unease creep into my veins. This behaviour was strange, with Jonas not telling me what was happening.

We pulled up with the brakes skidding on the gravel, stones hitting the rims. The cottage was rustic, hidden from clear view by large ponga bushes. It looked abandoned, although rather eerie, it held a welcoming effect.

"Jonas, why are we here?" I asked, a little curiosity hidden in my voice. The door creaked ajar, and a beautiful woman came out to greet us. I guessed she was in her late thirties or early forties, her skin radiant, with luscious wavy hair. She held an aura of mystique as though viewing us through a misted window pane. Seeing Jonas, she openly welcomed him with a gracious hug.

"Hello," she said warmly, her eyes burning into mine. "You must be Lily; soon to be Mrs Lily Blake?

"Beautiful girl, Jonas," she spoke with a smooth, soft tone while turning to look at him. "Come in, you two. I have been waiting for your visit. When Jonas returns from his travels, he always comes to see me before the mist places a shroud around him."

She knew about him. For a moment, I felt annoyed with Jonas for keeping secrets. I hadn't seen him as being unpredictable like this, but it was rather thrilling, like a part of dependable Jonas that I hadn't seen.

A man appeared at the door to the kitchen where we were standing. He was exceptionally tall and moved immediately to stand near the woman. My body was tense and animated as though I was waiting for a sentence to be passed. Scenarios were playing out in my mind, and I wondered why these two were intent on not yet introducing themselves.

Feeling this was a big moment, I turned to Jonas.

"What is happening here? You both seem familiar; should I know you?" The words were falling out of my mouth. "Are you travellers?" I asked, already knowing the answer.

Jonas turned to me. "Please meet our neighbours, and the couple who sold us the section our lodge is built on." "Sophia and James, please meet Lily Morris."

I was aghast. I thought Sophia and James were an elderly couple. Jonas had told me they were I'm sure. I moved forward; grateful for our property and their compassion in selling us the paradise we loved by the beach. The moment we hugged, my body trembled, and there was a silence as the familiarity of this couple felt like family. I pulled back to look at Sophia, and a force of power charged the room.

"Are you Sanura?" I stumbled, my words direct and blunt, hitting home like an adopted child finding her birth mother.

She nodded and reached out for me. "I have waited many years for this moment to acquaint myself with you. When I saw you on television, I knew we were kindred. Then, meeting Jonas and knowing he was my nephew, and James's son was such a revelation that we have been drawn here together. Love cannot separate, so it is a miracle. Please meet James. He was your uncle in our other world."

I swung to look at Jonas, who was conscious of the shock that must have been written all over my face. I had that feeling we were missing something. I possibly needed to look deeper into our family connections.

"Kalina, she is your daughter?" I questioned, my head now pounding with recognition of the enormity of it all.

"Yes, she is, and I have been denied the love of my child or a child here in this life. How is she? I am desperate for news. Jonas always gives me snippets, but his memories will fade."

"Come and be seated," James said as he led us into a comfortable open room with large windows overlooking the Pacific Ocean. We admired the spectacular view of the sea rising and crashing, releasing her fury on rugged rocks and the submissive beach below.

My thumping heart gave way to all the thoughts rampaging in my mind. I turned and moved directly to Sophia to open my arms and heart again to my beautiful aunty.

"Oh my gosh, do you know where my mother is in this life? She is a traveller, I know this," I spoke desperately. They would have the answer.

"We too, are searching, but she may not have come into this timeline," she said.

James then joined Sophia in telling us how important it would be to find her, to bring our family back from the brink of separation and devastation from what had happened to our brothers and sisters in Egypt.

"When my mother explained about her travelling, she told me she had been looking for me too as she never knew whose arms were holding me." I blurted out, trying to recall her words.

"My birth mother could not look after me as a baby, so my grandmother brought me up. I never had the warm arms she expressed to me. I never told her that," I said, matter of factly.

"Mother said she had been studying plant medicine to help those in ancient times. The place to look would be in natural therapy clinics or naturopathic learning centres," I continued.

"Come look in here," James said in a low, deep voice. He stood back, his arm extended to show us into another room. The back wall was covered in maps of Egypt and New Zealand. Markers and photographs with strings connecting places were like vines spreading across an old stone wall.

"Can you see what Sophia and I have been doing? We are tracking information to bring our family together in this timeline. You and Jonas were attracted to each other and having you here on the land is to all our benefit. We know your memories may fade, but we can help you recall as this is what we do. We are magicians and do past-life regression. Not that we recommend it for everyone."

Jonas never spoke. He just looked wide-eyed and fascinated with the outcome of today's events.

"Sophia, I have met Badru; he is my new bodyguard and a very handsome man. He is deeply traumatised by your transition, and even though it's been nearly two decades, he mourns you as though it was yesterday."

"Oh my gosh, he has been found, as I knew he had moved on. Sometimes I can reach through the veil and feel him, even hear his voice," Sophia spoke with sadness, looking far away as she focused on the maps before us. "You must take my words back to him when you next return. What would I do to see him again! However, that is impossible, but let us stay together and focus on our quest to continue reuniting our family here." She shook her head and looked at me as if to clear it.

"What is the point of this?" Jonas queried. "We have had other lifetimes."

"Yes, but we are on the precipice of a new way forward for our Earth, and we require the higher intelligence of ancient wisdom from the galactic realm," Sophia said. This realm is your forte, as High Priestess Akila, and we require the help of the ancient goddesses to do this to whom you commune. Sorry, I meant Lily. I still connect to you as my sister's daughter, for you were only a year old when I passed."

"Most precious of all is my daughter. Kalina is her name, Jonas tells me."

"Yes, named after a beautiful flower on a tropical island," I said.

We stopped talking, turned to look at one another, and realised we had discovered my mother's destination. Maybe it was on a tropical island, or she had been there.

"We will find her, or I will ask her on my return," I smiled, thinking why I hadn't known this before.

However, my mother was always secretive about her travelling, as though speaking of it would connect her to The Void. She was totally against discussing it. Her sister Sanura here could not penetrate my mother's adversity to discuss her travels. It was as though fate would open an abyss that would suck her into its depths. Sadly, it had, as she had lost her only sister.

THE
GOLDEN · DAZZLING
PYRAMID · OF · LIGHT

The beach, in its dazzling expanse, lay before us in the crystalline cocoon of the bay. Adjusting the blanket beneath us to be more comfortable, we spoke candidly about our most unusual relationship.

Feeling more like myself in this moment with Jonas, I fell into the lull of the rhythm of the evening.

Lips touching, we sensed each other and delighted in the renewed feeling of touch and the warmth of our youthful bodies as we huddled together. With each inhalation and exhalation, we exchanged breaths between us.

"Hey, babe," I whispered seductively. "I want you; I love being here with you and having this extraordinary relationship. Living two lives running together is bewildering, as I've never been in love in our other world," I said, feeling embarrassed as though I was betraying him.

"We are here now, and we must live this life and seize every moment," Jonas reiterated. "You are my Queen here; we are destined to be together and share such joy and fascination."

"Those two up on the hill; they are a little eccentric, though. Are they a couple? They must be," I stammered. "But yes, different lifetimes can have unique relationships."

I was trying to understand their relationship in Egypt: as brother and sister, Jonas and I, him a priest, and myself a high priestess, and we both are cousins.

It took a little adjusting to our connections in this life, yet I knew we would quickly become lovers again. We just needed some time. Our memories were strong, and we fully retained them now.

A soft yet haunting breeze ruffled her way across the ocean. As it reached the shore, it picked up momentum and started flicking the sand at us, reminding us of the windstorm. I felt the energy of my goddesses calling me to reawaken, to remind me of my other world. Hearing the whisper in the wind of Asim calling my name; 'Akila' roused my heightened emotions, urging me to return home through The Void. We quickly grabbed the blanket, shook it and ran for the lodge as the wind whipped up the sand, stinging our bare legs. My goddesses were hunting me, challenging me to keep connected to my duty.

Duty - it seemed life was full of duty. Had I lost my childlike joy? It was clear we were like lovers starting a broken relationship again, and although slightly uncomfortable, I had to let go of all the scenarios in my head and be present in this moment. We needed more spontaneity, fun and play, so we teased each other about the things we loved most about each other. We chose champagne tonight to celebrate our new beginnings.

The morning light slid through the windows, creeping in like a virgin mist to find us both cuddled and secure in each other's arms. I traced my fingers on Jonas's face, familiarising myself with the contours of his cheekbones. I knew his energy was coming alive again, and I welcomed it as we allowed the caress and touch to awaken our longing for more passion.

Lying secure and loved up, each contemplating what was next for us, I blurted out, "We must travel to Egypt and see if we can breach The Void and discover more about where Tani has travelled," I said rapidly, breaking the moment. "What do you think?"

"Yes, I have always dreamed of venturing to Egypt," Jonas sighed and stretched out, mulling over the plan. I could tell he was eager for this trip as much as I was.

"Last night, I felt Nef standing in front of the lodge, tracking me with sensory energy and dark eyes that could pierce the night. My snake wrapped around my neck, twirling and spinning and making me feel dizzy. Something is amiss," I said, trailing off.

The knocking on the door startled us, as it was an early hour. The Tui birds shrilling in the bush announced the arrival of visitors. They quietened as the knocking continued.

We both leapt up. "We will be there in a moment," Jonas yelled.

Sophia looked more alluring in the morning light as the sun flickered, the light playing over her skin, illuminating her delicate features. Her dark eyes were shining like starlight piercing the morning. We stood there gazing at each other as Jonas flung the lodge door open, welcoming their arrival.

"Come in," I said as I wrapped my silk gown tighter and tied the sash. I was excited to see Sophia and James and hugged them warmly.

"I'll make some coffee or tea. Which would you like?" My curiosity about why they were here was evident in my voice.

They admired the lodge interior with the soft colours, talking about how it felt homely and safe as it could be locked up and protected when we were away. I now realised why Jonas had built it like this as a secure fortress.

At last, we sat down at the wooden table. Our minds were all on the same scenario - a trip to Egypt, the four of us. James nervously cleared his throat.

"Sophia and I feel it is time to travel back to our ancient homeland; we are being called. We would love to take you both with us," he said as he leaned forward, blinking away his emotion.

Jonas and I looked at each other quizzically. "Just what we were talking about," Jonas said, surprised.

The jug's shrill whistle broke the silence as we started planning, while Sophia and I made tea.

"We will go back through The Void and arrange to meet on the other side. It will take strategic planning, Sophia," I squeezed her gently. "You could be close to Kalina, and perhaps I could bring her through to you, even Badru if you would like to see him again. We have a profound opportunity to allow our worlds to collide."

Tears of joy and heartache collected on her cheeks as she raised her hand to brush them away. "This is the opportunity of a lifetime, dear Lily. I want to take this chance," she exclaimed excitedly. "James is a master at quantum physics and a genius in his creative field, but there is only so much he can do."

From that morning on, we were inseparable. We shared meals at the lodge. We laughed and enjoyed stories as I relayed many memories of Kal as a baby. Sophia yearned for news about my mother and Keket.

Finally, I broached the subject, "I am at a loss as to why Keket turned on our family," I spoke solemnly. "She sent you through The Void, knowing you couldn't return when you were giving birth. Is that correct?" I shivered even though it was a warm afternoon.

Sophia took a deep breath through her pursed lips, the little dip in her throat wildly pulsing as she recalled the event.

"She was our good friend and companion. I often wonder what would have happened if she had not told me to go through the timeline to rest and gather my strength. Maybe Kalina would have died with me. I thought I could rest as Keket suggested. However, I could not propel myself back. I remained determined and gave an almighty push, a burst of energy. The push was enough to birth her into the world, my greatest achievement. I glimpsed her little body momentarily before I slipped out of my form and was drawn back here." Sophia gathered her breath to speak again as her faraway look returned her to her loss.

"I have travelled to other timelines trying to return in another person to you all, but it has not been possible to reach you. However, I have never blamed Keket; she was in love with our brother there," she said, pointing at James. "He wanted to be with another beauty. Still, James always loved Keket even though she was a maid servant, and they could not be together. He has never forgotten their clandestine meetings. I even used to cover for them so your mother never found out."

I clasped my hand over my mouth as though the shock of this revelation would jump out through my clenched teeth.

"You know she had a son," I announced softly. "James probably doesn't know, but the boy was carried in her womb in anger, grief and abandonment, and the boy turned evil as though to wipe us all out. She had to give him up to be raised by a village woman. He then went into the priesthood and into the military. I both fear and despise him, as he has tried to kill me. He has two daughters, whom Keket asked me to look out for. They may be travellers. I haven't met them yet, but James needs to know about his granddaughters," the words tumbled out of my mouth.

I described to Sophia the cruel death of Keket as if she was punishing herself for her treacherous behaviour.

"I am sorry Keket turned out that way," Sophia said softly. "We were very close, all of us. It was because we shared the secret knowledge of life-through-life. Your mother, Keket, James, and even your father's brother would hang out with us. We were inseparable."

I thought of our sisterhood with Kal and our circles of light as they briefly flashed into my mind, dazzling and alive - the six golden circles with the seventh circle in the middle dancing before my eyes. My circles powered up our feminine energy and sent it spiralling up our spines for enlightenment and connection to the oneness of all life. My meditation demanded this practice. This practice was releasing, sensual, and powerful.

"Oh, sorry. I was far away just now," I muttered, feeling the acknowledgement of my internal awakening energy.

James's planning was thorough. He considered our journey back to the ancient land and the timeframes needed to be at the exact place where we could encounter both worlds, thousands of years apart. We decided to meet at the Great Pyramid.

James booked our flights and accommodation. We were excited to return to Egypt in our modern day, but what would it feel like; and how would it look?

My energy had awakened again, and I felt the surge through my body. My breath was vital and flowing as my meditations grew stronger and spiralled within me. At the lodge, Jonas and I had found love again; like the joining of the river rushing over the rocks, we came together and abandoned all thoughts of our complex lives. Our bodies entwined, mingled with the scent of the forest behind us and the sound of the waves breaking and rolling onto the shimmering sand.

We slowly anchored in our unique sensory touch and kissing; it was an enthralling feeling, like lovers of different ethnicities without language. Leaving behind any thoughts of outdated concerns, we took our love to new heights. I trembled like I had felt the heavy temple doors closing on us with a resounding vibration.

After we lay together close and renewed with passion, I could feel my baby calling and I could hear him crying through The Void. I was helpless; he wanted me. It was as though I had abandoned him when he needed me the most. Jonas turned to wrap his arms around me, pulling me closer. My feelings of intense love were calling me.

The buzzing and trembling signalled travel, followed by the pulling of my cells as though they were breaking apart, splitting, spiralling, tumbling as we were thrust through the timeline.

Mother and Safiya were huddled beside us, my mother gently shaking me and softly calling my name. I could hear the close, plaintive cries of my baby becoming more desperate.

Herihor pulled away from me, shaken by our previous intimate encounter. Yet, here now, as my priest, he was reserved, as though portraying he was praying and blessing me.

I looked directly at my mother, trying to elicit words of support, but I was mistaken. She was annoyed. She cast Herihor a look of disdain and dismissed him with a wave of her hand; however, he didn't leave and stood to the side.

"Your son is in dire need of your milk and bonding from you. I can see what you have been through, but you must focus here and not get distracted."

"Yes Mother, please bring him. I want him," I said urgently. I had previously expressed copious amounts of milk to release any harmful poison, and now my breasts were laden again.

"Baby has been bathed and dressed, but we must be on our way before the storm turns her mighty fury back onto the desert. Your goddesses have kept the sands rolling, but the Theban priests will want to claim their future son and will be in pursuit, or they will send the wrath of the gods on us. Father has readied the camels, and we will be on our way as soon as you have rested and fed him." Eyeing Herihor with a sullen scowl, Mother left in a swirl of frustrated anger.

My memories flooded and pulsed back into my body as I glanced at Herihor, who was lovingly admiring his namesake.

We shared a moment of intense visual connection before he moved out of the tent. I still felt the sand and dust lingering on my skin but immediately unbound my robes again to feed baby Herihor. He pulled hard on my nipples, hungry, tired and demanding. He took the first thick milk, then settled, sucking contently.

Safiya, crouching in the background, moved forward, her dishevelled beauty even more glorious as she tossed her hair over her shoulders and began to plan our next move.

"I am so grateful to you for rescuing me during the sandstorm. How courageous you are." My eyes searched hers in acknowledgement of her risky task. "I am forever grateful, Sister," I whispered through a few gentle tears tracing down my cheeks. "I hope I can repay you somehow."

"My guides were with me," Saf said with determination. "Even convincing Mother and Father to come was tricky. I trusted and envisioned you drawing the golden circle and calling me. We have been travelling for months to be here," she said reassuringly. "It was worth the trip, as your baby would have been motherless if we had lingered."

I was under the spell of my son's hypnotic looks and energy. As the trickle of voices outside the tent filtered into me, I heard them whisper of the baby's magnetism as if he had powers that drew them into another world. Everyone was mesmerised by his skin colour; it was softer in texture, more pale, and his eyes deep pools of the green tones of the Nile. His hair was the rich sand colour of the desert. I sucked in a breath of awe and fulfillment. If only Asim were here to share these emotions of pure joy and gratitude for our baby's life.

I murmured, "Herihor," out loud. My baby's response was immediate, as though he had heard his destiny being called, and he stopped suckling and turned to give me an intense gaze of acknowledgement. I shivered as I listened to my revered goddesses reciting his name in response. "Herihor, Herihor be anointed," they whispered, summonsing his spirit and blessing him.

The gentle wind picked up the billowing tent as the stirring of the land wrestled with the sun's warmth in a warning to start moving away from this location.

Mother suddenly pulled back the linen flap of fabric and entered.

"Who is this child, Akila?" she asked with concern, continuing without allowing me to answer.

"This child is a coupling of two worlds; he is unusual, as if he knows his future. His task will be momentous, and he will need skills to protect himself. We will ensure he has the best instruction," she bent low and hugged my shoulders.

"Sorry for before, but it is unnatural for your priest, who is your cousin, to be around you constantly. Do you understand my concern? If it weren't for Asim to have named him, I would think you would have a closer bond. We must be on our way. We are being followed, and our scouts have given instructions to be ready."

Anippe entered with Amon, who timidly gestured to ask if he could come closer. I wrapped the baby and passed him to Amon.

Amon's tender, awkward grip holding him with one arm made me smile as Anippe moved to steady him. An orb of golden light was hovering above their colours; their aura entranced me. I watched the orb descend slowly and bathe them both in a single golden glow, a blessing from the divine.

"Saf, we must leave. Can you help me prepare? Let us hasten as my goddesses are urging us onward."

"Yes, let us gather our belongings," she said. However, before she could finish her sentence, the sudden whistle of a sharpened arrow split the tent's fabric and embedded itself into the flooring mat. The feathers on the quill were unusually evil, as though possessed, with a poisonous mist floating from them as they remained pierced firm through the carpet into the sand.

A chilling scream filled with terror reverberated around us. Saf, Anippe, and I cried out as we realised dark magic had been thrust amongst us, and we all fled from the tent in horror at the infiltration of evil in our camp.

Father's guards assembled in a formidable line and drew the flight of arrows in return, hurling them into the rolling sandstorm toward the unseen enemy. Eventually, we escaped the flight of poisoned arrows. No one was visibly in pursuit; however, travelling quickly in the day's heat was brutal. We pressed on to check if anyone was following.

At last, we made camp again in the desert. I was desperate to refresh myself with help from my mother and Anippe. I still had a lightheaded feeling from the residue of poison in my body, but I was grateful for my snake spinning the goblet from my hand.

Copious gourds filled with sweet beer were handed to us as we sheltered under parasols in front of an open tent.

"Father, who leads this attack on us? Do you have any information on their strategies?" I discreetly requested that he convene with the council of war. "Are our enemies men or the dark spirits? Is this war against the Pharaoh's protection? Who would be so daring?"

"Do not be concerned, my love. You are safe now," he responded, although his nervous tremor betrayed his confidence. "We will be here overnight and leave at the first call of the Ibis birds. Summons in your goddesses for the protection of our camp as my soldiers are falling to some illness."

"It is poison, Father. It was in the quill of the arrows which pierced our encampment. Mother will have an antidote, but we must hurry."

Cool-headed, my father demanded the energy to repel this unseen enemy. A single-minded man of control and diplomacy, he disappeared to gather the remaining troops and have them consult with his wife to be administered an antidote to the mist of poison.

As the evening settled in the camp before the stars lit up the sky and Goddess Nut, the goddess of the vault of the heavens, reigned with complete power; I requested a blessing from Herihor.

With a renewed sense of purpose, I knew my little prince had an impact on his journey here in this land. I was feeding him when my priest Herihor made his entrance.

Unlatching my baby from his feeding, I passed him to Herihor. He admired his looks without words, and with memories of our other world intact, he took a deep breath as our eyes locked in, knowing who he was.

"He indeed has the look," Herihor whispered. "This knowledge fills me with a protective passion. All my learnings have reached this point to fulfil my starlight purpose here. I will stay close to him as his priest and yours."

"When we arrive in our other world, we plan to be at The Great Pyramid, the thirteenth temple; let us not lose sight of this as our mission. Once we are in Memphis, we will calculate the transition time to travel." I squeezed my eyes closed as though trying to organise everything in my tired mind.

"I would like to speak with Kalina and Badru to see if we can go through The Void and meet with Sophia and James. We must acquire a scout to get word to Kalina to attend us as soon as we are back on course to Memphis. She will also meet her father. It will be a meaningful arrangement," I sighed. "The past cannot be altered, but we can re-shape future events. Our respectful designated positions here are to be upheld with baby Herihor as the child of Asim, which is rightful as we have not lain together in the same quarters. Asim has given him his glow and nourishment, so he will always be Asim's child. I understand that this conception occurred because of a miracle from my goddesses."

"The reason has yet to be revealed," Herihor whispered, keeping it low from all the prying ears.

The days flew by without further events of hostilities from Thebes. There was an eerie feeling from behind, as though we were being observed. Every time I spun around, a bolt of energy burst into my heart like a flash on the landscape, and my breath was short and rapid. Something unseen was following us.

Pressing our camels relentlessly onward, plodding through the desert, we mainly travelled at first light. We surrendered to the heat during the day, setting up camp and resting. My thoughts were constantly connected to Asim, Heqet and his mother. They would be troubled about me being taken away so suddenly. My hope was that those who caused this catastrophe to annihilate us travellers, would be held accountable. However, we may never be free if it were the dark forces and the chants of the priests summonsing them. Had Asim and Heqet been able to bury our baby's placenta in Thebes? These questions kept burning in my mind for the safety of my child's future.

As we approached Saqqara, the Nile was low, giving us a complete view. We were exhausted but never uttered words of discontent. I revered our rescuers. Osiris was connected to the fertility of the Nile, and this year's planting of wheat and barley would provide an abundant food source.

Arriving at Memphis was a long-awaited luxury. Anippe, in her element, fussed over us. She and my mother took on all the stress while looking after our newborn and looking after me.

Saf and I were planning our trip into the Northern Lands across the seas, in search of Tani. Safiya had all the ideas mapped out in her mind, so I left her to her strengths while I negotiated with the goddesses.

Kalina, waiting anxiously for a sighting of us, threw herself into the moment of meeting, and we all celebrated. Not letting each other go, we held on to our childlike way of drawing our symbols rapidly and then laughing.

Nef's magnificence as he strolled into the entrance captivated us all, especially Anippe, who practically fainted at his sight, and we had to steady her.

This act of endearment had not bypassed Nef, who strode over to be by her side. Love was blossoming like my goddesses had proclaimed.

"Kal, I have a special someone for you to meet; come with me," I whispered as I reached for her hand.

We strode out to the horses where Badru was stooped, preparing them for the next part of the journey home. The camels would be returned after a well-earned rest.

A neigh and stomping of hooves caught me off guard as I saw my stunning Khonsu pulling at his ropes and tossing his head, his mane dancing within his aura. Running to his side was most thrilling as we reunited with a connection of our spirits bathing in the magnetism that held us together.

I looked over to where I had left Kal. She and Badru had also reunited, each knowing who the other was. They were hugging, crying and inconsolable with the grief of what could have been.

Joining them, with Khonsu nudging my back, I reiterated the plan of what we had discussed in my other world. Both Kal and Badru were shocked that this could be possible. It would be easy for Kal as it was in her blood, but we would have to guide Badru through The Void to make the transition. We would not tell my mother; she was too afraid of what might happen. She had already forbidden me in her authority to take my sisters through.

Herihor and I ventured to the temple in Memphis. Clutching at our plan to reunite Kalina and Badru with Sanura, we went into the sanctuary where we would not be disturbed.

The god Ptah was sanctified by all the kings and was held with high esteem in Memphis. However, I was drawn to honour my goddesses for bringing us to safety. I knelt with my priest, Herihor, feeling the bliss surrounding us as my snake coiled around my chest, offering my heart protection. Still, the eerie feeling of being watched persisted. I visualised the symbols of the pyramid upward and downward and the swirls of the chalice above and around us while fully encased in the dazzling golden pyramid. The pyramids spun rapidly into the feminine sphere. We pulled the light energy to the centre and spun it outward to encompass Egypt. Like a sonic boom, I felt the temple walls reverberate in waves as my goddesses bathed the lands in their glory.

Silently, the Mer-Ka-Ba was spinning. Light, spirit and body were connecting.

"Herihor, are you ready to return? We are bound to honour our commitment." We sat our backs to the cold feel of the granite and reached to hold hands. As soon as the warmth of his fingers joined with mine, we hurtled into The Hush, The Void opening up to draw us in.

Our bed in the lodge was warm, and we were close. Jonas reached for me as we held each other, realising how normal this was becoming, as twin flames. There is nothing like an aura cleanse or a dip in the sea; we challenged ourselves. Chasing one another to the water's edge to refresh our bodies, we plunged in, diving like fish and offering our faces to the sunlight.

We returned to our lodge open-eyed and cleansed to plan our journey to Egypt. Jumping in the Jeep, we wound our way up to the homestead. On our arrival, there wasn't a sound. Jonas knocked on the door, calling out to Sophia and James, but there was still no response. The door swung open, inviting us in.

"Jonas, should we just enter? It seems we are intruding," I shrilled nervously. My snake had come alive and dominant, feeling my apprehension. Their car was in the garage, but no sign of the pair. The house had a familiar odour as if we had just walked into the Hypostyle Hall with the towering columns. The room with the wall of brightly coloured string held new information. There, we were signified with an additional baby, Herihor, depicted on the wall as Asim's child, connected to Herihor, and linked to Jonas, me and Akila.

"How did they know?" I stammered. "We have not revealed anything to anyone. The room was spinning, and my head was spinning. There must be an explanation here. There were other oddities, too - strings linking Sanura and Sophia and Badru and

Kal. Links were formed with James, Herihor's father, Keket and Dhoser, with thread leading to two pink pins named Eshe and Masika.

I left the wall chart to check the other rooms. A large room was meticulously kept with pure white linen draped curtains and a low bed like you would find in Egypt. It looked like a room in the grand house of the palace. The bright cotton of the floormat brought a splash of vibrancy to the room. Sophia had recreated her Egypt. Another room was decorated the same but with a baby's crib.

Further down was another room with the door slightly ajar. I felt intrusive as I opened the door a little more. There was a low bed in the corner and a large desk strewn with clippings and books piled high.

Closing the door to its original position, I felt I was being creepy as we moved through to the rear of the house.

A strange huge building was hidden with plants hanging over it. The door was left unhinged. It had an open retractable roof.

Calling out again to Sophia and James, my rapidly beating heart gave away my composure. I mastered my feelings enough to mutter to Jonas.

"What is this? It is a pyramid, yet no door or way to enter appears." It was pulsing with golden threads of light seeping from within. Place your hands on one of the faces, and I will do the same," I said softly, not to disturb a ruffle of energy.

"I will call the gods to protect us," Jonas said in his priestly voice.

"And I, too, my goddesses, please hear my call of protection."

My snake was roused but not alarmed, so we continued holding the space.

With both pairs of hands in place, we were immediately transported inside the pyramid, where a golden ambient glow lit up the inner sanctuary. We were viewing many scenes before us, which were fascinating. It was as though we had entered a time warp, and the visions were floating. *Were we creating these?* We were in a futuristic time chamber.

Jonas pulled me close as all his priestly ways had not prepared him for this escape into the past. James would have constructed this as he was deeply involved in quantum physics, the movement of energy fields, and past lives. We were now embedded within the field of light, the pyramid and the space between timelines. Waving my hands across the pictures was making them rearrange themselves. I was getting closer to our trip to the coast, and our mother was saying goodbye to Tani. It was right before us as the timeline drew us into her projections.

We focused on Tani and saw her untying the horses and trying to re-tie Khonsu to leave him. That would never happen with him, as he was the leader stallion of the herd.

We gazed in silence, my eyes riveted on Tani, her beautiful face stressed and anxious as her eyes darted nervously. I saw myself unlacing the tent and calling Khonsu, then sighting the massive form of Nef looming in front of me in the dark, shadowed night. He was lethal with anger, wielding a large knife and adrenaline pumping through his veins. He pushed me out of the way. I saw Tani running alongside her mare, flinging herself onto her back as she galloped off with Nef in pursuit.

The vision caught Tani lying low on her horse, moving fluidly, then connecting with Khan and his guards flanking her. There was no slowing until she glimpsed the riders behind her and reigned in, slightly slowing her steed using her legs only to balance. The sands were becoming thick now, whereas before, the hard-baked earth gave momentum on the hooves. She pivoted with precision and loosed two arrows in quick succession. Tani took her time with the other, carefully marking her target and steadily aiming.

We saw Nef hit the sand and crawl back to the other victims while Tani and her later pursuers continued. They were off the track now, using the stars for guidance.

Jonas and I were standing in front of the scene but also immersed in it, cloaked in the mantle between worlds. I felt my hand over my mouth in suspension, thinking, *what next, Tani?*

The swirling sandstorm was pounding, rolling between her and her pursuers as she turned directly to look at me. Her eyes pierced mine in a connection of knowing we could view each other through the lens of timeless love.

I focused on her as she battled through the sands with her allies. Her friends picked up a shrilling whirling noise as they whooped it up in response to following the sound.

She had arrived at an encampment just outside of the port. The next scene showed her patting Khonsu and wiping her fingers in thick, congealed blood from the gut of the freshly slaughtered lamb that was roasting.

Her emotions intensified for the first time; I saw sadness pool in the tears running down her face. She drew two entwining circles on Khonsu, slapped his rump and set him free. He reared on his hind legs, pawing the air, expressing a shrill, prolonged neigh. His upper lip peeled back, showing his strong teeth and elegant bearing.

His herd gathered and came to him as he repeatedly called to his mares without visual communication. The mares collected through the haze abruptly turned and galloped off in a dust whirl into the sandstorm as they followed Khonsu back to our camp.

Our attention returned to Tani devouring the feast with her companions. She looked subdued but animated. She was alert and aware of the danger from the men laughing and looking at her. Khan came to her side and brushed the hair from her face, holding her chin and looking deep into her eyes. He spoke softly and hugged her.

I involuntarily sighed while carefully noting Khan's movements to ensure she was safe.

We watched them journey the rest of the distance to the port, where Khan and Tani were guided aboard the waiting ship. It was an inspirational design much larger than the boats on the Nile, and Jonas beside me was trying to get a closer look at the hull. It was crafted out of reed lashed together with a main sail. She could not take her mare, and her grief at parting with her gripped my heart as I knew how I would feel leaving Khonsu for good. She passed the rope to a man, whispering and patting her mare goodbye.

We viewed the water journey across the Mediterranean Sea or Wadj-wr. The journey was the usual route where Egyptians traded Nubian gold, fine linen, papyrus, grain, and precision-made faience glass. Crowds cheered and chanted the name Khan as they disembarked and were ushered through the crowd. An older man cloaked in a colourful robe and wearing a strange round hat stepped through the milling people and clutched Khan, then stood back as Khan introduced Tani.

He didn't appear to mention who she was, as there wasn't any surprised or energised connection to her. Tani lowered her head in subservience to the man. Had they known she was the daughter of the head of the military, I'm sure there would have been a different response.

We learned no more from the viewing but knew it was time to leave this time portal. Jonas put his hand on my shoulder and urged us to leave. We turned and intended to go, being pulled back into the pyramid. Just as we were about to place our hands on the walls to exit, a golden shimmer of light appeared in the pyramid, and Sophia and James were beside us.

"You have accomplished the next stage," James said, smiling profusely. "You can see how all the frequencies link up here in this vortex. After years of research and trial, I have recently created this ancient space to bring through the timeline. As travellers, we can project our physical form across time and distance and view it in response to what has happened around us."

"This viewing is exciting. It's phenomenal, James," I hugged Sophia and said, "I haven't spoken to Mother about where she is when she returns here. She will be amazed at what you have here." Sophia glanced at James, and they both seemed distracted for a moment, even quieter than the most profound thought.

James cleared his throat. "We, too, have been viewing your journey back to Memphis. Although we can't intervene, we are very close to you. We were gauging your timing as to when to embark on our journey to Egypt. We must leave within days, the next flight we can get."

"Yes, that is why we returned to inform you of our position," Jonas responded. "We think that as soon as you book the flights, we'll know when to go to the Great Pyramid."

"We will stop for a few nights to rest. There are hotels near the pyramids in Giza, twenty kilometres from Cairo. I'll book one there," James said, taking the lead.

As we re-entered the house, it took on life again. Chatting excitedly, I paused next to the baby's room.

"How long have you had this room completed like this? It's beautiful," I spoke wistfully.

I could feel the pang in my heart as I felt those tendrils reaching out to my baby, Herihor.

"We had been hoping for a child to grace our lives, but now we live separately," Sophia sighed as she turned away and led us into the kitchen.

A vision interrupted me - the scene of Sophia holding a child, gazing into the baby's face. I was captivated in awe by the love she had for the baby. I could see the back of the child's head with soft sand-coloured hair. As I moved to get a better view of the baby, involuntarily, my body shuddered as I saw my Herihor gently cradled in her arms. What was this?

Immediately, I was pulled back into my mind and body. There were more questions and more secrets held here. I had to get away from this entanglement for a moment to breathe.

James stood in the doorway, mouthing everything that should be organised soon and searching my face for signs of discomfort.

My features gave nothing away as I smiled and asked Jonas to take me back to the lodge. The shutters of the lodge were still closed, ready to leave. I couldn't wait.

"Sorry I had to summons you away so abruptly, but a strangeness is happening here."

Jonas didn't feel anything out of place and shrugged off my discomfort in his excitement to return to the city and pack for our journey to Egypt.

ARRIVAL

Asim kept calm; however inwardly, he held brooding, anxious thoughts of what had transpired during the birth of Herihor. He had been thrown into a state of shock at the rapid changes that had occurred. His main concern was my health, how I had coped with the poisoning, and who had positioned the chalice to offer it to me. It must have been someone close to him, so now he no longer trusted any of his priests or helpers. His sister, Heqet, was his only true confidant apart from his parents. He felt the urgency for his family to travel to Pi Ramesses so that he could be with his son, with whom he hardly had time to bond.

Asim's passion for architecture had ceased. He admitted that even walking through the temples and great halls no longer fascinated him. His desire to hold his son and be a family with me were the only thoughts that occupied his tired mind. The very truth of his life had been squeezed of all its joy.

Heqet had been pestering for weeks to travel to the capital and seeing the frailty of her brother and after the sacred burial of baby Herihor's placenta near the temple, Asim's role in Thebes had come to an end. Asim was sinking into a state of depression, bringing a sudden stab of empathy to Heqet's life force.

They would wait until the inundation of Aur, the true name of the Nile, its meaning being, 'black as in the nutrient-rich dark sediment washed down in the great floods'. It was then that his parents and Heqet would make the treacherous journey. Asim's mother, who so desperately awaited the arrival of her precious first born grandchild, had also been devastated by the outcome of baby Herihor's immediate departure after his birth.

Heqet was deeply concerned about her brother; and as his emotional state intensified, she had all preparations made in advance to depart. As soon as the level of the waters lifted and the current flow was continuous, they would commission the most skilled navigators to cast off the flotilla and leave to sail north to Memphis to be carried on the swollen rapids of the impending flooding.

He had priests skilled in the sacred art of potions and tonics. Asim's father, full of anger for betrayal, believed that these were the priests who had made the deadly concoction for me, and he was determined to hunt them down. There would be no reprieve for Dhoser. He was wanted alive for public humiliation, and finally, his death would be brutal.

Dhoser's family had been arrested and held on account that they may have been involved in the treachery. His two beautiful, intelligent daughters were terrified; they huddled together as they walked down to the solitude in the outer rooms of the palace. The council interrogated and scrutinised his wife, intending to break her down.

Heqet had visited the girls' mother in their confinement, hoping to elicit some information from her. Whilst there, Heqet had let it be known that the girls were indeed related to Asim's wife, Akila. They would be protected and would not be held responsible. A flush of good fortune had come over Dhoser's wife as she realised her children may be protected by Akila's family.

She quietly told Heqet, "Dhoser was always distant and aloof, and I swear we knew nothing of his actions. I know that our lives have changed with so many secrets since the arrival of Keket. After Keket's death, Dhoser became defensive and angry and seemed possessed, like the ravaged dark spirits had engulfed his soul, his ba. He refused to consult with me, spent little time in our bed, and never even spoke of his leaving. It must have been on the spur of the moment he decided to cross the line and disobey his duty and security role as an officer. I cannot believe that, with his dedication to his position, he has acted this way." Her face was ashen, and the lines creeping on the corners of her eyes seemed to run down her cheeks in distress as she began sobbing.

The three females would travel north with the flotilla as hostages, to bring Dhoser to accountability. A death threat to an official or high-ranking family member was usually met with instant death.

Asim now spent his time in the temples honouring Hathor and Isis and connecting to them, sending information that would lead down the divine golden thread of light to be delivered to me during meditation. I could hear his stories in the sacred times of prayer. My goddesses uncovered Asim's true feelings and surrendered them to the whispers in the temple walls during my practice of going inward.

"I hear you, my love. I hear your account of the details and feel your ardour and passion. Keep your spirit intact and be strong, as there is no such thing as loss in the divine mind. Your will of strength is needed, my husband. Come to me. I will await your arrival on the rush of the waters creeping slowly to fill the dry, arid landscape and then rapidly to crush everything in its path."

I shook my head to connect back to where I was. I was grateful for the information about my Theban family, delivered from my goddesses.

We needed help deciding when to leave, to return to the majestic shining pyramid, and take Badru through the timeline. He was completely resistant. Three weeks of constantly being together, with Sophia eating feasts of delights of sweetbreads, meats, and delicious foods unimaginable to anything he had tasted before, was making him put on a little weight. We could see a paunch where his physical role and tight core muscles had previously kept him in shape.

Sophia was beaming with love. Her skin was glowing as her eyes followed him everywhere, drinking in his handsome features. He was passionately devouring her with every moment he thought they were unobserved. He encircled and held her, matching his body movements with hers, tantalising and alluring; he was seducing her romantically. It would be challenging to force him to return.

"Badru, we must discuss your parting as we return to New Zealand within another few days," I reached over and squeezed Sophia's arm in support of her for Badru's impending departure.

They were seated together, close and touching. Sophia's hair was pulled back; she held the countenance of a glamorous queen. The contours of her eyes were coloured with the black kohl pencil in the ancient art, looking gracious and seductive with a commanding look I had not seen before held in her eyes.

We were back in Cairo, and my intention to return to Saqqara again before we left Egypt was fresh in my mind. The noise and bustle of many honking horns, cars and millions of people was a cascade of vibrant, packed energies.

I had been so disappointed when we first arrived as I led the way back to Saqqara. The pyramid of Unas, close to the step-pyramid of Saqqara, had crumbled, but it did not detract from the power of the beautiful hieroglyphics in his temple within the pyramid. The first carved floor-to-ceiling image tells of the pharaoh's grandeur and his almighty power. The sacred energy beamed out of the centre of the rubble, and the written hieroglyphics had strength and power that could not be contained. With each stroke of his name held sacred within his cartouche, the oblong band that held his inscription brought chills down the spine even to voice his name, Unas.

Deep in my heart, sadness emerged as we walked around the crumbling structure of the step-pyramid. I could have ignored that, but the presence of the mother dog here suckling her pups in the corner of the ruins looked like a sad reminder of the grandeur of Saqqara. The great sand-coloured columns leading into the main courtyard were still present. Parts of the uraeus around the courtyard were also intact, but I could see where my sacred pool had been filled with the mystical hypnotic powers of the blue lotus. I felt grief at how time can wash away the richness of culture, obliterating feelings of grandeur to be left scuffing the sand in frustration and loss.

Jonas accompanied me this time to Saqqara and the pyramid of Unas as we silently disembarked from our vehicle and walked up to and through the entrance. I could smell the familiar odour of the desert and feel the thousands of footprints on this land as funerary processions slowly brought their kings and queens to their final resting places. I closed my eyes in the middle of the courtyard in front of the step-pyramid. In a flash, my thoughts returned to ancient Saqqara with young Amon as I bathed his forehead with lotus water. I could hear the incantations of the goddesses possessing my spirit for healing, becoming louder and stronger. I viewed myself looking into my eyes, knowing I was there, as the electrical charge of the water amplified in my body. The intense sensation brought enlightenment, and the cosmic power erupted from my crown, connecting me again to the almighty, I AM.

Suddenly, I felt peace and surrender as I let go of what was and focused on what would be. Jonas and I left with a stirring sense of clarity of purpose for our future.

After we had visited Saqqara, we would return to the Great Pyramid to directly access our portal.

The bell tolled, and the tones echoed over the city during prayer. We walked silently to the pyramid's base, our meeting point, waiting until tourists moved away from our space of reconnection for our travel.

"Sophia, we must depart with Badru; his energies are waning here, and he cannot withstand the pressure of his light body in two places. He cannot stay with us now as he has no travel documents or even existence here. We can bring him back here when the time is clarified," I said with care.

Individually, we were lost in thought as we sat down in preparation.

"Sophia, my love, you must release me, and I release you temporarily, for this is only the beginning of our second chance at love," Badru whispered. James stepped forward to help hold her up.

"James, take care of her until my return," Badru said in our ancient language. James's nod was enough. Sophia's quiet sobbing was filled with dignity and sorrow. We held hands, Badru in the middle, one last look at Sophia and James, and we spiraled like the many strands of DNA fractures of emblazoned light through the fringes of lightspeed travel.

Blinking my eyes rapidly, we were met with the same structure, but the white limestone on the pyramid reflecting the sunlight on the sand was stark in contrast to the strewn-cut stone we had previously leaned against. The river's proximity to the glorious structures was hauntingly beautiful, filled with wildlife and the call of the ibis and ducks.

Kal was up and moving, disappointed she didn't make the journey with us; however, she was excited to know she was already in a passive state in our timeline. She was a little dazed but helped me to my feet.

"Sister, I'm excited," she said. "I live in Scotland; my memories aren't strong enough, and I probably won't be able to hold them. At least you will know of my accent when I come to call on you."

"Your mother was sad she could not see you, but she has connected strongly with your father," I said, pointing to Badru, who was still coming around to being in control of his senses.

"Badru, you must document the memories of our journey, as you will forget them and Sophia very soon. Write them on the parchment to recall your connection in case you wish to return."

"I will return as soon as possible to be with my love. Nothing can keep us apart now we know we can be together. I will make arrangements," he said in a determined voice as he moved to write down his memories.

Nef was still organising the troops to take Dhoser away. All the while, Dhoser's resistance was causing chaos. He was thrashing uncontrollably, trying desperately to verbalise his thoughts trapped inside his mind. I felt he knew who my baby was. After seeing Jonas, he would know his lineage and that Jonas was Herihor. It played on my mind.

My star had graced the heavens, and the flow of the waters had begun. We could see by the measuring poles that the elevation had started. Farmers were preparing with anticipation further away from the river, with their culverts waiting to be filled with the dark sediment gushing from the waters. All was in preparation for this annual celebration. The waters brought festivals and collaborations amongst people from all over the neighbouring villages and cities, and they came together to honour the Pharaoh in his gift of calling in the rush of the waters.

We were celebrating; we were honouring the gods and goddesses. Feasts and finery were in splendid array in every courtyard of the great houses, and the celebrations in the people's quarters were also alive with drinking, dancing and music.

We would take the flotilla back from here to Pi Ramesses when the floods would make travel easier. The luxury embellishments of Memphis made our stay delightful. I had time to multiply my force of gathering women for our teachings and the principles that would govern our future - knowing that only a few would make the life-through-life transition, which could make survival more likely if they were cautious in not revealing their true intention until the right time. This was thousands of years of evolution aiming directly for when their greatest gifts would be revealed during the awakening.

Asim and his family were due to arrive in Memphis, and we would travel together to Pi Ramesses. The torchbearers were waiting at the docks, watching as Asims' flotilla arrived and sounded the trumpets. Excitement was everywhere as the first of the leading ships arrived from Thebes. I had the royal privilege of being amongst the people with a viewing advantage from the platform, alongside my parents and sisters. Kalina was with Anippe, holding up my baby Herihor to see his father disembark. Herihor, my priest, was next to Nef, who was carrying Amon on his shoulders. Amon was excited and positioned to have the best view whilst he kept glancing back to see if baby Herihor was able to see. For a moment, a fleeting warm feeling chased my apprehension away.

My nerves were causing chaos in my stomach as I smoothed my robes of the finest linen. I had a duck egg blue tunic ribbed with white bands of stitching as thick braids down the front. My gown had faience glass beads of blue and sparkling crystal sewn into the bodice to accent my breasts, flattering yet demure. My hair was twisted, wrapped in strips of dampened linen, then dried in the sun, and when unravelled, I had the most luxurious curls.

We were all dressed in our finest. My son looked the most handsome little prince dressed in a rich blue suit with gold edging. Now nearly three months old, how would Asim feel about seeing him after all this time? His hair had grown and was still the same rich colour of the sand in the shade. He was calling out to me, moving his chubby little fingers to come to him.

I moved towards him, and Badru and Kal stepped back and smiled at me. Suddenly, all sounds ceased, as everything was playing out in front of me without sound and in slow motion. I felt faint, but Nef's strong arms encircled and held me while offering his gourd of water to replenish my thirst. How many times over the years had Nef been there for me? Anippe and Nef had become extremely close, and I'm sure he would ask my father to take her as his wife.

There he was, my beautiful husband, disembarking from the ship. He was a shadow of himself and would need recuperation. Our son was shrieking with joy, holding out his arms as he practically dived into his father's arms. Even though they had only one brief encounter at birth, their souls enmeshed in each other, and baby Herihor immediately knew his voice. It was a joyous scene as Asim's mother came to embrace us.

It was so good to feel her welcome arms enfolding strongly around me. I felt calm and at peace, knowing she was present to hold her grandson, Herihor.

We melted into each other's arms. Asim was agitated in front of everyone as we moved towards our rooms. He kept kissing me as if I were an apparition. He needed to fill me up to feel his presence inside of me to reassure himself I was human and alive. I could sense his need to be connected immediately as we moved through the people, and our guard made the way for us.

Alone, we viewed our faces as if memorising every expression. Then Asim kissed my neck, my face, and around my ears and eyes as I closed them and drew in the tender feeling of his mouth slowly moving over my lips. He pressed himself closer, the familiar smell of him heightening my desire for more of his touch. Although he had lost weight, his body still held the strength of a lion as he picked me up and carried me to our bed. I trembled with expectation, closing my eyes.

"Open your eyes my love; let me see you look and desire only me," he passionately whispered. His kissing was deep and true, and I kept my eyes open, devouring our lovemaking with an urgency that consumed our bodies. He pressed deeper within me, claiming me like a triumphant prize. I could feel his mastery and that he was the ruler. I allowed his emotions to overflow, and I was receiving him with pure divine love.

We could not stop touching, and for the first time in months, I felt relaxed and secure as I belonged to the earth, moon and stars.

My life force was infused with love and warmth. Asim was home, and I was at peace, my body dancing on the inside.

After we had bathed and dressed, we would return to the festivities which were in full swing. I re-fastened my duck egg blue gown, but my hair needed re-fixing, so I pulled it up. Looking beautiful, I thought, just how I feel, with a flush on my cheeks, was the only telltale sign Asim and I had lain together.

We entered the feasting room, where our banquet was before us. The torches were lit, even though it was not yet dark. The glow illuminated the vast room as the musicians prepared their instruments for the next dance.

We knew how to celebrate this end of the country, and the celebrations were well underway. Asim looked relaxed and fulfilled as he grasped his wine and drank deep gulps from the beautifully crafted goblet.

Looking around, I thought baby Herihor must be with Asim's parents. I wasn't concerned; I was happy they finally could hold him.

Yet my mind was far away, and I had some unfinished business I would have to attend to. I too, picked up the chalice, took a sip of the red wine, and then suddenly, the chalice disintegrated and smashed into pieces as the glass spun from my fingertips. My dress looked as though it was splattered with blood. How clumsy, I had been preoccupied. With apologies, I excused myself.

My son was the only one who mattered. That his honour was intact; that was all I cared for and nothing to be against him. If there were a plot to discredit my son, only one person would be capable of this.

It was dusk. The sky was rippled with crimson as I slipped away from the festivities to go and change and then head to the confines where Dhoser's family were being held. The small white garden flowers seemed to all turn their heads to look at me as I walked lightly to the door where the guards were stationed. The next moment, Nef was beside me in all his glorious splendour, dressed in knee-length golden and black armour and displaying a thick golden neckband. He wore leather sandals, and his feet looked even more predominant with the flat surface of the sole. After eyeing him from head to toe and admiring his attire, I asked if he could assist me in talking with Dhoser's family.

We approached the guards, who, knowing who we were, could not deny our request. The large wooden door was pushed open, and we were led to the house in the confinement area.

Dhoser was imprisoned elsewhere. Suddenly, I saw a shaft of sunlight filtering across a great ocean. The vision was immediate, as two beautiful girls appeared charming and childlike. They graced the room elegantly as they moved curiously toward us. They didn't seem afraid of Nef; they were just curious. One was the age of marriage, maybe fourteen years, while the other looked a few years younger.

Their mother appeared short and well-looked-after; her beautiful large brown eyes ringed with long lashes peering reluctantly at me. She then, realising who I was, ran to kneel at my feet, endowing me with blessings and chants of hope that her life and that of her daughters, would be saved.

"Rise Sister, you are not responsible for your husband's actions, even if they are punishable by death. I will ensure you and your daughters can be free and live among the people in Pi Ramesses.

Your children are blood links to my mother's family," I said honourably, without letting on that they could be travellers. "You must remain here until they deal with Dhoser's fate."

I turned to face the girls, whose locks of wild, untamed hair framed their unusual yet dignified faces. "I will take care of you as my own sisters, and you will learn the way of life here in Pi Ramesses as you are related to our dynasty."

The deep eyes of Eshe as she was introduced, took me by surprise. She was spiritual and connected to the goddesses. My snake rose immediately, performing movements like a dance. This was without threat, and I was fascinated by her almost unwillingness to look directly at me. I covered my surprise as I introduced myself to her sister, Lapis. As the girls bowed, I said farewell to their mother, gathered my gown and left the house.

Outside, the scent of the well-manicured trees lingered like a soft perfume. As I inhaled deeply, I thought of how innocent my life was not so long ago - the immature joy of the two girls in confinement had reminded me. I was determined I would help them, as Dhoser's fate was already in the hands of the war gods.

"Nef, do you know what will happen to Dhoser? I must see him," I said earnestly.

Nef turned, looking directly into my eyes, scowling, "You cannot just go to the guard room and walk in. He is heavily guarded and has lost his mind. He is dangerous. I have seen him skirting the walls with a weird lopsided gait, hissing and screaming like a wild caged animal. What good will it do you to view him this way?"

"I must," I insisted. "Just to send his soul into the deepest depths without him releasing any resentment is cruel. I will do this for Keket, for no good has come out of this entanglement, and I want to bless and forgive him to set his daughters free."

Nef drew his shoulders up like only he could do to make his appearance look gigantic, and then with a great sigh and out-breath, he agreed to my terms. I knew he would let me have my way, as he always did. We walked briskly to the guard house, and the two guards stepped aside. The sunset drew jagged shadows on the walls from the flags hoisted from the corners of the prison walls. It felt like death again, and it smelled like death. For a moment, I could see the masked Anubis standing over the doorway, vigilantly, his jackal stance patient with sharp eyes and ears alert, hovering, waiting to devour his next corpse.

I shuddered involuntarily as we entered the chamber. The outer area was a walkway with two rooms opposite each other. Sentences were dealt with swiftly here, so there was no need for many rooms to hold prisoners. The stench of faeces and a foul odour were pungent, and I tried to block my nose and not inhale the revolting stench as we were led to the doorway.

"Are you sure?" Nef said.

I nodded. Nef unlatched the door, and the enormous wooden plank was lifted. There, in the corner, Dhoser cowered with his hands over his head. I cleared my throat.

"Dhoser, you are my cousin; I hold no malice against you. The torture you have put yourself through trying to take out the travellers has infested your mind. You have tried many times to kill us, but fortunately, our fight is strong within us to survive. I know you can hear me through the torment of your soul. I have come here to forgive you and set your daughters free from this vengeance you possess so they do not need to carry this wound through to their children. The masquerade is over; you can return to dust, and Anubis is waiting at the gates to devour you. I have come to set you free."

He began pushing himself against the wall, screeching and glaring at me with his bloodshot eyes. His lips pulled back in defiance as he hissed at us.

"To relieve your family of the indignity of having you dragged through the streets, we can put you to rest here. I have convened with the goddesses, and they have agreed to your demise this way if you are willing."

I drew the flask from under my bodice and passed it to Nef, who eyed me questioningly, and then he held it out for Dhoser.

"Here is the poison you administered to me. Your organs will bleed out, but it will be quick. This is for you to decide," I said. "But I assume you will agree to this choice."

I said prayers in the ancient rites of passage, reciting the incantations for the dead to summons the journey of the soul's release. Dhoser had not moved but was taking it all in.

"As Akila, High Priestess, I forgive your life here. You are accountable for your deeds, and now you can make amends and set your family free. Your heart has been filled with hatred because of your birth, and now I fill your cup with love for your family and your daughters. The goddesses will look out for your girls, and they will be free from your toxic betrayal of our family. Dhoser, I set you free," I said in a commanding voice.

Dhoser crawled closer like a creature and took the flask from Nef, but no words or fight were left in him. He knew this would be a more honourable way to go. His bloodshot eyes held my gaze. Tears traced down his cheeks as he sipped all the liquid from the flask. Slowly making his way to the corner, he curled up into a ball, his mouth frothing, murmuring, and clutching his stomach.

We waited. I placed the empty vial of the poison near his body and then immediately left the confinement. It was over. The taste in my mouth was as acidic as the poison, and I gasped for fresh air.

The tears on my cheeks were for Keket and James' forbidden lost love and the sadness for their granddaughters.

"We will never speak of this again Nef; it has been done!"

HEAT · OF
THE · RED · SUN

The stench of death was all over me, seeping into my pores, leaching into my soul. I could hear the rumble from the heavens above and knew my goddesses were questioning my title of High Priestess. The deed had to be implemented this way to allow Dhoser to choose himself. My part in offering him to take the potion was his chance to renounce his evil soul.

Like his mother Keket, Dhoser would surely make his dangerous journey into the afterlife, negotiating his final judgement. Would Anubis be kind to him after weighing his heart, or would his heart be thrown into the jaws of the devourer of the dead? Ahemait, the goddess with the head of a crocodile, a lion's body and a hippopotamus's hindquarters; a demoness, would be executing divine justice. I bowed to the magnificence of her role, waiting patiently for the sinners to be brought to her for punishment. Trembling, I hoped I would make my case heard when it was time for my heart to be weighed against the feather. Once more, I bowed my head and brushed off any impending doom.

After washing off the dank energy and changing my attire again, I re-entered the feasting hall. Herihor and Heqet were immersed in one another's energies. They were intimate, and she held an intricately carved scarab beetle - a lavish gift from Herihor. I tried to move away from their private moment and turned to go toward Asim when Heqet called out.

"Oh Sister, look what Herihor has given me. It glows with the opulence of shimmering crystal," she said as she moved it from side to side to capture the glow from the torches.

"It is beautiful, just like you," I laughed at Heqet. Catching Herihor's eye, I smiled and lightly nodded in an acquiesced response.

"My love," I stated as I sat down, smiling at Asim, with all threats to my family now concealed. "I am hungry and have a thirst for more wine." I licked my lips and squeezed Asim's leg, letting my hand wander into his groin.

"Let us fill our hearts and heads with a celebration that all is well now," I hesitated momentarily before continuing. "Now that you are here, you cannot escape from me again," I spoke lovingly. In the back of my mind, though, my thoughts turned to finding Tani in the faraway lands across the sea. Squirming in my seat, I brushed the thought aside. Soon, we would go back to Pi Ramesses, and I would languish at being home.

"Fill our cups," Asim called to our serving boy. "Tonight, we are celebrating my homecoming with my wife."

Father and Mother stood together, raising their chalices, and then everyone stood up. Mother eyed me intently with a newfound admiration. What a great night to remember - all was well in the divine plan that had been cleanly executed.

"I am anxious to go home," Saf quietly said as we walked through the gardens the next day. A gentle breeze wafted through the papyrus, which stood proudly close to the pond guarding the blue lotus. Their subtle perfume urged us to bend, kneel, and get closer to their intoxicating aromatic fragrance. Gigantic mosquitoes were beating their wings furiously at such a high frequency that the buzzing pierced the calm.

"You are missing your magician, aren't you, Sister?" I spoke as I inhaled deeply, letting the scent mingle into my mind. "You have been away for months, saving our baby Herihor and me. How can I ever repay you? I owe you my life, which is yours when you need me, life-through-life. I dedicate my heart to you, dear Sister. I share my son with you as I see how much you love him. We will leave soon. I too, have longed to be back in my room with my treasures, even for a while, until Asim and I have a new house." I felt lightheaded and relieved and agreed to her request to return home to Pi Ramesses.

Saf left and strolled back to the house, whilst Herihor's arrival at the pond where I was languishing was exciting. I wanted to hear more about him and Heqet and how the last night had captivated them.

"Herihor, we are leaving for Pi Ramesses soon. Will you ask Heqet to accompany us?" I spoke softly to let him feel into the request. "Come sit," I gestured, pointing to the ground beside me. I held out my hand to grasp his and pull him down, and suddenly, we were lurching, twisting, and falling through the spiralling timeline together.

James was comforting Sophia. "I am abandoned again, James. Do you know how that feels? It's like time is running out for me to be with my love."

I shook my head, returning to the present time, and saw James wince slightly as Sophia continued sobbing her heart out. Other tourists viewed us strangely, moving further away from our emotional gathering.

"I love Badru; he is my first and last love. I could not love or lose another. It will be hard to return to the solitude of our house when we are so close to our past. If only we could crawl through the pyramid walls," she cried.

I moved closer to Sophia to speak with her. "We can relay messages to him. He wishes to return to you, but I fear Badru will lose his memories, Sophia. It feels like all may be lost."

"No, I don't feel that way. Badru said he would come back to me. It is my dream, and I will keep manifesting his presence. I trust him," Sophia wailed as she shook her head in denial.

"He cannot live in two worlds as he is not a traveller. He would have to die in his other life, which would be hard for Kalina after finding her father again. He is also a professional soldier in the army with a killing instinct. Would he be comfortable living a different sedentary life here as ours?" I questioned with raised eyebrows.

Sophia wiped her arm across her forehead. She was hot in the burning heat and looked defeated. I promised her I would ask his counsel for his choice. We were destined to return to New Zealand to reconfigure our situation.

The blazing intensity of the sun seemed to suck every drop of moisture from the air as we struggled to breathe while walking back to our waiting vehicle. Our time here was over; so much had been accomplished, yet our visit had made it even more challenging to return to normality.

Jonas reached for me as we walked into the foyer of the plush hotel. Upon entering, a blast of cool air awoke us from our thoughts. His hand in mine gave me relief and strength. I was not alone. I knew I needed to go to an inner sanctuary, a temple, but none here were private. Life here had altered dramatically. I would have to call my goddesses from the foot of my bed.

The traffic and the noise below threatened to lose and torment me living this daily existence in Egypt. I gazed out of the dusty windows, taking in the entire vista to imprint into my mind. The pyramids were stark in the background, laced with the indistinct colour of the sand. Twilight now cast its soft shroud over the sky as I knelt beside our bed, praying to the almighty divine source to help us all.

The night was torturous, sending a tremor of insecurity through my body lest I wake and be alone. Aloneness was sometimes my greatest enemy, leaving me clutching at the familiar feelings of love as I moved closer to Jonas.

My morning prayer was also dedicated to my goddesses. "Thank you, Isis and Hathor, for your devout protection of my baby Herihor and your gifts of love in my other world that I eternally cherish," I muttered the words gently under my breath with reverence to Hathor and her constant protection as the morning light cascaded through the windows. Shivering as I was getting more of a download of my role in this lifetime, I panicked a little inside, wondering how to achieve such a shift in a short lifetime in this body of my human experience.

We spent the last day in modern Egypt, returning to Saqqara's ruins. Memories were intense for us all as we slipped back into our ancient language, where English was forgotten, and reminisced about the glory of this blessed place.

Standing still at the entrance, I could hear Hori, my cousin the Priest of Saqqara, reminding me, whispering to me from another world, "You will always recall Saqqara. It is your sacred soul place. I am here for you through many lifetimes, and my heart will support and guide you. Call me to come to you only when the time is in 'The Awakening', and my mother there will honour me and my intention."

Going home to New Zealand would test our fortitude.

Landing at Auckland Airport after a stopover, showed Sophia and James they were now worlds apart, lost in their thoughts about our Egyptian journey. James knew what would happen, and he would have to take the role of support if Badru came through The Void permanently. James would no doubt continue his obsession with quantum physics, which maintained his ability to build his spectacular quantum pyramid, his link to the ancient world.

I felt frustrated being around Sophia and James' energies, so Jonas and I stayed at our apartment for nearly a month whilst we returned to our work roles. His family was constantly asking about our wedding plans. These were the furthest thoughts from our minds. Jonas' mother, a family woman of Italian descent, was passionate and wanted to organise the event, and I was grateful and allowed her to take control of the occasion. I finally left my media position and went to waitress in Jonas' family's restaurant. It was interesting witnessing the intense passion of his family in the artistry and creation of their culinary delights.

I often compared Jonas with Asim and their families and had to tell myself we were in entirely different worlds. Asim was lustful, passionate, noble and proud, and I missed his forthright, sensual way. Jonas was full of affection and emotion, yet a longing emptiness occupied my thoughts. Still, Jonas and I were in love and had built our relationship on our eager interest in nature and tramping. Life at our lodge was our escape from the daily humdrum. We were now ready to return there for a few week's reprieve.

Kate and I had also reconnected, but she seemed worlds away. What was wrong with me? Did I prefer my other life? I needed to get a grip and find something more meaningful to achieve. Kate and I planned a much-desired dinner date.

"You look beautiful," we lavished the words on each other over our meal. I truly meant it. Kate looked ready for a lover. "Have you got a boy in mind, Kate?" I asked excitedly.

"Yes, yes, I do," she answered as she leaned forward enthusiastically. "I have been waiting to give you details about my new man when we were alone. He has moved into a flat down the road from us and jogs past our house. Who runs around the streets like that? He seemed to appear out of nowhere."

"We have been constant companions ever since. He asked about my friends, and I told him about you, my mysterious Lily. He seemed very intrigued. I would love you to meet him," she exclaimed breathlessly with a lilt.

I had never seen her look so empowered and think of herself for once. As I gazed at her, I thought, *this is how love makes one feel.*

"Oh yes, soon, let's do this. The four of us could meet at our favourite restaurant down at Mission Bay. You both will also have to come up to the lodge with us. It will be good for Jonas to have another male around," I replied eagerly.

A sense of anticipation and enthusiasm sent a shudder through my body as though this was a significant event; a promising occasion for Kate to have a lover after all her sadness.

Now, our lodge was drawing us back north, as though life there had an intoxicating pull on us, perhaps an obsession or addiction. It was the landscape, the land itself, a portal to the unknown. Even our lovemaking was more intense there as if we could abandon ourselves to the solitary, carefree life we loved. I sat back and caught my breath, thinking about our future. There was no use in planning; we must just let life play out for a while.

Already, I was held in the intricacies and patterns of the information in the continuous downloads I was experiencing from the pyramid. It left me in little doubt that so much more was coming for our world than we could ever anticipate. Control and greed still crept into the souls of corrupt individuals wanting a global takeover.

We continued up to Sophia and James' house to see how they were in the aftermath of our Egyptian journey. Those weeks of sailing down the Nile and spending time in the ancient ruins as the archaeologists scraped and laid bare some of the most priceless relics of a faraway time, reminded us of how precious those days were. Thinking of the last Pharaoh having to surrender the throne to the Persians, which dissipated our heritage. How had we handled that timeline? Seeing the abandoned broken temples and the Nile now controlled by the dam at Aswan was a grave loss. The tributaries of her foundation reached out like branches, ambling and flowing with crushing power from Nubia.

Sophia looked thin and hauntingly pale, vulnerable and delicate as she opened the door to greet us; even James was subdued.

"What is happening here, Sophia?" I questioned as we held each other at arm's length after our initial hug. "I feel you have so much to say. Please unburden yourself," I said quietly. I hadn't seen it at first, but now it was clear; her colours showed she was with child.

"Sophia, you are having a baby. You are pregnant, right?" I questioned, almost too loudly, looking wildly at James and Jonas. "When? How? Oh my gosh!" I could not stop saying those words. Suddenly, outside, lightning lit up the dim interior of the room, and then thunder shook the house on the clifftop.

"Is this Badru's baby?" I questioned; my hand clasped over my mouth. I knew it was so before the words left my lips. "Oh my gosh." There it was again. Only I seemed to be talking, and everyone was quiet.

Well, this sure was destiny. It was already written on the temple walls and hidden in the recesses of the tunnels under the Great Pyramid. A divine intervention had occurred, and Sophia and Badru would have another child together. The rain was falling now in torrents of unleashed fury as the wind forced the shutters on the kitchen windows to bang incessantly against the walls.

Sophia beckoned us to have tea as she smoothed the tablecloth and placed the hot pot brewing on the coal range on the table. James had excused himself to battle the winds and secure the shutters.

"You were expecting us," I acknowledged as we pulled out chairs and sat to discuss what to do next. Sophia was radiant now as she relaxed and started sharing her excitement. I had to admit James too, was animated as he burst through the door, taking off his dripping oilskin coat and rubbing his hands through his hair.

"Badru will have to know, and this will cause unsettled longings; that is, if he can recall his recent time travel to modern Egypt," James interrupted.

"How will we explain his presence if he comes to live here?" I turned to James, searching for answers.

"I have already been working on an identity and I have kept my young brother in the system records as 'Hunter Nobel'. He was 12 years old when he passed away. He was eight years younger than me."

I shuddered, as that was rather creepy, but then again James was undoubtedly unusual. His sadness was evident in the loss of his brother, as it had been traumatic for him. Did he want to keep him alive in his mind?

Jonas clasped his hand over his forehead in disbelief that this was all happening. The wind was shrilling now, carrying the spirits on the wind and trying to enter the house. My goddesses were arriving, and there would be a brimming celebration here.

"Bring out the glasses and champagne, James. Spirit travels on the wind to celebrate this hour with us. Oh my gosh!" *Stop saying that*, I thought as I pushed the chair away to stand and acknowledge this momentous occasion. My voice was not mine; I spoke from the ancient voice of my goddesses speaking through me as we gathered here.

"We have availed ourselves to support the transition of this ancient wondrous child as he gains a foothold in this timeline. We will surround and care for him here, to be unwavering in his protection," I spoke in the ancient language, which we all understood as we raised our glasses.

Just at that moment a gigantic lightning spark lit up the clouds and landscape, and thunder unleashed her fury again. Then, as rapidly as the storm had arrived, it faded away, leaving us planning how these changes would affect us all.

I could hear Herihor's cries in the wind as the leaves rustled the moist undergrowth of the forest after the storm wash. Back at our lodge, I had slipped through our hatch in the floor and wandered to where I had buried the beast deep in the earth. The crackling of broken twigs and bracken underfoot mingled with the call of the hooting owl was bringing my senses alive. I prayed for the beast and Dhoser, blessing him on his journey to the underworld. I kicked the wet leaves over the beast's grave and instantly caught a picture of the final look of Dhoser in the room, curled in a ball, frothing at the mouth, and then the visual of him here that night as I skilfully pierced the arrow through his chest wall. I sighed a deep breath of resignation that it was over. My son was safe; we were safe.

Herihor was Dhosers' brother, the other boy my uncle fathered to the commoner girl. James was this uncle, separated by thousands of years. It made me feel uncomfortable that Herihor or my Jonas here must never discover the part I played in Dhoser's transition to his afterlife. Suddenly, a rustle of leaves and the breeze picking up made me feel vulnerable. I got such a fright as Jonas put his arm around my shoulder, and I turned to him, trembling with tears in my eyes with gratitude he was here and our child was safe. My hair waved in the breeze around my face as we held one another locked together in an alluring embrace.

"Oh, my love, you frightened me..." I said, my words trailing off as we felt the frayed edges of our world spinning and pulling us back to Egypt through The Hush. Again, our worlds collided.

The ground was warm and inviting as we lay in the sunlight by the pond, the provocative scent of the blue lotus wafting around us stimulated awareness. I turned to look at Herihor; his charismatic charm made him irresistible. We reached for one another and held a moment, a heartbeat between us, an instant recall of a moment ago. Without a chance to speak, Heqet burst forward, interrupting our intoxicating moment.

"What is this? I have been observing you as though you are asleep or dead, with your hands clasped together. Herihor, you are a Priest, and Akila, a High Priestess married to my brother. What does this mean?" she shrilled with concern.

I tried to be present as I fluttered my eyelids. My cheeks felt flushed with the day's heat, or was it embarrassment? My heart was thumping, though I kept calm, and so did Herihor as we sat up abruptly.

"We were talking about you and your impact on Herihor, dear Sister. Come sit with us in the sunlight and feel the warmth on your face," I assured her as I patted the ground between Herihor and myself as we shuffled apart. "The gentle scent of the blue lotus has mesmerised us. Come and experience it, too. We have been through much together, and we appreciate that we have lived through the challenge of the desert storm." Her look of astonishment seemed to vanish as we three lay down together, holding hands connected like a child's daisy chain.

"We must live these significant moments and cherish them together as Herihor and I are like brother and sister, and you, dear Heqet, he tells me you have captured his heart," I spoke softly.

"You are two of my favourite people in the kingdom," she said, turning both sides to look at us and squeezing our hands. "I was just surprised as you both lay so still; I had thought you had gone together and had departed from this world."

I laughed reassuringly, then breathed a sigh of relief that my guilt had been overwhelming and unnecessary. A twinge of jealousy briefly gripped my heart as I saw Heqet's admiration for Herihor. We would have to be more cautious of our spontaneous touch in the future.

The days turned into weeks as we travelled back to Pi Ramesses. Baby Herihor and I relaxed on the journey. Our outer world was slowing down, and without any resistance, we celebrated life as a family in the evenings, lounging in the tents erected for the journey home.

Grand celebrations of immense proportions were heralded upon our arrival in Pi Ramesses. With our sister, Heqet, we prepared for the festivities. Our hands were painted, and our lips were coloured with red ochre from hematite mixed with fats to apply sensually over our lips. Our eyes were elaborately and expertly lined with kohl, while eyeshadow from crushed malachite preserved with animal fats protected our eyes and enhanced our beauty.

Looking stunning, we practiced our dance, adding harmonious hand-flowing movements to depict our beauty and elegance. Heqet shone in the adornment of her newly made faience beads, with silver clasps and prized silver earrings hanging delicately from her ears.

Mother beckoned me to sit before we were escorted to the main hall. I dreaded these moments because they had serious overtones and seemed to bring me down.

"Akila, you are a woman now, and there is nothing I need to advise you on, as you have already learned a great deal during your journey south. You are a High Priestess and practising in the arts of the initiation temples; however, there will be various undertakings you must adhere to and not let your free will be so explorative and unconventional."

I sighed and looked wide-eyed at her, agreeing to her wishes. If only we could talk more openly, I was sure she would have revelations about her own life. I boldly took the chance to ask her about her other world.

"Mother, where are you living in your other world? We are searching for you. Your sister Sanura, Kalina's mother and your brother have found each other. They live close to us in New Zealand, a small country in the Pacific Ocean," I stammered to get it all out before I lost my heart to speak up. She immediately stood and looked exposed and agitated.

"You know where Sanura is?" she exclaimed almost too loudly. "And my brother, are they together?"

She swivelled to check that no one was in an earshot. "Where? I, too, have been searching for her. Is she happy and healthy? I was not sure she had travelled and survived. After I had left my tropical paradise, I now live in a magnificent villa in Italy. We will want to connect when this day is over, my Akila. I am thrilled to hear of this outcome," Mother spoke as she enthusiastically showed signs of letting her guard down.

We stood and held hands, and she looked at me directly with hope and joy. For the first time, I saw the excitement in her eyes, and I felt we had broken through the heavy facade of our life portrayal as mother and daughter.

Our evening was a great success, with welcome celebrations creeping into the early morning hours. During the evening, I tried several times to contact Badru to let him know I wanted to speak with him, but as a royal guard, he was preoccupied. I would have to wait for the appropriate time.

TALISMAN · OF · ISIS

The galactic presence of the ancient light beings probed my mind, tapping into the recesses of my hidden thoughts. I felt these thoughts sift from my mind like sand falling through my fingers, unstoppable and gaining momentum until every last grain was filtered through my hands.

My mind was being emptied of all ideas, deeds, and actions. Light beings thousands of light years away extracted and copied the collection of past concepts in my mind. Yet, standing with bare feet on the cool stones, I was reminded of my task throughout many lifetimes; to gather information on humanity and then allow the knowledge to be released like dissipating mist into the star dome, the home of my Elestial Crystal Star.

I was spiralling now, drawn up into the pathway of the heavens, the portal to my ancient Elestial Crystal Star. Like silken frozen liquid, her structure crystallised with the rainbow light fractures hidden within her form. Her magnificence, the feminine liquid light vortex, glistened in the depths of the universe. Her partner Sirius wrapped around her form, hiding her and protecting her. Only those with the unique frequency could detect a trace of her.

The towering ancient light beings held boundless wisdom and knowledge, casting a radiant presence over all humanity. These collection points were connected to Earth and the global pyramids, serving as demarcation points for the light beings. They were all synchronised with Earth's sacred geometric patterns. The light beings were collecting relevant time data for the future. The knowledge of humanity's future was held in the walls of temples and pyramids as laser light imprints of a language and knowledge of galactic power. We were visiting each other tonight.

I wrapped my warm cover tightly around my shoulders to avoid the cold early morning darkness, broken only by the shimmering starlight that enveloped me. I was one of many galactic source interpreters chosen to assist with the activation. My home was in the crystal foundation of my Elestial Crystal Star. Venturing to other galaxies and dimensions gave me complete reverence for the ceaseless level of work the light beings were connected to on a galactic scale.

Delivering concepts and impressions as a messenger held great reverence in my stardom role. I left myself keys of information locked into energy vaults in varying locations on the planet. I then retrieved them to prompt me on my work. The transfer of knowledge up to the light beings was a continuous process governed by the pull of the moon cycles. Yet, I would recall this commitment repeatedly throughout my many timelines.

Before Goddess Nut released her hold on the night sky, I had crept slowly back to my husband's loving arms. He knew I was communing with the galactic light beings and never interfered with these connections.

"You are cold, my Priestess. Let my love warm your heart and body," Asim lovingly whispered as I snuggled in beside him, replenished in my renewal and upgrade.

Our bodies were electrified as we collided in one another's aura. Asim's warm, tender touch covered my skin with goosebumps and tingles like feathers, brushing lightly and raising the delicate hairs on my arms. Asim's body was filled with romantic affection and impassioned, ardent movements as he surrendered to my caress. I brushed against his alive maleness, recalling all the details I missed as I had journeyed homeward with baby Herihor. The early morning light lifted her veil of translucent fineness to view the beauty of our lovemaking as we were entwined together. Our bodies and spirits lifted the energy in the room to wash over our little son nestled in his woven basket beside us.

The great eagle soared across the landscape, her majestic extended wings filtering the airflow. Representing Goddess Nekhbet, she was the wise protector, especially of the Pharaoh, but today, she was aligned with Badru.

I was holding the rope around Khonsu's neck. He was restless, tossing his head and stomping his hooves. The dawn was still breaking in a breathtaking vista of beauty across the horizon viewed from the side of the palace walls. The fresh awakening of the morning called the heron birds to span their delicately splayed wings and glide over the river below. Herihor, Badru, Nef and I were to be riding along the banks of the waterway to be out of earshot for a very private meeting. Nef held the other horses' reins as they were restless and ready to respond to our ride.

Alone, except for the guidance of the eagle, Badru strode up to the great walls of the palace to be our guard for the day. His body was erect, but his head was down, looking somewhat dejected. His aura colours were flat as I tried to analyse the reason.

"Dear Badru, you look lost in your thoughts," I quickly engaged in the meeting.

"I cannot get Sanura out of my thoughts…" he said, his voice trailing off. "She has been haunting my visions. I dreamed I was picked up by the great eagle and flown on the wind currents. I was transported to a place where I could see her animated face. Sanura whispered she was carrying our child exactly as she told me when we were expecting Kalina."

I must reveal the truth to Badru; this meeting must be now. Earlier this morning, I took my daily ritual to the temple to pray and acknowledge reverence for my goddesses, so I was inspired to speak directly.

"Badru, as High Priestess, I say these words with the utmost respect for your decision either way. Your vision was a reality through our timeline quantum leap thousands of years into the future. When Herihor and I took you and Kalina on the journey through The Void, even though you may not recall the events, you met with Sanura at the Great Pyramid."

"Kalina has reincarnated and been transported to another light body. You, dear Badru, spent fourteen starlight cycles with Sanura. Do you remember any of this?"

He looked at me intently, his big hands trembling as he covered his face. "I have been revisiting those dreams repeatedly to keep them alive, for fear of Sanura slipping away again. Yes, I recall some of the journey," he said with emotion etched on his face.

"How would you feel to be able to be there again, permanently, with Sanura and your new child?" I hesitated, taking a deep, prolonged breath while waiting for his response.

His eyes flew wide open as he once again cupped his hands over his face, his big shoulders heaving with distress.

"How could this be possible? I am here, and she has left for her afterlife," he shuddered.

"Sanura is alive and pregnant with a child in our other timeline as we gather for The Awakening and our new Earth. I can escort you through The Void, but we will have to release your body here to your afterlife once you are in our timeline. After communing with my goddesses, you must surrender your light body here in Egypt through the vicious bite of a poisonous snake. Your spirit will be set free from this timeline. You would be afforded an official burial of the highest-ranking honour; however, you can never return to Egypt as you know her."

The great eagle called loudly and circled briefly before returning to the lush farmland.

Badru fell to his knees, talking rapidly and gesturing at his desire to leave here and be with Sanura.

"Let us ride and work out how this can come to pass. We must keep this secret within our circle. It is of utmost importance that we execute this ritual effectively. There is one more we need to consider. That is Kalina. However, if she is a part of this conversation, it will be transmitted to her Magus, and all will be revealed. Be careful, Badru, we must not give anything away. Your heart will still be weighed against the feather here; however, as you will be on another timeline, this should not affect your transition into the afterlife. Be certain you know there will be no return to this land. Your combat and trained executioner skills will be of little use except perhaps as a hunter-gatherer." I took a deep breath, waiting for a response from anyone.

By this time, our horses had moved closer to the river. Neither a bee nor a butterfly listened to our conversation as Badru coughed and spat on the ground. He was deep in reflection of what this may mean.

"I am ready today, however, I will see my beautiful Kalina, and at sunrise, after three nights, we can meet again on a similar journey. We will be far enough away to have no interference or assistance to save me." Badru spoke with clarity as though executing an order.

Herihor shook his head, not in defiance, but in struggle, as it was against his principles. Nef remained calm and self-assured, knowing this would be done. Nef never questioned these situations, as he knew Badru held a fire within him to be with Sanura, and that would only be extinguished when he died here.

I cannot imagine how Badru would say his last farewell to Kalina or her response. I kept in my world with Asim and our son strolling within the city and taking a felucca ride on the Nile. I filled these three days with the delight and joy of loving our child. With infinite patience, I embraced motherhood, sending signals of calm and strength to my little prince. Several times, I noticed his eyes flicker rapidly out of nowhere. I was anticipating he was preparing to travel. Amon spent much time with baby Herihor, and his unusual language always brought Herihor to stillness in wonder and listening as though he understood their strange, faraway connection.

The first light broke through the dim shroud of darkness. I had had a restless night and woke perspiring but ready to leave for the temple with Herihor, my priest. Communion in close spiritual connection with my goddesses had a vital impact today as we prepared the ritual for Badru.

Nef would be out early, before sunrise, acquiring the deadly viper. Each snake had a different way of killing its victim. The god of snakes, Apophis, was the most lethal and painful with his four fangs, so Nef would be looking for one that would bring rapid death with less pain.

We solemnly journeyed to the river and prepared the scene for our ritual. Badru was bold and unwavering in his decision. He was freshly bathed and shaven, looking handsome and alert. My mind flicked over to where we would end up, which was in the forest by our lodge. It briefly crossed my mind that he would still look like Badru, as he had on our previous journey.

I called my goddesses to be with us and protect our passage through The Void. We held the Talisman of Isis and individually blessed the soul of Badru. I blessed him from the feminine aspect and Herihor from the masculine. I requested that my goddesses protect Herihor and myself from the snake's reaction. As soon as it unleashed its venom on Badru, Nef would truss it again in the thick sack. Nef said prayers of intent that he would encourage the snake to poison only Badru, as we would be in such close confinement. It could be tricky.

"Nef, you are a good man, and I know you will find happiness with Anippe. She has spoken fondly of you to me on more than one occasion. She would embrace your attention should you allow yourself to favour her company. Do not waste a moment of this life; be the best version of yourself, having been loved," Badru spoke with reverence to Nef as we all bowed our heads as they embraced.

The horses exuded restlessness, sensing the snake's presence. As Herihor and I sat with Badru between us locking arms, Nef nodded to us.

The three of us huddled tightly and suddenly, I caught a fleeting glimpse of Kalina stepping into the clearing. We were instantly whisked into The Void, enveloped by The Hush as all sound ceased. The whirling and spinning felt endless, with light flickering intensely.

Minutes after my embrace with Jonas, we stood, the three of us - Jonas, Badru, and myself - wide-eyed and holding each other tightly, unbalanced but intact, outside our lodge. It took a few minutes to gather until Badru broke the silence, standing naked and trembling.

"Where are we? The pungent smells in the forest and the rich vegetation suggest we are not in Egypt," Badru spoke in our ancient language.

He would have a whole new language and life to learn about, and I am sure James is well equipped to teach him, I thought.

We went under the lodge and through the trap door as night fully blanketed us. I passed the clothes we had prepared for Badru's arrival, heated some soup, and showed Badru to his room. He was impatient, but it was late, and our meeting with Sanura would fill him with anticipation until the morning.

I was perturbed, being the only one to see Kalina enter the clearing; I hoped she was alone. By now, she would know we had travelled with her beloved father, and he would not be returning if Nef was to continue with the plan. My goddesses agreed with the transition, so why would Kalina be there to stop it? It made no sense.

Backing the Jeep out of the garage the following day sent sputters of fumes into the lodge. I closed the door, thinking to myself that we must repair that smelly exhaust pipe, as we left immediately, winding up the road to the house on the hill. There was nothing I could say to Badru; even if we had told Sophia he was coming, it would not have mattered. He was here, and permanently. Badru was nervous, fidgeting, rolling his thumbs around each other, something I had not seen him do before.

It was eleven in the morning, and even though we had been at the house on the hill the day before, it now looked abandoned and overgrown. What was happening here? Nervously, Jonas and I climbed out of the Jeep. The foliage around the house was entangled with vines, which we cleared to go to the door. The grass was overgrown, and all the shutters on the windows were closed. Badru spoke openly, suggesting no one lived here.

"Yes, this is the home of Sophia and James, but it is strange and looks as if they have not occupied this house for months," I said with curiosity laced in my words.

The door was locked, as expected. What were we to do? Jonas and Badru went to the side and back of the house; everything was closed.

I jumped onto the back fence to see the shed roof. It was open, but it too, looked wind-blasted and overgrown. Climbing the wall, we saw everything was dark inside the shed, with no glimmering golden lights as before.

"We must climb onto the roof to get inside and see what is happening. Can you help Jonas up, Badru?" I said, on edge. Only my fast-beating heart gave me the energy and capacity to keep pressing on to find out what was happening. Maybe this place was an illusion, unreal, but definitely strange, and now Badru is stuck here in our world.

The leaves cluttered the top of the pyramid, hidden inside the shed, and broken branches from the nearby trees covered the floor.

"Nothing is happening here; no power, nothing. It feels eerie as though no one has been in here for months, although it has been bolted from the inside here," Jonas yelled as he unlatched all the bolts on the door from within the shed. The doors creaked open like a haunted house, welcoming strangers. I just wanted out of here. My snake too, had surfaced as the trepidation became more real.

"Let us go, guys," I shrilled. "I am sure we will discover what is happening here in time but let us go home to the lodge right now." Jonas had to lock everything up again, and then Badru helped him down.

I elbowed Jonas. "This was not like yesterday; months have passed to have this much overgrowth."

"Yes, but do not alarm Badru. He is not any the wiser," Jonas whispered.

"Badru, are you sure you will stay here before your light body is consumed with poison in your other life? We must quickly return if we are to save you there. Already, Nef may have acted as we had planned," I said, feeling the necessity of quickening our journey back.

"I will stay here no matter what," Badru said, his face stoic in his decision. He stood with his arms crossed, a curious combination of determination and unflinching attitude.

Back at the lodge, Badru started clutching his stomach as if in agony. His eyes were bulging, and his tongue was hanging out.

"Quick! Water for Badru!" I called out to Jonas whilst I placed my hands on Badru's chest to help him heal and calm down. The process of the final transition of Badru shedding his light body has been set in motion, thousands of years in the past.

It was late in the evening. While Badru was sleeping, Jonas and I sat on the couch and held hands to travel back to see Badru's fate.

The energy tossed and twisted around us, pulling us closer into the heat of the clearing. I was hot, irritated, and annoyed, which had allowed me to propel us more directly through The Void.

Herihor leapt to his feet while expressing his sorrow and said prayers over Badru, who was in a terrible state of imminent death.

There was chaos. Kalina was holding Badru, who was dying very slowly and painfully. He was gagging and moaning, blood oozing out of his eyes and mouth. Kalina seemed calm and concentrated on nursing her father.

Despite the tears streaming down her face, she appeared resolute as she tenderly provided him with the utmost care and attention in his final moments.

"Kal, I am so sorry. Your father wanted to be with Sanura, and it was inevitable he would not let anything stop him. In our timeline, he is in good health and resting." I spoke slowly to let it sink in. She looked up at me, her eyes like saucers, filled with gratitude that he was alive.

"Has he seen my mother yet?" she probed, her words hinting at hope. "He told me last night of his pending journey. Even though I was in denial at his foolishness, I realised he would never be content without her. No other woman could fill the void in his heart. I had to help ease his suffering here as he plunged into his new world."

The lone eagle overhead circled above our gathering in the clearing. The ancient symbols of the majestic Nubian eagle on the temple walls were overshadowed by the flight of this eagle's magnificence. The great emotionally wounded bird with her broken heart was weaving her pathway to glory, lifting Badru's spirit and calling him home. She lamented endlessly, haunting cries of profound loss. Known as The Mother, Goddess Nekhbet's protection of Badru was nearing finality as Badru allowed his seeping life force to be released from his arched body.

We knelt and embraced one another, each lost in our thoughts of the heroic decision Badru had made for love. The snake, still thrashing in the sack, kept the restless horses at a safe distance. I rose to stroke Khonsu, soothing him with my words. I used similar words on Badru before his final death throes to calm him on his flight of the spirit. We now must leave to return to the palace and pass Badru's body over to the priests to be prepared for his journey to meet Anubis.

Kalina sighed and spoke of Dakari and how he was visited by the eagle, who expressed Badru's decision to leave this timeline. Dakari had taken it to mean his soul brightness would be extinguished here, not knowing of his travels. How could Dakari write eternal life into stone for Badru if he thought his spirit still existed in another timeline? Kalina's magician knew what happened today but did not know the continuation of his new life. Would the gods approve of Badru's actions?

"It is up to you, Kal, to ensure that Dakari does not know the full extent of our actions here. It would be best to cover yourself with the shrouded veil of secrecy. We will keep your father's decision private, especially from my mother. She would be horrified that we have assisted in Badru's transition," I said sadly.

Hundreds of tapered lantern holders lined the streets with their flickering flames, in high esteem for Badru. There was a strange combination of sorrow and celebration from the people, as they knew Badru would be honoured by the gods and goddesses. Asim and Herihor were mounted on the most proud of noble steeds, riding up the front of the procession to hold respect for Badru - the great eagle called hauntingly with her high-pitched whistle. At the same time, she encircled the slow-moving ceremonial parade, diving downward towards the chariot and then elevating at such speed and soaring into the cloudless sky. Her massive wingspan and gripping talons brought gasps of awe from the townspeople.

Badru's body was carried on the back of the chariot, and two magnificent horses slowly pulled the golden chariot with much celebration from the villagers. The chariot ventured towards the Nile for Badru's journey south toward Saqqara. Kalina, Safiya, Dakari, and I were carried on couch litters, moving solemnly behind the chariot.

In Saqqara, the priests would extract his four organs and prepare him for embalming and wrapping. Badru would be honoured for a well-lived life, as he had dedicated it to serving the great Pharaoh. Badru, who had defeated Egypt's enemies on the southern borders, would hold a powerful burial at Saqqara.

After the feasting and before the entertainment, Kal, Saf, and I returned to Kal's room to celebrate Badru in our own way. My goddesses held the space, raising the energy in the room. We felt this was all an illusion; had this actually happened?

"Badru had saved my life and that of my unborn child. I will forever hold him in my heart," I said with reverence.

We had dry eyes. There would be no mourning here tonight. We had prepared a feast of our own, with sweet beer and wine to keep us satiated as we lifted our arms, entwined them, and sipped the nectar of the gods. We sang and danced in the moonlight as the wash of moonglow bathed us in her inspiration. We celebrated Badru as a father, a warrior, and a lethal assassin, but most of all, we were grateful for the generosity and respect he held for everyone. Now was his time to find happiness.

As I called Tani in from the heavens to join us on the golden thread of connection, I could not help but feel the weight of her distress. The chill of the evening seemed to echo her feelings as I slowly saw Tani's eyes pierce mine, silently pleading for help from thousands of miles away.

Looking into the starlit night, I could not shake the image of the single ring Tani had drawn surrounding the moon - the same moon she was gazing at across the ocean and beyond the treacherous mountains. It was clear that Tani needed rescuing, and my heart went out to her at that moment.

We are coming for you, our princess. The time draws near for us to bring you home. Your message has been recognised. You are calling for us. Hold strong, little one. Your sisters here acknowledge your prayer. A sudden glimpse of a misty vision showed the cherub face of a newborn child snuggled at her breast. The intense eyes caught mine in recognition of our bloodline with Khan's unmistakable, dazzling, piercing blue eyes.

TATENEN

"Herihor, we must return together right now," I said, clearing my throat as my voice sounded unnaturally shrill.

I had walked in on Heqet and Herihor languishing on a comfortable lounger. Herihor looked at me with frustration as if he were in the midst of a personal moment.

Heqet's sighing made me realise they wanted time alone. Did she think I was jealous of her always requesting Herihor's time? I did feel somewhat irked though, that Herihor had not jumped up immediately.

"Where must you return to Sister?" Heqet asked inquisitively.

"To the Temple of Isis to honour Badru's life and help guide him to the underworld. We must depart immediately to prepare for his earthly release." I squirmed as the half-truth seeped out of my mouth.

"Yes, you must fulfil your duties. As the High Priest and Priestess, you are both required to communicate intimately to reflect on the recent events," Heqet said to Herihor as she looked lovingly at him.

"Asim calls for a meeting with you Sister; he requests your presence if you are available." I relayed the message to Heqet.

I left the room, hoping Herihor would be in quick pursuit.

Walking down the long sphinx-lined avenue was familiar and heartwarming. I lifted my nose to take in all of the scents of the landscape, wrapped in the emotional security of knowing I had survived Thebes and was home. Beside me quietly, without interrupting, walked my new guard, Tatenen. He moved with my moves, step for step. He was not behind or in front, but to my side. I felt a light-hearted connection with him, as though he accompanied me of his own free will and not under instruction from the military or Nef. His youthful appearance, muscular biceps, and quickness of stride left me without a doubt of his physical agility. Nef had trained him like Badru to be an elite assassin. When he turned and smiled, I felt an instant connection; we aligned. Explicitly trained for my protection, he showed me his lethal weaponry; a battle axe tucked into his waistband, which hung loosely by his side and his knife in a pouch hanging from his shoulder. His smile revealed a twist as though he could instantly launch and activate his fury if provoked or attacked. I smiled warmly in return, in appreciation of his prowess and the feeling of safety.

The North Temple loomed magnificently by the water, with the immense obelisks piercing the sky with triumph and the statues of my goddesses standing proud and steadfast.

We strode into the Hypostyle Hall. The fast pace had left me slightly out of breath, so I sat to await Herihor's arrival.

Tatenen moved to converse with the temple guards, which to my relief, gave me time to calm my breathing and rapidly beating heart.

The relief of being back in the familiar Temple of Isis was overwhelming. This place was my anchor; the scent of the stone and the sand I loved. Inhaling deeply, I closed my eyes, and a vision of Tani immediately gripped my heart. My snake was now fully alert. Tani had been crying and looked dishevelled and alone. Where was Khan? Her child was handed to her as she pulled down her shift to feed the baby - a daughter, I presumed by the angelic features. Tani's strength had diminished as frailty took a grip on her body. I could see her collar bones jutting out from her shift; this was not clothing fit for a highborn of a foreign country.

Tuning into my sister, she lifted her beautiful face in response and squinted to view me. Then, she turned her head to hear anything I might say. I whispered clearly to her.

"I am here and I am coming for you, Sister. Hold onto the courage and strength of your training and your dream to fight in the battles."

She then lifted her shoulders and pushed them back. The fire in her now blazed in her eyes like a furnace out of control. A woman came into view. Her face was sharp, and her countenance severe. She spoke harshly in an unusual tongue, which Tani seemed to comprehend. Tani challenged her verbally, her eyes intense with anger. If she had a weapon, I am sure she would have used it on the woman. Immediately, the mist rose and obliterated the scene, but not before I called out in anguish.

"I will come for you Tani; wrap yourself in the strength of Goddess Sekhmet."

Tatenen suddenly appeared in wild aggression to be in combat with the unseen enemy as he heard me cry out.

"Who is our enemy here? Let me see them if they are before us, for I cannot fight an apparition or the unfavourable gods. However, I will try. Tell me, who is our threat?" He knelt earnestly, trying to fend off that who had made me cry out.

"I do not seek or have an enemy here; it is a vision of my sister far away in the lands across the sea," I squirmed in defeat. In the next few minutes, I blurted out to Tatenen all that had transpired with my sister's disappearance. He nodded as though he already knew of the circumstances.

"Nef has given me full knowledge of the situation; he says you will risk your life to find her?" Tatenen raised his voice in question.

"I will attend to and protect you and be your companion if you cross the ocean. Nef's figure and presence stands out, and he would attract too much adverse attention. As I am less noticeable in appearance, I have an advantage. However, he has trained me to protect you with my life."

Placing my hands over my face, I gave way to an emotional outburst of gratification for Tatenen's support. After seeing Tani so vulnerable and defeated, I knew I would soon go to her. As Sisters of the Light we must protect one another. Tears of sadness brimmed in my eyes as my snake slowly curled around my heart for comfort. Tani was my only priority now. Something terrible had descended upon her.

Herihor's entrance was perfectly timed as Tatenen had returned to standing strong beside me. I felt as protected as if Tatenen was Nef himself.

Herihor gazed at me, wondering what had taken my composure.

"Let us enter the sacred chamber; we must return to Badru immediately. We will ward off the forces of chaos and bring the universe's divine order back to us in our other world," I said emphatically.

Herihor and I entered without Tatenen needing to check the sanctuary. The pure white light of Isis connected us, plugging us into the glorious crystalline light. We simultaneously perceived the inverted and upright tetrahedron spinning around us and within us in a perfect Mer-ka-ba, illuminating every facet of the dazzling symbol. Our bodies felt electrified as Goddess Isis's commanding presence once again was clear and precise. Her warmth flowed into our connection, blessing us with holy power and for the collaborative relationship we held as Priestess and Priest. We opened our minds and hearts to receive accountability for our part in Badru's transition. We were exonerated and released from the experience, knowing that we had held the sacred Talisman of Isis to bless Badru when it was time for him to move into his new light body.

The sanctuary lit up in pristine crystalline energy so fine that faience glass would have shattered with the intensity of the heightened pressure.

It reminded me of the initiation training schools and the twelve energy temples along the Nile where, as initiates, we were forced into fearful situations so intense that they would forever hold our courage for the new world. These calculated experiences through the mystery schools were dedicated to initiating the highest order, and passing all tests was necessary if one was to be enlightened. I was still engaged in this training.

I was breathless, as though all the air had been crystallised and frozen, so I was only sucking the smallest amount of air possible. I could feel Herihor was in the same situation. It was like having your face pressed against a granite statue with only the slightest amount of air drawn into the lungs.

Herihor and I reached for each other. We were summoning the courage to die together as the fiery pain gripped our lungs. Our transition into the territory of The Hush was immediate after we passed out. Slipping and spinning, I could feel the DNA channels circling us until we woke from sleep on the couch in our lodge.

We both stretched, and I stood up rather wobbly as I had not fully returned to my form. Pulling Herihor up, we moved to our room, tired and breathless. I drew in long, slow breaths, drawing the energy into my being, expanding light and warmth through my body. I was still cold and shivering now as if we had experienced something profound and traumatic, like death itself. Releasing the fear, I realised we had gone into the mystery school of the highest order at the second temple, one of breathing and sexual energies.

Our intimacy that night was heightened, and we felt a cosmic connection as we moved with the breath of life. Jonas and I felt the sacred rise of the Ankh and the wrap-around effect of the powerful projection of eternal life. The energy poured out of us, leaving us fully connected to the higher self. We held the absorbing and releasing breath; we ascended on a shaft of light to Sirius. My Elestial Crystal Star was welcoming us, the feminine aspect hidden in the dark recess of Sirius light years away.

I leapt out of bed, abandoning Jonas's comfort. It was early light, and the Tui birds had just begun their morning song. Something was amiss. All my senses were energised as I knocked, waited, and opened the door to Badru's room. It was empty, as though he had not slept in the covers. An indentation was evident where his body had been lounging. I checked the front door. It was locked, and I saw he had left through the trap door. That was the simple exit for him. I had noted he had been intently watching everything we had been doing since he had arrived. We had yet to show him the beach, but I am sure he would have heard the crashing waves and the calling of the gulls along the shore.

"Jonas, quick, Badru has gone. Let us go up to the house on the hill. He would have gone up to see if Sophia was there," I expressed in a frustrated voice. "She does not know he is here. The house gives me chills, too. If I were to go alone, I feel I would disappear. It is like living in a time warp. We are on this powerful, sacred land, caught up in something extraordinary. The hill with the rock face and tangled vines behind it has a feeling of extraterrestrial energy. Could this be true, Jonas? We are immersed in some unusual activity, and Sophia and James are involved too," I let my breath go, not realising I was holding on to it.

"You exaggerate, Lily... but yesterday, it was odd that everything around the house was overgrown. There is the situation of when I purchased the lodge. Sophia and James were an older couple. They were not the only ones living in the house. There was another man and a younger man that I thought was the gardener, but now I am unsure. Until I see a different situation, I will not speculate on what is happening here. Let's go then," Jonas said reluctantly.

Rumbling up the well-metalled road in the Jeep, we came to a slow halt outside the front door. It was very odd. The vines had gone, the shutters were open, and the house looked lived in and welcoming - certainly not like yesterday. The door opened, and Sophia stood there smiling, looking demure and beautiful; pregnancy had given her a radiant glow. Oh my gosh, my hand flew to my mouth. Her belly was huge, looking about seven months into her pregnancy. She was standing with her hands on her hips, stretching her back.

"We have not seen you for months," she said enthusiastically as she reached to embrace me. I felt a jolt of an electrical current pass between us, and my belly felt like there was a baby inside kicking like Herihor used to do. I pulled back suddenly and looked at Sophia. "Did you feel that?" I responded in shock.

"Feel what, Lily? My baby was just kicking, so he must be delighted to see you."

"Oh, are you having a boy?" I asked cautiously, not knowing what was happening here.

"Yes, he is a boy. I have met him in my visions. Come, come inside. It is so wonderful to see you both, isn't it, James?"

James was quiet, but this was not unusual - unless he talked about his passion for physics or the philosophies of life. He did have an odd look on his face but was welcoming, nonetheless.

"I am not sure what's happening. Yesterday, we came to visit you here, and the house was tangled with vines and overgrowth as though the mountain behind you was reclaiming it," I spoke rapidly.

"You have not been to visit for months," Sophia spoke calmly. "We went to the lodge to check on you, but there was no sign of life. Let us not be concerned about this now."

Sophia and James glanced at each other as if the secrets were not to be revealed.

"It is lovely to see you both looking refreshed and well," Sophia beamed as she reached for my hands. "We have missed you both. Have you been back to our homeland? How is Badru? Did he come back with you? We have been waiting. I am excited, but he isn't here with you," she spoke questioningly.

"He is here but was gone this morning when we woke up. I have no idea where he is but let us go in the Jeep to find him," I nervously responded. Whatever the outcome, there was no return to our ancient homeland for Badru.

Driving down to the beach entrance, we saw him sitting on the rocks in the distance. A lone large hawk, a Kahu, or swamp harrier, a dancer of the skies, circled him and drew our attention. The hawk was celebrating his arrival. Squawking in a high-pitched call, the bird rocked in the undulating air currents. Badru rose from his sitting place on the rocks as we leapt out of the Jeep to greet him.

Jonas and I ran towards him, momentarily forgetting Sophia, who was slowly coming behind, with James steadying her on the rippling sand.

"Badru!" Jonas called out. "Look who is here to welcome you. Your beloved Sanura."

Stopping to let Badru move forward and greet Sophia, we allowed our ancient language to flow thick and fast, slipping off our tongues. Their embrace was magical. The sun lifted the clouds in the sky as though an amplification of light had occurred. This was an unusual, magnificent connection between two lovers who had been separated through tragedy and were now reunited forever in this lifetime.

I saw their complex triple Mer-ka-ba's spinning in unison, with golden light fractures spiralling at light speed from their bodies. A sonic boom came as a thunderbolt, collecting momentum like a roar. The sand on the beach was twisting and stinging our legs. James, Jonas, and I stood back on the swirling foreshore as the waves lapped on the surf spray.

The couple's auric colours were magnificent shades of purple and gold, wrapping around their bodies like cloaks of silken shields.

We waited until the calm, and as Badru placed his hands on Sophia's belly, he quickly viewed her face as though he had felt the baby kicking. I could see a glow of golden hue around her as though she was a golden orb.

We all strolled to the water's edge, arms around each other in a familiar, loving embrace. We walked into the ebbing tide, feeling the sea wash over our feet, cleansing and releasing old energies.

Badru stood in awe as he gazed at the breathtaking panorama before him. It was a sight unlike any he had experienced, with the pristine beach stretching before him and majestic rocks rising from the shoreline. The vibrant colours of the ocean shimmered under the golden sunlight, creating a mesmerising scene that filled Badru with a sense of wonder and admiration. We were grateful to view this scene as though we had never before cast eyes on such a spectacular sight.

Back at the lodge, we shared breakfast. Jonas cooked up a feast of bacon and eggs while we discussed what life could look like and that we would have to stand firm together. Badru would live with James and Sophia, while James could educate and teach Badru the ways of life in Aotearoa.

His new name, Hunter Nobel, would take some time to get used to, but we will practice it from now on.

I took James aside. "How are you coping, James? You will be an uncle to this child. This blessed child will seal the destiny of all of us with his unique connection." Little did I know then how much this boy would hold a deeper meaning in all our lives.

Sophia decided to travel to the city closer to the delivery, and we planned to use Hunter Nobel's documentation to register him as the father. Since it was revealed Sophia and James were not married, we thought a registry wedding would be a good option for Sophia and Hunter, who was now using his new name.

Our apartment was compact, but we made space to settle in for Sophia's last month of pregnancy. The rapid time warp to complete a nine-month cycle within a few months was eerie and thought-provoking. What was happening at the house on the hill? Or was this happening to Jonas and me? Were we the ones who were losing time? My thoughts of this time warp had me checking the dates on the milk in the fridge and the shopping we had last bought. These dates did suggest we were months out of the time zone we thought we were in. Where did we go? Was it all of us out of synchronicity with time?

Driving around, we familiarised ourselves with the city's sounds and sights while teaching Hunter as many phrases and ways of adapting to his new world as possible. It was easy for us to lapse into our ancient language as we laughed and planned our futures.

EYE · OF · HORUS

Gathering to joyously celebrate Sophia and Hunter's union at the registry office in Auckland for a Thursday midday wedding was a highlight. Kate and her new man, Sean, were invited. I had already summonsed my ancient goddesses to be present to hold the space at the wedding signing and to bring a sparkling celebration to the after-party in the evening; one I hoped my aunt and uncle would never forget.

It was an electrifying moment when Kate and Sean entered the beautiful wood lined chapel room. All sound dimmed, and I sensed the energy of yearning for an elusive love, a cry of longing or excitement. I could not decipher why this feeling possessed me. It was the same excited feeling I experienced when I saw Asim for the first time.

I saw him walk in with Kate, and my heart raced. The divine power of the creator brought him in. His hair was blond, and his bright blue eyes did not hide the potent energy of his reincarnation. I had to suck in air to breathe more calmly and let go of my nerves to greet them properly. I had to trust and release expectations and attachments to this moment. I shook my fingers to release energy.

"Kate, I am so happy to see you. It's wonderful to meet you, Sean, and welcome to this special day," I stumbled over my words. As Sean and I hugged, a flash of insight into an echo of a faraway time or another dimension infused this moment with magic. I moved away from the unease of the intimate connection. "Sean, come and meet Jonas, you two should get on famously," I smiled, thinking how crazy this situation was.

I wondered if he recognised me. By his smile and knowing look, I could see he had some idea we knew each other from a past life. I pulled Kate aside while Jonas and Sean connected, and I bubbled with enthusiasm to talk about her new love.

"He is so gorgeous, Kate. I can see you are entranced by him. Perhaps this is a deepening partnership with someone with whom you can truly express your freedom and explore what you have together. He has an old worldly look about him," I said admiringly.

"Yes, he is so beautiful and passionate; you are making me blush, Lily," she said as she squeezed me.

As my universe rocked, my mind sought a healthier way of looking at this situation. This time belonged to Kate. He had come to be with her, but it was a miracle he had found his way into our present timeline.

"Come, Kate, let us celebrate these two lovers here right now," I said, radiant with happiness.

"Lily, who is this couple? You mentioned you bought the lodge from them, but Jonas said they were elderly. They are having a baby and seem quite young; it's never too late to experience life on their own terms. Where is he from? You said his name is Hunter," she questioned.

"Yes, he is Egyptian and has been working over here," I thought at least here with this explanation; my heart would not be weighed against the feather. Still, I was stretching the truth.

I put my finger to my lips to signal to Kate and led her over to meet Sophia. I noticed Sean, Hunter, and Jonas were getting on famously, as if they were old friends, even though Hunter could not grasp the words. Sean was looking at Jonas quizzically with an undeniably puzzled expression.

Kate, Sophia and I admired the transformation of the restaurant. The ambience was enchanting. Long, exquisitely decorated tables were adorned with fresh flowers and colourful streamers, and abundant red wines and champagne flowed freely. The air was filled with the melodious sounds of traditional Italian songs, creating a truly magical atmosphere. Jonas's family and some family members I still needed to meet, were gathered around the tables. This was what I loved about Italian culture, as it was steeped in music, dance, family, art and home life. The scene was set to make this a night to remember.

The highlight of the evening was held with family celebrating the spirited traditional dance, 'La Tarantella', which infused the room with energy and joy. As the dance unfolded, I thought this was excellent practice for our upcoming wedding. Although Sophia had to sit it out due to being close to giving birth, she was fully engaged in the celebrations. She cheered on her loving husband as he quickly learned the moves and clapped the dancers enthusiastically.

Hunter was getting used to his new name and, deep in the festivities, was thoroughly enjoying himself. Even though he could not comprehend any of the conversations, his adept sense of observation kept him involved in all the exchange of celebrating activities. I noticed Hunter did not partake in drinking the available alcohol; even in Egypt, the abundance of rich wines and beers had never passed his lips. Hunter was very much the old Badru here; he was always on guard and poised for action. His killer instinct, a primal urge to protect his loved ones, was dominant tonight. His eyes were skirting the room, and it became overwhelming with so much of an explosion of noise, clapping and stomping.

The finality of the evening came with the symbolic act of smashing a crystal vase into tiny fragments. The room was overflowing with applause as each piece of the shattered vase represented the happy years that Sophia and Hunter were destined to share. Sophia was transfixed on her intention for a happy life as the vase was dashed on the floor. It was a powerful and unforgettable moment, and I felt a sense of pride in having chosen such a meaningful crystal vase as a symbol for their celebration.

Suddenly, Hunter, with the agility of a leopard, sprang into action. He was holding the sharp cake-cutting knife in a threatening way, brandishing the blade with a killer instinct at anyone who came close to Sophia.

He threw his body into a rhythmic display of athletic agility, gracefully marking the audience with a threatening performance. Suddenly, the room fell silent, except for Hunter's low guttural growl, like nothing anyone would have heard before. He stepped up his performance, enticing anyone to cross his imaginary boundary around Sophia. Sophia moved to calm him, speaking in our ancient language, and Sean came forward mesmerised by their language. They held a challenging gaze, but Jonas immediately stepped in, and diffusing the situation with light-hearted banter, he then turned, raised his hands above his head and clapped. Immediately, more applause and cheering exploded around the room, with everyone thinking this was part of the ceremony.

As Jonas extracted the knife from Hunter, his aggressive stance diminished. All the while, Sophia was still standing awkwardly, explaining the custom to Hunter. I should have considered outlining these traditions with him earlier.

In a quiet moment alone, I filled my wine glass, and my heart reached out to my time-travelling mother, who lives in Italy. *Can I find her before my wedding to celebrate with me?* My birth mother would be present, too; she was such a beauty, and I was excited about this as I had not seen her for some time. Sean looked at me inquisitively from the other side of the room as I waved, smiled, and walked away. There would be a better time to delve deeper into our connection.

Sophia's labour was intense; however, she remained calm in her desire to have a birth that was natural and free from the trauma of her last memory. We were prepared with birthing oils, and I supported Sophia in squatting to open the canal for the baby to descend on his barque into delivery. We used visualisation and relaxation techniques, with breathing and hypnosis, whilst I calmly spoke to Sophia as I called in my goddesses for the anointing rituals. With relief, I recalled what I had learned from the wise birthing women who had helped me. I remembered my birth and being poisoned when I had baby Herihor and shuddered, then put aside all thoughts to be present for Sophia and Hunter.

He was born in the hospital in the early hours of November 11; it was a life-changing moment as he entered our world. Once again, time stood still. I had not realised I had been holding my breath as I supported Sophia and released a long exhalation. As I connected to the little boy being born, I could not help but cry in awe, putting my hand over my mouth. I felt our baby Herihor's energy filter into the room like stardust trickling from the heavens.

He was travelling on his horizontal timeline to be here as Sophia and Hunter's baby. Smiling at Sophia, mixed emotions flooded through me.

The nurses wrapped and passed the little dark-haired baby to her to suckle. Hunter needed all his senses on alert to strengthen them both as their emotions spilled out into the delivery room. I pulled the curtain aside slightly and opened the door.

Leaning against the wall on the other side of the corridor, my emotions too welled up, with so much to take in. I was anxious to return to my ancient world and my little boy.

I expressed my excitement about the baby to Jonas and James, who were waiting restlessly in the waiting room for news like anxious fathers. The hospital was quiet as morning was still a few hours away. Just a few plaintive cries from the newborns stirred the rooms to life. I had to smile at the complexity of the situation. It flitted through my mind that most have no knowledge of life-through-life and would not even have a clue of this crossover of lives, relationships, and reincarnations that was happening all around us.

Finally, we headed north, and my urgency to return to be with baby Herihor dragged me to the edges of my life here. As Sophia and Hunter had named their baby Travis, I smiled, knowing the French meaning 'to cross' or 'crossroads' was appropriate for him. I could not help but continuously turn to look at him as he slept in the back of our Jeep between his doting parents while James followed us in his new Cortina.

"Jonas, I must leave the first moment we have to ourselves. Are you willing to return with me? I must begin preparation to cross the seas to look for Tani and bring her home," I whispered.

After locking the lodge and drawing the shutters, we sat back on the couch and held hands, reminding ourselves where we had last begun our journey back here from inside the temple. I recalled it had been terrifying not being able to draw breath. Would our light be strong enough to survive our return?

The Hush pulled us through as though with urgency. The current, like the flow of water, was therapeutic and anointing. Gasping for breath, we both felt the impact of the closeness of death delivering her final judgement as we were hurled back into the past. The temple now was still and calm compared to the last moments of entering The Void. It felt complicated back here, but not more so than in our modern world, where many hidden situations overlaid reality.

Tatenen stood ready at the sanctuary entrance and momentarily glanced at us with a questioning look before indicating we would return to the palace. He used Nef's familiar hand signals, which I knew well as he directed us back past the languishing sphinx.

The evening sunset lit up the tops of the palms, shrouding the lower foliage. It was as if the fronds were stretching and preparing for a long night's sleep. As a little girl, I had listened to the date palms sending me messages. The overarching leaves protected the fruit hanging in massive clusters.

The whispers of the night had been captured, and I could hear their subliminal messages relayed in the gentle dance of the lush green foliage. Every living element that graced our country was in perfect harmony as the insects heralded in the night.

We had left the sacred temple to head back to feast for dinner. However, I immediately returned to our rooms to be with Asim and see my little son. Picking him up, I looked into his charming eyes, hugging him like I could never let him go. I saw through to his soul and knew love could not separate, and so, of course, he was destined to come back and travel to be close to us.

"You are mine," I whispered to my baby, not realising that Asim was so close.

"He is yours, and you are mine," he spoke lovingly, his breath warm on my cheeks.

The night held the magic in our touch. I brushed the long Ibis feathers over Asim's body. Speaking in my modern language, which Asim loved hearing, I murmured of enchantment and took him through a meditation of profound enlightenment. We unleashed our sensual, loving connection on a frequency of crystal light. The experience was soul-touching, as though two lovers had glimpsed one another from afar, magnifying their soul essence. I could feel his heart beating faster, inhaling in shorter breaths.

"Take me with you, my love, so that I may see the many facets of your world," Asim whispered huskily.

"This is our world, here, my love; leaving it would be too difficult. Let us share this endless time right here, right now," I responded.

Words evaporated into the mist as our bodies felt the rhythm of the energies building to take us both on a heightened desire for love. We kissed, holding the sensory feeling of each other's breath.

Keeping eye contact increased our connection. There were tears in Asim's eyes as he relinquished his glow. Holding on to me tightly whilst his breathing subsided.

I could not take Asim, for he would learn that Jonas (or Herihor here) was my lover in the other world. It would be heartbreaking for him, and he would see the likeness in baby Herihor's eyes.

"I will find you in the future. I will reincarnate and come to you when you need me," Asim whispered. I shuddered, knowing he was already there and had fulfilled his promise to return.

"My love, my sun, moon and stars, I must leave soon to find Tani. She has been calling me to come to her as she is held captive in foreign lands. Saf and I will go. We will leave within the week. I am prepared for the danger and know my goddesses will harbour me from the storm. We will follow the path, and I will call upon my goddesses to protect us," I forced the words from my lips with conviction, knowing nothing would change my mind.

"I will not try to stop you, for I know the sacred seed of the sisters flows through you. Your bond is immeasurable, and it would be useless to insist you abandon this pursuit," Asim said quietly, resigning himself, knowing this would happen.

I lovingly cradled my son, listening to his voice as he sang and murmured in harmonic sounds. I would sing to him timeless ancient songs of strength and prowess.

"I will see you in our other world when I come to you," I laughed as I tickled him. Sophia's baby, Travis, would know who I was, which would be the only way I could visit him.

Nef, Tatenen, Saf, and I gathered in the stables as I brushed Khonsu. We lowered our voices to not let the stable hands know our intentions. Khonsu shuddered as I brushed his forelock.

"Saf, are you prepared? We will leave in two cycles of the night, in the afternoon; as the sun sinks low in the sky, we will only take what we wear. Our weapons will be minimal so as not to arouse suspicion. Mother will be distraught, but Kal will support her. She will try to load us up with supplies, but we must stay light on our feet and reject all help. This is a dangerous mission, and it may take months to rescue her, Khan, and their child. We are unaware of the environment or even where we are heading, so we will only use our natural ability to be concealed by looking like travelling drifters."

Suddenly, Khonsu started neighing and getting restless. An eerie sensation prickled the skin all over my body, and Eshe walked into the stables. She was clothed in a light animal skin, hugging her petite frame, and had a strange smell about her. Her eyes were darkened and shrouded as she lifted them and looked at me with distaste. Immediately, my snake was roused; this time, he did not dance but lashed out furiously, his tongue spitting venom. Eshe fell backward onto the stable floor. Even though no one could see my snake, he packed a powerful strike when threatened.

"Eshe, what are you doing in the stables? You would have had to get past the guards," I questioned.

Eshe collected herself and stood up quickly. Animated and defiant, Eshe clasped her hands behind her back. "I can move like a mouse. This is a tremendous gift, a legacy my father has left me. He trained me to creep silently with great speed, but when moving as a mouse, my life is always in great danger. I have heard your plan to leave, and I wish you to take me with you," she said, smiling, now looking like a sweet angel.

"I came to tell you I know what happened to my father. I was there. I followed you that night when you came to visit," she spoke slowly, letting her words impact Nef as she looked directly at him. She then turned and walked out, leaving us all stunned, looking at each other.

I could see the questions in the minds of Saf and Tatenen as Nef gave a noncommittal grunt, as though he did not care about or believe the situation.

When I followed her to explain, I had no doubt she was looking to cause trouble or threaten us. But when I left the stables, there was no one there - only a tiny mouse scurrying away as the guard attempted to squash it.

"We must take care. There is ancient magic here. What has happened to Eshe? Something has changed in her. I will need to commune with my goddesses," I said quietly.

Asim and I spent the time reflecting together on all that had transpired in such a short time. We touched and held each other as though we could not part. I joined him and our mothers in the sacred garden for strength and healing, where Herihor awaited us and performed protection rituals. Kal's magician had summonsed the three of us to place mystical protection around our auric field and sent us blessings from the lineage of mystics. He pressed an udjat amulet, the Eye of Horus, into each of our hands to heal and ward off any harm.

"Mother, I must speak with you in private. Can we walk in the garden?" I questioned.

The pool in the centre attracted a few annoying mosquitoes despite the growing geranium bushes, lemongrass, and citronella throughout the gardens. We had covered our bodies in geranium and lemongrass oil to repel the insects; the scent on our skin was divine. Dragonflies and water beetles, which thrived in the warm climate, hovered around us. Their presence symbolised strength, luck, and precision, which was comforting. Lotus flowers danced on the pool's surface, bringing the pond to shades of vibrant blue. My mother pointed out poisonous plants that we must avoid. She circled her hands, saying all these on this side had medicinal properties, and tried to name them to me.

"Mother, you are avoiding this chance for us to speak. I can only contact you through travel to our other world. You must seek me out so I can communicate with you. Come to my country and meet me there. The Italian restaurant Sol Mio is in Auckland, New Zealand. Ask for Lily Morris; that is me. I will not be in the restaurant, but my fiancé's family owns it. They are Italian too, Mother, and know how to contact us. They have a key to our apartment. Do you have a husband in Italy, Mother? Is he Italian? You may stay at our apartment, as we spend much of our time at our lodge, where your sister Sanura lives in the house on the hill. Her name is Sophia. How will you recall this conversation, Mother?" I asked passionately.

Grasping her hand, I led her to the pond where the blue water lilies were abundant. "My name is Lily Morris, and I will soon be Lily Drake," I pointed to the water lilies and the male ducks with their colourful plumage. "You can recall with this memory, Mother," I said.

For the first time, we talked about our life through The Void, the secret place Mother never spoke of or alluded to. She still did not commit to coming to New Zealand, but I knew her desire to see her sister would be an instinct to pursue this journey. Why was she so hesitant?

"I will leave it up to you; there is nothing more I can do to persuade you. This may be the only way you will know what has transpired outside our kingdom in our pursuit of Tanith," I said, pronouncing her name just like Mother loved without shortening it.

Finally, my mother emerged from her complex, hidden world, facing me and speaking from her heart she had softened.

"I remember our other world, Akila, just as you do. But I rarely speak of it, for it stirs up a deep sadness that we are not all there together. I have held back from revealing the truth, fearing it might be too much to bear. Yet perhaps it is not as terrifying as I have imagined. This could mark the start of a deeper bond between us, for you, my daughter, have a profound understanding. I hope this will bring us closer," she said, her voice tinged with the weight of her emotions.

"I am proud of my four girls and wish my children peace and prosperity. However, I see a burning desire in you to rectify wrongs and try to change the future. Each of you girls has immeasurable gifts, and I am sure they will support you when you need them. There are prophecies written about a strong woman, a High Priestess who challenges all customs, continuing her legacy to support Goddess Isis and to keep her memory alive even when the great Temple of Isis on her island in Philae has been overtaken."

Knowing of these prophecies, I bowed in awe, allowing my mind to wander to this most sacred, beautiful temple. Originally a small temple to honour Goddess Isis, to the most recent that had not even been built yet and would not be for hundreds of years into the future. It was this alignment we worked towards to hold this holiest sanctuary safe. To maintain the freedom and soul retrieval of the divinity and power of the feminine glory of Goddess Isis, life-through-life.

I had pictured the Sacred Temple of Isis as it floated into my consciousness. The temple looked as though it was suspended on water.

My thoughts returned to our modern world, where the temple is set on an island in Egypt. Jonas, Sophia, James, Badru, and I were escorted through the eighteen-metre-high structure of a pylon, then through the second pylon. Into the hypostyle open court, antechamber, with the musical scenes in the temple of Goddess Hathor and through to the inner sanctuary of Goddess Isis. Two granite shrines stood here, where a gold statue of Goddess Isis had been mounted on one, with the barque on which the statue travelled, mounted on the other. We walked up the stone staircase to the Osiris chambers, where the stunning reliefs of Osiris's death were depicted.

Before its relocation, the Nile's waters submerged the temple and had risen dramatically during the construction of the Aswan Low Dam. All the ancient treasures were lost as the dam engulfed all in its path.

My Goddess Isis was drawing close to weaving her magic as my last journey to the temple in Pi Ramesses was uplifting and powerful. At no time did I feel fear; I had brushed it aside only to claim the prize of our return home to safety with Tani.

Tatenen accompanied me once again. I asked Tatenen to be with me in the sacred sanctuary to hear the authentic truth about the journey ahead of us. Entering the sanctuary, I was awash with reverence, deep respect, and admiration for Goddess Isis and her sister Goddess Nebet-Het or Nephthys. I could feel the presence of Goddess Ma'at, symbolising truth, balance, order and harmony.

Sitting gracefully before the symbolic statue of Goddess Isis, I invited Tatenen to do the same. We bowed in reverence and expressed determination for our journey to find Tanith. Would we be protected? My request was straightforward. As the sanctuary lit up with brilliant illumination, it refracted off the walls. Our ancestors' orbs or small moons were present, floating in the radiance. My snake, fully alert, seemed to revel in the warmth and glow.

The voice of Goddess Isis was rich in tone and all encompassing. Her form softened, revealing her feminine power.

"There is treachery amongst you; it is growing in the seed of the tiniest flower. You must release the hold of the lineage. Therein lies the blood of the tormented adversary. Release the pain with forgiveness, and you will have a powerful ally. Your journey will be heart-led but treacherous. Your bond with the seed of the sisters will unite your force. Never give up, for you will be challenged. However, you will need to call on the strength of your ancestors, and you will define wisdom in the stages of seeking the truth," Goddess Isis's words reverberated around the sanctuary.

Goddess Ma'at's words surprised us as we heard the tone shift. "Your guard here, Tatenen, is faithful and dependable. Stay together as you navigate this treacherous terrain, for betrayal lurks within those you trust. You must see behind the words of others to fully expose your reality. Your companion eagle, Goddess Nekhbet, will guide you. Return with our daughter Tanith to her rightful place here in Pi Ramesses. The harmony of the universe is always seeking coherence."

Listening intently, I memorised the prophetic words. I would need to decipher their deeper meaning later.

As the luminosity faded and the chamber returned to its solid entity, the statue of Goddess Isis still felt warm and loving.

"I had never expected to hear the language of the goddesses. They were passionate yet dominant. I will heed the knowledge portrayed to us," Tatenen said, bowing his head in admiration and respect. My heart felt lighter, leaving the temple as if all was known in the divine mind.

As the afternoon of our departure moved forward, like the unstoppable flow of the Nile, time weighed heavily upon me.

I felt the sharp knife blade close to the back of my neck as Nef held my hair, sliced through it, and turned to Saf to do the same. He would bury our hair as protection close to the Temple of Isis. We were dressed in our old, familiar, tattered attire, the look we had perfected over our childhood years. Having removed our makeup, we looked surprisingly young. We wrapped and bound our breasts.

Relinquishing my mothering role until I returned, I had laboriously stopped feeding baby Herihor a few weeks ago as his wet nurse took over the feeding. I was surprised how my body shape had changed since I had given birth, so it was now harder to disguise my womanly figure.

"Nef, please take care of my son with the help of Anippe, Asim, and my priest Herihor. I trust you to keep him safe from the poisonous snakes and plants. There are other dangers to be aware of, such as Eshe, Dhoser's eldest daughter, who is a risk as she appears to be a shapeshifter. You recall she came into the stables as a mouse and crept past the guard," I said reluctantly, sounding somewhat strange.

Nef nodded, fully understanding Thoth's magic and how, being the god of wisdom and magic, he may have granted her this ability. "I have baby Herihor's protection. Anippe and I are together, and we are watchful of the young prince and Amon, my new son," Nef stood proud to make this announcement to me.

I smiled and reached to hug Nef. "I also have you as my protector," I patted my chest, in reference to the protection of my snake.

I listened intently to the rustle of fabric and the low, solemn voices of Tatenen and Saf as we quietly made our way into the streets. The evening brought forth the twinkling of stars, and as the opal moon rose in the night sky, we were guided out of the city limits towards the sea.

Nef would meet us outside the city, and together we would travel to the oasis on Khonsu and the other horses, continuing our journey to the port. After that, we would be on our own. My Elestial Crystal Star beckoned us forward as Sirius shone brightly in the star-studded sky.

THE · HUSH

Become the seeker of the timeless state that allows the subtle energy
to move and flow, capturing the essence of past and future worlds.

Here lies the ability to manipulate space and time to connect
through a portal or vortex, enabling physical energy to transmit
into the spiritual Soul Light. The essence of this light is fractured
so that the initiate can pass through the millions of fine particles
of matter through the void and spaces between matter. Spaces
can be magnified to allow vast physical transmission.

For those who have liberated their souls, the perfect moment
at the perfect time becomes a gateway to the miracles of light
transformation. In this state, the soul can exist, breathe, and
thrive in other realms, at different times, and in other worlds.

Sound magnification, always resonating at a specific oscillation,
facilitates the release of outdated programming. Engaging
with these frequencies, whether through playing, listening,
or becoming at one with them, elevates the soul to create
a potent life that manifests in any chosen dimension.

To be the Light Ones or Light Beings, one must pass through the
temples of higher existence to be fearless, release the earthly, and
travel the universal spectrum; This allows the subliminal coding
of the mind-body connection to complete the unification for
soul travel. The ultimate is to be weighed as light as a feather.

www.ingramcontent.com/pod-product-compliance
Lightning Source LLC
Chambersburg PA
CBHW072119020726
47501CB00003B/884